The Stream: Discovery

BILL JONES, JR.

Published by Panthera Press

Panthera is a trademark of Panthera Press.

ISBN:
ISBN-13: 978-0615594880
ISBN-10: 0615594883

For my Father.

1 – GOOD MORNING IS AN OXYMORON

Charlie hated mornings. This was due, in no small part, to his having the sleep habits of a caffeine-addicted owl. Often, he was just falling asleep as the neighborhood's early birds were awakening. For Charlie, getting up was a thing to be savored over the course of an hour or so. He always started his day the same way: by hammering his alarm clock with a closed fist, falling back asleep, arguing with his sister who had been sent to get him up, and then stumbling out of bed, eyes closed, into the bathroom, to empty his bladder.

Those were the good old days.

Recent mornings meant a surreptitious sprint to the bathroom. As if starting the day shortly after falling asleep were not bad enough, lately, he woke up … *like that.* Once, his dad had caught him before he could pee, stopped, saluted, and said, "Ten Hut!" Charlie had no idea what he meant at the time, but when everyone else laughed, he knew it could not be good. His mom had chastised the family, and consoled him by stating it was a perfectly normal thing for an eleven-year-old boy. Still, the damage had been done, as his red cheeks attested.

Though he had inherited his mother's caramel color, Charlie's skin seemed to flush at the slightest embarrassment. It was a gift, he reckoned, from his father, along with curly brown hair, deep dimples, broad shoulders, and spectacularly average height. It was one thing to be humiliated by virtue of a joke he didn't understand. It was worse to have his entire family be able to read his embarrassment.

Charlie staggered into the bathroom, and after completing his mission, opened his eyes for the first time.

What's the refrigerator doing in the bathroom?

He had the right to be confused. Charlie, as it turned out, was in the middle of an excellent nightmare. It took him a full ten seconds to realize he was standing in the kitchen, dressed, facing the open refrigerator. He was certain there was a toilet there moments ago. He hoped he had not just peed into the open vegetable crisper; however, he decided against looking down to check. He was certain his mom would let him know if he had.

Breakfast consisted of a single kernel of oat cereal in a big bowl of water. Even in his dream, Charlie thought his breakfast a bit odd, but apparently, not odd enough to awaken him from his deep slumber. His hunger sated, he walked the quarter mile to his bus stop, and stood there, alone, waiting. After eternity passed, after the sun grew to a great orange ball of sputtering hydrogen, after the first two planets melted in admiration, and all the stars in heaven were visibly moved, the bus finally showed up. It was a Greyhound with "Middul Skool" on the front panel.

Middle school is going to rock.

Charlie's excitement lasted exactly ten seconds. The inside of the bus reeked of cigarette smoke and cheap perfume. As he passed, the bus driver growled in his direction, but he didn't stop to listen. He was too busy trying to find a seat, while avoiding making eye contact with anyone on the bus. It was fortunate he was looking down, as a shard of clipped toenail grazed his face, just missing his eye.

Charlie looked up to see a swing set in the aisle of the bus. Fat Mrs. Martinez was sitting on the swing, humming a tune in Spanish, and trimming her crusty toenails. Charlie wondered how he knew her song was Spanish since she was merely humming. As he squeezed past the swings, all the while ducking toenail shrapnel, he found a seat in the very back, next to, of all people, the guy from The Twilight Zone. It wasn't the old chain-smoking guy with the creepy black shoe polish hair, but the newer, cooler one. Charlie found this not at all surprising.

The bus navigated an unfamiliar highway, past ramshackle houses and barren neighborhoods. At the distant end of the highway stood a set of high mountains. They sat in two rows, the first reflecting a pinkish hue in the morning sunlight. Behind them, rising ominously until they disappeared into the clouds, were mountains of black rock. Gray clouds slumped down the mountain slopes, obscuring the highway ahead in a blanket dense fog. A faraway part of Charlie's brain began to cry out that he had never seen mountains like these in eastern Virginia. Still, that is not what drew his immediate attention.

Instead, he wondered why there was only one other kid on his bus. He could not make out the shadowy figure near the front of the bus, except that it was obviously a girl, with long, dark hair. She sat with her back to Charlie, dressed head-to-toe in black. She never turned around, which Charlie decided was probably a good thing. From his position, she too-closely resembled a few Japanese horror movies he had covertly downloaded onto his computer.

It was she; he was certain. He had been dreaming her all summer. She never spoke to him, though lately, she had begun to smile on the rare occasions when he made eye contact. Charlie always woke himself up, or, if that did not work, would look down and hurry away. The girl never did anything out of the ordinary. In fact, most of the time, she would watch him, silently, as though his dreams were created solely for her amusement. Still, he guessed serial killers smiled at their victims too, once they decided to go in for the kill.

That thought birthed a creeping anxiety, which he soothed by making spit art on the bus' window. At the precise instant he was about to put spit eyes on a spit head, the driver slammed on the brakes, and Charlie sailed from the seat, coming to rest directly under the Twilight Zone Guy's left leg. Twilight Zone Guy flicked a cigarette ash in his face, and deadpanned, "Off the shoes, kid." He was no longer the hip, modern host, but a black-shoe-polish-haired relic of an era Charlie estimated to be the 1930s, before God invented color TV.

Shoot. When did Mr. Shoe Polish show up?

From the front of the bus, Charlie could hear the female bus driver honking the horn, and ranting, "Move! Stupid freaking sheep!"

I've heard that lady's voice before.

Charlie tried to recall her name, but it danced just out of reach. Whatever the name, her voice made him shudder.

Standing, he strained to see what halted the bus, but it was too dark, and the fog surrounding the bus obscured his view. Charlie sat, slid along the seat, and craned his neck through the open window. The air was crisp, cool, and smelled of wet wool. There were no sheep, but rather an immense flock of small children slowly crossing the wide highway. They were moaning, and their cries echoed in the morning stillness like the bleating of a hundred sheep. Tall, slim, shepherds in hooded cloaks followed the flock.

One small boy wandered directly under Charlie's window, but did not look up, even when Charlie called a concerned, "Are you okay?" A hooded shepherd turned in Charlie's direction and snarled, his teeth bared. It had the face of a wolf, though its hands, clenched around his shepherd's staff, were human. Charlie drew back inside of the window. Within moments, the shepherd had prodded the boy into rejoining his flock, and the group disappeared into the darkness beyond the highway.

Charlie sat in silence for a time, as the bus continued on its way. He was beginning to fear, perhaps, this school would not be as cool as he had hoped. However, within minutes, he was lulled into a renewed sense of security by the bus' gentle motion. Unfortunately, as soon as he began to relax, the bus screeched to another stop, banging Charlie's head, hard, against the window frame.

Ow! Jeez-o-flip!

In addition to now having a headache, he was choking on cigarette smoke, as the open window had drawn Mr. Shoe Polish's smoke in his direction. The cloud of smoke drifted into the form of a skull, which hovered over Charlie's head before dissipating. He turned to Mr. Shoe Polish, who shrugged, and flicked his cigarette butt in Charlie's direction.

"Don't look at me, kid," he said, lighting another cigarette. "It's your dream, not mine. Your stop, by the way."

Charlie rose, and crept down the aisle, by now harkening to the sound of a chainsaw or knives being sharpened. As he approached the front door, he glanced back, and saw Mr. Shoe Polish still seated, obscured by a rancid smoke cloud. No knives. Charlie, however, was not reassured. The back of the bus was now ensconced in black and white, which he knew to be the dominion of absolute evil. Movies had taught him that.

Charlie hesitated at the bus' front steps, craning his neck to see the three-story entrance to his new school. "Welcome to the ZONE!" was emblazoned in dripping red over the enormous double doors. He gulped, hoping against hope the sign-maker had used paint.

"Wow!" exclaimed the dark-haired girl behind him.

Charlie had forgotten she was there, and responded to her excitement by screaming in a lovely soprano.

"You are so funny," she responded, grinning, and ruffling his curly hair.

Charlie stood clutching his chest, checking for angina. He couldn't find it, as he wasn't entirely certain what it was. He had never seen the girl up close. She was a Cute Girl, with lightly tanned skin, large eyes outlined with black mascara, and dark hair that fell in loose curls around her face, from under which Charlie could make out three earrings on one side, and none on the other.

"Um, I-I think you lost an earring," Charlie offered, hoping his helpfulness would prevent her slashing him. Her eyes seemed to change from blue to hazel as he watched, but he decided against mentioning that. One never knows what will set off a psychopath.

"Oh, my left ear wasn't in the mood for decoration today," she said, without a smile. She poked him casually in the rib cage as she walked by. "Come on, silly, you're gonna be late for school." She descended the stairs without so much as a backward glance.

Charlie stood dumbfounded. She didn't appear to be Japanese, but, rather, Hispanic. Importantly, though her poking had caused a second, smaller yelp, he wasn't bleeding. He was unfamiliar with Spanish-language horror movies, but thought he should look them up for future reference. This could still be a trick.

"Off!" yelled his former second-grade teacher, apparently now moonlighting as a bus driver, as she kicked him in the seat of his pants. He landed with a splash in a fresh mound of (he hoped) mud and looked up. Standing over him was the biggest, ugliest kid he had ever seen. He thought it might be a girl … or a goat.

Maybe both, because it does have one of those goatee things.

Goatisha (he decided the she-goat was called) picked him up with one hairy-knuckled hand, and yelled, "I liked my new dress yellow, not mud brown! You are dead, kid."

For the very first time in his life, Charlie learned what "saved by the bell" means. As one ham-sized fist (with spring pomegranate polish) entered gravity on a collision course with his smile, the school bell rang.

"I said, mama said, 'Wake up!'"

It was the unmistakable siren song of his sixteen-year-old sister, Layla, who was holding Charlie's ringing alarm clock and earthquaking the bed. It was possibly the first time he had ever been glad to see her. He always believed she yelled so loudly in the mornings in the secret hope she would scare him into wetting the bed. She had only been successful in that endeavor once.

"Look, boy," Layla continued, "Mama said if you are late to school today, you don't get to visit the Senior Center this weekend. And that'd mean you might have to get an actual life of your own." Layla dropped the still-ringing clock in his lap and stormed off, muttering, "What kind of kid wants to spend his whole weekend hanging around a bunch of old folks?"

Layla treated Charlie as if he were an alien species, despite the fact that they were the spitting image of each other. Of course, neither of them would admit to bearing any familial resemblance at all.

Charlie sat on his bed, his eyes blinking at his orange and green walls. "Yay," he said, dully, as realization set in. "I get to be the only kid in the world to go to my first day in the sixth grade twice."

Based on his past experience with school, he held little hope that the second first day would be much better than the first. This had been the third disturbing dream of the week, each more vivid than the last. Charlie had been prone to nightmares when he was six, but it had been years since he had a dream he even remembered. Now, entering middle school, the dreams had returned — in spades. As the summer had progressed, he found himself in one nightmare after the other. His hope that it was just a symptom of puberty was beginning to fade into a fear that perhaps he was going crazy. Or worse.

The fact that his dreams seemed to be coming true made him dread school even more than normal.

2 – FRESH STARTS STALE QUICKLY

I'm going to a new middle school.

The words had become a chant that declared his liberation from the tyranny of elementary school and its bus rides full of three-abreast first graders. It was the 27th of August, and he was officially a big-time-middle-school kid. The sixth grade was halfway to college, and halfway out of his parents' house. He was psyched. A new school meant a new start, and possibly, an end to his interminable loneliness. Charlie was a bright, personable boy, whom almost no one knew. Ignored at home, bored at school, and without a close friend to speak of, he had become so accustomed to feeling invisible that he had adopted it as part of his persona.

Charlie was biracial, though he rarely thought of himself as such. His father was of Scottish descent, by way of Boston, and his mother was of African American origin, via the nation's capitol. Charlie thought the whole idea of ethnicity a bit silly. He had never seen his father wear a kilt, and his mother's closest connection to Africa was a collection of dusty wooden masks that gave him the willies. His sister, Layla, self-identified as black. Charlie self-identified as Charlie. It wasn't that he did not feel black. Rather, he did not believe he had to choose just to make others feel more comfortable. He had felt as close to his late paternal grandmother, Kate, who had alabaster skin and blue eyes, as he did to his maternal great-grandfather, Joe, who was the color of dark chocolate. Now, surrounded by a sea of multi-hued students, he delighted in his ability to blend in and disappear. His skin was his camouflage.

Tan American, that's me.

Charlie had attended the same elementary school for six years, and the closest he had come to developing a friend was Jannet Rogers, whom, he believed, sat next to him his entire school career for the express purpose of getting on his nerves. He had been able to tolerate his lack of a social life by spending weekends at the Senior Center with his great-grandfather Joe, who was a life-long adventurer, a great storyteller, and a first-class grump. Charlie adored him. His great-grandfather was Charlie's one bright spot; however, lately, Joe had begun to slip into the unforgiving arms of senility. It was, to Charlie, like watching a brilliant light bulb slowly dim. He intended to enjoy every bit of light he could before the shadows took over.

This day, unfortunately, was not the weekend. It was a school Monday. If weekends were a bright spot, then school days were a dark abyss of endless torment – at least to a genius kid with no friends.

New middle school.

The words sat on his tongue much in the way a long line of spit did when he let it dangle inches from the ground. Like drool, the words had a sickening aftertaste he tried hard not to think about. What if his new school were no different than the old one? What if the chance for a new start that his great-grandfather had promised was an illusion? What if being a lone wolf was to be his lot in life?

Still, the idea of a new school, and the hope it implied, made his heart pound in his chest.

New.

The irony of that word was not lost on Charlie.

How can they call it my new school, when I'm pretty sure that slaves built it?

Sadly, his southeastern Virginia school was not named "The Zone." Instead, it had the mundane name of "Upper Peninsula Middle School." The building was an old two-story cinderblock structure, painted over in what could only be described as cream-of-puke green. The windowsills were painted a forest green that complemented the puke walls, while covering sixty years' worth of old paint. The nauseating color ensured no one could stand near enough the walls to notice the shoddy paint job. This produced the secondary benefit of keeping you from noticing how musty the old building smelled. Yes, from a distance, one would even think people who had possessed the gift of fire built the school.

Unh, skool good!

By now, Charlie was daydreaming, picturing how the builders would have celebrated finishing construction ... perhaps by sacrificing a goat. He squinted at the ancient cinderblocks and decided the school must have predated slavery — even ancient Egyptian slavery.

Adam and his sons Cain and Abel probably directed Neanderthal migrant workers to build it. They could have used ground-up leaves for the paint color. I can see their ads now, "Adam and Sons Construction, building schools since ... the Beginning."

Charlie was standing pretty much to himself, nearest the side entrance. There were groups of other kids talking around him, as he silently scanned the crowd. He was an average height to slightly short sixth grader in a sea of eighth graders. Nearest him was one kid with a goatee who had either been sent down to the minors from high school, or was a precociously young teacher. The torn t-shirt and the semi-glazed stare suggested he might not be too bright.

"Yup, teacher for sure," Charlie giggled to himself.

Shoot.

Not to himself. (He really needed to work on that.)

He could feel Jannet (the Plannet) Rogers somewhere behind him roooollllinnng her eyes at him. She was a copper-haired, pencil-thin girl with all the charm and fashion sense of an eighteenth century schoolmarm. Charlie called her The Plannet (in his head) because of her world-class ego.

You'd think straight A's for life meant you were smart or something.

Charlie wasn't impressed with grades. That took way more paying attention than he wanted to deal with. He had taught himself to read at age four, mostly out of boredom, so had never acquired the skill of learning from others. Generally, he just daydreamed, and wished teachers would *shut up* so he could think.

Charlie's dad would yell at him because of his grades, when, unbeknownst to Charlie, he was prodded by his wife into energizing his son's ambition. Charlie's mom would just give her famous "Do better baby, okay?" speech, and Charlie would, for her. A grading period of daydreams was almost always followed by a period of all A's except one B. Charlie hated straight A's. Only followers got straight A's as far as he was concerned. It was important to establish a healthy sense of independence when dealing with teachers.

As this was an important day, Charlie was dressed appropriately. He had on his lucky jeans with the torn left knee, a red polo shirt, and his favorite red canvas sneakers, with "Charlie" signed in ink, just above Chuck Taylor's signature. That little bit of art had gotten him a First

Rate Butt Slap, his first since he was eight years old.

"Charlie, how many days did you go to work this week?" his father had asked,

In his defense, the literal-minded Charlie often did not get the concept of the rhetorical question. He had made the mistake of answering, "One," since he had been at work with his mom that Thursday. Being a "Smart Alec" (whoever he was) was generally not tolerated in the Patterson household, it turned out. Still, looking at how awesome he looked in genuine Charlie Autographed sneaks had made it worthwhile. He did hate that Alec guy though, he remembered, absently rubbing his bottom.

"What doesn't kill you makes you stronger," his left brain reminded.

Charlie called his left brain Chuck.

Now, it should be noted here that Charlie never thought of Chuck as his left brain. At eleven, the concept of left versus right brain was still alien to him. Nor did he think of it, exactly, as his logical side and his emotional side, though the two halves of his personality had been battling for control for as long as he could remember. No, to Charlie, he simply heard his mother's logical voice, Chuck, and his father's emotional one, Charlene. Chuck was tough, cool, and efficient, like his mom, while Charlene was sensitive and emotional, like his dad. His dad wasn't gay, but he thought Charlene might be. A little. Chuck reminded him quite a bit of his Uncle Alexander, who was.

"Hey!" he heard himself yell, as he was crammed against the open door. He wondered, not a bit embarrassed, how long it had been open. The kids were in their first-day rush to establish territories in the new class rooms. It was positively the only day any of them would rush into the building when it wasn't raining.

All of the sixth-grade English classrooms were on the musty first floor except Charlie's. Due to an influx of newcomers in the area, there were more sixth graders than ever, and one lucky English class got to be on the second floor with the big shot eighth-graders. Charlie ran up the stairs, two at a time, looking as casual as he could make his face look. This decision could make or break his year. He couldn't mess it up.

Charlie hoped to sit in the middle of the classroom, the absolute center, nearest the windows and the faded pea-green walls. This was his strategic spot, the perfect placement. He rushed, in his most casual, "I don't care where I sit," walk that was, of course, about twice as fast as a casual walk should be. He didn't know for certain that anyone had figured out the perfect seat, but he reasoned he couldn't take chances with a decision as critical as location.

If he sat too close to the front, he was doomed on two levels. First, all the kids behind him, and they would all be behind him, would think he was a suck up. A teacher's baby. A sissy. Or worse of all, a "you think you're smart, don'tcha?" kid, the kind who is automatically a target for anyone who thinks in fact they themselves are not so smart. But he wasn't really so worried about them. If he sat way up front, Mrs. Taylor would know for sure he wasn't paying attention.

Mrs. Taylor had been Charlie's fifth grade teacher. She had probably been a sweet lady back in the old days — the 1980s — when she started teaching. However, too many years of the teaching the same thing had taken its toll on her patience, especially with smart-mouthed boys who did not seem to know their own potential. Still, even though she made picking on Charlie in class her hobby, and once made him cry, he could tell she liked him. That made it even worse.

Just when he was celebrating making her a faded memory, she announced she was following her "favorite goof-off" to teach in Middle School. Charlie had being having school nightmares ever since. Being supernaturally lucky — in the way that deer are lucky on dark roads when trucks are near — he had managed to get Mrs. Taylor for English.

"Yay." Charlie gave a flat-line cheer in his head at the thought of sharing puberty with her. Maybe it would stunt his development, and he'd never have to suffer through liking girls. No, anytime a girl would try to steal his soul with her dark magic, he'd just picture ol' Mrs. Taylor's pudgy red face. And her voice. The voice that made cats cry. He actually saw her make butter melt once just by singing to it. Really.

If he sat in the front of the classroom, she'd probably call on him just to embarrass him when he was drawing his important sketches in the margins of his notepaper. That was just ... sick. He could imagine her scratchy, "I got you now, boy," voice, with her smug little half-smile.

He could almost hear the kids giggle behind him as he sweated under her gaze. "Um, could you repeat the question," he would ask timidly. Her face would contort into a raptor's grin, and she'd actually begin to drool with the thought of fresh boy kill. And, with the appropriate perverse delight, she'd repeat the question, and add a second part to it since he wasn't listening.

Then, he knew, there would be an almost perfect silence. The room would fill with the sweet smell of anticipated humiliation. There would be nary a sound, as the kids behind Charlie wouldn't want to miss a second of his fumbling answer. The corner of Mrs. Taylor's mouth would begin to curl in an up-turned, knowing smile …

Then he would answer the questions. Correctly. He would then add some stuff she hadn't taught yet. Man, would they all hate his stinking guts — again. No, he'd been down that road before. The front of the classroom was right out.

As he entered the classroom, Jannet Rogers gave him her usual look, which he knew meant she considered him to be an alien life form. Jannet snapped her head away, her hair strands moving in unison, none daring to fall out of step. No, a misplaced hair would suffer the humiliation of a firm brushing, followed by chemical warfare. There were two kinds of hair in the world: good hair, and hair that you beat into submission. If you can't be good, at least be quiet. Jannet had quiet hair. Quiet and red was an odd combination, to say the least. The thought of that made him snicker.

Jannet turned her eyes toward him, somehow not changing the position of her head, and gave him a full three-second eye roll before turning away. "Pa. The. Tic," was all she decided he was worth. She was wearing a long white dress with small, tan polka dots. Her freckled face was fixed ahead, ignoring him. Charlie thought it odd that a pale girl dotted with freckles would choose to wear a dress the same colors as her skin. It was like some weird Rogers camouflage.

"Would you stop staring at me, Patterson?" Jannet startled him by saying. "You. Are. So. Creepy."

Charlie hadn't realized he was staring, and hoped she wasn't stupid enough to think it meant her liked her. To disprove that notion, he decided to ignore her back, and began putting his new pencils neatly on his desk, and grinning to himself in his inside grin. Outwardly, he had a look that resembled someone whom had just smelled cheese for the first time. But inside, he was grinning — big time. It was his perfect-middle-desk-spot grin.

Charlie could have probably lived with being stuck in the front, although the prospect of going through another year labeled as the weird, smart, all-day daydreamer made him cringe. Even worse than that would have been to be stuck in the back. First of all, you had the same problems as in the front. Only this time, Ms. Taylor would call on you quicker since she was sure the only reason any kid would sit back there was to goof off.

She obviously never smelled her own breath.

Even scarier, in the back was where the Tough Kids sat. They were big, they were mean, they were dumb, and proud of it. The back was Willie Green (teeth)'s territory. (But you never, ever, called him green teeth to his face. To be safe, you never brought up the subject of pimples either, lest you make Willie start feeling self-conscious, whereupon he would pound you into dust.) If Charlie sat back there, in between getting smacked in the head, or punched in the arm, or just kicked all day long, he'd have to choose between answering wrong on purpose and living, or answering right, and risk getting killed after school. You do not come into Willie Green's territory and make him look bad. You also don't stick your tongue in a light socket.

I'd do that before messing with Willie Green.

Willie had failed the third grade twice (rumor said) and so he was actually fifteen (supposedly), which is why he was huge.

"His mama is why he is ugly," Charlene offered. Charlie snickered again, which evoked a deep sigh from Jannet.

Charlie just couldn't risk being asked a question in the back of the classroom. He had rarely answered anything wrong on purpose in his life, and he was really afraid he'd forget. Once, in the second grade, he had tried that and got so scared he forgot what answer was wrong. So, he froze, and said nothing. The teacher made him stay in the classroom until he gave her an answer. Charlie sat in the classroom, with the teacher, listening to the sounds of students' joyous departure. He heard the buses leave on by one, their diesel stench wafting through the windows and mixing with the classroom's normal musty smell.

His teacher had simply glared at him, and every ten minutes or so would wave her flabby arms at him and ask, "Are you ready to answer now, Mr. Patterson?" Of course, by then, he had remembered the answer, but couldn't think of a way to answer it and still save face. So, he kept his silent vigil, and tried his best not to make eye contact with her. His mom finally came and picked him up at 5:30. She was pissed. He would quit school before risking that again.

So, after much consideration, he had found his perfect spot — right in the middle with the normal kids (except Jannet, who was abnormal, but sitting right next to him), next to the window for a good sunny daydream, and nowhere near Willie Green.

Yep, this looked like it was going to be a normal, quiet year. Heck, if he were lucky, no one would even remember he was there.

***

Charlie, for being a thoughtful, insightful boy, had a knack for being absolutely wrong about many things. Maybe it could be attributed to his age, or the fact that he was smarter than he was wise. Whatever the reason, it was not at all unusual for him to be absolutely certain of a thing's occurrence, only to have the opposite happen. Quiet year? Hardly.

This became evident to Charlie, when upon climbing onto the bus for the trip home after his victorious first day, he looked up to see Mrs. Thornwood, his snarling second-grade teacher behind the wheel. Charlie almost jumped back off the bus, but remembered he didn't know the way home.

"Charlie Pee Pants," she sneered, her sallow teeth gleaming in the afternoon sun. Charlie could swear he saw a line of drool dangling from the brown edges of her tobacco-ravaged teeth. He resisted the urge to check the front of his pants to check if she was referring to a current... incident.

"Interesting to see you, Pee Pants," she leered. Her craggy smile was anything but pleasant, and Charlie shivered. Mrs. Thornwood was no more than 42, but looked 55, her face an intricate spider's web of cracks and crevices. Her cheeks hung from her as if they no longer wanted to remain a part of her face and were attempting to blend in with her loose neck skin. Mrs. Thornwood's attempts to beautify herself only added to her garishness. The cracks were filled with a layer of makeup that reminded Charlie of when he'd helped his dad spackle his room before painting. The cloud of tobacco fumes that surrounded her in elementary school had been replaced by the putrid smell of old-lady perfume that made Charlie want to gag. The pale color of her made-up skin contrasted with the deep ebony of her hair and made her look even less alive than she was. In short, she looked a bit more like a zombie than a bus driver. Even so, Charlie didn't like her.

The teacher-turned-bus-driver had dropped from a size twenty-two to a six, losing 110 pounds (as well as some of her left lung) after a bout with cancer that left her too broke not to work, but too weakened to teach. Charlie had heard his mother speak of her illness. Apparently, Mrs. Thornwood's love of children drew her to a career that would keep her close to the little darlings.

Yeah, just like how the witch kept close to Hansel and Gretel.

"Sooooo good to see you Charlie lad," she purred in a voice that tasted to his brain like syrup mixed with vomit and nails. Fortunately, Charlie's compulsive need to be first to claim a seat meant no one else was actually in the bus to hear the Pee Pants comment. After all, he had only done that once, and he was seven then.

"Double P!"

Crap. The unmistakable voice of Cody (nicknames for life) Bullock, official class clown with an idiot savant's memory for embarrassing details.

"Thanks, Mrs. Thornbush," Charlie mumbled, trying to ignore the laughter now building like a wave behind him. He plopped himself down in the nearest burnt-orange seat, his backside hitting the hard bench with a concrete thud. In addition to attending the oldest school, he apparently had the honor of riding on the oldest school bus in civilization. Charlie wondered if Henry Ford had built it himself with used Model T parts.

He sighed, and filled his ears with music, shutting his eyes tight, and hoping against hope that idiot Cody would forget Just. This. Once. Charlie was upset enough that he had even forgotten to count the seats to make sure he was one past the center seat. He'd have to do better tomorrow, he reasoned.

Double P, rather, Charlie, listened to his Jamaican Ragga music while the bus squeaked and swayed in an equally hypnotic rhythm. Charlie was soothed enough that his mind did what it did best ... it wandered.

He began to wonder if he should be concerned that Mrs. Thornwood had turned up as his real bus driver. Of course, in his dream, she barely fit in the seat, and was now slim. Still, in the dream, she had been both smaller and meaner than when he knew her in elementary school. True, he had never been her favorite, but she had never called him names in public before. Even in the classroom "answer me" standoff, she had called him Mr. Patterson. Moreover, he had no idea she'd become a bus driver. That was too many coincidences.

He reassured himself by remembering how different his dream was from reality. This was certainly no Greyhound he was riding. There was no luxury to be found. In fact, Elena Martinez was sitting on the dusty floor in the center of the bus, rocking back and forth, and humming to unheard music. Elena was a sweet girl with large, chocolate-brown eyes and jet-black hair. Charlie liked her, and thought it a shame that no boy had given her his seat. True, she was heavy like ...

He sat bolt upright, his left earplug flying out and hitting the tow-headed boy next to him in the eye.

Her mom. It was the dream again.

Charlie was starting to feel agitated. He would actually be glad to be home for a change, where things were predictably boring.

3 – NOTHING COMES TO SLEEPERS

It was after Coach Traynam's giant gym shoes kicked Charlie in the butt for the third time that he decided this wasn't an excellent nightmare. True, it was somewhat amusing the way they scampered about, giving orders that smelled vaguely of old fish. But they seemed overly enthusiastic with their work in his opinion.

"Move along Charlene," the dirtier left shoe ordered, its long tongue flapping in a silly, lop-eared bunny sort of way. Charlene was the name Coach gave Charlie during his one tryout for Pee Wee football. It had stuck in Charlie's head ever since.

Charlie took solace in the fact the coach had two left shoes. That probably explained why his stint in the Pros didn't last more than four games. Coach Traynam was a huge, oily, bear of a man, who always seemed to be sweating, even in the coldest weather. Besides an impressive streak of consecutive losing seasons coaching youth football in the area, he was best known for wearing white socks and sneaks with his suit.

Charlie could picture Coach Traynam's rationale — you never know when an exercise emergency might break out, and you had to be ready. Okay, so that probably wasn't the reason, but still it was more amusing that guessing coach couldn't afford size 15EEEE dress shoes on his paltry part-time teacher's salary.

Coach himself was nowhere to be found, but left his butt-kicking shoes in charge of hall duty. As Charlie made the turn towards the looping corridor that housed the science classes, the shoe gave him one last swift kick in the butt.

"What was that one for?" Charlie whined, grabbing his cheeks with both hands.

The dirty left shoe hopped away without a word, giggling with the familiar fish-breath, Coach-is-crazy laugh that kept the boys with good sense away from his football team. Charlie looked to its sparkling white twin left shoe for consolation, but it was busy breaking itself off in some knucklehead boy's butt. Charlie recognized Willie's dirty blond hair immediately. Willie was spending his first year in middle school in much the same way he spent the past five years.

By this point, Charlie was actively willing himself awake, as he often did when his dreams didn't go his way. For some reason, however, this time it wasn't working. True, it didn't always work right away; he often had to wake up from a dream two or three times in a row before his subconscious would relinquish control to the real world. Still, just knowing it was a dream would usually be enough to make it change in a direction he liked.

He walked along the corridor, counting the lockers, even though they were already numbered. The science geeks' locker numbers were laid out in beautiful algebra equations. The geeks were busily tapping in their handhelds, trying to match the equations with the answers they had been given. First week of school was still a bit rough on the science geeks.

Charlie had the misfortune of being assigned a locker right in the Jocks' Wing. Now, in his actual school, there was no Jocks' Wing. But to kid with no visible athletic prowess, it seemed natural that the fawning public would build them one. He walked as quietly as he could, looking at his feet all the while. Somewhere in his mind, he remembered someone telling him not to make direct eye contact. That story carried some vague warning about the Jocks being able to smell fear, and considering eye contact to be a threat.

"Hey mouse!" he heard someone call him from his left.

Charlie bristled, but kept silent. He never started trouble, but he was definitely not one to run away either. As he continued his march, just now noticing that he was further from his locker than when he started, he considered telling the Jock he was more cat than mouse. Instead, he decided to stare the him directly in the eye, the equivalent of tugging on Superman's cape. For a genius kid, Charlie was pretty dumb.

Fortunately, the Jock, a blonde six-footer named Lars Somethingswedish was preening in the full-length mirror in his locker, and had already lost interest. Charlie caught enough of his reflection in

Lars' mirror to notice that he was, indeed, a mouse.

"Hmm," Charlie mumbled aloud. It seemed Lars was being genuinely friendly. Maybe some Jocks weren't too bad.

Before he could even finish the thought, the top half of Lars' body turned 180 degrees, facing Charlie, while his legs continued to face his locker. He gave Charlie a wink, and then showed a toothy grin that featured at least three rows of pointed teeth. His body began to morph, with his skin turning to scales, his eyes changing to an inhuman gold, and his jaw extending until it was a leonine muzzle. Within seconds, Lars was more reptile than human. Charlie staggered back, trying to make his back as small against the corridor wall as possible. Without warning, the Lars creature leapt, leaving the smaller boy only time to clench his eyes, and await death.

"You're awfully tall for a mouse," said a soft, familiar voice.

Charlie, still crouched against the wall, opened one eye. No sign of the jock. He opened the other eye, and turned. The hallway was empty, with the exception of the first Really Cute Girl he'd ever seen in his school. She had huge hazel eyes, full lips, and long dark hair that started out straight and ended in bouncy curls. She smiled at him, mouth full of braces, and repeated her comment. Charlie instantly recognized her from the Greyhound bus dream.

"D-did you see a tall, b-blonde kid?" he asked her. "Or, a lizard man?" His voice was a trembling squeak, but he was too shaken to feel embarrassed.

The girl frowned, and shook her head. "Nope. I've only seen some smelly basketball shoes, and now, a talking mouse." She grinned, and turned to enter the nearest classroom. "This is a really weird school. I like it."

Charlie began to shrink. The Cute Girl grinned even harder.

4 – THE CUTE GIRL AWAKES

Cute Girl giggled, assuming Charlie changed into a mouse and shrank just to show off for her, and decided that boys were silly. This one was at least amusing, if a bit weird.

All that talk of blondes and lizard men when he was standing and talking to himself.

When she finally made it home from her wonderful new school, she'd have to remember all the interesting "people" she had met. She had never actually played basketball with a pair of basketball shoes before. You would think they'd be better at it. This pair was slow, and kind of smelled like farts.

She did wonder, however, how she got to this school from New Mexico. Her mom was going to be all mad at having to pick her up from school in Virginia. "Okay," she thought, "That clinches it. I can't be in Virginia already, or else I can't be awake." This little realization disturbed her very little. She was increasingly aware that she might be asleep, but decided not to wake up, just in case it got weirder. She liked weird quite a bit — it made her feel at home.

She found it not at all odd that geography violated her sense of logic, while talking mice and basketball-playing shoes seemed normal. This place had its own set of rules, she decided, and she would go with them. If logical things seemed troublesome, so be it. Logic was so overrated.

That's why boys are stupid.

The Cute Girl's name was actually Robin Mercedes LeBeaux, although she would have loved having been named Cute Girl if her parents had enough foresight to think of it. Robin entered the classroom, and was immediately hit with a wave of nausea that not even the puke green walls could explain. She heard the weird, mumbly mouse-boy say something, but then the school bell rang, and whatever he was saying faded to a dim buzz behind her.

No, not behind her, it was next to her — where her nightstand was. That buzzing was sounding suspiciously like her obnoxious alarm clock. Her mostly asleep brain warned her to wake up before the buzzing became unbearable. It was a whisper now, but it would advance to chainsaw volume in a minute, and then Mommy would come yell for her to get her "skinny butt up." Then Mommy would smile, but Robin's smile was broken before eight o'clock, and she never smiled back. Unless she smelled pancakes.

"Oh, shucks," Robin giggled. "It was just getting fun. If Virginia is anywhere near this weird … "

"*You'll fit right in,*" her inside voice finished.

"Oh, shut up," Robin said softly, almost to herself, but not quite — not really. She swung her right arm towards her alarm clock, and pounded it into silence with one blow from her slender fist. This was moving day, her big day, and she needed to be ready. It was a week before school was to start in her bustling New Mexico town, and Mommy had told her just last week they were moving across the country. They'd be a week or so late for the start of school in her new Virginia home, but Robin was a quick study ("mi genio hija," her mom would say) and Mommy wasn't really worried. The absolute last thing on Robin's mind was school work. She was leaving her best friends!

Of course Robin's initial reaction was tears, followed by horrified phone calls to her crew of equally pretty twelve-year-old girls, followed by more tears, followed, inevitably, by heart-felt promises to Always Write and vows of Eternal Friendship. Robin at least, was sincere, though she doubted Lindsay Waggadorn could be consistent about anything for much more than six weeks. Becky, her best friend, would write, and they would webcam, and still be sisters and stuff. She'd probably need to find another Number Two to replace Lindsay, just in case.

In truth, most of Robin's dramatics were for Becky's sake, so she would never doubt Robin's love. But Robin's house, pretty though it was, was not a Good Place. It was full of clutter, and cat hair, and tears, and memories dripping from the stucco walls that refused to fade. When Mommy told her of The New Job Back East, and her chance for a New Start, Robin almost dared to hope.

Almost.

So now was the day the movers would come, and she'd hop on a plane, and be east (or north, she wasn't quite sure how to properly measure Virginia) for their New Start. She made herself think of her start in capital letters, because it just had to be. It had to, because she couldn't let herself fail. Not this time.

Not like with Reyna.

Immediately the tears came. They flooded from her bright eyes, green, the color of sadness, of disruption, of heartache. The tears raced a familiar trail down the sides of her small, perfect nose, leaving a salt-stained path down peach-colored cheeks, and bounding, joyously, to her satin pink pajamas. Her tears were rapturous, delirious in their conquest of her. She cried until she shuddered, her diaphragm contracting, doubling her over in pain. She gasped for air, and begged the tears to stop.

But still the tears came, until she could make no more. And, when the tears were done, she was washed of it. She was finally clean of the sadness … at least until the next time she thought of her sister. She reached under the mattress where she kept Reyna's last photo, and held it to her chest, hugging her with both arms. She'd almost forgotten to pack it — almost left her big sister behind.

"I won't forget, Reyna. I promise I won't," Robin vowed.

She was an only child now, after a lifetime of being the "funny-looking little sister," her Reyna's little bird. Now as puberty awakened the long, lean beauty she would become, she was the pretty one — the only one left. Reyna's death had left Robin a wounded little bird, but it had freed her as well. She would fly from this place — her lovely little piece of Hell, and make her sister proud. She'd promised that, and she wouldn't forget her promise. Last promises have to be kept. They do.

And the tears came once more. This time, they threatened not to stop, until Mommy started coming down the hall. The tears were afraid of Mommy, and they never came when she was around. Mommy wouldn't understand the tears. No one would. No one ever could.

'Cause she'd never tell.

5 – "FAILURE IS NOT THE FALLING DOWN, BUT THE STAYING DOWN" — MARY PICKFORD

A still-dreaming Charlie watched the Cute Girl turn the corner into her classroom, stop, and hold her head, swaying as if she might fall. Charlie called out, his voice making only an embarrassing squeak. "Are you okay?"

Great, thanks voice. Change now, why don'tcha?

The school bell rang for first period, and the Cute Girl suddenly perked up. Charlie at first thought this dream girl might be another book nerd like Jannet, but then she started raving to herself about alarm clocks, silly dreams, and waking to pancakes.

Cool. She's normal like me.

At that very instant, she disappeared.

Charlie correctly surmised he was dreaming that she was dreaming all this. He could not understand why he would dream that a kid he didn't know was having a dream. He couldn't be awake, so this must be somebody's dream. Cute girls in the real world do not disappear like ghosts. Besides, if he had dreamt, she wouldn't have vanished when she began talking about waking up. Heck, if it were his dream, she'd still be here — at least until he had found the courage to ask her name.

But I'm not awake. He looked down at his mouse body. That was pretty clear.

Charlene also insisted he was not awake. *"Grandma said there's no such things as ghosts, and she used to talk to Jesus all the time, so she'd know."*

So, he was asleep, and the girl seemed to be having her own dream at the end, apart from him. That meant she was asleep too. There was only one explanation.

Maybe she was dreaming him.

Oh. My. God. What if there is no Charlie Patterson? What if my whole life, all 11.9 years, is just a brief instant in some girl's dream?

"Wait a minute, genius," offered Chuck, now tiring of Charlie's emotional ranting. "The only logical explanation is that you somehow ended up in one of her dreams, just like she showed up in yours."

Now in firm control, his left brain woke him up.

Good old Chuck. You rock.

He was on the bus, and the early morning sun told him he was heading to school. He had forgotten that he had awakened and boarded it. Indeed, he had forgotten the entire morning to that point.

The bus stopped at his school with a lurch, and an unceremonious "Off!" from Mrs. Thornwood. Charlie stepped off, head down, counting his steps, and bumped headfirst into what felt like his Aunt Carmel, with the huge … things.

"Hey kid, watch the tits," grunted the tallest ugly girl he had ever seen. She was built like an upside-down triangle, with massive shoulders and chest to match, along with a face that could only be described as gorillish. Though only thirteen, she was already almost six feet tall. Perhaps she was the ugliest tall girl he had ever seen. He was trying to figure out which when she pushed him ass over baseball cap into a mud puddle that was busy trying to convince itself it was a garden.

"Leave the kid alone, Tisha," came a voice from slightly behind, as a small hand tugged gently on her frayed lavender sweater.

Tisha turned, and grunted. "Yeah, he ain't worth the detention, little perv."

"I doubt he put his head between your boobs on purpose," her friend calmed. "He doesn't look like the suicidal type."

They both laughed, and Charlie curled himself into a little ball in the puddle, trying very hard to be invisible. His rescuer, a beautiful girl with shining gray eyes was looking at him with a sad smile, that he sensed wasn't vindictive. She was tall compared to him, and slim, and …

Crap. My dream.

Charlie recognized her as the Cute Girl from his dream, although she appeared to be much taller than he remembered in his dream. He felt — awkward — and not only because his dreams had begun to freak him out. It was just, well, she made him hurt. Inside. And his teeth felt itchy. He wondered if he had brushed his teeth after

24

breakfast, as that could have been the cause.

The girl cocked her head to the side, and looked at him with a strange frown that registered surprise rather than anger. At least he was not the only one surprised to meet in real life. She followed Tisha through the ugly green doors, never taking her eyes off Charlie.

He was left alone in the drizzle as the first school bell sounded. He was cold, and wet, and muddy, and a little teary-eyed. Most of all, he was confused. He needed order, needed to know what to expect. One thing was certain, however — this was going to be anything but a normal school year.

Charlie wondered, as he wandered to class, if, perhaps, he had seen the girl around town before without realizing it. That would certainly explain her appearances in his dreams, and her sudden appearance at school. Having dreams about a pretty girl you forgot you'd met was certainly more logical than a dream-invading serial killer.

Or thinking you somehow entered the dream of a girl who wasn't even asleep.

Still, it wasn't just the girl.

First, Elena Martinez and Mrs. Thornwood then Goatisha, now the Cute Girl.

Charlie's left brain tried to tell him these were coincidences, that there was a perfectly logical explanation. He just needed to get on the internet so he could find it. Yes, there was probably some dream research … but Charlie was not buying it. Logic wouldn't answer this puzzle.

Worst of all, the cutest girl on earth just saw him get his butt kicked by a female Wookiee, and it wasn't even nine o'clock yet. Too much of what happened reminded him of recent dreams. He thought about the other dreams he'd being having lately — the stupid, awful nightmares — and began to get worried.

Crap. I hope I don't meet any lizard men at school today.

Some dreams were not meant to come true.

6 – ON THE RIVER, BLUE

After an eventful few days, Charlie was determined to never dream again, even if it meant never sleeping. To make sure, once his parents were in bed, he snuck into the kitchen and made himself the strongest cup of coffee he could stand. Horrified at its taste, he sweetened it "a bit" with four teaspoons of sugar. He was quite pleased with himself as he sat sipping the concoction in his bed.

This is perfect. I'll worry about being drowsy in school tomorrow. I just need one day without worrying about a nightmare coming true.

Charlie continued sipping, even as his eyelids began to droop from the warmth in his belly.

"Feels good going down too," he muttered, as he drained the last of the liquid. He settled himself in bed, and switched on his laptop. He had planned every detail of his all-nighter, even pre-selecting movies to stream that he was certain would keep him riveted. It would be a glorious night of sleeplessness.

Which is precisely why he was horrified when he "awoke" in the midst of a dream, no more than five minutes after drinking his coffee. At first, he was terrified, as he was certain he must be awake. After all, coffee, according to his dad, was guaranteed to get one going in the morning. Even so, he found himself standing on a wooden raft, in the midst of an ice blue world. If he was still awake, then he must be insane. Being a logical boy, he quickly discarded that hypothesis.

That girl! She must have kidnapped me into her dream again, somehow.

Charlie looked around, but saw no sight of her. What he did see, however, was marvelous. The raft on which he stood seemed to be hand hewn from logs, judging by the ax marks, and tied together with twine and leather straps. It was six feet wide by ten feet long, and drifted with the gentle current of the blue river on which it sat. Charlie sat down, facing the very front of the raft, and took in the view.

Wait. There's no current.

The river itself looked more like a sheet of blue glass than water. Even though the raft moved without Charlie's assistance, the water showed no movement, not even a ripple.

Maybe it's a ghost boat. Charlie regretted the thought as soon as he allowed himself to think it. He scanned the edges of the river, looking for threats. The river was bordered on both sides by snow-covered rocky peaks, which also gave off a bluish hue. The sky was clotted with thick bluish-grey cumulus clouds that hung low over the mountains. At the farthest point ahead, where the river took a sharp bend to the right, sat an enormous blue moon. It looked like the moon he was used to seeing, except its color, and the fact that it was larger in the sky than the rising sun.

The moon illuminated the landscape as if it were bathed in blue daylight. The reflections of the rugged mountains painted the still river. Odd, bubble-headed fish poked their noses above the surface of the river. Their random movements caused interlocking ripples that made it appear the water had decided to dance. The moon danced there as well, seeming to touch the water, and cause it to glow. It was bitterly cold, Charlie knew. The entire landscape looked frigid. Small islands of ice dotted the river as he passed, and his breath hung heavy in the air with each exhalation. Nonetheless, though this world looked as if there had never been a sun to warm it, Charlie could feel none of it.

"Must be the stupid coffee making me warm. A lot of good it did keeping me awake." Charlie was speaking aloud, and the sound of his voice echoed from the surrounding mountains.

"Did y'all check to see if it was decaf before you made it?" The voice came from behind him, and Charlie whipped around quickly enough that his movements made the raft rock from side to side.

"Jeez-o-flip!" Charlie said, holding his chest, and panting. "You scared the heck outta me."

"Steady there, Charlie boy. You like to made us flip over."

"D-do I know you?" Charlie squinted at the figure behind him. It was a tall lad of around fifteen, dressed in bib overalls and a blue-checkered shirt. Despite being no more than three or four years older than Charlie, he was a least a foot taller. He was also quite familiar.

Charlie turned his body to face his companion. He leaned in, and the taller boy slid his straw hat from his head, letting it hang on his back from the cord tied around his neck. The boy grinned at Charlie, his pearly teeth contrasting his rich chocolate complexion.

"G'pa Joe?" Charlie asked, calling him by the shortened form of great-grandpa he'd used since learning to talk.

"In the flesh," his great-grandfather answered. "But seeing as how I'm just a kid in this place myself, might as well call me Joe." He pushed off against the long pole he held, and the raft glided forward. "Seems a bit odd being called G'pa by someone near about your own age."

"How … where did you come from? You weren't there a minute ago."

"I was here. Sometimes it takes a while to tune in. You'll get the hang of it soon enough, I reckon."

"But … I … where are we? How did you bring me here?"

Joe chuckled, his rich baritone resounding off the rock walls. "One question at a time, Charlie boy. First of all, the where is a bit hard to explain. Let's just say we're in a place where dreams are real, and what you think of as reality is just a different sort of dream."

Charlie looked around once more, his eyes stopping at the moon. "So I am dreaming. That explains the ginormous blue moon."

"Well, it wasn't blue until you showed up. You sleeping with the air conditioner turned all the way up again?"

Charlie smiled and shook his head. "Mom won't let me. Said I made the house feel like a refrigerator. I have my own fan, though, and it's right over my head."

Joe smiled. "That explains the cold, I guess."

"But you still haven't told me how I got here," Charlie said. He stood, and carefully walked over to his teenaged great-grandfather. "I mean, it's better than my usual dreams, but I was hoping not to sleep at all."

"Whoa, I didn't bring you here," Joe replied. He stopped pushing off against the river bottom, and allowed the raft to drift along the quickening current. "I was going to ask you how you found me here."

"But … but I even drank coffee to try to and stay awake."

"Your daddy's coffee?"

Charlie nodded in the affirmative.

"Thought so. That hippy only drinks unleaded." Charlie's left eyebrow slid up, signaling his confusion. Joe responded with, "Decaf."

"Decaf? But he's always talking about how he needs his coffee to wake up."

"That's because he don't know your mom's been giving him decaf, so's he don't get on her nerves as much. You probably should have asked her."

Charlie shook his head. "She'd never understand about my nightmares. She thinks I should have outgrown them by now."

Joe placed a large hand on Charlie's shoulder. "Don't sell your mom short. She might just surprise you."

Joe's voice was interrupted by the sound of a thunderous screeching in the distance that echoed off the mountains. It sent chills down Charlie's spine. "E-eagles?" he asked, looking up in the indigo sky for the giant-sized bird that would have made a sound that large.

"Maybe the fire-breathing kind," Joe said, scanning the sky. Charlie frowned at him, by way of asking for clarification, but none came. Satisfied that there was no impeding danger, Joe resumed guiding the boat along the river. "Well, you here now, so you may as well get ready," he said.

Charlie was less convinced of their safety than Joe. "Re-ready for what?"

Joe reached back, and prodded the craft around the right-hand bend they had been approaching. As it cleared the small mounds of ice that blocked their path, Joe pointed. "Ready for that."

Charlie could make out a small flotilla of boats a half-mile ahead. The center of the group comprised a half-dozen barges strung together with chains. The barges carried large structures covered in canvas. Accompanying them were long boats with high sides, in which stood large figures that Charlie could not make out. There were several in each boat, and nearly two dozen in total. At the rear of the caravan was a solitary canoe, in which sat a cloaked figure with his back to Charlie and Joe. Despite there being no signs of a motor, or anyone propelling the small craft, the boat glided effortlessly through the still water.

"Better take a seat. Things could get hairy from here on out," Joe said. His voice had dropped to a whisper.

"Why? What's going on? What's on those barges?"

Joe hesitated, then pulled his long pole from the water, and sat next to Charlie. "I've been reading in the news about a bunch of little kids that are showing signs of brain damage. Some docs even think it might be some new kind of early Alzheimer's."

"Okay." Charlie raised one eyebrow, then looked again at the boats ahead. "I don't get it."

Joe sighed, and motioned toward the barges. "I think that there is a new load of those kids."

Charlie's eyes widened. "You mean there are little kids under those covers?"

Joe nodded in the affirmative. "That's my guess. And those creatures around are there to make sure they get delivered."

"To whom? For what?"

"Batteries."

Charlie found the response puzzling, but something in G'pa Joe's eyes made it clear it was all the answer he would get.

"I don't have time to explain everything now, Charlie. You just need to trust me."

"I always trust you, G'pa, er, Joe." Charlie thought for a moment, then exclaimed in a breathless gush. "My bus dream! I saw a bunch of little kids being herded like sheep."

Joe nodded. "That explains why you showed up here. You shouldn't be here, Charlie. It ain't your time yet. His energy must be pulling you here."

"Whose energy?"

Joe stood, and stuck his pole deep in the river. The raft stopped its forward progress. Charlie rose to his feet as well, and the two watched the flotilla pull further in the distance. Charlie looked up at his companion, but met only the side of his head. Finally, after a full minute, Joe spoke. "That's about far enough, I reckon."

"Far enough for what?"

"There is good and evil in the world, Charlie. Sometimes, you have to be really careful about which one you call to, even by accident."

Charlie laughed, despite himself. "What, like in Harry Potter? We can't say the bogeyman's name?"

Joe met Charlie with a stare that froze all the laughter cold. "Some fiction is truth, Charlie."

Charlie gulped.

Joe placed a hand on the boy's shoulder, and bent low, placing his forehead near Charlie's. "Don't you worry none, this here is the family business. You'll do just fine. It just looks like you running up against the evil part of the world earlier than any of us expected."

"Family business?" Charlie echoed.

Joe leaned forward, now almost whispering in Charlie's ear. "I guess you more like your mom than any of us knew."

"That's the second time you mentioned mom. No offense, but my mom isn't exactly the type to have crazy dreams about people."

"First of all, this ain't your dream. I done told you that. It's mine, and you somehow stumbled into it."

Charlie mouthed the words, "Your dream," but no sound came out.

"Second, your mom ain't happy, that's her problem. Tell you what — she used to be the silliest, happiest, kid you ever wanna meet. Creative as all get-out, too."

"My mom? Name's Charlotte, dark brown hair, light brown eyes, really pretty? Maybe you're thinking of someone else." If his mother had ever had an imagination, Charlie had not seen it.

"Nope, that's her, skin like caramel and all. Right up until she was about sixteen, Charley was a mess of fun. Always up to mischief too. Popular, track star, you name it. Your mama was a lot like you, boy."

"Why did mom change?"

Joe stared at the rising moon, but made no sound; it was long enough that Charlie began to think he had not heard the question. After a while, he turned to Charlie. "Sometimes, dreams don't work out the way you hoped. This place," he said, his arm sweeping at the landscape, "can be whatever you want it to be. But it can also be a prison if you're not careful."

"Like those little kids?"

Joe nodded. "Your mom, well, I reckon she learned that the hard way."

Charlie looked into the older boy's eyes, and saw, for the first time, the eyes of his wise great-grandfather. There was a quiet determination there he knew very well. "You're here to stop them, aren't you?" he asked Joe.

Joe did not answer. Charlie did not need him to.

Ahead, the sky began to darken, as small dots descended from above the clouds. As they drew closer, Charlie could make out the rising call of birds.

"Firebirds," Joe said. There was little emotion in his voice.

"F-fire what?" Charlie stuttered. There was quite a bit of emotion in his.

"They must have spotted us." Joe stepped back to the center of the raft, and instantly, he was transformed. His coveralls disappeared, and he was garbed in a long purple robe. His head was wrapped in a silk purple turban that looped below his chin.

"What are you going to do?" Charlie asked. Joe's sudden change gave him confidence, though he was not sure why.

"Onliest thing I can do – fight fire with magic."

"Don't you mean fire?"

"Can't burn birds made of flames, Charlie." Joe turned toward the sky, as the roiling dark cloud of birds formed a wedge, and began a dive toward Joe's small raft. Then the sky ignited. The birds, in unison, turned to flame, that intensified from a cool blue to white-hot as they flapped and dove. "Hang onto your hat, Charlie. It's about to get hot. If the flames get to close, don't be ashamed to dive in the water."

"But I can't swim," Charlie protested.

"Boy, this is your dream too. Figure something out."

Charlie's first act was to dive onto the floor of the barge, as a firebird swept over the space he'd just occupied. He could feel its heat as it swooped by. Even before he could rise, a second, then a third swept by. They were nothing by bird-shaped flames, with wings pounding the air. Another descended, and this time, fire trailed from the bird as it passed. The ball of flames narrowly missed Charlie's head, setting a small fire on the base of the barge.

"Jeez-o-flip! They're pooping fire."

"That's what firebirds do," answered Joe.

Charlie sat up, and was knocked backward by the force of energy whose source he could not immediately discern. It did not hurt, but tingled, as if every nerve ending in his body was activated.

"Sorry Charlie boy. I couldn't help that. Need to keep this barge from burning."

Charlie looked up, and saw Joe, with his arms churning in the night air. He was emitting a dim light that pulsed from his hands into the air. From his vantage point, it seemed as if his companion were shooting fireworks into the sky from his hands. From every direction, the birds swooped in, expelling fire. The once-calm river was now aflame, with patches of fire surrounding the craft.

"Behind you Charlie!"

Charlie turned and saw another part of the raft aflame. He rushed to it, stomping on the flames until they were extinguished. No sooner had he done so than two more small fires erupted. He rushed to the first, and felt heat singing his back. His jacket was on fire! Charlie fell to the barge's floor and began rolling from side to side. In a few moments, he put out the fires on the barge, and on his clothing.

He sat, panting. He was in pain, but otherwise okay. "You should have made this raft out of metal or something," he called to Joe, who was still fighting against the firebird flock.

"Didn't … think of … it," Joe managed to say, in between thrusting balls of energy into the sky. His aim was improving, and he managed to knock several out of the sky. However, there were hundreds now, and he was making little headway. "I could use some help, Charlie," he called.

Charlie looked around for something to throw, but came up empty. "What do I do?" he asked. He had never felt so useless.

Joe motioned with his head. "You can put out that fire for one thing."

Charlie spun, and saw that the entire rear of the raft had been pooped aflame. He reached into the icy water and scooped some at the flames, but with little effect.

Crap that water is cold!

"This isn't working," he said, flinging water as quickly as he could. We need a metal boat."

Joe turned, and a large firebird flew straight for him. He reacted just in time, managing to strike the bird with his fist, knocking it to the barge's floor with a metallic clang. Joe paused, rubbing his burned hand. "How the hell'd you do that?" he asked.

Charlie was momentarily confused, until he looked down. Their raft was gone, and in its place was an aluminum boat, complete with a large outboard motor.

"I-I don't think I did it," Charlie replied.

"Well it sure as heck wasn't me. Don't just stand there, use the pump."

Charlie looked to his left, and sure enough, there was an enormous pump with a six-inch nozzle. On the pump was a small sign with a single word, "Push." Charlie did as it said, and a jet of water breached the night air, shooting four hundred feet into the sky. No longer was he a helpless boy trying to dodge flammable bird poop on a small craft. This was a game he knew.

He stood on the deck of the ship, his dream now having turned to a three-dimensional video game. Charlie was hit a firebird with the water jet, and it would sizzle into nothing more than a pocket of steam. After a few hits, Joe ceased his own war, and instead, began keeping score, lighting the night air with his point tallies. He awarded ten points for a normal bird, fifty for an eagle-sized firebird, and a whopping one thousand for hitting a bird in full power dive. Within a few minutes, the flock was gone, having left no trace of themselves except for steam, which settled onto the river like a fog.

Charlie's grin competed with the moon for brilliance.

"What do you say we hit the motor and see if we can go catch us some bad guys?" Joe asked.

"I say, hit it!" Charlie enthused.

Joe gunned the engine, and the swift boat glided along the smooth river. They were moving fast enough that the craft barely touched water, spending as much time airborne as it did water bound. In no time, they had caught up with the flotilla. Joe cut the motor, and let his boat drift, as the group ahead turned in his direction. Joe lifted his hands in the air, and expelled two more bursts of energy. These arced high in the sky, and drifted back toward the river like twin flares. With the added illumination, Charlie could see the creatures in the boats that accompanied the barges. He wished he hadn't.

They were tall, long-limbed beings with torsos to match. Each was easily eight feet tall, with thin arms and legs, and oversized hands that were as long as their forearms. Charlie could see their long fingers ended in sharp points. He could imagine their shredding his flesh with one swipe of their hands. It was not clear whether they were male or female, as their thin bodies displayed characteristics of both. They had feminine faces, but no breasts, or any obvious sex traits.

Their faces were red, even in the bluish light, with long noses. Their hair and eyebrows were as white as snow, and made, it appeared of feathers. Their eyes were not human, but wide, with irises that registered red in the dim light. From their scowls and hissing, it was clear they were not happy.

"I sure hope those birds we destroyed weren't relatives of theirs," Charlie whispered to Joe.

"I hope they was," Joe replied.

"Why are they moving so slowly?" Charlie could not help but feel this was a trap. Surely with all the time they had spent on the firebirds, these creatures could have been long since gone. "All they needed to do is find a motor like we did. However we did it."

"They move slowly because the kids' minds a resisting them. It takes a tremendous amount of energy to trap a mind like that, much less a bunch of them."

"So the kids are dreaming this, but those creatures are really trapping their minds somehow?"

"Something like that," Joe said. "Now, I've gotta tell y'all. I've met these fellers before, and my energy didn't do much to stop them."

"What? You're just telling me this now?"

"Well, with this fine metal boat you conjured up, I figure we might just get a head of steam, and sink their little wooden boats. Once we do, all you have to do is grab the chain on the lead barge, and we'll tow those kids to safety."

Charlie nodded. He was not at all convinced that was the best plan he'd ever heard.

The solitary figure in the last boat sat with his hooded head bowed, silent. Joe hit the motor once again, and the aluminum boat took off with a lurch, heading for the tall creatures on the right. The hooded man turned, with his body rotating one hundred eighty degrees, although he neither rose, nor bent. It was as if his torso were on a swivel.

"Hold on!" Joe called, leaning forward, as the swift boat went airborne.

The hooded man lifted his arms, holding a metal staff in one with some kind of bird's skull for a handle. A bolt of what looked like blue lightning emanated from the staff, traveling in all directions as once. Several bolts hit Joe's boat as it descended toward the flotilla, and knocked the craft out of the air. Charlie heard himself scream, and then felt himself hit icy water. The shock of the frigid water overloaded his system, and he began to feel numb.

The feeling was surprisingly pleasant. As he descended into the deep river, he blinked, and smiled at the curious fish that floated around him. They were the same ones that swam alongside the boat. Charlie reached out to touch one – his arm moved sluggishly, as though he were floating in gelatin. Then all went black.

He awoke, what seemed like an instant later. He was shivering, and wet. Joe had wrapped him in his robe, and had managed to start a fire. Next to the small fire was a sizeable haul of wood. It was large enough that Charlie understood he had been unconscious for some time.

Joe had aged seventy years in the time Charlie had slept, and now looked every bit the octogenarian he was in his waking life.

"I thought I lost you, boy," he said, and hugged Charlie so tightly, that the boy disappeared into his great-grandfather's massive frame. "I couldn't wake you up here, and couldn't send you back."

"Back," Charlie repeated. His mind was spinning, as was the world. He lay there for a few moments, watching the blue moon, now high in the sky, swirl above him.

"Yes, back to Virginia, your mom, the real world. Thought maybe you'd ..." His voice trailed off, and he turned away from Charlie.

"I'm okay, G'pa," Charlie responded. He touched his great-grandfather on the arm. "We'll get them next time."

G'pa Joe shook his head. "Ain't gonna be no next time." All the humor had left his eyes, for good, it seemed. He stood, and stepped onto the same raft Charlie had seen when first he arrived.

Charlie sat up. It was too fast, and his head began to spin. "G'pa? Do you think we can maybe dream together again?" he asked, holding his forehead.

G'pa Joe pushed the raft off from the shore, leaving Charlie behind. "I hope, as God is my witness, that you never find this place again. Promise me you'll try to stay away." With those words, he slipped into the rising fog, and disappeared. From the mist, Charlie heard, "Time to wake up."

Charlie did awaken, moments later, drenched, in his sweat-filled bed.

"Not a chance I'm staying away," he said.

This dream world was better than any video game he had ever played. He sat up, still headachy, but excited.

"Don't worry, G'pa," he said to his empty room, "Nobody wins a game the first time they play."

7 – THE INVISIBLE MAN

Much to Charlie's surprise and relief, the next school week passed mostly uneventfully. If he dreamed, he didn't remember it. He barely remembered the dream with G'pa Joe, in fact. Mrs. Thornwood continued to drive the school bus, and, apparently, to hate all the children on the bus — Charlie in particular. Charlie managed to stay below the radar in class most of the time, and if he concentrated very hard on being still and silent, teachers seemed to forget he was even there.

In fact, his one trip above the radar came as a result of his being too effective at being invisible. Just before math on a Thursday afternoon, the teacher had shut the classroom door in Charlie's face, not even recognizing him as one of his students. For a time, Charlie considered not entering at all, but became concerned that the teacher would later refuse to admit him during a test. His failing math would give his father a fit, and he would never believe it wasn't Charlie's fault.

So, after fifteen seconds of deliberation, Charlie turned the doorknob to enter the classroom. He kept his head down as he entered, in part to avoid eye contact with Jannet, who would be watching — and, of course, snickering — but also in blind hope that old man Bachoven would not notice he was there. Unfortunately, the squeaky wooden floors (and giggles from the class) gave him away. Bachoven, already in the process of creating a hazardous cloud of chalk dust, spun in Charlie's direction and looked over his reading glasses.

"May I help you young man?"

Charlie kept his eyes down, and shook his head "no" rapidly.

"Well, let me try again." Bachoven pointed his frowning forehead at Charlie like an accusing finger. "Why are you tip-toeing into my classroom?"

Charlene answered in Charlie's head. *"Because your breath stinks and I was hoping to keep your back to me."*

Charlie had to stifle a smile, and Charlene's response, answering, "Uh, I-I just didn't want to interrupt."

"Mission not accomplished." The classroom burst into giggles once more. Bachoven spoke slowly, as if to a moron, "Why are you in my classroom in the first place? Do you have a message for someone?"

"I'm here because I'm suicidal, and I was sure you could bore me to death." Charlene again. Charlie once again nixed that response.

Instead, he answered, "Huh?"

The class burst out laughing, and Bachoven held his hands up. He gave a condescending look that Charlie assumed meant the teacher felt it impolite to laugh at the special needs student. "Is there something you need, young man?"

"Uh. (Pause.) No, I'm in this class."

"Oh. Oh, I see," Bachoven answered. His words were curt, as if it hurt to speak them. "Well. This is *advanced* math class." He paused, as if waiting for Charlie to run, screaming in fear. Charlie stood by his desk. Bachoven sighed. "If you are new to the class, I should advise you it begins at precisely at 1:15. Please be on time in the future."

"Dude! I was here, you brainless twit. You slammed the freaking door in my freaking face! If you weren't so freaking high on chalk dust maybe you would recognize folks. Especially when they've freaking been in your class for three freaking weeks!"

Nope. That time it was Chuck. His logical mind was offended that Bachoven would assume he was new rather than the more obvious, late for class. He had tired years earlier of teachers' surprise at his being the smart kid. Melanin, his mom said, did not affect his math skills.

Charlie spoke to, but did not look at, Bachoven. "I've been here since the first day." He almost added the words, "getting A's," but choked them down as if though they were made of glass shards.

The class erupted in laughter. From the back, someone shouted, "The Invisible Man lives!" Charlie would have been proud of the name were he not feeling completely exposed at the moment.

Bachoven told the students to be quiet, and Charlie to be seated. What he did not tell Charlie was that he was sorry for closing the door in his face, for embarrassing him, for failing to pay any attention to the best math student in the school district. Charlie was now feeling much more of an outsider than he had on the first day. Being bullied by teachers was much worse than the normal bullying to which he had become accustomed. He stole a glance at Jannet, not being able to resist seeing her inevitable victory smirk. To his surprise, she was not laughing. In fact, she was staring at him, and looking as if she might cry.

After class, Charlie was heading to his locker, and considering spending sixth period inside, when he ran into, of all people, the Cute Girl.

There was Robin, by herself, standing in front of her locker. She looked sad, but otherwise, perfect. Charlie was looking at his feet, the place he normally looked when he walked, and met a pair of ankle-length, tan, suede half boots with two-inch heels and frills where the laces should be. The frills reminded Charlie of the ruffles he'd seen in drawings of Elizabethan England. As he looked up, he saw two very long legs in dark gray stockings, and further up, a tan and dark gray checked skirt with a belt the dark gray of the skirt. It was three inches wide, and featured what looked like half a flower. She wore a light gray blouse with black lace near the buttons. On it was a flower the precise color of her shoes embedded with grays from the skirt. It could have been hand sewn, as it was made from cloth, and had been stitched into the blouse. Charlie loved that it took his eye from her neck to the belt and then the shoes, pulling the whole perfect picture together.

That he had time to notice all these details should help explain how very slowly he had begun to walk once he saw her – and how long he was staring before he realized it.

"Photos last longer," a voice said. It was hers.

Charlie's heart sank. She was looking straight at him. His right brain immediately began offering clever things to say like, "*Yeah, but you look better in 3-D,*" or "*Well, I was really hoping to make a video,*" but logical Chuck refused all suggestions.

Instead, he simply averted his eyes, and mumbled. "I-I'm sorry. I was … I was kind of daydreaming."

"Oh," Robin answered, looking disappointed. "I spent the entire night making the stupid flower to match the stupid belt and the stupid shoes. You should *want* a picture." Her face said it all: boys never notice anything. She began twisting her hair violently.

Charlie, being not at all unobservant, picked up the change in expression and mannerism. He thought he should say something to her like … like, "*I want to have your babies,*" Charlene offered. His eyes got as wide as the blue moon. For a horrifying second he thought stupid Charlene had actually vocalized that, using his mouth. He wasn't even totally sure what it meant, but he knew it wasn't possible. Robin, meanwhile, had turned back to the locker, bearing the same sadness she was wearing when he arrived.

Charlie paused, took two steps away, and then stopped again. "I … I'm sorry I was staring at you … and for lying about it. It was rude." One more step. Stop. "Y-you look great."

Whoa. Patterson swings blindly, and gets a base hit. The crowd goes wild!

Robin looked up, suppressing a smile. She was clearly pleased he *was* looking at her. "Well, you should be sorry. That was very rude," she said, hazel eyes beaming through her stern expression.

Mustering every ounce of courage he had, he looked Robin in the eyes. She wore a look that almost made him faint, or bleed internally, he wasn't sure which. His eyes itched and he wanted to scratch them, but resisted the urge. As he blinked however, he could tell she wanted him to say … *something.*

Charlie knew this would be his chance to be a man, to step up and take charge of something he wanted for possibly the first time in his life. And, he almost did — almost. Her eyes widened in anticipation, and he could tell she wanted him to talk. For once, it wasn't fear that stopped him. Truthfully, her presence felt … familiar. Unfortunately, for the first time in his life, all the clutter inside his head stopped at once, and he could think of nothing to say.

Rather than responding, he gave a shrug, looked down once again, and settled for remaining a mouse.

"You still wearing that stupid flower?" came the voice of DeShaun Yancy, the bully, the purveyor of insults, the haver of very bad taste.

Charlie looked up just in time to see Robin smiling coquettishly.

"*Smiling? Sir Thugsalot walks up, insults her, and she's smiling?*" Charlene was outraged.

"*Well, you could see she wanted you to talk to her, and you didn't. What did you expect?*" the unsympathetic Chuck countered.

Charlie responded defensively.

I can't help it if I couldn't think of anything to say. I have all this noise going on in my head, and when I finally need words … nothing.

"*It seems like the logical thing would have been to ask her name. Or to have thanked her for not letting the big girl kick your butt by the bus earlier,*" responded Chuck.

Charlie decided that he freaking hated his freaking left brain. Behind him, he could hear more flirting from Robin, and more insults from DeShaun. Charlie decided to leave before he threw up.

"This year is going to really suck," Charlie said out loud. He didn't care if the other kids heard him say it either.

8 – ONLY THE SMALL THINGS MATTER

Joe Tettleton, Charlie's eighty-five year old great-grandfather, sat against the wall of the third floor lobby of the Southside Senior Center. Joe was seated in a wheelchair that looked as if it would be overpowered by his massive frame any instant. He was tall, just shy of six foot six in his prime, though age had stolen a couple of inches in recent years. Even so, his lean, muscular frame gave him the appearance of a much younger man — until, that is, you looked at his face. Joe perennially appeared as if he had forgotten to shave, white whiskers dotting his deep chocolate face. His semi-circle of white hair and broad nose gave him the appearance of an outsized, chocolate Gandhi.

Joe was watching a trio clustered in the corner. There his friend Bernard "Sarge" Sargent was being spoiled by his granddaughter and daughter. The women were on their bi-weekly "Saturday picnic" visit, although it had been awhile since they had actually gone outside with him. Instead, they had brought him a fine lunch of turkey on croissant, with not-quite-homemade cream of chicken soup from the upscale deli about a mile from the center. Sarge sat wide-eyed, brow furrowed, as the women set up their feast. To an untrained eye, it appeared that Sarge was either frightened, or had little idea what was going on. Joe knew differently.

Sarge deserved a bit of spoiling, Sarge did. That distant, wide-eyed look was all that was left of excitement, dimmed by the ravages of dementia on Sarge's once razor-sharp mind. Sarge knew who the two women with him were, today, and he even remembered where he was this time. It was a good day for Sarge.

The lobby was a surprisingly cold place, more hospital wing than home. The yellowed linoleum floor gave the room a sickly ambiance. Some administrator had long ago decided the once-white flooring would be in the seniors' best interest, since the floor would bounce the harsh, unfiltered fluorescent lighting back to the residents. It did, but now, aged, made most of them seem jaundiced. In the corner immediately to Joe's right, was a small lounge area, consisting of two loveseats and an armchair, all a handsome red and blue striped pattern. They matched absolutely nothing else. Close by sat a coffee table with reading material the residents had mostly memorized, stacked neatly. There was a display case that held mementos of the nursing center, but little of the residents who lived there. The air was stale, with an ever-so-faint smell of urine from the far end of the hallway.

They were on the third floor in the D wing, the Disappearing Wing, as the orderlies called it, where those residents who needed constant monitoring or serious medical care lived out their lives. This was a "graduated living" facility, where the residents started out in their own apartments then gradually moved to the equivalent of dormitories, and eventually, hospital beds or the intensive care unit. As such places go, this was a relatively nice one, clean and certainly bright. When he got away with it, Joe would sit in his sunglasses in silent protest of the glaring lights. Protests in D wing were silent by definition. The nurses and the orderlies took no backtalk from the residents. Indeed, most of the orderlies seemed to think their jobs were the equivalent of prison guards rather than caretakers. The nurses were well trained and well equipped to do their jobs. But they were also overworked, underpaid, overtired, and oftentimes in pain from lifting, pulling, and cajoling elderly patients who couldn't care for themselves.

It was not coincidental that the Senior Center residents always sat facing the elevators. Most of them had few guests, some none at all. Their enjoyment was in welcoming visitors as they entered the third floor lobby, and inquiring for whom they were intended. Gathering that information was the sole purpose of the nurse's station, but the nurses knew that sharing in the excitement of a visit was as close as some of the residents would ever come to being visited themselves.

At times, a lovely, rare-souled visitor would sit in one of the empty chairs and visit with the crew of residents, asking about their lives, and, for a bit of time, giving them someone who cared about them. Charlie was one such rare soul, and it was his day to visit. The residents sat

43

waiting in anticipation, along with Joe. Maybe, just maybe, Joe would be willing to share today.

Some Sunday nights, a local church group would stop by and chat for a while. It might as well have been Christmas on those nights. To the residents, it wasn't about the church, or even about God. It was about being needed, talked to. It was about being important to someone once again. There were blessings and hugs all around, small gestures that mattered.

One fine day in April, another rare soul brought in an old Labrador retriever that was being trained as a service dog. The dog's name was Dusty. He visited the group, and each resident he touched perked up, became more alert, alive. Dusty had whimpered when he came to old man Grady, sniffing him vigorously, and whining. When the trainer tugged at the dog's leash sharply, Dusty turned, pulled at the leash, and let out a brief, but ferocious snarl.

The embarrassed trainer scolded the dog into submission with a wagging finger and took him away for "a little more training." Neither the trainer nor Dusty had been back since. Perhaps if they had returned, the trainer would have discovered that doctors had found an advanced cancer in old man Grady's right kidney some weeks later. Perhaps he would have learned his special canine companion was a rare soul who could smell cancers that even MRIs couldn't detect. Perhaps the trainer wouldn't have returned the dog to the Pound to be euthanized. Perhaps the old man's roommate wouldn't have died of a similar cancer three months later.

Perhaps.

Charlie could not smell cancers, but his great-grandfather knew he had the same spirit as that old dog. He would fight his parents tooth and nail for the chance to make the old folks' lives a bit better.

Rather than being repulsed by or bored at the Center, Charlie seemed a bit of an old man himself, and would spend almost as much time with Joe's crew as he did with his great-grandfather. The sun and moon rose because of Charlie in G'pa Joe's eyes, and made the end of his long life's journey worth the trip. Today Charlie would be by, and the world would be just a little brighter.

G'pa Joe was seated in his usual spot in his oversized wheelchair. His position looked like a master sergeant reviewing his troops, perfectly parallel to the troops awaiting inspection. That was, of course, because G'pa Joe had spent years in the Army doing precisely that. These were his troops, albeit a bit withered at the edges.

"Old habits die hard, or they weren't hardly worth having," G'pa Joe would say. None of his crew minded G'pa Joe's large-and-in-charge demeanor, and a few even thought it amusing that a black man from the then-segregated US Army would find himself the de facto leader of a crew of mostly Jewish retirees from New York.

"At our age," G'pa Joe's friend Abe Singer offered, "we learn to be friends with whomever is available, can talk, and has the interest."

"Besides, we're too damn old to fight anyway," G'pa Joe added. Lovely sentiment, but it never stopped the two from constantly bickering. "C'mon over and eat with us when Charlie comes by, Singer," G'pa Joe said. He liked Singer, though he would never admit it to him.

"Thank you, but no. I don't want to intrude on your family."

"Man you know we share family up in here. None of us has so much we can afford to be stingy with it. Besides, what else you gon' to do with yourself on a Sunday?"

"I got plenty to do, Tettleton," Singer said, placing his thumbs in his suspenders.

"What, watch the soap opera reruns with the ladies? Real men don't watch soap operas, Singer."

Singer waved G'pa Joe off and pulled his round frame to its full five feet five inches. "You apparently also think real men don't use soap, Tettleton. And it's Saturday, you old fool. If you read, you'd see that on the calendar over there."

"Hey, I bathe, Singer. I even take showers." G'pa Joe ignored the reading comment. Just because he *could* read, didn't mean he *did* read.

"I'm sorry, Tettleton, but using wet naps after Charlie brings you KFC chicken does not qualify for a bath."

"Okay, that was a good one," G'pa Joe said, laughing. "But just for that, I'm going to tell him not to bring you any more chicken when he comes. In fact, maybe we'll just have a nice intimate pig's feet dinner," G'pa Joe shot back with a wry smile.

"You know, even Schicklgruber didn't serve those things in the death camps."

Joe decided to end the game there, knowing no way to respond without being on very dangerous ground. Some things, you couldn't joke about — lynchings were one, the Holocaust another. Singer could; he was a survivor, and that was also his way of saying "Game's over." Joe had been a good leader in his middle years, and a good leader knows how to listen, when to follow, and when to shut up.

"Okay, Abraham, I hear you," Joe said softly, returning his gaze to the trio who was just now finishing their picnic. He wanted to make sure he would get first dibs at the table once Charlie showed up.

Singer bristled at the mention of his first name. No one, but no one ever called him Abraham, though no one quite knew why. "Don't call me that, Joseph," he warned. "It's Mr. Singer to you."

"I'm terrified," G'pa Joe returned. They exchanged a warm smile. Both men irritated the heck out of each other, and that made life a little more interesting.

9 – CHARLIE BRINGS THE LIGHT

The elevator's bell sounded at precisely four o'clock, signaling Charlie's arrival. He had never been late. "Just like his mama, that one," G'pa Joe said with a grin.

Charlie stepped out of the elevator into the bright lobby and blinked, adjusting his eyes to the glare after riding in the slow, dark elevator car. He was carrying a large bag of KFC's finest, a gift from his mother to her grandfather. She would be by exactly at five o'clock, not a minute later, but always gave Charlie his hour of alone time with his favorite person on earth.

Charlie had visited his great-grandfather almost every weekend for as long as he could remember. G'pa Joe would regale him with stories of leaving his sharecropper home at age fourteen with little more than the clothes on his back and a mind full of hopes. He had met a young man who called himself Tennessee Toot while on the road north. It was originally a shortened form of his given name, Toussaint Hebert, but G'pa Joe would tell Charlie most thought it referred to the tarnished horn with the slightly bent bell from which he managed to coax "heaven's own noise" for enough coins to eat. "That old boy," G'pa Joe would enthuse to his enraptured great-grandson, "saved my life more'n once. He was a bit of con artist, a liar, and a thief ... later even a pimp and a convict. But he treated me like a little brother. Got me to Detroit in one piece."

G'pa Joe would tell Charlie about the adventures in the juke joints in 1942 Detroit, where he decided there was more opportunity fighting Hitler than there was at home. And the war stories — Charlie's mom would be horrified to know he heard them, but to a boy of eleven, G'pa Joe was the only true hero he had ever met.

Lately, when Charlie visited, it seemed as if G'pa Joe was lost in his past. The stories that used to fascinate him now only made him sad. Visiting G'pa Joe had become like watching an old photograph fade. Still, Charlie came as often as he could. If G'pa Joe were going to disappear, Charlie would make certain that he went down fighting. And after the dream he'd had, even if he imagined it all, he were more determined than ever to help G'pa Joe.

"G'pa!" Charlie shouted enthusiastically. He ran over to give his great-grandfather a warm hug, without the slightest hint of embarrassment. G'pa Joe braced himself on the arms of the massive wheelchair, and stood, stooped forward at an angle a full five degrees short of vertical. Even stooped as he was, he stood six foot three and a half, and embraced Charlie with his long, broad arms such that the boy seemed to disappear into his chest.

"Missed you G'pa."

"Missed you too, Charlie boy."

Every single resident smiled in unison. Seeing a boy so obviously in love with his relationship with his great-grandfather was a prized to be shared. The ladies turned in their chairs, waiting for their hugs. Charlie was always good for a hug or two. For some, it would be the only hug they would get for a week, until his next visit.

At the small table across the room, Sarge's granddaughter, Cathy, gave her first almost smile, looking at and waving to Charlie as she cleaned the remaining mess from the picnic. Old Sarge, appetite sated, was now slumped in his wheelchair, leaning to the right side. His eyes were no longer wide, but drooping sleepily.

"Diggin' the scene wit' a gangster lean, Mr. Sargent?" Charlie asked with a smile. Old Sarge had no idea what he was talking about, judging by the confusion in his eyes. He smiled nonetheless.

"Boy, we've got to get you some friends your own age," G'pa Joe grinned. "All your references are as old as I am."

"Not even Moses' references are as old as you are," Singer slipped in.

G'pa Joe turned toward Singer, pretended to scowl, and dropped himself back into his chair, his large frame threatening to overturn it. He turned to Charlie and whispered conspiratorially, loudly enough for Singer to hear. "We got to get a bell to put around that cat's neck." He gestured toward Singer with a sideways nod of his head. "You a pain in the you-know-what Singer," he added.

"Yeah, I love you too. Now where's my chicken?" Singer asked. "You didn't forget my wings, did you? You know the dark meat gives me gas."

"Hell, breathing gives you gas, you old bag of wind," G'pa Joe responded.

Charlie shook his head, his knit cap flapping back and forth. "Do you guys do this all day?" He already knew the answer; still, it amused him to ask. The ladies smiled and watched, also shaking their heads. The Joe and Singer Show was their favorite weekend form of entertainment, next to reruns of "Cops."

Mary, a slight woman with shoulder-length white hair and fair skin, pushed herself up from her chair, and sidled over to the men. "Room for one more, gentlemen?" she asked coyly.

"Always room for you Mary," G'pa Joe replied with a broad grin.

Charlie looked at his great-grandfather and tried to gauge his interest in Mary. Practically all G'pa Joe's teeth were showing. However, the food was getting cold and if he asked any questions, they'd never get to eat. Besides, he really wanted to spend some time alone with G'pa before his mother came back. No time to waste then.

"C'mon, Mr. Singer, I got your potato wedges."

Singer put a finger to his lips, and furrowed his brow, shushing Charlie, and looking over his shoulder at the nurse's station. There was no one there.

"You know those prison guards don't let me have fried foods," Singer whispered.

"Oh, I'm sorry, I-I didn't know. I can eat those then. Can you eat corn on the cob?"

"Yes, I can eat corn on the cob. I have teeth. See?" Singer reached in and took out his uppers, and thrust them at Charlie.

"Gross!" Charlie groaned, turning away.

"Put those things back, Singer," G'pa Joe countered, his eyes averted and hand extended in front of his face. "Pay that fool no attention, he's just trying to make you lose your appetite so he gets your share too."

Singer mumbled, looking annoyed. "I need a new friend. This one knows me too well," he said, nodding his head toward G'pa Joe. Singer reached in the box and pulled out a huge chicken breast, looked over at G'pa Joe, and thought better of it. He took a couple of baked chicken wings instead. Then he took the potato wedges and immediately popped one in his mouth, closed his eyes, and made a sound that Charlie thought must be a sound of pure joy.

"I thought you couldn't have those," Charlie objected.

"No, I said the guards don't let me. I can have whatever they don't see." He stuck the little box of wedges between his legs, just in case the nurses came back. Singer looked up in time to see Charlie slowly shaking his head at him again. "What, you want I should starve?"

By this time, G'pa Joe was eyeing Mary, who was still standing in the same spot. He waved at her, gestured for her to come over. Mary just stood there, eyes vacant, not seeming to notice.

"Charlie, go tap Mary, and get her to come eat," G'pa Joe said with marked tenderness.

Charlie did as instructed, a chicken leg in his hand. He gently took Mary by the elbow, and led her toward the table. She took two more steps, turned toward Charlie, and smiled, a warm, familiar smile. Then she began to scream. She screamed until her throat was raw. She screamed until the nurses came then the orderlies. They tied her to a gurney, wheeling her down the hall, away from where she usually slept.

Charlie, having fallen over a chair at the first shriek, was visibly shaken and trying not to let the tears show. "What happened?" he asked the two silent men. Neither had moved, save for feeding themselves. "Why was she screaming like that? I didn't hurt her did I?"

Singer stopped nibbling on his second wing and looked up at the boy. "No, son, that wasn't you. Nothing happened that doesn't happen all the time around here. She just went somewhere, that's all."

G'pa Joe shot his friend a look that made the smaller Singer wince. Neither said a word for long moments. They didn't have to.

"Don't mind me," Singer said, filling in the growing silence. "I talk too much. Sometimes, there is … darkness even when the lights seem to be on. Maybe she remembered something dark. She'll be okay."

"Where did they take her?" Charlie was concerned, but sat down to eat his now cold food.

G'pa Joe answered in his most reassuring voice. "They probably just took her somewhere to calm her down, and maybe scan to make sure nothing was causing her pain. I'll check on her later, but she'll probably not even remember screaming. Heck, she'll probably be mad we didn't save her any chicken." It felt to Charlie like a lie, was a lie, but he readily accepted it. Sometimes, truth is overrated. G'pa Joe tried to make his face smile, but it refused. Charlie knew he was worried, and not just a little.

Charlie looked at the line of residents in wheelchairs sitting opposite the elevator. There were ten of them, all with their eyes closed, most rocking forward and back. He could not hear any sounds, but was sure their lips were moving. On the far wall was Mr. Patil, G'pa Joe's friend, standing, eyes closed as well, with hands slightly uplifted on either side of his face. He was not rocking back and forth like the others, but every few seconds his head would waggle side to side, looking very much to Charlie like an Indian bobble head doll.

Charlie frowned, his eyes darting from one to the next. "What are they all doing?" he asked.

Singer answered without looking at the group at all. He was still gnawing on the chicken bone. "Praying."

"Singer, shut the hell up and stop chewing that bone before you break your new teeth. You look like a old-ass Chihuahua with a chew toy."

Singer didn't respond, but stopped chewing, turned, and wheeled toward the group. Within a few seconds, his eyes were closed, and he was nodding back and forth in the same rhythm as the group.

"Wow," Charlie said, not sure if he was impressed or just uncomfortable. "Folks sure are religious around here. Is it the Sabbath or something?"

G'pa Joe did not answer.

Charlie cocked his head to the side, watching his great-grandfather's worried expression. On impulse, he leaned closer, and asked. "Do you think maybe Mary has dreams like the one we had?"

G'pa Joe squinted at Charlie, but showed no signs he remembered their rescue in the blue dream world. "Everybody dreams, Charlie, especially in here. Folks even dream when they's still awake. Sometimes getting old ain't much different than being a little kid."

Charlie considered pushing the subject, but he was not at all certain he had shared the dream with G'pa Joe. It was far more logical to assume it had happened solely in his mind. "Everyone dreams, but not like I do." He sighed, his shoulders slumping. "I hate dreaming. Mine are making me go crazy, I think."

G'pa Joe wrapped a long arm around Charlie, and spoke softly. "Lemme tell you something about dreams, boy. My daddy, God res' his soul, worked hisself till he dropped. He'd get up to work 'fore the sun got up, and come home when it was already dark. And when he got home, he owned less than when he left in the morning. My daddy was a sharecropper, and that man didn't even own the dirt under his nails.

At his funeral, I half expected somebody to come scrape his fingernails to collect the dirt. He was a good man, and strong. But see, his granddaddy was a slave, and his daddy worked like one. Workin' was all he knew, all any of us knew.

"But when I was fourteen, I had this dream, see? I dreamed there was a world out there where I could work for myself, and die free. Now I don't mean no Martin Luther King, 'I Have a Dream' stuff. I was really dreamin' this — droolin' on the pillow and everything." G'pa Joe stopped to laugh. "I dreamed even though I didn't go to school much, I would still rise up and be somethin'. So you know what I did?"

"You left home?" Charlie asked, already knowing the answer. He was beginning to fear he had lost G'pa Joe once again to his colorful past, which was much more intriguing than his gray present.

"Damn right. I left home. I left my family and everything I knew. All I had in my pocket was ten dollars. But I also had my dream, and that was worth more than any money or any fancy education. My dream is what got me through. First saw ol' Toot in that dream."

"Really?" Charlie held back a grin that wanted to control his face. "I … I met somebody in a dream too."

"Well then. That must be a pretty special friend. If the dreams make you smile, then believe in 'em. It's the scary ones that lie."

"You think so?"

G'pa Joe nodded. "Maybe God is tryin' to tell you somethin'. All's you got to do is keep dreamin', and listen." G'pa Joe pointed to his chest. "And when that voice in here says now is the time to act — well then you make sure you do." G'pa Joe pointed a long finger at Charlie. "Dreams ain't just for sleepin', Charlie boy. Dreams are for travelin' from where you are, to where you s'posed to be."

G'pa Joe's words resonated with Charlie. "Maybe Mary had a dream that took her where she didn't need to be," Charlie said, his eyes traveling down the hallway where they had shuffled her away. "Maybe she's lost on a blue river of her own."

G'pa Joe eyed Charlie, and nodded. "Something like that," he said, following the boy's stare.

He was there. He remembers the blue river.

"G'pa, maybe this week we should cut the visit short so you can go check on Mary."

"No, this is your time."

Charlie knelt down, and met his great-grandfather eye-to-eye. "She needs you, even more than those kids did."

G'pa Joe frowned, but then his expression eased. "We kind of failed with them, but maybe I can see about her, huh?"

Charlie nodded in agreement. "Don't worry. I can just spend time with Mr. Patil and the ladies until mom gets here to pick me up."

G'pa Joe slapped his hands on his thigh, and brightened. "Just when I think you couldn't do one more thing to surprise me, you do." He leaned over, and kissed Charlie on the cheek, then turned, and wheeled himself toward the room where they had taken Mary.

Charlie cleared the debris from the table, leaving the remaining chicken in the box. He knew it wouldn't go to waste. After wiping his hands on his jeans, he stopped, staring down the empty corridor. Charlie was crazy about Mary: she was funny, unpredictable, artsy, and he got the feeling she was once exceptionally smart. She still was, when she was lucid. Today was not one of those days. Her outburst had rattled him more than he wanted to let on.

What he needed, more than anything, was to be out of D wing, and in a hurry.

"C'mon ladies," Charlie said, calling to the group of lonely grandmas sitting in their wheelchairs. "What do you say we go down to the sun room and watch some TV?" The ladies all tittered in delight, and wheeled their chairs to the elevator with Charlie.

I need some sun anyway. Suddenly it's too dark in here.

10 – NOTHING TO FEAR

Mary had been thinking how delightful to be having a picnic with her best friends on a lovely Saturday. Having Charlie was always a gift — he was such a clever boy, and always kind and respectful. Such a leader, he was, just like Joe. She had closed her eyes and inhaled, wanting to cherish the rare morsel of anticipation in a life that had become mundane on even the good days.

With her eyes closed, she could hear Charlie chattering excitedly, and Abraham — she was the only one who got away with calling him that — was whistling softly.

Abraham always whistles so wonderfully. He had been a clarinetist for years in the New York Philharmonic, and never lost his musician's chops.

"I see I'm not the only one in a good mood," Mary offered cheerfully, her now-open eyes bright with anticipation.

"No, mommy, this is going to be fun!" It was the voice of her five-year-old son, David.

Mary looked down in dismay at her two boys, dressed in matching dungarees and their lightweight navy blue London Fog jackets. Little Davey had on his favorite shirt with horizontal blue and white stripes, and his younger brother, three-year-old Michael, was wearing the only shirt he would wear at age three — his lucky red pullover. Mary knew exactly what year it was by the crimson of that pullover shirt. It was 1973, and that made this France. The family had spent all of 1973 and 1974 in northern France, living near the Ardennes, courtesy of her young executive husband's stint in the French wine industry. He had worked for two years, without much success, trying to build a relationship for the U.S. distributorship for which he worked. By late 1973, that lucky red shirt had been washed to faded tatters.

These memories were rushing in, washing away the grains of her nursing home existence like so much sand at ebb tide. She was disconcerted, and grabbed handfuls of her thick curly hair that shone copper in the sun. Mary had always run her hands in her hair when she was stressed. Sometimes she would twirl it absently, other times she would comb and re-comb the locks with her fingers. Those rare occasions when the thirty-year-old Mary would become very agitated, she would clamp the curly locks between her fingers as if she could press the unwanted curls out through sheer force of will.

She paused, two fistfuls of copper threading her thin pale fingers. Her hair had not been long for years, and hadn't seen its natural red color for decades. It was interlaced with bits of mousy browns, and the summer sun would bake the ends a copper so bright it would shine yellow in the sun. No hair salon she could ever have afforded was capable of matching the gift God had given her at birth. The impact of her hair — her long-lost natural treasure — overwhelmed her.

True, it had been forever since her sons were that age, but they were always her baby boys in her heart. The hair, however, meant she was young again, and beautiful, and alive. She couldn't wait to show Joe … no, wait; she would still be married to Stanley at this age. Stanley was 1973. Stanley wouldn't have noticed her hair if the copper strands were licks of fire dancing with the febrile heat of Hell.

Mary threw her hair back and laughed. It was more than laughter; it was a song, lyrical, passionate, beatific laughter. Her hair was tied in two perfectly formed tails that framed either side of her face. Her skin was alabaster — fragile, translucent in the bright daylight. Her lips were pale crimson with matching eye shadow, the only makeup she wore in those days. She had eschewed her usual jeans for a summer dress: a pale, almost white shade of pink that looked more appropriate for mint juleps on a hot turn of the century day than a 1970s picnic in the forest. This was a special occasion for her to have dressed up so, though she couldn't remember what the occasion might have been.

"Mommy, when we gonna eat?" It was Mikey, the always-hungry one.

"Why, I don't know what we have for food," Mary began looking around, trying to remember what she had brought with them for their weekend outing.

"I still have it!" Davey held up a basket with both hands, struggling with its weight. "It's not too heavy," he added, bravely.

"Oh good honey. Here, let me take that, and you can hold Mikey's hand so he doesn't get lost." Mary knew Davey would object unless he had another equally important mission to fulfill.

"K. C'mon Mikey." Davey took his brother's willing hand and they began to march, giggling, toward an opening in the forest. It was a huge expanse of forest, even larger than she remembered. The trees towered in a lethargic race to touch the sky. The air was thick with the fragrance of pine, mixed with the perfume of rich earth and decaying leaves. The ground was scattered with them, a carpet of gold, and brown, of yellow and orange covering rocky ground and yellowing grass.

The trio walked in silence, listening to the sounds of birds and the chittering of small animals angered at being disturbed in their afternoon peace. At the edge of the trees, the forest opened into a vast clearing of green hills, dotted with soft flower petals that recently abandoned their stems — a kaleidoscope of autumn's warm colors. They walked on, marveling at the solitude, the beauty of the place. This was Mary's church. God was strong in this place, she thought.

"Well, we might as well set up here, I don't think there's a more perfect spot on earth," she beamed at her sons.

The boys sent up a cheer, grabbing the picnic basket, and pulling from it a soft blanket they had carried with them. Mary let her boys eat, preferring to lay back and stare at the cloudless sky. She thought of Stanley, wished he could have come, and wondered why she couldn't quite seem to remember his face. As she closed her eyes, the gentle autumn air kissed her skin, and she knew she had found her home at last. She was a child of the forest, a wood nymph, and this was her domain. She …

… heard her sons scream.

They screamed as if the world had suddenly become fire and shattered glass, and they were made of soft paper. She sat bolt upright, heart pounding, and eyes wide. Her lips were pursed to form, "What's wrong?" but there was no need. Her boys, both, were lying on the blanket, eyes wide with fear, covered head to toe in spiders. They were a rust orange, gray, and brick red swirling mass, engulfing the small boys like a wave. The ground was spiders – undulating in a chaotic wave that flooded the grass. They swarmed around the boys in numbers so great she could hear the scrabbling of their tiny feet. Mary grabbed her sons, each by one arm, and tore them violently from the mass of arachnids. They were sobbing now, but they were moving, and moving was going to be important.

She was standing, not remembering getting up, and she was running, holding Mikey under her left arm, and practically Davey dragging by his. They leapt over the islands of spider clusters that spanned the sea of rolling green. No, not a sea: a vast, Atlantic Ocean of green. The Ardennes were no longer recognizable, this was some … other … place. Behind her, she could hear the rustling of the dry grass as the spiders moved en masse to the only food they were likely to find before winter's winds set in and ended their season. Mary couldn't understand how she had mistaken them for flowers, why she could not see. She had put her sons in harm's way, and could find no way out. She stopped to get her bearing. In the classroom, she had always taught her students that panic was the first step to ruin. She must be calm, and think.

There was an incessant drumbeat in the distance. For a brief moment she expected some Tarzan-movie-borne painted natives to emerge, weapons in hand, to rape, or kill, or worse. The beating increased, and she placed a hand to her slender chest, steadying herself. Her heart pounded to the rhythm of the drums as she bent over to catch her breath. The rustling of the spiders was behind her, softer, but there. They would not pursue; they would simply wait.

"Do you boys hear those drums?" Mary tried her best to sound nonchalant. She couldn't bear it if they started screaming again.

Both boys stopped whimpering and listened, turning their heads toward each horizon. After a brief while, they looked at each other and shrugged.

"I don't hear nothin'," Davey offered, shaking his shock of red hair.

"Me too," Mikey chimed in.

"You're sure? You don't hear anything?" She could still hear the pounding beat, it sounded like … her heartbeat. The sound was coming from her ears, the blood pulsing through her arteries. She had been on the verge of panic, and panic could cost her the boys' lives. She mustn't panic. Could not panic. She turned to survey the surroundings, to form a plan of escape.

Directly behind them, the pastoral hills were still swarming with spiders. To either side was of the same, as far as she could see, to either horizon. Ahead, past a rise, she could just make out the tops of trees. That had to be the way they came, through the forest, and back to the

Ardennes.

"Okay, this way Kiddos," she smiled at the boys.

It was a painted-on smile, but one that they needed to believe. If mommy wasn't scared then they were safe. Her smile meant they were going home.

"I wish I coulda kept one of them 'piders," Mikey offered. He liked pets, and had never had a spider for a pet.

"You're crazy," was Davey's only response.

Mikey started up the hill, looking over his shoulder all the while, one eye on his mom, and the other on the spiders that had begun to move in their direction. Mary and Davey followed his gaze as his eyes began to widen, and they quickly followed him up the hill. Mary scooped up both boys, and ran up the hill toward the edge of the forest. The colorful treetops became thick trunks, broadening as the trio neared the peak of the hill on which the trees lived.

Five more feet.

Mary urged herself on, her legs and back straining with exertion. At the top of the rise, she could finally see the massive roots of the trees, and among them, eyes. Glowing, angry eyes were visible in the darkness of the dense trees. Mary stopped, and, unthinking, dropped the boys in a whining heap on the ground. She could not run; there was nowhere to go. From behind the trees emerged a large gray wolf with eyes the color of tarnished gold. It stood five feet at the shoulders. The wolf bared its massive teeth with a low snarl. A line of saliva could be seen glimmering in the declining sunlight. More emerged, one to the right, another to the left, further way.

In each, there was hunger, a visible clarion call of hunger. Mary could not escape. The wolves had strategically placed themselves between Mary and the forest. She could not risk their hunger, for her children were too small to outrun them. There was no turning back, for behind was a tsunami of spiders amidst the sea of grass. It was still daylight, but the sun was fading, and its sister moon had already shown herself. Night was near, and death was nearer.

The pack was attempting to encircle her and the boys. She knew she could not let them get behind her. There was something different about these wolves. Something ... intelligent.

Mary moved slowly, as slowly as she could, and tucked the boys under each arm. They were crying, but soundlessly, their eyes fixed on the wolves. They were their mother's sons.

The wolves began to howl, and it was beautiful — a song, chorus, a crescendo of anticipation. It was hunting time, time for singing.

11 – THE MOTE IN CHARLIE'S EYE

Charlie lay in bed, tossing and turning for what seemed like hours. Sometime after midnight, desperate for sleep, he decided that staring at a single point on the ceiling would make his eyes tired enough for sleep. Unfortunately, not only did it not work, he began to see little floaters appear in his line of sight. He soon stopped. He was worried his staring was doing permanent damage to his sight. At around one a.m., he decided he no longer cared about vision; he cared only about sleep. Floaters or no, he would stare himself to sleep.

Though he was certain he was causing himself to develop glaucoma (the only eye condition he knew), the floaters held a sort of fascination for him. He attempted to watch a floater fall all the way to the ground to see where they go; however, as soon as he would tilt his head, it would either dance back toward the ceiling, or move to the other eye. That both eyes were now engaged was problematic. If he just lost one eye, there would be inevitable depth-of-field issues, certainly. Still, he was already lousy at baseball and did not hunt, so he reasoned binocular vision was not really that critical. However, if he lost both eyes to glaucoma, that would be a problem.

"Don't be stupid," a small voice said. It was as clear as his own voice.

Charlie initially assumed it was Chuck, telling his Charlene side to stop being emotional, but he realized the voice was distinctly Caribbean. "I am not glaucoma, you idiot." It was the floater, hands on hips, and small wings clearly visible. Charlie could not understand why he hadn't noticed the wings before.

"Are … are you talking to me floater?" Charlie knew that was a stupid question, but he figured it was as good an opening line to a floater as any.

In response, the floater, its hands still on hips, came to rest on Charlie's nose. "I and I prefer to be called a mote," it said. "Mote don' float, me 'ave wings, seen?"

Charlie squinted, noticing a small brown creature with a bald head, wearing an orange robe, and carrying what appeared to be a microphone.

"*You do realize we must be dreaming, right?*" Chuck chimed in. Dreams bored Chuck, however, and he decided to go to sleep.

"Just you and me kid," the mote said. "Do you always start a dream by telling yourself you are dreaming? Seem like dat would spoil de fun."

"Well no, that only happens when I think I might be having a nightmare. Would you happen to know how I'm having a nightmare when I've been awake all night?"

"Shush, now, we don' have time for your foolishness. Do you want to go or not? We only have a little time you know." The mote was now looking at what appeared to be a very small cell phone. "It's 'leven-seventy-tree o'clock."

"Huh? Okay. I went to bed at nine, so I've been lying awake for …"

"Bway, would you shut you face and come?" The mote was really getting impatient now. Its accent thickened with anger, and Charlie could no longer understand what it was saying. Charlie did recognize that the mote was very agitated, so he didn't ask. The mote took flight through a door that wasn't there before, to the left of Charlie's bed. By the time it reached the door, it had grown to be around three feet or so, and Charlie could make out it had brown fur and a face like a bunny — a winged bunny with a bald spot. He wondered if there were bunny ears under the robe's hood, but didn't dare ask. As it reached the other side, it turned toward Charlie and placed its hands on its hips once again.

"Would you come on?" the mote yelled.

Charlie shook his head no, and decided to pull the covers over his head. Unfortunately, his feet and legs had been asleep during all this, and didn't get the message. So, when the mote yelled for him to come, they immediately woke and jumped out of bed, dragging Charlie along for the ride. So there was Charlie, dressed in large gray t-shirt and black sweat pants, no shoes, walking toward the door. His legs and feet were in a hurry to catch up to the mote, while the upper part of his body leaned impossibly backward trying its best to get back under the covers. Given the upper half of Charlie was the half with the brain, back to bed was probably the smarter decision. Nonetheless, the head tends to go wherever the feet go, and Charlie was too confused to think to tell his feet to stop and return to bed.

Once through the door, he gave up fighting, and decided to stand straight, less he develop a bad back to go with his obvious psychosis.

"*At least you can rule out glaucoma,*" Chuck yawned.

Charlie straightened, bent side-to-side to stretch out his crumpled back muscles, and turned to go back through the door to his bedroom. His bed sat looking forlorn, lit romantically by the light of the moon. Soft music was playing, and Charlie longed to be back in the bosom of its lovely down comforter.

He said, more to himself than the mote, "This is nuts. I'm going back to bed."

"You can't go dat way, bway," the mote corrected, pointing to the door.

"Why not? That's the way I came."

"Read the sign," said the mote.

It was pointing to a wooden sign above the door, on which was carved the words: "NOT AN EXIT"

"See, you haffe go dis way bway."

Chuck chimed in. "*You know it's impossible to read when you're dreaming. This is troubling.*"

Charlene responded. "*That's the part you find troubling?*"

Charlie was embarrassed and frustrated by the exchange, as the mote seemed to be able to hear it. To the halves of his brain Charlie said aloud, "This conversation is not at all helpful." To the mote he added, "I'm having a lot of trouble understanding your accent. I caught about half of the last thing you said. I'm sorry."

"Oh, that's quite alright. New travelers tend not to be very perceptive at first. I said, 'You have to go this way.'" The mote was now speaking in a perfect British accent and pointing ahead of him. "By the way, is this one better? I can also be from Texas or Japan if you prefer."

Charlie glanced again at the sign. Now it read, "You Haffe Go Dis Way," with a large red arrow pointing away from Charlie's bedroom.

"N-n-no, this accent is quite fine," Charlie stammered. He turned, and ran to follow the mote, who had begun walking. "What did you call me by the way?" Charlie asked, panting. "A traveler? I-I wasn't traveling at all. I was trying to fall asleep."

"And so you have. I must tell you, lad, you should really try to focus while you're in here. Things have a way of happening the way you think they will, even if that's not the way you meant for them to happen." The mote stopped walking, which was good for Charlie, since he was having a great deal of time keeping up. It walked over to Charlie, and looked him up and down, as if sizing him up for something.

The mote was indeed brown, and, as it threw off its hood, Charlie could see it was in fact a bunny — a run-of-the-mill, brown, lop-eared rabbit, with a bald head. It had the cute wiggly nose, the whiskers, the whole bit. Its feet were large, but since it was wearing high-top basketball shoes, Charlie couldn't really tell if it had normal rabbit's feet. It did have rabbit paws for hands, although it had furry fingers, and Charlie was certain normal rabbits did not have fingers. Even if they did have fingers, they wouldn't wear black nail polish, like this rabbit.

Charlie found himself asking blunt questions, which was uncharacteristic of him. "Why do you call yourself a mote? You really aren't very small for a rabbit. In fact, you're fairly tall as rabbits go."

"I never called myself a mote."

"You absolutely did. You said 'I prefer to be called a mote.' Well, actually, I corrected your grammar, but it meant the same thing."

"No, you rude child, I said I prefer to be called A. Mote. That's my name — Abner Mote. Don't you prefer to be called by your name?"

"Well, yes of course."

"What if I decided to call you brown onion-head-doo-doo breath? It's a fairly accurate description, yes, but rather rude don't you think?"

"I never called you names, and I don't have doo-doo breath, rabbit." Charlie was getting impatient with this ... whatever-it-was' illogic. "I use mouthwash every night. I was simply trying to understand what you are."

"I am not a rabbit. That's what I are."

Charlie clapped his hand to his forehead and exhaled. "Okay, that makes no sense. How can you explain what you are by saying what you aren't? That's like my saying I am not a mouse when someone asks me if I am a boy or a man."

"Well in your case, saying 'I am not a mouse,' would be a lie."

Shoot.

Charlie had the horrifying belief that he had somehow turned into a mouse again. He had forgotten the mouse episode at school.

Wait. Not in school, in a dream about school.

"I know what you're thinking," said Abner, who was attempting to suck a piece of carrot from between his teeth. "You're wondering if you changed into a mouse. Admit it."

Charlie answered honestly, as was his norm. "Okay, well, the question had crossed my mind ... only recently though. I had a dream about being in school and turning into a mouse. It was quite embarrassing."

"You haven't had that dream yet."

"Jeez-o-flip! Would you freaking stop that? I know what dream I had. You are the most annoying rabbit I've ever met."

"And yet, I am not a rabbit."

Charlie groaned, wondering if killing a rabbit that was not a rabbit was illegal in this place. As he considered that, he noticed for the first time he was not actually in a place. In fact, it just seemed to be him and the rabbit-that-wasn't. "If I ask you where we are, will you just tell me where we aren't?" Charlie asked, hoping for a truce. His head was starting to hurt, and he was afraid that might wake him up — or worse, it might cause his brain to hemorrhage in his sleep.

"Of course I wouldn't answer that way, child. It would take too long to explain all the wheres we aren't. Besides, you aren't in a where you are in a when. And the when is some time ago, as it happens. You were a mouse in your school next week. So you see, you haven't had that dream yet."

"Ow." Charlie was holding his head.

"That might be a tumor," said Abner. "If you like, I can have exploratory surgery done on your head, just in case. I have it done all the time." Abner leaned over and showed Charlie a long curved scar on the top of his head. It appeared to be infected, as it was tinged with crimson along its left side.

"Jeez-o-flip!! That's gross! Do you actually have surgery on your head all the time? Why on earth would you do that?"

"We're not ... "

"Do not say we're not on earth," Charlie said, his finger pointed at Abner like a dagger.

"Okay," said Abner, his voice even. "Then where should I say we are not? We are not on Mars either, if that helps."

"I'm going to kill myself." Charlie was now holding his forehead with two hands.

Chuck, the left brain, woke up, and hearing the discussion, offered a bit of advice. *"Why don't you just ask him where he was taking you instead of trying to make sense of what doesn't matter?"*

For once, Charlie thought, Chuck was turning out to be useful. "Why don't you just tell me where you were taking me," Charlie said. Thinking quickly, he added "Or to when you are taking me."

"Oh, I'm taking you to France. You would like France," Abner had shifted voices and sounded very much like a girl.

Charlie raised one eyebrow and stared, as he did when he was nonplussed. "Why do you sound like a girl?" he asked. "I am sorry if I'm being rude, but some questions need to be asked."

"I don't know, why do you act like a girl?" came the reply.

"Arrrgh! Just once, do you think you could answer a question normally?" Charlie practically shouted.

"The answer to that question is yes. And since you requested it, I will only do that this once."

Charlie threw a rock at the not-a-rabbit, not once wondering where he had gotten a rock. His aim was true, and it hit Abner straight in the forehead. Abner immediately fell over backward, motionless. Charlie ran over to him, gushing apologies.

"Oh crap. Oh shoot. I'm sorry, I'm sorry, I'm sorry. I am so sorry. I just lost my temper for a minute. I didn't even know I had a rock. It was an accident."

Charlie bent over Abner, and touched the bunny's wounded forehead. There was a small cut there surrounded by a huge bruise. Charlie didn't so much as touch the bruised forehead as he poked it. Repeatedly.

"A-are you alright?" Charlie was certain he didn't want to find out what jail was like in this place.

"No I'm not alright. You have quite effectively killed me. Congratulations." Abner kept his eyes closed, and folded his hands over his chest. As if on cue, a single, perfect white lily appeared in his left hand. It smelled like cheddar cheese.

"I didn't kill you," said Charlie.

"You threw the rock, so you absolutely did. Besides, there is no one else here yet."

Charlie was once again exasperated. "I admitted to throwing the rock. But you aren't dead!"

"Guilty! Guilty!" called voices from the dark void ahead of them. Charlie looked up, and realized he was now at the edge of a large forest. The guilty verdict had come from somewhere amongst the trees.

"How did we come to be in a forest?" Charlie was more concerned with this bit of illogic than he was the guilty verdict, or wondering what creatures might be condemning him. As it turned out, Chuck had become fascinated at the puzzles and was figuratively sitting on the edge of his, well, brain. Charlene, meanwhile, was trying to change the channel to something a bit more Disney-like, without success.

Abner answered without moving, or opening his eyes. "We didn't come to be in the forest, the forest came to us. That's why we weren't in a place. The place hadn't shown up yet. Now we are in a place."

"Okay, great," Charlie said. "Now we're getting somewhere. What's it called?"

"It's called The Forest," Abner said.

Charlie shouted a minor obscenity, and then clamped his hands over his mouth. Abner continued, unperturbed. "It's the forest long ago, in France. I wish you hadn't killed me so I could see it. I do so adore France."

"I didn't kill ... look, you aren't dead! Jeez-o-flip, if you just open your eyes, you'd see you're alive. Well, assuming you were alive when we started, you are alive and just fine."

A voice from the forest shouted again, and louder. "Guilty! Hang him from the nearest tree!"

The nearest tree, which happened to be named Frank, objected. "I beg your pardon, if you want this thing hung, why don't you hang him from yourself? I, young lady, am not a Christmas tree, and don't appreciate having things hung from me."

Charlie sat on the ground next to Abner, and started to giggle. This wasn't a puzzle; it was schizophrenia. If he was going to be psycho, he may as well enjoy it. He lifted Abner's hand, and began stroking it. The soft fur was as soothing to Charlie as the stroking was to Abner. As he continued gently stroking Abner's furry hand, he looked in the direction of the forest, which was becoming bathed in light. It was not as if the sun was rising exactly, more as if the night was setting. As night sank below the horizon, the very top of the sky began to shine brightly. It was as if the nighttime sky were a big curtain that hid daylight behind it. As the curtain of night fell, day appeared in a straight line across the entire sky. Within no more than ten minutes, the noon sun was overhead.

Abner, having been sufficiently soothed by all the stroking, opened his eyes, looked up at Charlie, and said "I forgive you, but I promise I will be dead again if you throw another rock at me. Besides, did it occur to you that the rock might have liked where it was sitting?"

"What? What are you talking about?" Charlie asked, smiling this time.

"Do you know how long it takes a rock to get to a place? It could be another million years before it gets back to where it was, and you just … casually fling it at any random head you see about."

"I didn't move it, it just showed up in my hand. And I already said I was sorry." Charlie stifled a giggle.

Abner continued, as if Charlie had not spoken. "What if it had a family? Don't you think the kids will miss their dad when he's gone for a million years or so? His wife will probably have remarried."

Charlie noticed for the first time, now that the light was strong, that Abner was wearing a hooded bathrobe and wings from an old angel costume like the one Charlie had worn on his second Halloween. "I am terribly sorry," Charlie said, "and I do apologize to you and Mr. Rock. I will gladly transport him back to his family if need be."

"Oh don't be silly. Rocks don't have families. It was an illustration for goodness sake. You are very literal aren't you?" Abner was shaking his head and making clucking noises with his tongue.

"I've been told that, yes." Charlie admitted. He had, in fact, been told that all the time. "Can I ask you a question? Well, I have several, but one is sort of more urgent."

"That's why I'm here, to answer your questions," Abner said, his expression sincere.

"*That's why you're here?*" Chuck interjected, having managed to work Charlie's mouth before he could stop it.

"Certainly," Abner said. "You ask, I answer. It's just that your questions are not the boss of my answers."

"That scares me, because I actually understand that."

"As well you should. There is hope for you yet. Good. Your education has begun; congratulations." Abner gave Charlie what was clearly a rabbit smile.

"Huh? Okay," Charlie said. He cleared his throat, not for effect, but because it seemed to him to be the equivalent of a change in paragraph. This conversation needed a new paragraph desperately.

"New paragraph." He was being literal again. "My question is why are you wearing angel wings and a robe? I hope that isn't a rude question, I still don't quite know the etiquette in 'The Forest.'" Charlie made quotation marks with his fingers when he got to "the forest" part.

"Oh," said Abner, "I was being an angel of death."

"Oh."

Pause.

"Um … "

Longer Pause.

"Why were you being an angel of death?"

"Dunno really, I just show up dressed the way you guys want me to be dressed. You were dreaming of floaty stuff, and I thought 'Fairy', or 'Angel of Death.' Angels of Death are much cooler. I wish you had been thinking of motorcycles. I could have been a Hell's Angel of Death."

"Again, that somehow makes sense," Charlie said. "Is this place making more sense, or is it me?"

"It's you. This makes no sense at all … well it does, but it shouldn't to you. Not yet." Abner stared at Charlie, and then broke out in a broad grin.

Charlie had closed his eyes and cocked his head at a 45 degree angle. He was thinking. In fact, he had his index finger on his temple, which meant he was solving — hard. "So, you come in wherever my dream is, and you have to first be part of my dream then you bring me here. Right?"

Abner nodded. His grin widened.

"So why am I here? And did that tree talk back there? Well both those trees?"

Abner walked over to the nearest tree, and sat on one of the broad roots that looped above the ground. "This is Frank. Say hello, Frank."

Frank the tree, being a smart Alec, replied, "Hello Frank," in a booming voice. The sound seemed to come from an opening two-thirds the way up the trunk in what could have been a mouth, but which also was a home for a family of swallows. Frank was a rather handsome oak-apple tree, with both acorns and green apples currently in ripe abundance.

Abner patted Frank affectionately on his trunk. "Frank is my oldest friend." He paused, apparently expecting laughter. "That's a tree joke." Charlie looked at him blankly. "Never mind," Abner continued. "The other voice, however, is not a tree. I thought she was a friend of yours, although the 'hang him from the tree' comment does give me pause."

Frank dropped an apple directly on Abner's head. Abner frowned, but didn't rub his head, refusing to acknowledge the insult. The tree then lifted the entire set of looping roots on his right side, and a small figure appeared from behind him. It was the Cute Girl again. She was wearing a lovely brown skirt with a red top.

Charlie loved the color red.

12 – ROBIN IN WONDERLAND

"Hi," Robin said. "Sorry about the lynching thing. I thought you killed the rabbit and I wanted to scare you so you wouldn't do something like that again."

"It's okay. I wasn't really scared," Charlie lied.

"I didn't really mean it, I'm actually non-violent. I am relieved you are only guilty of felonious assault. The kids would have missed you."

"Kids … " he said, his voice trailing off.

Abner waved his hands at Robin, shaking his head vigorously. Robin looked confused, but stopped talking. "I guess I should introduce myself," she said, after a pause. "I'm Robin, and I'm dreaming you. I am sorry about that."

Charlie laughed out loud. "No, I'm pretty sure I'm dreaming you," he said.

"That's not true. Why are you arguing with me?"

"Well, first of all, we've already met – at school," Charlie said. "Second, there's your name. A tree and a Robin? It's too good to be real. I mean, who on earth would name a girl after a bird? Clearly that is something I made up."

Robin gave Charlie a hard look, and walked straight up to him. She was about four inches taller than he was, her long legs ending slightly above his waist. She leaned her nose until the tip touched Charlie's. Charlie could just make out the fullness of her lips as he looked down to avoid eye contact. Thinking he was about to be kissed, he closed his eyes and tried not to faint.

She slapped him. Hard. Twice. He had a knack for being profoundly wrong at the most inopportune times.

"Do. Not. Make. Fun. Of. Me." She was speaking through clenched teeth. "I have to take that out there, but I do not have to take it in my own dream. No siree, Bob."

Charlie was rubbing his left cheek, and trying hard not to let his eyes water lest she think he was crying. He looked up towards the sun and blinked, pretending it was a light problem his eyes were having, rather than an "I just got pimp slapped by a girl" problem. After composing himself as best he could, he responded in his most calm voice (that only quivered a very little, to his credit). "Why did you slap me?"

"*Twice.*" Chuck corrected.

"If you were upset with me, I pretty much got that message from the first slap. And my name is not Bob, by the way. Perhaps you have me confused with Bob."

Robin looked at Charlie as if he had two heads. "No siree, Bob is just an expression, Einstein. Hello. It's called an idiom."

Charlie smiled. "I consider being called Einstein a great compliment. I think you should know that for future reference. I suspect it takes a little off the sarcasm." He paused, trying to think of something else to say. He wasn't used to having responses when people talk — not girl people anyway. The sting of his cheek was subsiding, and his ability to think was starting to return, as the blood eased from his now pink cheek to his brain. After an uncomfortable silence of exactly seventeen and a half seconds, he added, "For what it's worth, I like birds."

"You are such a dork," Robin surmised, shaking her head, her long hair swinging from side to side in counterpoint. Her hair was syncopation to Charlie, and he stood hypnotized for a second. "I said I was sorry for slapping you, okay?" she finally said, when she realized he was staring at her, mouth agape.

"Uh, no you didn't."

"No I didn't what?"

Robin's eyes bore into Charlie's face, which made the light brown skin of his cheeks flush red once more, this time, for a completely different reason. The girl made him intolerably uncomfortable, but in a good way, he decided. She was creepy. "You didn't actually say you were sorry," he said.

"Oh. I thought I did. In that case, I'm sorry you made me slap you."

"Only a girl could apologize to me for something, and still make me feel like it was my fault ..."

"It was, but that doesn't mean I'm not sorry."

" ... but few people ever apologize to me for anything, so I guess I should just accept it."

"I hit you pretty hard."

"Twice," Charlie added.

"Oh, I know, but I'm only apologizing for the second one. That was only a one slap insult, but ... I got carried away. I never hit anyone on purpose."

"Oh, now I feel special," he said.

Robin looked away, toward where Abner was busy in a heated discussion with Frank the tree. For a time, they both appeared to have forgotten the kids completely. She glanced back at Charlie, who was looking at her with a strange puppy expression, tilting his head from side to side, as he looked at her. She frowned at him. "You're kind of weird," she said.

Charlie's expression drooped, and for a moment, he was certain he might die.

Robin was looking at his face, but did not seem to notice his change in demeanor. "I like weird a lot," she said. "I like you, though usually I hate boys that make me like them."

Charlie exhaled in relief, and smiled. "You are even more confusing than the not-a-rabbit," he said. He was staring at her eyes, first at one then the next.

"Did you always have those dimples?" Robin's mouth asked. This brazenness apparently horrified her eyes, which widened like a deer's in headlights as soon as she asked the question.

Charlie answered, still staring at Robin's eyes if she were a science experiment. "I dunno, I guess so. I don't really smile at myself in mirrors, so I never notice them myself."

"One should always smile at oneself in mirrors," Robin proclaimed. "I do that every day."

"Well, you have a reason to," he replied, having spoken before he realized what he was saying. It was now his eyes' turn to widen in embarrassment.

"Stop flirting with me," Robin said, smiling shyly. "It's weird."

Charlie considered reminding her she liked weird, but instead decided to change the subject. "I-I was about to ask you if your eyes are always such a deep green, but they just now turned blue. Is that part of my dream? My dreams usually aren't this detailed."

"We really need to sit down at some point and discuss exactly who is dreaming whom," she said. "While I can understand how you would mistake me for a dream — as I'm very cute — I can assure you I am not a dream. I am Robin Mercedes LeBeaux, Mexindirishfrenchican girl, and I am very real."

"Mexind-what?" Charlie asked, laughing.

Robin was talking, and as was often the case when she was talking, she was not listening. "I, in fact, am the only Mexindirishfrenchican girl remaining in existence. I am a rare, but not endangered species, as I am quite certain to have daughters one day."

"Wow. You talk really fast."

"Keep up, Dimple Boy."

"Um, are you insulting me now?"

"Why? Do you feel insulted?"

"Well, I-I'm not sure. It's just you called me 'boy.'"

Robin blinked at him. Twice. "You are a boy, silly."

"I-I know, but my … well I've been told that being called boy is demeaning."

Robin blinked twice more. "That's ridiculous. Dimple Boy is your superhero name. You know, like Astro Boy, Hellboy, Superboy …"

"Okay, I get it, I get it. Like Robin, the Boy Wonder. But I don't think having dimples is much of a superpower." Charlie smiled out of half his mouth, the way he did when he was trying not to smile, and made exactly one dimple with his face.

"That is very annoying." Robin said. She immediately followed her statement by contradicting herself, her voice deepening. "Yes, it is pretty cute."

Charlie frowned and scratched his head. The girl was confusing. He wasn't even sure she moved her lips the second time. "What kind of girl, exactly, did you say you were?" he asked.

Sigh. Pause for effect. Longer sigh. Place one hand on slender hip. "Mexindirishfrenchican."

Charlie looked at her for another seventeen-and-a-half-second pause. They pretty much just blinked at each other, although Robin did, from time to time, raise her eyebrows and roll her neck a little. Then she grinned at him, her cute, full lips pulling back to reveal perfectly lined teeth covered by braces with pink bands. Charlie had a stroke. Well, it wasn't exactly a stroke, but it felt like one. He tested it, whispering random words to check his speech center. He had learned to do that after G'pa Joe's stroke two years ago, the one that sent him to that stupid Center.

"You are such a mumbler. Why do boys mumble so?" Robin was

frowning now.

"Well, usually it's because we aren't sure which things we say might get us slapped, so we kind of test them out before we hit the "send" button that's attached to our mouths."

"Good idea, that. You should have thought of it earlier. You could have avoided hurting my hand with your face." She rubbed her hand as she spoke, apparently completely serious. "Mexindirishfrenchican. It's my heritage."

"Oh! Wait, wait, don't tell me!" Charlie loved a good puzzle. "You're Mexican … indirish, Indian, Irish … frenchi … French, and … that's it. How'd I do?"

"Not bad," Robin answered. "It's Native American, by the way, not like, from India, but Native American made it too long."

"No, you're right, it's just the right length now." He paused two beats. "Do you know what your eyes remind me of? A chameleon."

"Do you mean like a chameleon in terms of colors, or are you saying my eyes bulge? Before you answer that, consider that the entire future of our friendship may depend on your answer." Robin now had both hands on her hips, and had pulled herself up to her full height for effect.

"The color definitely. I mean, now they are a brownish color. So far I've counted green, gray, blue then brown." He chose not to mention they changed on the bus dream, as he wasn't sure she would remember the other dreams. It was also embarrassing to mention he repeatedly dreamt about her.

"Hazel," she said. "They're never brown. My eyes are actually a mixture of blue and hazel. They appear to change color depending on the light, the sky, my clothes, and makeup … mostly they change when my mood changes. People tell me that's impossible, but my eyes don't care what people think."

"Oh. My. God. You have mood eyes. That is so cool!"

"Good call, Dimple Boy. You get 100 points. That, added to your 1000 demerits from earlier, means you're only 400 points in the hole. I neglected to inform you about the demerits."

"Um, that's negative 900."

"I know, but you earned 500 points in school for liking my outfit. But now you just lost 100 points for thinking I can't do math. Anyway, my eyes are green when I'm mad, the madder, the greener."

"Like the Hulk," he said, grinning.

"So not funny. They are hazel when I'm happy, which I am, at the moment, to your good fortune. Gray is just blah, and means nothing really."

Robin was on a roll now, and was beginning to talk even faster, which is what she did whenever she was on a roll. Just as she started, Abner gestured for them to follow. He was walking down a path that wound around the tall trees in the forest. This looked odd to the kids, since the not-a-rabbit, who looked like a rabbit, was walking on two legs, rather than hopping. His large shoes (and presumably, feet) gave him a clownish appearance. It was also odd that there would be a path that wound through the forest, and around the trees, given the fact that the trees could walk, and were polite enough to move out of the way if you asked nicely.

"What does blue mean?" Charlie was still on eyes.

"What?" Robin wheeled around, facing Charlie, wide-eyed.

For a moment, he thought he was about to be slapped again, and instinctively leaned back. "I just wondered what it means when your eyes turn blue. They did right before you starting talking about superheroes. I figure the information might come in handy to avoid more slapping."

"Never mind blue. It doesn't mean anything, probably just reflecting the sky."

Charlie looked up at the sky, which was mostly blocked by trees. "Oh," is all he said. "Are you really a real person?" he asked. "I mean, I know you're real, I saw you in school. You kept that girl from pounding me, in fact. It's just I'm wondering if I'm making all this up in my head, because it seems pretty real."

Robin spoke softly. "I told you I'm real. This is who I am, and I'll remember the dream. Besides, you aren't making this up, I am."

"Why are you so sure of that?" he asked.

"In real life, you don't actually talk."

"I do so talk," Charlie said defensively.

"No, I distinctly remember that you walk up to people and say nothing."

"Well, I'm usually a pretty good talker in my head." Charlie thought for a second, and added, "just not so much with my mouth." He winced, thinking he had given a perfect description of a loser. He resisted the urge to touch his forehead and see if there was a large capital "L" there. Instead, he went for a quick change of subject. "Do you think we're having the same dream, or is one of us psychic? I was thinking that maybe you're dreaming and I'm somehow reading your mind ... or vice versa. I had insomnia before this not-a-rabbit showed up so maybe I'm not really asleep. The other possibilities are, one, we are both asleep and dreaming, or, two, only I am dreaming, and somehow you are controlling my mind through some dangerous girl power you have."

Robin considered that for a minute before she answered. There was a long silence as she pondered the options. Charlie was impressed, as most girls he knew seemed to speak long before they thought. "I'm thinking there are other possibilities, she said, "like we are both lying in bed awake and somehow are connected, but I don't think those fit. I distinctly remember having a migraine tonight, and my mom gave me stuff that always makes me fall asleep. So, I'm sure I am asleep ... or was. In fact, I was told I was being taken to France, but ended up here in Never Never Forest."

"I was told the same thing," Charlie said with a scowl. "Not-a-rabbits are such liars."

"I can hear you, you know," Abner interjected. "Rabbit or no, I do have rabbit ears, and they work quite well."

"Sorry, dude," Charlie said simply.

"For the record, we are in France. It's the when I'm not sure of," Abner continued. "I was debating that with Frank, but he's so old, I can't trust him with dates. He thinks in terms of '100 years give or take.' I say 100 years too far would be overshooting the mark an unacceptable amount."

"Undoubtedly," Robin agreed.

"Robin, do you own a rabbit?" Charlie suddenly asked.

"No, why?" she answered.

"I was just wondering if Abner might represent a pet you have."

"I've had a ton of pets, but never wanted a rabbit. "

"How rude," sniffed Abner.

"Sorry guy." Robin answered emotionlessly. "I know I was asleep. So, either you are hacking into my dreams, which makes you a perv, or we are both asleep. You appear to be younger than me, so I'm guessing you aren't a full-blown perv yet. So that leaves we are both asleep."

To Charlie, Robin had the most illogical logic he had ever heard; yet, it made sense to him. "Agreed," he said simply. "So the question is why are we having the same dream? Bunny boy said something about choosing me I think. So this must be about him somehow."

"Maybe he's dreaming both of us."

"Are you aware you keep saying 'bolth?'" Charlie asked, too

distracted by Robin's non-native Virginian accent to notice what she was saying.

"Huh? Okay, what's with wrong with both?"

"Well there's no letter 'l' in both for one thing. It's b-o-t-h."

Robin frowned. "That's what I said. Both."

"No, you said bolth," he insisted. "B-o-l-t-h."

Robin laughed. "It's how I talk, I'm from New Mexico. Leave me alone."

She poked him in the shoulder until it began to get sore, all the while, smiling.

Charlie was about to complain about being poked when he saw Abner stop at what appeared to be the edge of the forest. He put on sunglasses, and pulled off the hooded robe and artificial wings he had been wearing. Underneath, he was wearing what appeared to be a military jacket with the name "Morris" on the lapel and olive green slacks. On his shoulder was an insignia of a snarling black panther and the words "Come Out Fighting."

"I've seen that before," Charlie said to Robin, pointing at the patch. "My great-grandfather has one of those."

As they watched, enraptured, Abner pulled off the rabbit ears one by one. They did not slip off like the fake wings had, but instead, required serious tugging until they came out with a loud "pop!" followed by a short gush of blood.

Abner winced in pain at each pull, but took them off nonetheless.

"Won't need those anymore," Abner said. Good thing, that, since they were now laying on the ground, each tipped in blood, looking like a pair of used gloves from a serial killer.

Charlie turned to look at Robin who was making a crunched up face with the tip of her tongue sticking out.

"Vomitocious," was all the speech she could muster. She dry-heaved once or twice, but nothing came out. "Shucks," she said. "I usually feel much better after a cleansing puke."

"Do you have anorexia?"

"No, silly. It's bulimia, and I love food. I get migraines. They make me nauseous."

Abner reached into the breast pocket of his jacket, pulled out an electric razor, and began shaving all the visible hair from his body. When he was done, there was a pile of rabbit fur in a fluffy pile at his feet, and he looked quite remarkably like a hairless ape. In fact, as they leaned in to stare at him, he looked like a hairless man. His rabbit nose fell off, revealing a rather ordinary nose underneath. He grew lips, lost the whiskers, had man ears, and grew taller.

Abner, as it happened, was nothing more exotic than a middle-aged, balding man. He was indeed, not a rabbit. Anymore.

13 – ROLLERCOASTER OF LOVE

"Dude! What in the heck are you?" Charlie asked, half horrified, and half enthralled. To him, Abner was like a video game. "I thought you said your name was Abner Mote. Now you're some army dude named Morris. Is Morris your real name?" Charlie, as much as he loved video games, was beginning to tire of this particular one, which seemingly had no discernible rules.

"I have many names," Abner answered, all the while looking down and buttoning his jacket.

"I want to hurl," Robin said, holding her stomach with her right hand, and pressing into her right eye with her left hand. "You made my migraine come back too. I can't have a migraine, I have a test in the morning."

"I am sorry about your headache," Abner said, without a trace of empathy. He turned to Charlie. "I already told you kid, I am not a rabbit. Why was that so hard to understand? If you had been paying attention, you would not be surprised now."

"So you're just an old dude in a bunny suit? Charlie asked, wide-eyed.

"Yes, except that I am not an old dude, just like I was not a rabbit." He paused. "I just play one in your dreams. You might want to ask yourself why you dream about older men." Abner considered Charlie with squinty eyes. "Have you ever considered that perhaps you might be gay?" Charlie's left brain tried to nod half his head yes, while the right brain tried to shake the other half no. The net effect was for Charlie to look as if he were having a petit mal seizure.

"Epileptic," Abner continued. "That explains a great deal. I must make a note to avoid too much excitement too quickly."

"I am not epileptic; you just get on my frigging nerves," Charlie fumed, now deeply annoyed. "For the record, this stuff was much cuter when you were a bunny. Now you're just a pain in the butt."

"That is so shallow, Dimple Boy," Robin interjected. "He can't help it if he's ugly. Not everyone is naturally beautiful like, well, you know."

She was smiling, which Charlie felt was a good thing. He also thought it odd, since she was on the verge of vomiting no more than thirty seconds earlier, and she had one finger poking just above her eye, trying to stave off her headache.

"It's Charlie. My name's Charlie, in case I didn't tell you."

Robin shook her head. "I prefer Dimple Boy. That's your new name."

"Um, okay. You're the dream girl."

Robin began twisting her hair. "I told you to stop flirting with me. It's really weird." Her eyes were blue again.

Abner looked over his shoulder at her. "Now you've got her all excited, kid."

Charlie's eyes widened with the realization that he was actually *talking* to this girl; in fact, he was *flirting*. Moreover, she seemed to be enjoying it. G'pa Joe would be proud. Truthfully, he never meant to be flirting. In fact, his reference to dreams was little more than an acknowledgement that he was not yet convinced she was more than a dream he was having. Plus, he was trying to hint she had been a frequent guest star in his dreams, without looking like the perv she hinted he might be, Still, while awake, it was a great effort for him to string more than two sentences together to anyone but G'pa Joe, so this was invigorating. "I'm, I'm, uh, sorry," he said. "I didn't even know I knew how to flirt."

"Well you do," Robin said, still smiling.

Abner, who had been watching the two of them, shook his head, and started walking deeper into the forest. Without turning to look at them, he said, "If you two are finished being in puppy love, we really are late."

"Ew," said Robin. "We just met, and he's too young for me."

Charlie tried not to be crestfallen. He had flirted, and that was a victory in itself. Now was time to retreat, with dignity. In response, he said, "It's called being friends, Abner-Morris. Maybe if your best friend weren't a tree, you'd have better conversations with people."

"*Score!*" Charlene called in his head, while Charlie was careful not to smile and ruin the moment.

"I stand corrected, " Abner shrugged, walking faster now. " You aren't in love. You're bloody twins. Look, it's almost time to leave this place, and we haven't even gotten there yet."

Charlie, suddenly intrigued, ran ahead, and caught himself even with Abner. "Gotten where yet?"

"To meet the old one, who named you Charlie."

"G'pa's here? Why?"

Robin touched Charlie's shoulder. "Who's Geepa?" she asked softly.

"It's short for great-grandpa. It's what I call him." He turned to Abner who had finally cleared the trees, and was standing in an open field of rolling hills. "You didn't answer my question."

"I did answer it. You just haven't seen the answer yet."

Charlie was again considering strangling Abner, when Robin pointed to a large tree in the distance.

"Who's the lumberjack?" Robin asked. "Is that he? It can't be, he looks awfully young to be a great-grandfather."

Charlie spun in the direction she was pointing and looked. In the distance, he could see a young version of his G'pa Joe. He appeared to be in his mid twenties, was indeed dressed like a lumberjack, and he was swinging wildly with an amazingly long knife. As they watched, G'pa Joe continued raging against at what could have been ghosts — or perhaps invisible ninjas.

The young G'pa Joe was a huge, muscular man, all wrath and vigor, fighting against nothing, tilting against imagined windmills. There was sweat staining his entire back, and blood trickling down both arms. Charlie guessed he must have torn his flesh on the bark of the tree, not even knowing he had done so.

"What is he doing?" Robin asked gently. "He's not a little ... ill ... is he? Maybe I can help. I have some experience with violent men."

"He's not crazy," Charlie said, his heart pounding. He turned to Abner and grabbed his jacket with both fists. "What are you doing to him?"

"I am bringing *you* here to him. That's what I am doing. The rest, he is doing to himself."

"Why is he acting like that — fighting nothing?" Charlie asked.

"Oh I assure you, it's not nothing he's fighting. And, sadly, he has no chance of winning. You should have listened to me." Abner brusquely removed Charlie's hands. "He wanted to be a hero, and now he'll have to pay for it."

Charlie glared at Abner, but said nothing. Instead, he took off toward G'pa Joe in a dead run. Abner, trailed by Robin, quickly darted after Charlie, catching him just before he reached G'pa Joe's pantomimed struggle. Abner held him as he flailed in frustration. "You are too late. I had hoped you can talk him out of it, while there was still time."

"Too late for what?" Robin asked.

Abner pulled a pocket watch from his pants pocket. "I kept telling you to hurry, and now look what happened."

"Enough of the white rabbit bit," Robin said, her eyes flashing green. "What's going on?" Abner ignored her.

G'pa Joe reached up to the trees as if lifting something up, smiled, and collapsed.

"G'pa!" Charlie screamed in fear and rage, the full brunt of his emotional energy surging. He had watched his Grandma Kate die, and now, he feared, it was a repeat performance with G'pa Joe. Charlie's anguished cry shook the trees, and rushed past the inner planets to the sun. The radiant energy from his voice made the fiery orb glow momentarily brighter, the way a campfire will when one blows into it. The cry sailed past the solar system, faster than light, and into a cluster of nearby stars, causing one to crash into another with the force of a supernova. Somewhere, at the edge of the galaxy, burgeoning, still unintelligent life on an entire planet in this land of dreams, ceased to be, because Charlie had unleashed the entire force of his pain and fury.

Abner looked to the sky, and the brief, but distinct, distant flare of light, and winced. He looked at Charlie, and shook his head in disbelief. "You have no idea what you have done," he said. The words were not accusatory, but weary.

Charlie looked from G'pa Joe to Abner and back. "I didn't do this," he said, hoping he was speaking the truth. G'pa Joe was not moving. There were no breath sounds.

"Not this, no," Abner said somberly. "This pointless attack was the old man's doing, and he will pay for it." Abner looked up at the small empty darkness where light had been. His eyes flashed with fury. "This is no place for children or impulsive old men. Leave, and never return. This will be your only warning."

Abner transformed into a shimmering figure of blinding light, and was gone in an explosive flash.

Robin, who had been holding her ears since Charlie's cry of pain and sorrow, stood quietly by, her gray eyes streaming tears in a torrent like a thousand bitter seas. "They are all dead," she said, tearfully, her eyes fixed to the heavens.

Charlie's eyes widened in horror, and his eyes searched the skies where the girl looked. He found only the cheerfulness of a midday sun. Robin looked at her new friend, and turned his face to hers. Despite her tears, she managed to smile at him beatifically. Her lips moved, as if searching for the perfect words. Finding none, however, she wrapped her arms around him, as if the world depended on the embrace. She clenched her eyes and pressed her cheek to his, whispering, "Wake up."

Charlie did.

It was morning, his alarm clock was buzzing, and his pillow was damp with tears or sweat. It carried the crisp scent of Robin's perfume. He was no longer certain he had been dreaming, as dreams were not supposed to leave smells on pillows. He was sure of one thing, however; if he was dreaming, he never wanted to do so again.

14 – FEAR ITSELF

Mary was in a deep but fitful slumber on the night of Charlie's visit. In her mind, it was 1973, and she and her boys were under attack. The meds given by the nursing staff made her sleep but did nothing to assuage the images that had taken over unconscious mind. She knew nothing of Virginia, or Charlie, or of being a 69-year-old woman. For her, there was but a single reality — the pack had begun to hunt.

Mary grabbed her boys, and began to run.

As the wolves encircled her, Mary watched each one, noting their positions. First would be the alpha, which must be avoided at all costs. She had noticed one to her right that lagged behind. It was away from the rest of the pack. Perhaps it was old, or wounded – maybe the omega, more timid than the rest. She knew wolves could sprint up to 40 mph, faster than she could ever hope to go. They possessed stamina and ferocious determination. They would never give up, and they would not be outlasted. She feinted in the direction of the beta male that stood directly to the alpha's right. She appeared to be playing chicken with it, on a beeline in its direction. It reacted by sprinting toward her, and the horrified boys screamed, no longer holding onto their mother, but holding their eyes shut instead.

The alpha saw Mary's move instantly. It took one step, and leaped a full fifteen feet in the air on an interception course with dinner. A split-second before both wolves would have tackled Mary, she cut right, heading toward the timid wolf in the shadows. The alpha, just landing, did not have time to alter its course, and barreled into the beta that had been running full speed at Mary. They tumbled in a swirling, snarling, angry ball. The other wolves began to chase, but they were distracted by the two lead wolves – the alpha female and her mate, the beta male – that were busy chastising each other.

Mary charged the sole wolf ahead of her. It seemed more inclined to run away than attack. Mary shouted fiercely at it, using words her sons had never heard her say before. It turned and bolted. It was just another outcast in dangerous territory.

She had chosen well, and her sons had survived because of it. At the base of a tree with deep, thick roots, Mary practically threw her sons into the lowest branches. The wolves were on her heels. She could hear the snarls and feel their humid breath against her legs as she pulled herself into the tree. One solitary tooth snagged the flesh of her heel, leaving a crimson trail streaming behind.

They had tasted her, and she was warm, and it was good. Exhausted, heart pounding, full of fight, and tears, and hugs, the trio climbed deeper into the massive branches of the tree, away from the wolves, and toward salvation. She rested, and pulled her children closer to her breast. Her boys were brave now, safe in their mother's arms, and almost calm enough to stanch their tears. Below, the wolves circled and waited, circled and waited. They were forest sharks, and the little family was adrift in a deadly sea. The pack followed a protocol of snarls and leaps for a while, before settling down below the tree.

They are hungry, but not starving. They can wait. Wolves are patient beings.

Mary pulled off the few remaining leaves from the middle branches of the tree and tore off most of her skirt to make a bed in the manner that she had seen chimpanzees do. They were twenty feet above the ground, and safe as long as they stayed in the tree. The wolves would tire of the hunt — she hoped. In the meantime, they would sleep.

"It's okay kiddos, we're safe here." It was as much a prayer as it was comfort.

The wolves were quiet, all save the alpha, which pawed at the tree, never taking her eyes off the group above. The alpha had a pack to feed, Mary a pack to save. Mary and the alpha made eye contact, neither blinking. The wolf showed her teeth in a warning, and Mary answered with a middle finger. It was an impotent gesture, but it made Mary feel stronger. The two watched each other for a long time, until both settled down to a restless sleep.

Around ten o'clock, with the moon high in the night sky, Mary awoke to a rustle in the leaves above. Squinting, she could just make out what appeared to be a branch moving above. Mary looked at the boys, who were sleeping quietly. Mikey had his thumb in his mouth, something he hadn't done in months. Davey was sleeping with his arm around his little brother, protecting him even in sleep. Mary sat up, not wanting to disturb the boys or waken the wolves, now invisible below, deep on the forest floor.

Something moved below. Another sound overhead. Below, a small branch snapped, and a whimper shattered the still night, followed by a loud thud. Above, the moving branch had become two, and one had a mouth.

It is no branch. There are snakes in the tree above.

Below, Mary heard a low growl and saw angry amber eyes fifteen feet below her. They were looking straight up, and met her gaze with a coldness that chilled her. She had seen those eyes before. They were the eyes of an alpha female gray wolf.

The wolves had learned to climb.

15 – WATCHING THE WATCHER

Time is a very strange thing in dreams. While it used to be common knowledge that time passes more quickly a dream than when awake, sleep research did not show that to be true. In fact, for those rare beings who could dream lucidly, and while dreaming perform some pre-arranged tasks like counting, there was no real difference between the time tasks took to accomplish while asleep and awake. In other words, it takes just as long to think while asleep as it does while awake. Dreaming, it seemed, was far more ordinary than anyone suspected.

Travelers in the Stream, that stream-of-conscience world of dreaming into which Charlie, Robin, and Mary had stumbled, knew better. Certainly, one could travel, count, do any number of mundane tasks and never experience a gap in time. But for the very experienced, time was very different. While time may move at the same speed in a dream when one is doing little, very active dreams are different. More recently, scientists have learned that physical activities performed while dreaming take more time than the same activities while awake. It was as if movement in the dream world moved at a different speed altogether.

Oddly, the more strenuous an activity was in the Stream, the more difficult to perform, the more time would bend around it. Five minutes spent on a dreamtime walk in the woods would take no more than walking five minutes while awake. However, a daylong war in the Stream, with all its exertion, stress, blood, and horror — that could be completed in the real world time it took to sneeze. Counterintuition was part and parcel of the nature of the Stream. It was disconcerting for the beginner, to say the least. Like moving underwater, it took the average Stream traveler quite some time to become accustomed to being able to fit an hours' worth of physical dream activity into the blink of a waking eye.

Robin's sister Reyna was only now beginning to get used to it.

In the months since her death, Reyna learned much about the Stream. Freed permanently from the restrictions of a waking mind, she had learned that time was not linear in the Stream. Past, present, and future were concepts with little meaning here. It took no more effort to travel to the past than it did to travel to the corner market. Indeed, with practice, one could do both things at once.

Reyna had always watched over her little sister. She found her unfortunate demise no reason to stop. Though despairing, she was able to follow both Robin's and Charlie's dreams, and the hooded stranger who followed their every movement.

Reyna's watching had taken her to Mary. Mary was fighting for her life, and the life of her boys. But this was no ordinary pack of wolves. The alpha wolf was but one of many manifestations of the dark one. Siri, he was called. He meant to have Mary, and would stop at nothing to get her. Reyna understood what was at stake. Mary would lead to G'pa Joe, and G'pa Joe would lead to Charlie. Charlie would lead to … well, that was too much to allow herself to consider. Reyna allowed herself to be near the pack — an outcast, looking for scraps.

Reyna would watch Mary, this night. She would find G'pa Joe, and call his mind to his friend. It could lead him to a dangerous conflict with the dark lord whom had begun to master the Stream, true. But it must be done. All of creation depended on Charlie and Robin's coming together, and the quest they must undertake. They must be as one, those two, and they must choose the work themselves. Some things, even a being beyond death such as Reyna, could not change.

Reyna could not make the choice for her little sister, neither would she want to. There is a link between life and death, between dreams and reality. Siri did not fully understand that link, but, in time, he would. Robin and Charlie's work must be complete by then. Failure could mean their death, and far worse.

So much depended on the little sister whose hair she now sat stroking. It was just before dawn, and Reyna had once again led her younger sibling to Charlie. Almost nightly, since her death, she had pushed Robin to Charlie's mind, much as she had pushed her mother to move to Virginia. Because time moves differently in the Stream, she could join a dream Robin had in August with one Charlie dreamed in

September. And now, Robin, Charlie, Mary, and Joe would share a dream that each had at different times in the real world.

Powerful things are dreams.

Reyna had whispered to Frank – timeless, grumpy Frank, whose fruit he claimed once tempted a Middle Eastern woman in defiance of God himself. Frank had taken Robin to Charlie, because Reyna knew he must. So much depended on their bond. More than anyone could ever know.

Reyna bent over and kissed the sleeping Robin, who was moaning and whimpering in her sleep, her hands over her ears. Even asleep, the feel of Reyna's full lips against her cheek made Robin smile. Robin always smiled at her kisses, Reyna remembered. She allowed herself a single tear, and whispered, "Sorry, little bird. For leaving, for bringing you into this, and now, for letting you handle it without me."

Robin muttered a soft "no" in her sleep, frowned, but did not awaken.

"Don't be afraid, little bird," Reyna said. "My little brother will watch over you. He loves you already, you just have to meet him first." She kissed her sister once more, and wiped away another tear, which fell to the floor as a perfect pearl. "I'll be watching, but I can't help you." Reyna stood, looked at her sister, and then disappeared, with the light in the room warping into a single point. For a moment, the room itself seemed to curve inward then snapped back to its normal shape with an audible "pop" as Reyna departed.

***

Robin's eyes shot open, and she sat erect in her bed. She had felt the many creatures cease to be, her heart breaking with each ... not death, but un-life. Their existence was erased as though they never were. And though the pain was unbearable, it could not match the heart-pounding sadness of awaking to the smell of Reyna's familiar "Turquoise and Silver" perfume. Robin knew it was only her imagination; it was just one more morning of awakening in tears, as she had done most mornings since Reyna's accident.

Robin forced herself from the bed, and stumbled to her bedroom mirror. She loved looking in the mirror these days, now that she was in puberty's full embrace. No longer the awkward little girl, she was, more with each passing day, the image of her lovely sister.

I don't have my Reyna, but at least I have her face.

Robin forced a weak smile, her braces grinning back at her. She pulled her long curls aside, turning a full cheek to the mirror. There, clear as the morning sun, were two full lip prints stamped by a deep purple lipstick. It was Reyna's favorite — a color her mother Gloria hated now. Reyna was still out there, somewhere, still watching over her little sister. Robin had no doubt.

She began to cry, and this time, the tears were welcomed.

16 – "REALITY IS MERELY AN ILLUSION" – ALBERT EINSTEIN

Charlie was sitting in a window seat on the old school bus on a rainy Monday. The streets shone like stained glass from the combination of rain and the thin layer of engine oil pulled from the asphalt by the slow mist. The sky was dark and gray, as if the sun had decided to sleep in. Inside Charlie's school bus, however, was bright, with a clattering of energetic babble from dozens of shared-weekend details. Charlie, as usual, spoke to no one, but this was a silence even deeper than his norm.

He sat hypnotized by the reflection of headlights on the road's surface. It was morning, but could have easily been evening. The world outside was dark and gloomy, but no one else seemed to notice. Charlie thought it silly to be worried about his great-grandfather based on two stupid dreams, but he was rattled nonetheless. True, nothing had really happened in the last dream, nothing that he could remember anyway. He recalled a pantomime by G'pa Joe, followed by … something. Still, it was enough to give him pause. Something, that vague whatever, was very wrong. For once, he wished his dreams did not melt away upon waking like morning frost. He needed to remember.

Seated next to him was Bryan Flynn, a reed-thin, sandy-haired, ruddy boy of thirteen. Bryan was busily bopping his head and a singing off-key to music from his cell phone. His twin brother, Brandon, was seated across the aisle from him, and was likewise singing to music from a matching phone. On a normal day, Charlie would have guessed the boys wanted to sit together and offered his seat. Charlie knew Twin

Flynn, as they were known, were normally inseparable. This was no normal day. Charlie was barely aware that Bryan had joined him several stops earlier.

Charlie pressed his forehead against the cool glass of the bus' window and stared at the patterns of the raindrops being blown on the other side of the glass. It was a little after eight a.m., and he was still tired. Instead of a restful night's sleep, he felt as if he had hiked uphill all night. The bus was bouncing in its usual rhythm, and he found himself drifting to sleep. As soon as sleep overtook him, however, the bus shuddered to a sudden stop. Mrs. Thornwood, the driver, had apparently been distracted, and had almost passed a group of ten kids who were standing in the rain. She braked late, as if considering just passing them by, rather than risk spinning the old bus out. But there were parents there as well, and splashing a group of angry parents while leaving their kids in the rain wasn't good for one's job security. The kids climbed on the bus, now filled to capacity, with their usual rancor.

Charlie pulled his mp3 player from his camouflage backpack, and looped the sound-dampening headphones over his ears. He stared at passing cars, his eyes fixed on the double white lines, the sound of hip-hop in his ears, and diesel fumes offending his nose.

His dream had been vivid; that he remembered. It was more real than any dream he had ever had. He could remember smelling flowers as they approached the edge of a forest. Never had he had the sensation of smell while in a dream. And the Cute Girl had a name, Robin. The details from the dream were escaping, but he remembered she promised him she was really there.

Unless I'm crazy. Or maybe she's psychic, or, like a witch. I read once how witches can get in your mind, and turn you into a serial killer.

Fortunately, Charlie still had Chuck on duty in his brain, and his logical side assured him if he were a serial killer, he would be thinking about knives or something by now. Mostly, he was thinking about a girl with mood eyes. What if he really didn't meet Robin in his dreams? How could he find out without risking look like an idiot? He could just imagine the conversation:

Me: Hi, good to see you again, Robin. Nice dream we were having huh?

Her: Uh, I've never seen you before, kid, and my name is Shaniqua.

She would think he was nuts. This was a no-win situation if he had ever seen one.

Wait, Robin. She told me her name, but only in the dream. If that's her real name then I really dreamt her.

"Which could mean you're psychic, dummy. Doesn't mean she was actually in your dream." Chuck was crawling through the holes in Charlie's logic.

The bus squealed to another sudden stop, throwing kids toward the seats in front of them at thirty miles per hour. Charlie had relaxed his grip on his mp3 player, which went sliding under the nearest seat. Bryan had fallen into the aisle, and was on his knees, smiling at and punching his brother, who was laughingly asking if he needed a car seat. Charlie had to reach all the way under the seat to recover his player, collecting the mp3 player and about a week's worth of dust. The knees of his black corduroy pants were gray with filth, as was the front of his favorite red sweater.

Charlie stood, brushing off his pants and shirt, and occasionally looking toward the driver's mirror in an attempt to see if Mrs. Thornwood was laughing. It would have been her idea of a practical joke, he reckoned.

When the last of the kids got on the bus, Charlie was standing, head bent over, as he tried to clean his previously pristine red sweater. Charlie, being Charlie, never once looked up, never noticed Bryan staring ahead with a goofy grin. He sat back down, relieved he was able to get off most of the dust, and immediately made another greasy forehead stain on the bus' window. The last stop meant ten more minutes to school on a normal day, but traffic was slow. This was the south, and there was bad weather. A slow trip to school suited Charlie just fine — just fine indeed.

***

As a consequence of dropping his mp3 player, Charlie had been noticed by one tall, slender girl with long dark hair. Robin spotted him almost the instant she was on the bus. It was less good fortune than careful planning. Rather, it was as careful as any of her plans. She had awakened frantic over her friend's well being. Though her visit from Reyna had brightened her mood considerably, Charlie seemed despondent at the end of her dream. She had, in fact, imagined his cry made suns collide and worlds crumble in a wave of misery and destruction. She had, after some debate, decided to believe it was her imagination. Her immediate instinct had been to pick up her cell phone and text him an "r u ok?" but on picking it up, she remembered she didn't actually know his number. She didn't know his last name, or him, for that matter.

Still, Robin was nothing if not loyal to her friends, and she had decided that Charlie was a friend. True, she had only dreamed him, but he had assured her he was really there, as had she, and that was good enough for her. She didn't trouble herself too much with the logic of the situation. Maybe they were psychically attuned, or whatever, but having an entire summer full of dreams about a kid you never met must mean something. Okay, they sort of met at school, but he had barely said three words to her then. But if God, or Reyna – whom she was certain, was her guardian angel – wanted her to look out for this kid, there must be a reason.

As she moved toward the back of the bus, she did a quick scan, and saw the only empty seat was in the back, next to some smelly gym rat type she had met her first week. This had been her first time on the bus. Her mom insisted on driving her to school initially, but Robin had finally convinced her she'd never make friends unless she took the bus. True, she never had any difficulty at all making friends when she wanted to, but that wasn't the point.

Robin watched Charlie, head to glass, staring out the window, and trying to be asleep. She was standing in the aisle next to his seat, but he never looked around. He looked sad — like a little brown puppy. She couldn't recall everything they talked about in the dream, only that she liked him — or he annoyed her — she could not quite remember which.

"He's a boy, so he annoys you. What part don't you get?" It was her inside voice.

You know, I already have enough problems without having some Goth chick stuck in my head.

Her inside voice objected, insisting she was more Emo than Goth, but Robin was trying not to listen. Mrs. Thornwood chose that moment to hit the accelerator, splashing muddy water on the remaining parents, and Robin stumbled backward, falling on Brandon. His brother Bryan, being ever so competitive with his brother, grinned, and offered Robin his seat. Bryan squeezed in next to Brandon, who immediately dug his elbows into Bryan's bony rib cage. "Get off!" Brandon said, through a wide grin.

"No way. If girls are gonna fall outta the sky," Bryan said in response, "I'm not letting them fall on you."

Robin smiled a sweet thank you (without revealing her braces) and took Bryan's former seat.

So, through crafty feminine wiles, or just the luck of the female of the pretty dork species, Robin found herself sitting next to a still-oblivious Charlie. Now Robin was kind, but not desperate, so she pretended not to notice that Charlie was not noticing her. After about five minutes of this, and with the school no more than five minutes away, she decided they needed a Plan B.

"So let's try this again, Dimple Boy. Are you going to talk to me this time or what?" Robin still wasn't very adept at Plan B's, or at subtlety, as it turned out.

Charlie jumped in his seat, banging his head loudly against the metal frame holding in the window. "Crap! Ow," he complained, rubbing his aching forehead.

Brandon and Bryan were grinning at him in twin Cheshire cat expressions. "Dii-mple Bo-oy," Twin Flynn chimed, echoing Robin.

The game was afoot. Charlie glanced at the twins, but quickly looked away from the twin grin-down, which left his eyes nowhere else to look but into Robin's eyes. "Gray. That means ... I don't know what that means. I don't know what I'm talking about," Charlie mumbled softly. He was speaking, and looking into her eyes, yet he still appeared to be talking to himself.

"You do know you're not actually talking to me, right?" Robin asked.

"Uh, um, sorry. Hi," Charlie said hesitantly.

They sat like that, in silence, for the next four minutes, right up until the bus sat, stuck in traffic, two blocks from school. There was an accident there and no one was moving until the police cleared the scene. Robin decided she needed to break the silence, or she'd look like a dork for starting a conversation with a kid who basically just brushed her off. Cute girls did not get the brush off. This was especially true given he obviously liked her a lot. She could not understand why that was such a hard thing for boys to admit.

"You know, if you just go ahead and admit you like me, it would clear up a lot of this awkwardness." Still not subtle.

Charlie gasped in response. "I-I ..." His voice trailed off, then his eyes darted again towards Twin Flynn, who were busy sharing a pair of earbuds and singing off-key. "I never said I didn't like you," he whispered.

Robin was certain he was blushing under his caramel skin.

Good, we've got that settled.

"So, are you okay?" she asked.

"Yeah, no, not really. I had a rough night. I can't stop thinking about it, but I also can't remember it exactly. I'm sorry."

"Why are you apologizing exactly?"

"I'm not making sense. I hate it when I don't make sense."

Robin frowned, but her voice was gentle. "You're doing fine. Sheesh. Hard on yourself much?"

"I apologize a lot, yeah," he said, flustered. "I'm sorry."

"Well, you looked down, so I thought I'd cheer you up." Robin put on a big, braces-covered grin. "Consider yourself cheered Dimple Boy."

"That's the second time you've called me that. I'm not even smiling."

"Uh, I'm pretty sure it's been more times than that," she countered.

For a second Robin thought maybe she had dreamed the whole thing, and Charlie had no idea who she was. She considered asking him if his name was in fact Charlie, but that would prove nothing. It never once occurred to Robin — she being adept at believing in the impossible — that Charlie was not in her dream. He was there. However, crush or no, he didn't appear to remember their dream. That thought made her embarrassed, and more than a little bit insulted. Did he really not remember her? She was not vain; in fact, she was mostly false bravado and a thin layer of self-confidence. Liking a friend who didn't remember you was too much, especially when it was her dream in the first place. Boys, it was turning out, were uniformly annoying.

"Your eyes are green all of a sudden," Charlie said, interrupting her thoughts. He looked nervous. "What … what did I do now?"

Robin cocked her head and smiled. He was there, and he remembered. "Welcome back." Of one thing, Robin was certain: dreams could easily be forgotten, but color-changing eyes were a life-long memory. Even her own family found them fascinating. "What's my name?" she asked him.

"Wow, how did you know to ask me that?" Charlie looked at her, a fresh wave of nervousness washing over his face.

"How did I know to ask you if you remember my name?"

"Well, yeah. I mean, you could have asked me a lot of things. Why that?"

"Because, silly, I want to know if you know my name."

"Um, R-Robin?" His voice practically squeaked.

"Sheesh. Not very confident, are you?"

"Are you going to hit me again?"

"No, why would I hit you?"

"Well, you kind of make me nervous when your eyes are green. I don't want to say the wrong thing and get hit again."

"I told you, I'm only violent in my dreams, Charlie." She smiled at him. "You do remember, don't you?" she asked.

Charlie nodded then glared at the Flynn brothers who were staring in their direction. Robin followed Charlie's gaze to the twins, and both immediately stared at their laps. "See? I told you those green eyes are scary," Charlie said.

"Some people think they're pretty," Robin huffed at him.

"I-I didn't say they weren't pretty, it's just ..."

"It's too late to flirt with me, Charlie."

Charlie blushed a deep crimson, and turned to face the window. After a few moments, he returned his gaze to her. "How do you think we had the same dream? I mean this kind of stuff is impossible."

Robin shrugged. "Impossible stuff happens every day. So do nightmares," she added, softer.

Charlie's eyes searched hers. "My great-grandpa — did you dream about him too?" he asked.

Robin nodded, as the bus jerked to a stop.

"Get the heck off my bus!" yelled Mrs. Thornwood. It was her usual early morning greeting. Afternoons she would advise them all to consider dropping out to make her next morning easier. All the kids, except Charlie, loved it.

Charlie and Robin sat talking for a bit about their shared dream then stood up when the smelly kid from the back row passed them. As they walked to the front of the old bus, Charlie looked down, obviously trying to stifle his emotions. Robin thought boys were generally masterful at that, full-fledged emotion-stifling wizards. However, Charlie was struggling. It wasn't hard for her to guess why. He was worried — about his great-grandfather, maybe his sanity. She, however, felt the opposite. He had remembered her from their last dream, and maybe he would remember the others. That meant that she wasn't going crazy after all — at least not alone, anyway.

Robin put her hand on his elbow, and leaned toward him. "We'll talk later, Charlie. It'll be okay. Don't try to be in control, just be in the moment."

"This is real, isn't it?" he asked.

"Of course it's real, silly," Robin answered, smiling. "I'm your best friend." She did not exactly know why she was so certain of that fact — maybe it was just a vestige of the dreams that Reyna had showed her. Nonetheless, she knew the instant she spoke the words that they were true. They were real. They had barely met, but she was his best friend.

"Thanks," Charlie said, blushing once more.

Now at the front of the bus, the pair of newly found friends drew a glare from Mrs. Thornwood that made Robin cower. "Off. My. Bus!" she bellowed, pointing to the open door.

Robin couldn't wait to get off the bus, even if it meant being in school. As Charlie reached the door, Mrs. Thornwood reached over and pulled it closed in his face, trapping him. Charlie turned to face her. Mrs. Thornwood leaned in, grinning at Charlie, her yellowed teeth bared. He took a hesitant step backward toward the door. Just as his back touched the door, she pulled the door's control lever, opening it, and spilling Charlie backward, feet over baseball cap. Into the mud. Again.

Just as before, there was Tisha. This time, she had been splattered with mud. She gave Charlie a savage grin, and socked him in the right eye.

Happy Monday.

17 – BLUE MONDAY

Even sitting in his perfectly chosen seats in each class, Charlie was not having a perfect day. It was third period, and the single positive thing he could think about third period was that it was followed by lunch. That was also the worst thing about third period — no lunch until it was over. His mind was adrift; he was a small craft in an ocean of thought. It was midday, and the safe shore of the end-of-period bell was a distant land below the horizon. He was profoundly bored.

He was in World History, normally a seventh-grade social studies class, but Charlie was in the "Gifted" program, having failed to score lower than the 90th percentile on the standardized tests he took in the third grade. He hoped to achieve a higher level of mediocrity with the upcoming sixth-grade version of the tests. In fact, he had convinced his dad to purchase a study guide from the local educational supply store. Both his mom and dad had been impressed by his ambition.

His mom, in fact, had privately spoken about "her genes finally kicking in," and how he was "on his way" to greatness. The truth of the matter was that Charlie guessed quite a bit on the third-grade tests, and decided that he must have accidentally guessed right too often. His new strategy was to know 100 percent of the subject matter, and purposely get just enough wrong to score in the 88th percentile. Charlie aspired to be in that tier just above average performers — extra medium he called it. It would force school administrators to decide his performance did not warrant his being permanently abandoned to the relative desert of "dumb" classes, but it was still not quite gifted enough. It was to be his ticket out of the land of nerds for which he was being trained.

Charlie was a smart kid who hated smart kids.

"*Hate is too strong*," Charlene said, reminding him once again why he had given his emotional side a girl's name.

At the front of the class was a cluster of teacher lovers. These were the kids who, according to Charlie, so desperately wanted approval they sat in the ringside seats. This was the equivalent of the people who paid top dollar at a fight just to have huge, angry men flick sweat all over them every time they were hit. The sycophant section was directly in front of Mr. Nagatomi, who had been teaching world history as long as anyone could remember. The small, gray-haired man with the hypnotically soft voice was currently lecturing about something or other regarding the Fall of Rome. Or Greece. Charlie had stopped listening fifteen minutes earlier.

Mr. Nagatomi's real claim to fame, however, was his wardrobe. He wore the same brown herringbone tweed sports coat with the dark brown elbow patch, olive drab dress slacks, yellow short-sleeve shirt (though no one ever saw him without the coat), and brown loafers, no penny. Rumor had it that he first wore that combination in 1969. Another equally plausible rumor was that he had ten sets of each clothing item, and wore them in rotation. He was never dirty, never smelled, never varied his routine.

Charlie thought history was the perfect subject for a man who didn't believe in change. He also guessed Mr. Nagatomi was so adept at facts and figures because he had studied at Herodotus' side in ancient Greece. Or Rome. Charlie couldn't remember which.

The suck-up crew was all as nattily attired as their teacher and idol. At least two of the sycophants, a boy whose name Charlie never learned and a rather chubby girl with stringy hair and a cute face, each had tape on their glasses. Since they were sitting so close to the teacher, they had — poor saps — no alternative but to pretend to listen attentively, never taking their eyes off him. Mr. Nagatomi had failing eyesight, but not the sense or wherewithal to buy glasses, so he constantly looked at his front row fan club, as he really couldn't make out the expressions of kids much past row two.

Charlie was in the middle section, where all the kids were normal — all except Jannet the Plannet. They were doing what normal kids do. Some were listening, most were not, two were texting each other, and one kid named Darius appeared to be sleeping with his eyes open. Charlie now considered Darius to be his hero.

Charlie would have been amused if boredom had not reached the critical point. He imagined that his brain cells were currently committing individual acts of suicide, starting with his auditory cortex. He wondered why God, in his infinite wisdom, gave man eyelids, but no ear covers. When he died and went to heaven, he'd have to offer God his suggestions for improvement in future evolution. Man 2.0 would be vastly improved, indeed.

Behind Charlie was a combination of normal seventh graders, and eighth graders who had managed to fall behind in their social studies. They were two years older and taller than Charlie, and a bit intimidating physically, but not the Willie Green type. Willie, as far as Charlie knew, only took English and gym.

Charlie's name for the eighth graders was "kids with their priorities straight." Charlie was an honor roll student, always had been. But he never quite got the point of history class. If he wanted to know what happened he could either Wikipedia it, Google it, or worst case, History Channel it.

Heck, I can just ask G'pa Joe. He was there for most of it.

"Mr. Patterson," called the voice of Mr. Nagatomi.

"Uh, yeah?"

"Please describe three factors that led to the Fall of Rome."

Shoot.

Charlie took in a deep breath. "Um, failures of leadership, money problems, and Religion."

"Ohh! Ohh!! Mr. Nagatomi." It was the hand waving, stealth suck-up Jannet, the Royal Pain in the Plannet.

"Yes, Miss Rogers." Mr. Nagatomi was so polite. Charlie liked that about him.

"I believe it should be Imperial Decline, over-expansion and inflation, and the rise of both Christianity and Islam splintering it into different factions."

Mr. Nagatomi merely nodded, eyes slightly closed. Jannet gave herself a Plannet-sized self-satisfied smile. Charlie imagined her red hair was glowing with pride.

Charlie raised both hands, palms facing him, and frowned. If he were skin, Jannet would be a rash. "Dude!" Charlie practically shouted.

Mr. Nagatomi, who had walked to the chalkboard to make illegible scribbles of the answers he'd just been parroted, turned, thinking Charlie was calling him. He noticed the boy was facing Jannet, and returned to his chicken scratching.

"Dude." Charlie repeated for effect, hands still outstretched, but lower. "You said exactly the same thing I just said. You're like a red-headed freaking parrot." Charlie surprised even himself with his outspokenness. Invisible kids did not lose their temper.

Somewhere deep inside him, Charlene was shouting a combination of *"Danger! Danger!"* and *"Mess her up!"* Apparently, his right brain was not totally opposed to hitting answer-stealing girls.

Jannet had ignored his first "dude" but felt compelled to address his "tirade." She would not give him the satisfaction of looking in his direction, however. "You gave abstract answers, and I clarified them. Perhaps the text would be a good reference point for more precision," she said. She genuinely didn't care if he was mad or not, she then informed him. In fact, she thought it only proper to educate him thus.

"Abstract? I said 'money problems,' you said 'over-expansion and inflation.' What do you think money problems meant?"

"I don't know. Perhaps you felt the ancient Romans lost too much money at the gaming tables in Reno." The class began to snicker. "My answer added that it was that they had been rich, but had grown too quickly to sustain it. And I did so with the same level of conciseness as your vague answer."

"Dude, why are you such a pain? The point was getting the answer right."

Jannet looked at Charlie for the first time. "The point was explaining what happened, to the class, not showing you are a great guesser. Even a broken clock guesses right twice a day." Jannet huffed, and turned away, her folded arms plastered to her chest. Her face was beginning to flush as red as her hair.

"Yeah, well guess what I wanna to break right now," Charlie half-mumbled under his breath, but loudly enough for Jannet who, of course, was sitting right next to him. The kids nearby laughed out loud at his response, which caused him to turn in surprise. He had never been funny, to the best of his recollection.

Charlie decided to let it go. He was surprised (and a little impressed) to see that Plannet had a temper. Perhaps a small part of his brain also remembered being slapped — twice — and thought better of antagonizing another angry female. His lightly bruised right eye certainly remembered Tisha clocking him in it. He thought it wise not to risk angering a second female today. Besides, Jannet was in all of his classes except gym, so he needed to pick his battles if he was going to stay below the radar all year. He had enough troubles already.

18 – "IN SOFT REGIONS ARE BORN SOFT MEN" - HERODOTUS

Despite his intentions to the contrary, Charlie and Jannet spent the remaining sixteen minutes of the period bickering, which was one of the longest continuous interactions that they had ever had. That fact itself was remarkable, given they had known each other since pre-school. The two had battled for intellectual supremacy since before either could spell IQ. Until this day; however, it had been a remote control war. Each lofted missiles of erudite enlightenment over the vast distance that separated their personalities. Being mutually conflict adverse, however, neither had ventured into the dirty business of hand-to-hand combat. Yet, today, this rainy Monday, this day of post-phantasy depression, Charlie was not in the mood for a long-distance war. This day he would begin to become the man he needed to be.

Today, Charlie would not surrender.

"*I will quit no more, forever,*" thought his right brain.

"*Heck yeah,*" answered Chuck, in surprising agreement. "*We can never achieve greatness by continually marching backwards.*"

So, on this day, Charles Robert Spencer Patterson became a man. Sort of.

Jannet had the initial advantage as she was seemingly unaffected by Charlie's increasing criticism of her air of superiority. To Charlie, she was an automaton. His right brain wondered — aloud — if she might, in fact be a robot. His left brain just thought she was kind of hot.

In truth, in the seven-plus years she had known him it was the first time Jannet had seen an indication of the passionate human being underneath. That he would care about anything long enough to argue for sixteen minutes surprised her. Though at the surface she appeared to despise him, Charlie got the sense she enjoyed realizing their mutual affection for abstract concepts (even though her opinions were wrong and stupid).

They had almost reached the point of global escalation (having moved to the full on writing of insults on a shared piece of notebook paper) when the lunch bell rang.

"This isn't over, Plannet," Charlie said angrily. He had never, before today, called her that out loud before.

Jannet looked at him, not getting the reference at all. She slightly raised her two red eyebrows and shook her head in the negative while shrugging her shoulders. "You are so weird, dirt nap," she said.

"Dirt nap?"

"Yeah," she answered, reaching the door. She held the ugly green doorjamb and looked at him one last time over her shoulder. "Because your brain died years ago."

Charlie was going to respond, but saw Willie Green waiting to walk her to lunch. She lost interest in the battle as soon as she saw Willie. Mr. Nagatomi, who to this point had been pretending not to notice World War Dork, walked up to Charlie, and put one small hand on his left shoulder.

"It's about time you stood up for yourself, young man. But she was right. If you answer such that it isn't clear whether you are knowledgeable or just guessing, no one will take you seriously."

"I know," Charlie replied, his anger subsiding. He knew he was as angry with himself as Jannet. "I'm not sure if I always know myself."

"In the wise man, the difference between knowledge and guessing is often confidence," Mr. Nagatomi said.

"That makes sense. Is that an ancient Chinese saying?"

"I don't know. I'm Japanese. Besides, I just made it up."

"Oh, okay," Charlie said through a smile. "Sorry about the Chinese thing. I should have known that."

"Yeah, you should have," Mr. Nagatomi agreed, smiling.

Mr. Nagatomi smiled and patted Charlie's shoulder again then left for the peace of the teacher's lounge and his usual lunch of tuna and lettuce on rye.

Charlie smiled to himself as he walked along the quiet corridors toward his locker, where he kept his lunch. Mr. Nagatomi was a rarity in Charlie's life — he was a teacher Charlie actually liked. To Charlie's way of thinking, being considered a favorite teacher by a student who hates your subject says quite a bit in your favor. He would have to remember to find a way to tell Mr. Nagatomi that, without actually admitting he hated history.

The halls of the old school were wide, dark, and empty, except for the custodian at the far end of the hall. The lights emitted a yellowish glow that, when combined with the light green and white paint, gave the walls a nauseating pea soup hue. Charlie stopped at locker number 714, and pulled the greasy brown bag his mother had insisted on packing his food in. Today's special was a cold chicken sandwich, an apple, and a granola bar.

Charlie looked at the rather unappetizing bag, and wondered if he would get poisoned from warm chicken. His mom was still of the opinion that all morning in a warm locker was somehow a perfectly safe place for food. Still, he was hungry, having a bad day, and didn't care if he got sick or not.

Charlie slammed the locker shut, which rattled and bounced back open, killing all the intended drama. His red sweater, still covered in dried brown mud, fell on the floor, leaving a round dirt mark that looked like he had pooped there.

"Great," he sighed. He hoped that Cody Bullock wouldn't come by before the custodian got there with his mop.

He closed the locker gently the second time, and walked toward the cafeteria through the maze of hallway. After a left turn and two rights, he saw the sign reading "CAFBTERIA," his destination. Long weeks ago, some kid had hand-painted the first "E" into a "B" and the cash-strapped Administration pretended not to notice.

All the other students were already in the cafeteria, which was a joyful cacophony — silly or overly earnest conversations, the tinkling of silverware, and a mixture of music and laughter. The room was large, and was the most well lit part of the school.

Charlie blinked in the bright light, and shielded his eyes with his left hand. He tried to look casual as he scanned the room; first in the unlikely hope of seeing Robin then looking for an uninhabited part of the room. Robin had told him as they'd entered the school that she was in the seventh grade, which meant she would be in the second lunch period that immediately followed his. He wasn't sure he had the courage to try and sit with her anyway, but at least wanted to make eye contact and see how she responded. She was new, and maybe wasn't surrounded by a clique of wannabes yet.

Charlie found an empty table near the front of the cafeteria. He had known most of these kids for years, and spoke to many of them, but was close to none. Today, he just wanted to eat and leave. The sooner he ate, the sooner he could go to the school's office to see if they would allow him to call the Senior Center to check on his great-grandfather. His mom forbade his taking his cell phone to school. She knew him well enough to know downloaded games would hold his interest far longer than lectures.

As he sat with a dejected thud — being a lone wolf didn't mean he didn't want a pack He was joined by the massive Ray and Jay Romatowski, who had been christened "Double Trouble" by Coach Traynam for their football heroics since their earliest youth league football days. The dark-haired, round-faced boys with permanently snarling countenances were a force to be reckoned with on and off the field. Future NFLer and early high school player Ray's favorite pastime was blind-siding quarterbacks in the hope of inflicting his first "clean" concussion. Jay was less skilled on the field, being destined to fill up his remaining football days in small college football followed by a thrilling career at a convenience store. At age thirteen, the boys were an outsized 5 foot 8 inches tall, and around 190 pounds each. Jay made up for his lacking football prowess by being the official school bully. Sure there were pretenders to the position galore, but Jay had a plaque declaring his position in the Coach's office. Actually, it said, "UPMS' Bad Boys," with a picture of the boys in football uniforms, but Charlie knew what it meant. No one had ever challenged either boy — neither student nor teacher.

Spotting Charlie's lunch, and having had only two of his own, Jay quickly snatched the brown bag Charlie had been holding. Charlie had held the bag absentmindedly; his grip had been light. At the loss of his lunch, he was shocked, barely having had a chance to notice the boys were there.

"Looks like I have another lunch," Jay grinned.

Charlie merely sat with his hands in the exact position they had been. He stared at Jay with a blank expression, not moving.

"What? You got a problem with it?" Jay asked, not expecting to be eyeballed.

Charlie didn't have a strategy. For the first time in his life, he was … being in the moment. He continued to look Jay in the eyes, not moving his hands, not making a sound, expression, or gesture.

"What you gonna do about it? You gonna take it back?" Jay looked at Charlie, his eyes seeming to boil over with hatred. Ray sat at his brother's side observing, but saying nothing.

At this point, Charlie's heart was pounding in his ears. He was committed. If he flinched now, he realized he'd probably get beaten nearly to death.

"At some point, when you've committed all your resources to war, you have to go forward, because back is death." It was Mr. Nagatomi's voice in his head. Charlie was at war for the second time today. He would not flinch.

Jay looked a bit nervous at this point. Generally, his angry look had been enough to get him what he wanted from life. Charlie was seven inches shorter and almost 80 pounds lighter than Jay. Yet, there he sat, quietly, looking Jay in the eyes, his hands waiting for the bag to return.

There was a heart-wrenching five seconds of silence. Charlie wanted to blink, to run, to scream. He waited for the inevitable huge fist to smash into his face for the second time today, making the two hits from his dream come true. His eyes begged, pleaded with his rational left brain for permission to blink. *"Permission denied, sissies,"* was the surprising answer from mission control.

"You crazy, boy," Jay said. "You nuts." Jay Romatowski then did something he had never done before. He flinched. He put the bag back in between Charlie's hands, and tried to keep a straight face.

"You're lucky I'm not hungry," Jay said. His brother Ray sat quietly, looking from Charlie to Jay, and back to Charlie.

With the bag returned to its rightful place, Charlie told himself not to react, nor gloat. He needed to play it cool to survive. His eyes now lowered, he just opened the bag, took out his chicken sandwich, and took an enormously satisfying bite. It was the best chicken — and game of chicken — ever.

Jay watched Charlie eat for a moment, and then rose, lifting his leg over the chair's back, macho-jock style. Ray watched him, and then stood himself. Charlie allowed himself to look up, meeting Ray's eyes for a second. There was no defiance, no machismo. Charlie simply looked at him. Ray returned the gaze then nodded, almost imperceptibly, and followed his brother out of the cafeteria.

For the first time in his life, Charlie was a bit of a minor celebrity. Quiet rumors of Charlie's run-in in the cafeteria had spread quickly. The emperor had no clothes, and Charlie was the kid who exposed him. Immediately after Double Trouble had left the café, or, more accurately, a safety net of thirty seconds later, first nerds then normal kids came over to pat Charlie on the back, and congratulate him for his stupidity, rather, courage.

"I thought you were dead, man," Cody Bullock told him.

"Me too," Charlie confided. "I wasn't trying to be brave, I just wanted my sandwich back."

Charlie spent the remaining four classes, Science, Math, Spanish, and Art in an emotional mixture of the same dread that had plagued him all day, and a gnawing confidence that just maybe he could deal with whatever lay in store. Between classes, he would wander the halls as quickly as he could, scanning the crowded mass in search of Robin. He needed to talk to her about the dream, and knew he would never get enough privacy at home to discuss anything remotely so important.

At 3:55, as the last bell rang, dismissing the kids, he finally spotted Robin. She was walking by herself, but being followed, paparazzi style, by Bryan and Brandon Flynn. They walked a safe ten feet behind the girl, as if she would suddenly turn and ask them to join her. Every few steps or so one of the boys would nudge the other and shove him forward, each egging the other on to break the ice first.

Charlie thought about Twin Flynn, who were genuinely good kids, and Double Trouble, with whom he'd had his run-in earlier, and wondered how two sets of twins in the same school could be so different. Actually, Charlie suspected that it was only Jay Romatowski who was different, perhaps from being cast in the athletic shadow of someone who was supposed to be his identical match. The Flynn brothers were different; they loved being twins, but reveled in their small differences. Brandon was the jokester, and Bryan, the good-natured butt of jokes.

As they approached the door, it was mostly Bryan who was being shoved in the direction of the oblivious Robin. She walked slowly, her head down and books clutched to her chest. Her hair swayed as she walked in counter-balance to the movement of her torso. Charlie had another stroke. He understood his reaction to Robin about as well as a monkey understands quantum physics — which is not at all. She was just a girl. True, she was cute — horribly, awesomely cute, but she was kind of skinny, "freakishly tall," which meant, of course, taller than him, and she wore braces.

She's perfect.

Robin was wearing a pair of black leggings that were complemented by a deep sky blue top, and a half jacket that stopped at her small waist. Over the leggings was a blue miniskirt that was technically no longer in style, but seemed to fit her outfit perfectly. She wore her hair in loose curls down to the small of her back, with a headband in front the exact color of her blouse. Being not quite thirteen, she wasn't allowed to wear makeup yet, but her mom allowed her just a bit of blue eye shadow to highlight her eyes. On her feet was a pair of boys' black gym shoes with a blue and black graphic design. Her mom had ordered those online straight from Japan. She wore no jewelry save a turquoise bracelet on her left wrist that was inscribed on the underside with the single word "Be." That was a gift from her sister, delivered a few days before her death.

Charlie noticed every visible detail. He then looked at his wrinkled gray shirt, no sweater, hand-inscribed sneakers, and marginally clean pants, and sighed.

As his heart pounded in his chest, he realized he had spent the entire day looking for someone he was now too terrified to approach. Robin had reached the wide main hallway that was bordered on the right by the school's gymnasium, and on the left by the main auditorium. The students called it the Echo Chamber due to the resonance caused by the wide hallway and the tall, cold walls.

Charlie was approaching Robin quickly from her left rear, but suddenly slowed, realizing he didn't know what to say. She reached the front doors, twisting her way past other students to where the buses were waiting. Charlie decided he would follow her on the bus and ask if the seat next to her was taken. He had no Plan B for if she sat next to someone else, especially if she sat next to another boy. With his luck, it would be Jay Romatowski, who would then kill Charlie in front of her. That thought made him shiver.

"Hey, it's Dimple Boy!" shouted Brandon, grinning in raving-idiot-moron-dork style. He was pointing to Charlie as if no one could reason who Dimple Boy was unless he pointed him out.

At the mention of the name "Dimple Boy," Robin stopped, and spun on her heels. She spotted a red-faced Charlie — and he was red-faced, it was just hidden under all the light brown skin — giving Brandon the old stink eye. To Charlie's amazement, Brandon stopped grinning, looked down, and walked past Robin without a glance.

"Good for you," Robin said. "Besides, no one gets to call you that but me."

Charlie tried to smile, but his lips were broken.

"You're supposed to say, 'of course Robin' there." She paused for a smile, but Charlie's face had begun to melt from the first sun of the day, and his smile drooped into what looked like a frown.

"What's wrong? I heard about a sixth grader named Chucky something who backed down these big huge Evil Twins somebody or other and I thought it might be you."

"Uh huh, yeah, kind of. It wasn't anything really. I was mostly just caught off guard."

"That's not how I heard it," she responded. "I heard you sent them packing."

Charlie shrugged. "Maybe bullies really are just cowards. Or, he could have just been trying to mess with me. He could've killed me if he wanted to." Charlie felt he could be honest with this girl. In fact, he felt *compelled* to be honest. She claimed to be his best friend, and it was the first one he'd had.

"It still sounds pretty brave to me," she said.

"The truth is I was scared to death. But I wasn't going to let him know that. I just decided if he were going to kick my butt, he would never get to see me afraid. So, I'm not brave, just good at faking it I guess."

Robin would not concede the point. "My sister used to tell me that not being afraid doesn't make you brave. Not being afraid makes you stupid. She said being brave was being afraid, and choosing to do a thing anyway."

Robin looked sad, a faraway expression crossing her face. Their bus was late, so they just stood in front of the school not talking while she gathered her emotions back into the blanket she wore over them. Charlie looked into her deep green eyes, the angry, sorrowful green, and imagined he could see dried tears she could never weep.

"So you see," she said, taking in a deep breath, and turning her head in his direction. "You were brave. You chose not to let fear stop you." Then after a beat, Robin added, "Fear or common sense, apparently. I heard he was huge."

Charlie's face finally had stopped melting, and he was able to smile at her.

"Yeah, I kept noticing his fist was around the same size as my whole face. I wondered if he punched me, would my face stick to his fist like a tattoo."

Robin laughed. It was loud, way too loud to be ladylike. When she laughed, her eyes opened wide, and she tilted her eyes toward the sky. It was raucous, abnormal. Charlie loved her laughter immediately and decided that making more of her laughter would be his mission in life.

"Yeah, I can picture that. Then he'd, like, have the letters H-A-T-E tatted on his knuckles so that everyone would see your face and know what happened to his enemies."

"Ew, God. I hope I don't dream about that tonight."

"Why would you want to dream something like that?" she asked, frowning.

"I can't control what I dream about," he answered, puzzled at the question.

"Of course you can, I do it all the time. Like last night, I dreamed I was Eve, of Adam and Eve, except I was wearing a very cute outfit. I don't do nude dreams."

"Good thing," he answered. "That would have been embarrassing."

"Ignoring you. Anyway, it turns out Adam was clueless, so I went to the Tree of Knowledge and said, 'If you're so knowledgeable, find me someone I actually like,' and he took me to you." She paused, and then grinned. "Shows what he knows. I don't like you at all."

"No, I didn't think you did," Charlie said, smiling.

"So, what was up with you and the rabbit?" she asked.

"I don't know what was up with that." He was about to jump into a discussion about the nature of dreams, when he remembered why he had been looking for her all day.

"My G- my great-grandfather; did he look ... dead or something to you?"

"I couldn't tell, I thought he might have just passed out. Why? You superstitious about dreams?"

"No, not superstitious, it — it's just my dreams have been sort of coming true. Well, pieces of them have, and all in weird ways."

"Mine too."

"I'm just worried about him and whether he's okay. I haven't been able to stop thinking about it all day." Charlie considered stopping there, but took a deep breath, and dove in. "I dreamed about him before, but he had to go before we could talk. I tried dreaming again last night, but ... nothing."

Robin nodded, as if nothing he said was out of the ordinary. "Why don't you just call him on your cell?" she asked.

"My mom won't let me bring it to school. She thinks I'll play games all day." He did not add that she was correct. "I wanted to use the phone in the office, but they wouldn't let me. My dad won't let me call when I get home, because he thinks I spend too much time with G'pa already."

Robin reached into her purse and pulled out her pink cell phone. "Here, use mine. Do you know the number?"

Charlie smiled, and reached for the phone. Just as he was about to dial, Robin's mom rode up in her brand-new, secondhand Toyota.

"Merced!" Her mom, yelled, loudly, despite the fact they were only a few feet from her car. She was the spitting image of Robin, except she was "pleasingly plump" and her hair was light brown with blond streaks.

Robin looked at her mom and gave a "What the heck?" gesture with her hands. Her mom responded with a gesture of her own. Robin turned to Charlie and shrugged apologetically. "It's my mom."

"It's okay," Charlie answered, and handed her back the phone. He was lying, like a true gentleman should.

Robin took a step toward the car then turned and added, by way of explanation, "She always calls me by my middle name when she's annoyed. It's Mercedes."

"Like the car."

"Well, like Spanish. It means 'mercies', like favors from God." She turned to her mom, and grabbed the door handle, almost yelling into the open window. "Mommy, why are you here? We said I could ride the bus."

Gloria Cruz LeBeaux looked at her daughter then leaned past her to frown at Charlie. "The school's automated phone thing called. Your bus broke down and isn't coming. Did you not notice it isn't here?"

Robin sulked herself into the beige passenger seat, fastened her prison chains, rather, seat belt, and gave Charlie a sad wave. Charlie watched them drive off and was hit by a wave of disappointment.

"Oh great," he thought, "no phone call, and I still don't understand how she came to be in my dreams."

Charlie's left brain, which was bored up until the puzzle of the dreams was mentioned, kicked in. He wondered what the chances were that his dad actually picked up the phone when the school called him to say the bus wasn't coming. He lived almost three miles away, a far walk for a kid with a poor sense of direction. Charlie turned and re-entered the school. He would go to the office, and ask, no, demand to use the phone to call his mom at work. She could call his dad.

"Dad always takes her calls," he said. "Unless they've been arguing."

It was going to be a long day.

19 – "COME OUT FIGHTING" – 761ST TANK BATTALION

Monday morning had found G'pa Joe wandering around the fourth floor of D-wing. He was still wearing his long flannel pajama bottoms, a white t-shirt, robe, and brown leather slippers. He was shuffling slowly, his wheelchair still in its place in his room. Nurse Nora Radcliffe had found him headed for the elevators, though it became quickly apparent that he had no particular destination in mind. In fact, he seemed to have no idea who she was, and she was not certain he even realized she was talking to him.

The staff was accustomed to sudden changes in coherence among the residents, but Joe was a particularly lively soul. He was one of the D-wingers' group leaders, a favorite with most of the residents, and, grudgingly, the staff. Nurse Radcliffe wrapped Joe's long arm around her shoulder for support, her knees buckling under his weight until two orderlies rushed over and gently led Joe to his room.

Joe turned to the younger of the two male orderlies. "Sergeant, we beat 'em back at Morville-les-Vic, and now we done took Tillet that all them white boys couldn't take," Joe said. He was grinning, but his eyes were blank.

"Sure, pops," the orderly replied. He wasn't really paying attention; he had long ago stopped listening to their nonsense stories. G'pa Joe was not really there anyway. His mind was replaying the weekend's dream in a loop.

To Joe, the early 21st century was a future he could not even imagine. His mind was stuck in the final Winter of World War II, and he was a battle-seasoned man of seventeen years old. He had joined the

113

army at the tender age of fifteen, though the service genuinely believed him to be nineteen. Toot knew exactly where to go in Detroit to get good-looking papers that would have passed even the most rigorous muster. But in the middle of a global war, the truth is no one was too inclined to challenge the service of a strapping young man who was built like an iron ox and stood well over six feet two inches tall.

Joe had been assigned to the 761st "Black Panthers" Tank Battalion, which was now in the course of making invisible history in Patton's Army. Joe was too large a man to fit comfortably in a light, or even a medium tank. The 761st had, at its full strength, some fifty-four Sherman tanks and fifteen "mosquito" M5 General Stuart tanks, along with associated artillery and support vehicles. Joe was assigned to the Headquarters Company's Mortar Platoon. He probably would have been assigned to the infantry straight away, but he grew three full inches after enlisting, and after the army had invested in his training.

The Black Panthers' initiation into World War II combat was to be sent into what was expected to be a suicide mission. The German army was holed up in Morville-les-Vic, France, and General George Patton had largely passed it by, not wanting to get bogged down in a dirty house-to-house battle. Patton himself did not think much of Negro troops initially. Thus, the 761st had been sent in, essentially, as cannon fodder: "throw a few grenades," draw enemy fire. The army had hoped the Germans would use up all their ammunition on the 761st. Then the town would be cleaned up by the white infantry. War, though, is not racist. War hates everyone equally, even if Hitler did not. The men of the 761st surprised everyone but themselves by taking the town.

Months later, Joe had been directly involved in the bloodbath that was to be the Battle of the Bulge. Joe's Battalion had taken the town of Tillet near the Ardennes Forest. One after another American unit assigned to take the town had been sent packing by the German forces. U.S. tanks, artillery, and infantry inside the Ardennes Forest had assaulted Tillet, but had only contributed to the massive graveyard the Forest and the battle had become. In January 1945, the 761st was the next unit to be sent into Tillet. After a week of steady fighting against battle-hardened SS troops, after having seen continuous action since they had reached France in October 1944, the 761st took Tillet and drove the Germans out in full retreat.

Some 19,000 men were to die during the months-long Battle. Somehow, a teenage boy named Joe, a poor sharecropper's son from eastern Alabama, had managed not to be one of them. Joe had left home a boy, but returned a man. He rarely talked about his war experiences, and never spoke of the Battle of the Bulge at all. "Too much death to be celebrating," was all Joe would say about that.

Family rumors had it Joe had been wounded on a cold winter night, and, instead of his usual place as lead driver, he was with the medics getting patched up for a return to the fight. A German mortar shell had hit Joe's truck, and his whole crew had been killed.

In his dreams, Joe would return to that place; he would be running behind the truck and waving wildly, trying to get them to stop. Just as they would spot him in their mirror, the truck would explode in a thunder of angry sparks and fireballs. He could hear the screams of the driver, still alive, but engulfed in flames.

Some nights, Joe could see the dead crew afterward, walking slowly homeward. He would face them, try to apologize, but they would never acknowledge his presence. He wasn't one of them anymore. He had quit them, and, now, they would quit him in return. The return to the hell of the Argonne Forest was a journey he would make on the loneliest of nights. It was his penance for having survived. His trip to the third floor elevator of the Southside Senior Center was just such a journey. He had taken the familiar dream-state trip back to the forests of Ardennes countless times. Most of the time, his conscious mind spared him the memory of the trip; his dream remained buried harmlessly in his subconscious mind. This trip, however, was the first time he would take a nightmare journey to Ardennes and not return upon waking. Joe's body was in the Senior Center, but his mind was still a long way from home.

The Senior Center orderlies sat Joe down on his bed, and removed the slippers from his hard, dark feet. They eased him backwards, and Joe's body yielded, lying back down. He had been up late Saturday night and most of Sunday seated by Mary's bed, fretting over her. He remained despite being advised that there was nothing he could do, and she likely did not even know he was there. But Mary was part of Joe's crew now, and he wouldn't leave her behind. "Never again," Joe would say.

The vigil had left him worn, stressed, and vulnerable. The medical staff assumed it was nothing more extraordinary than exhaustion that caused Joe's relapse. True, he was eighty-five years old, and he was under a great deal of stress. But Joe knew something the medical staff did not know. Mary was lost somewhere inside the world her mind had created, and he needed to find a way to bring her back. He knew she had not gotten there on her own, nor could she return alone.

As Joe lay on his hard mattress, his heavy-lidded eyes drooped closed, sleep took him, and his subconscious mind began to roam. The subconscious knows neither reality nor fiction. It simply believes whatever it sees or hears. When Joe's subconscious mind took control, there was no soundtrack of sinister music, no cigarette-smoking host providing an introduction. Joe simply lay down in the autumn of 2012 and opened his eyes a split second later in the winter of 1945. His mind believed him to be there and so there, he was.

"Corporal Tettleton!" Joe's day officer Lieutenant Morris was calling him. Morris was a short, balding man with a long scar on the top of his head from a previous run-in with a German soldier. According to official versions of the story, Morris had surprised a German SS officer during a house-to-house search in a small French village. Morris had managed to shoot the German, but not before suffering a glancing shot to his hard head that had split his helmet. Now Morris, having refused to be shipped stateside, wore the scar like a badge.

Unofficial versions of the story, however, said that Morris had been shot from behind, as he turned to run away, terrified. Wounded, and in pain, he fell over a thigh-high wooden table, all the while shrieking. As he hit the floor, his rifle discharged accidentally, striking the German and killing him. Morris, in exchange for not being brought up on charges of cowardice and dereliction of duty had agreed to be transferred to the 761st.

"Sir?" Joe Tettleton snapped to attention. He was standing by a small cot in the medic's tent near the battle's front lines. Joe was shirtless, his thick dark muscles in stark contrast to the white bandage that covered a recently stitched wound on his left shoulder.

"Why are you still here, son? You're supposed to be sent home. You know the rules, only three weeks at the front at a time," Morris said, a rather insincere smile across his face.

"Well, suh," Joe answered, "With respect, none of the other boys in the Platoon has had a break since we come to France, so's I'd rather wait until we're all sent home together — after we sends these Krauts to Hell."

"Well, that's admirable, but the other men haven't been wounded. That sniper's bullet," Morris said, pointing to Joe's bandaged shoulder, "was your ticket home."

Joe looked to the ground, and responded softly, but with his head shaking a firm no.

"Again, with respect suh, the doctors say I'm good to go back into the battle anytime I want. This ain't more'n a scratch. And suh ..." Joe hesitated, taking in a deep breath and blinking as if the tears he held back threatened his very life. "I need to get back in."

"I'm afraid that's not possible, Corporal," Morris said.

"My boys didn't come back," Joe insisted. "I need to get a jeep and go back and find 'em. No one knows for sure if they're dead." Joe paused then gathered his composure, pulling himself to his full height.

Morris considered Joe closely. He stared him in the eye for any trace of open defiance. Joe knew he was looking for an excuse to bring him up on charges. Insubordination was as valid a reason for sending a man home as being wounded.

"I can't leave one of my own behind, sir. I'm sure you understand that sir. I'm sure you'd do the same thing if you had the chance."

Morris flushed red then turned away, answering Joe as he walked away. "Very well Tettleton, it's your neck. The transport back to the beaches leaves at 1500 hours. Be on it."

"Thank you, suh," Joe enthused.

"Don't. I hope to find someone who can talk some sense into you before then." Most of the men Joe encountered in his WWII dreams were only memories. Morris, however, was no memory, but an intruder into Joe's dream. Soon he would shed the guise of Morris, and would retrieve young Charlie, but to no avail. Joe would not be stopped.

Morris walked out into the bright January sun. Joe hesitated; he had not been sent home, but he hadn't been given a clear answer either. He had to get back in there. He needed to find his m-m-me ... Mary.

And, in a blink, the dream shifted. Joe grabbed his shirt and gear, opened the tent flap, and exited — deep into the forest. For the first time in days, there was no noise from artillery shells, no small arms fire, no sounds of death. Instead, there was the clarion call of the songs of nocturnal birds wintering in the forest. The day had become night, and the light of the full moon illuminated the forest floor like a silver spotlight. Joe was on stage now. It was his dance.

Goddamn, I know it was day when the LT left just now. He said he was going — to get somebody — before 1500 hours.

Joe's mind had made the leap again; he was in the Stream now, and his journey was no longer solely his mind's to control. He furrowed his brow, trying to remember more details, but the conversation with the lieutenant was fading like sand sliding down a wind-blown dune. Joe placed his hands on his hips and looked east.

"She must have gone that way," Joe said aloud. "Mary has got to be there, and I need to find her and bring her back. No one gets left behind. Not my crew."

Joe had forgotten the Battle of the Bulge, or Headquarters Company, or his long-dead crew. It was no longer January 1945, it was 1973, but somehow Joe was only a few years older than he had been during the war. This was Joe of the Stream, Joe the Warrior. He had the wisdom of eighty-five years, and the strength of his twenty-five-year-old self. That he was cool — James Bond cool, John Shaft cool — that was just Joe's mind being Joe. This was the Joe that G'pa Joe Tettleton wished to be. In the Stream, the difference between fantasy and reality was desire. If your mind wanted it enough, it could be. Joe wanted his Mary back; he wanted that very much.

Joe looked at his rifle, his sidearm, and the hunting knife strapped across his left hip. He was dressed in jeans, hiking boots, and a red flannel shirt. He twisted his massive neck left then right, hearing the satisfying crackle of his loosening joints. Joe's six-and-a-half-foot frame rippled with anticipation. He would get another chance, finally, for redemption.

He would bring her back. She would be safe. Joe was on a quest to save his Mary, the horrors of World War Two lost, once more, in the echoes of his weekend's dream.

His mind would play this sequence in a loop for the next few days.

20 – THEY SAY THAT CAT JOE IS A BAD MUTHA ... SHUT YO' MOUTH

Joe was jogging through the woods, exhilarated. He had walked in the Stream his whole life, but never so easily, or vividly. It was as if some external force had supercharged his mind. Had he tried, he could have traced the moment his dreams changed to his blue river adventure.

The night air was crisp. There was a smell of pine, and mildew. Above was the distinctive warbling cry of a nightjar. Joe was alert. His mind was sharp; he could recall details of his past or reach into his imagination as if they were ripe fruit on a low-hanging branch — in his dreams. Something was giving his mind power. Something named Charlie Patterson.

Awakened, he was just an old man with failing memory and awareness. Prior to Mary's bad turn, he had decided to stay away from the Stream. He was old, and needed to let God's will be done, he figured, rather than try to hold onto the past by living in a fantasy world. Dreams were for the young. His dreams were a drug, one he needed to quit. However, now Mary was trapped in the Stream, and he needed just one more Stream walk — just one.

The forest was filled with lanky trees spaced in irregular clusters that reached up to the dark sky. Moonlight cut through the forest curtain, bisecting the woods into areas of gray and black. The trees were six or more feet apart, allowing Joe to see into the distance. Toward the horizon, there was a light, subdued, but visible against the darkness. It was in the wrong place to be the moon.

Joe guessed it meant civilization, and the way to find city-girl Mary. Surely, she would not have wandered this deep into the forest of her own accord. He would start where man meets the forest, and search from there. As he walked, the trees' outstretched limbs made them look as if they were surrendering to the night. Leaves had begun to fall from branches that towered overhead, but the ground was soft and damp, and he traveled soundlessly. The entire forest floor was covered in a downy moss that gave the ground an eerie green reflection in the filtered light.

Joe walked, as the forest began uphill, ever so slightly at first then gradually steeper. His stride lengthened, and his exhalation came in white, moonlit puffs. He looked like a sable locomotive steaming up a forested hill. As the hill steepened, Joe's muscles strained in exertion. He paused, and breathed in the cool night air, invigorated. He was young and strong again, and it felt good — damn good. He resumed his journey, his pace quickening as the hill grew steeper against him.

Joe was aware of the danger feeling young and strong presented. Recapturing his robust youth through his dreams was what drew him into the Stream in the first place. Initially, they were just dream memories. Then, they became increasingly vivid — longer, more powerful, invigorating, sexy, darker, dangerous. He was alive and young in the dreams, and even though he did not remember them when awake, his subconscious found refuge there, and he began to spend more time in deep sleep than ever before.

Eventually, he discovered he could initiate or manipulate the dreams. He could be anywhere, any time he desired — or anyone for that matter. Joe learned that if he concentrated, he could walk from dream to dream. It was as if there were other dimensions apart from the limitations of space and time that could only be entered via the world of dreams. Joe could enter the Stream via his dream, and travel into the dreams of another. He was like a dark, benevolent Freddy Krueger.

By the time he had learned of the dark side of traveling in the Stream, it was too late. He was hooked on the adrenaline rush, and more importantly, he had become a target. This needed to be his last trip. It was a rescue mission, his last journey into Mary's dreams and a last-ditch effort to save her from them.

At the top of the rise, Joe turned and looked back into the dark forest. The moon was visible only in glances. Ahead of him, the forest was thinner. The few trees there were larger than the ones behind him.

The plateau on which he stood went on for about a half mile then retreated into another valley similar to the one he had just left.

Joe could see a clearing near the base of the hill where the forest seemed to stop in a line. Joe walked ahead, a solitary figure in the almost noiseless forest. Above, a cloud relinquished its position above the forest and the bright moon burst through. In the distance, Joe could see movement near a base of a massive tree. A single beam of moonlight breached the gap between the branches and Joe caught the sight of glistening gold. It was some distance above where his senses told him the ground must be. He squinted in the night, his eyes by now adjusted to the darkness, and thought he could make out the figure of someone standing in the trees — a small someone with hair of copper or gold.

Mary!

His adrenalin surged, and he thought to run, to shout, waving. But he was in the forest, minutes from war, and his training told him that caution and patience were the order of the day. His enemy could have followed him here, or preceded him, and Joe must err on the side of good judgment. He bent his large frame lower, shouldering his rifle, and holding the hilt of his long knife with his left hand. He ran silently toward the figure, careful to watch for movement as he approached. He could not snap any grounded branches or crunch dried leaves. He must run through the night like the wind kissing the darkness, caress the ground like a silent, hunting lover.

At around 100 yards from his objective, he could see eyes; several eyes were there, and they were watching him. From the darkness, he could hear a low, angry growl.

Joe froze. If he had now turned from hunter to prey, he would make them work at it. Joe moved slowly to his right; the eyes followed his movements. He took five paces forward; a pair of eyes grew ever so much larger. He moved to his left; all eyes shifted leftward. He was being tracked.

Silently, Joe pulled his rifle from his shoulder, and aimed at the nearest pair of eyes. For the briefest of seconds, his mind asked him what if he was wrong, what if that were Mary. But Joe had been to war, and he had learned to hunt in the backwoods of his Alabama home. One thing he knew for certain, when you stalk prey, it doesn't stalk you back.

Joe squeezed the trigger. The report was loud, violating the stillness of the night air. A quick yelp and silence followed. The eyes scattered and reappeared. Joe found another set and fired; another yelp, and this time, a scream from somewhere above.

Mary! Joe's mind screamed again. She was in danger, and he was running out of time. He now had two options. He could stay back and try to pick off whatever it was he was killing, and hope that Mary was still safe when he reached her. Or, he could act now, and deal with whatever comes up.

Now, no one to that point had ever accused Joe of thinking too much. He had flung down the rifle, pulled out his pistol, and un-holstered his long knife on a dead run before he even realized he was moving. He faced the first being, a large gray figure with red eyes charging him. From the snarls, he guessed dog, but from the smell and the size, he knew it was something worse, something larger. At five feet away, Joe aimed his .45 caliber pistol and squeezed.

The wolf was airborne. The bullet from Joe's pistol hit it in the left flank, turning it in mid-air. It fell directly toward Joe who had just enough time to sweep his long knife upward through the animal's midsection. Warm blood splattered against Joe's upstretched arm, and the wolf practically roared in pain and anger — then disappeared.

"What in the Hell?" was all Joe could say.

From his right, two more wolves leapt. Joe rolled forward, in the direction from whence the wolves had come, just enough that they overshot their mark. A third wolf had circled behind Joe and was now charging. Joe rolled once more and rose to his knees, firing his gun wildly. He did not have time for precision. He had learned in the artillery that close was sometimes good enough.

One bullet of the four hit its mark, and the closest of the three attacking wolves "poofed" into non-existence. The remaining two attackers rose, circling in tandem, and were joined by two smaller wolves that had been circling the enormous tree. From above, Mary could be heard screaming, calling to someone who was apparently in the tree with her.

Joe watched the four wolves, trying to pick out the leader, the one who would attack first. Just as he had decided on a large brown male, he felt himself knocked to the ground with the force of a sledgehammer. It was the alpha female leaping from the tree above. Sharp teeth punctured his right bicep as he held his arm above his face. The defensive move had kept the wolf from biting through his neck. As Joe felt the powerful jaws clamp on his muscle, his grip on the pistol loosened, and he felt it drop with a disheartening thud to the ground. It was now just Joe, wolf, knife.

Joe punched the gray bitch with his left hand as it continued biting down on his right arm. He could feel hot breath in his face; a combination of saliva and his own warm blood trickled on his cheek. Joe heard a sickening crunching sound, accompanied by a sharp jab of pain. The wolf's strong jaws had shattered the bone in his right humerus. As Joe bellowed in pain, the wolf clawed with its hind legs, jockeying for position. Once again, Joe punched the wolf, trying to get enough distance to turn the knife for the kill.

As the two wrestled on the forest floor, the large beta male grew impatient, ran forward, driving himself into the mix. The brown wolf bit into Joe's right boot, severing his large toe. The pain was instantaneous, releasing a flood of adrenaline into Joe's system. Joe screamed in anger and pain.

The large alpha female turned and bit her mate for his impudence, choosing to keep the pack's order ahead of ensuring their survival against a common enemy. The beta male, enraged, launched himself in retaliation and the two wolves were a sudden snarling mass.

Joe turned his attention to the remaining wolves, which were now swaying back and forth waiting to see who would become or remain their leader. They were beautiful — golden-limbed god creatures with dark gray fur on their backs and head. They watched Joe with interest, their eyes curious, intelligent. Two stood at alert, their haunches ready. The third sat silently behind the trunk of what appeared to be a poplar tree.

Joe could never coldly kill so beautiful of God's creatures. Sadly for them, he knew these creatures were almost certainly not from God. Joe screamed what he imagined a Zulu warrior cry might be, and grabbed his long knife with both hands. Broken arm or no, he was at war. He swung at the wolves as if they were trees and he were Paul Bunyan with his mighty axe. The closest wolf lowered its head as it ran, aiming at Joe's thighs. With a two-handed backhand, Joe caught the wolf at the base of its neck, separating the flesh and muscle from the bone. It fell away dead, and disappeared into the night with a poof.

Blood and fur and bones and teeth flew, each wolf disappearing the instant it was cut. The pack had attacked much prey during their time, but none had attacked back. None except Joe. The score was Joe five, wolves zero. Joe was a sweat-dripping, bloody, wolf-spittle-covered stinking mess. He had never had so much fun in his life.

From behind him, he heard a loud growl. Joe spun and found

himself face-to-face with the large alpha female. She was standing straddling the now-dead male, her muzzle darkened in blood.

"What the hell kind of wolf are you?" Joe asked, panting. This wolf was some new breed — tiger shark wolf perhaps. Joe could count two full rows of teeth as the wolf pulled its lips back in anger. The eyes made Joe shiver. They were not angry; they were cold, calm, amber eyes that studied Joe as if he were of no more interest than a passing squirrel. It had just killed its mate, watched its entire pack killed, and still the eyes were coldly empty.

Joe held the knife tighter, and waited. He could see the pistol shining on the ground behind the wolf.

From above, Mary called his name for the first time. "Joe, is that you?"

Joe reacted to his name by looking up ever so briefly. It was long enough. The large female charged and knocked Joe backward into the tree trunk. The full weight of the animal hit Joe in his diaphragm, knocking the wind from him. Joe bent over involuntarily, trying to catch his breath. As he did so, he felt teeth sink into the base of his skull and a matching set near his forehead line.

He was being eaten whole.

Joe was a strong man, and brave. As a teenager fighting the Nazis, he had developed a reputation of being fearless. That he saved his men on more than one occasion was common knowledge. However there was no preparation, no training, and no degree of bravery that could have prepared him for the pain, the absolute horror of an animal attack. As the sharp canine teeth tore into his soft flesh, he screamed in agony and fear. It was a high-pitched cry that even Joe would not have recognized as his. From the tree above, Joe's scream was echoed by Mary's own cry of fear for her beloved friend. It was only knowing that she was listening — that, and the surge of adrenaline from the wolf's bite — that brought back his reason.

Heart pounding, still winded, he thrust both hands upward, his eyes now blinded with dripping blood. The knife met its mark, thrusting deep into the wolf's chest, puncturing its aorta. Canine teeth bit deeper into Joe's skull, dragging him to the ground. Joe tried to blink the blood from his eyes, and thrust upward with the knife again.

This time, however, he felt nothing; the wolf had moved. Joe staggered forward, and wiped his eyes with the bloody sleeve of his shirt. He saw nothing in front of him, and fell backward in a panic. Nothing.

It was gone, presumably dead.

"Joe, there are snakes up here!" Mary cried out.

"Then come down, woman," he said. Joe was a hero, but he was a tired hero. Joe leaned against the tree and closed his eyes, concentrating. With Mary safe, he had become fully aware that he was dreaming, and now focused all of his considerable energy on securing her safety. As he focused, the forest behind him began to fade, and the bright surroundings of the Senior Center came into focus. All he had left to do was pull her mind back through.

"My boys, Joe! They have my boys!" Mary shouted, climbing down to the lowest branch, trying to get Joe's attention.

Joe, misunderstanding Mary's intentions, reached up and pulled her from the tree, smiling. Mary wiggled and struggled against him, trying desperately trying to get back up in the tree.

"The boys — the snakes have my boys!"

Joe had just enough strength to shove Mary roughly through the opening he had created behind him before collapsing from his own loss of blood, and before Mary, after thirty-nine straight hours "asleep" in the Intensive Care Unit, woke up. She was back in the Senior Center, disoriented, and babbling about having lost her boys in the woods. She was frantic, insisting that Joe was right behind her "with the boys."

The boys the childless Mary never had.

The nurses in the Senior Center gave her a mild sedative, and put her on their watch list. Simultaneously with Mary's emergence from her catatonic state, Joe had first begun losing his own grip with reality in the Senior Center. He had been the knight in shining armor. He had rescued his lady fair from The Stream, and he had gotten lost there himself. The same energy that trapped Mary — produced by the Overlord's strong mind — now entrapped the weakened Joe.

Charlie had been right to be worried. G'pa Joe was not alright. He was not alright at all.

21 – WILD HORSES

At the insistence of the nursing staff, Mary spent most of the day in her room. She had recovered from her "episode" over the weekend, and was alert, though despondent. It didn't help that Joe, her closest friend at the center, had suffered a major decline that the doctors could not understand.

Val Andrews, the Senior Center's thin, harried director, had called the Henderson Research Institute regarding Joe at around two o'clock Monday afternoon. After both Joe and Mary had sudden unexplained changes in status, Val had become concerned about the safety of the drug trial in which both Joe and Mary were participants. A thirty-minute personal call from Dr. Henderson had reassured her. Dr. Henderson could not reveal who was given the meds and who was given the placebo, "of course," but she assured Val that the dosage given to the recipients of the drug would never be enough to cause any serious side effects. Dozens of prior trials, in fact, had only shown a limited ability to bring some Alzheimer's patients, like Mary, to greater alertness and coherence.

If Joe had a sudden decline, the meds were not to blame. What convinced Val most of all, however, was Dr. Henderson's explaining that if she had to alter the control group, she would have to stop the trial entirely and start over with a new set of patients. The not-insubstantial funding to the center for the project would be in jeopardy. Better to continue, Dr. Henderson advised. Joe knew the risks, and had signed the waivers himself.

After her conversation with Dr. Henderson, Val insisted the center's medical staff perform a complete physical on Joe. If the drugs were not to blame then it was possible that his sudden change in mental condition was delirium, which could mean he'd suffered another stroke, infection, or any one of a number of medical conditions. Joe's physical, however, turned up little. He was as healthy as a horse. Officially, Val attributed Joe's condition to fatigue or depression. Privately, she just prayed Dr. Henderson was right. If the drug trial was to blame, she and the center could be in very deep trouble.

No sooner had they returned Joe to his room than the nursing staff found Mary walking to the elevator, claiming to be going to "check out." Mary believed she was on vacation in France with Joe and children she'd never had. It had taken strong sedatives to calm her down when she learned the truth.

Some hotel.

Val inhaled a furtive drag from her first cigarette in weeks, waving her pale arms to disperse the smoke as she exhaled. Smoking was expressly forbidden — she'd written the rule herself.

I'll fire myself later.

Val sighed, her brow wrinkling as she ran her fingers through her graying hair. "Mary may be back from vacation, but whatever trip Joe took, he's still there," she said then threw the cigarette out the window in disgust.

***

Monday night at the Senior Center was movie night, and the residents were usually in a pretty good mood. Tonight's selection was 1951's "A Streetcar Named Desire." The center's staff was determined to play the American Film Institute's 100 Best Movies in order, if only to give the residents something to look forward to.

Mary was only eight years old when the movie was released, but Marlon Brando had always been a favorite of hers, so the staff was concerned when she declined to see the film. However, given her delicate emotional state, they did not insist. She was more responsive than she had been over the weekend, but that was only small comfort given she had been in what they feared would be a long-term catatonic state. After awakening from the dream, rather, having been forced out of it by Joe, Mary had wandered the halls looking for her sons, wanting to "get out of this damned hotel." She was awake, almost. After considerable time spent demanding the staff tell her they done with her boys, Mary awoke — fully. One moment, she was in her thirties, looking for her two young sons, the next, she was sixty-nine, and had remembered that the children she loved with all her heart never existed. Her sorrow worsened when she remembered that she had married not Joe, but Art.

Mary sobbed, for the better part of an hour, until the sedative she had been administered put her into a peaceful, dreamless sleep. When she awoke, she tiptoed to Joe's room, sat by his side, and held his hand. Every so often, one of the nurses would take her by her slender shoulders, and guide her to her room, or to a cluster of her other friends — Abe Singer, Jay Patil, or Sarge.

Mary would allow herself to be led, and would nod when the staff told her she needed to let Joe rest. They told her that there was nothing she could do; he likely wasn't aware she was there. Joe would rest, and she must rest and gain back her strength. Mary would nod agreeably, and sit with her friends. For five seconds. Then she would look each in the eye, and smile, and say, simply, "Wild horses."

She would stand; she'd raise her head with a bearing befitting a lifetime spent on center stage. Were she leaving to headline at the Boston Opera House, no one would have been surprised. She did not shuffle as she had in the past. She strode, barefoot, back to room 318, Joe's room. There she would pull the single chair that sat in his room away from the wall, and back to its place next to his bed, and there she would sit, take his hand, hold it to her cheek, and sing.

"Wild horses couldn't drag me away."

Her eyes would close, and she allowed the tears to cleanse her pain. But she would not let Joe's hand go. When the staff came to retrieve her, she ceased her song, and played another round of the game. The chase continued thus for hours, until the staff finally tired of the chase.

"She's harmless," they surmised.

Mary had never talked much since she first arrived at the center three years ago. In fact, due to the advanced state of her Alzheimer's, the staff was positively overjoyed that she had been able to make friends with Joe and his buddies. She would chat with Joe, and laugh when the crew laughed, but the far away, wounded look in her eyes told her secret. She was not with them, not truly. There was a small island on which her memories had taken refuge, and much of her conscious mind had joined them there. Mary was lost at sea, forever adrift, a body floating along, its memories lost long ago.

In her prime, she had been more than a brilliant poet and artist. She was more than a charismatic teacher, having spent decades teaching English Literature at Harvard. She had been more than the youngest fully tenured professor on the staff. Mary had been magic and joy, laughter and light. The winds of Mary's optimism had carried stardust with it, and all that it touched were changed forever. She had taught three Pulitzer Prize winners, and one Nobel Prize co-author, who dedicated his prize-winning book to her.

She had been a force of nature, she had.

At age twenty-four, already an associate professor, she had taken a year's sabbatical and traveled to Haight-Ashbury in San Francisco. It was the summer of 1967. Mary was no hippie, though you could not have known the difference, save she was never stoned, and always clean. She sat with the hippies and sang their songs with them, her guitar never out of reach. She wore no shoes, but Mary had never liked shoes — and she usually had on nothing more than a pair of denim overalls and an occasional t-shirt. When there were no police, or if they didn't mind, she would forgo the t-shirt and wear only her waist-length, frightfully curly copper hair over her small, but lovely breasts.

Mary spent the summer, and the autumn that followed, writing their stories in poems and songs. To her, they were not smelly, drug-influenced dropouts. No, to Mary they were modern wood nymphs, and satyrs, and fairies. Mary always found the magic, and if there were no magic, she would bring her own.

It was in Haight-Ashbury that she would meet her future husband, he with the small beard and big dreams. His name was Art, Arthur Galloway to be exact, and to Mary, it was destiny; she had always been in love with art. Together they were to conquer the world. And for a time, they had.

Then came miscarriages. Mary had her first miscarriage during what was supposed to be a vacation trip to France, but which had turned out to be more of a working trip for Art. He had neglected to tell her he would be scouting potential suppliers for his growing wine distribution business. She had been on a picnic by herself in the Ardennes Forest when she began to bleed.

Mary had always blamed herself for the failure, which was unfortunate, since Art blamed her as well. Someone had to be blamed, and it couldn't very well be him, could it? After two more years, she worked up the courage to try again, with the same unfortunate result. She had been on bed rest for two weeks when she began to hemorrhage. Art had been at work, his work apparently involving bedding the senior vice president of marketing for the beer distributorship he was courting.

Mary managed to call an ambulance, but there was nothing they could do. The damage to Mary's uterus from the bleeding was too great; she was told if she tried again, it might be at the cost of her life.

Good old Art, he came through after that, however. In fact, he felt so guilty for not having been there for Mary, he made sure she was well taken care of in the divorce settlement. The last time Mary saw him in person had been in 1988; he was still with the senior VP, now CEO, and their two lovely children. Mary had never loved another man after Art - or before Art for that matter. It's like she always said, "I was made for my art." He was her Art.

Many years later, no longer a force of nature, but still full of magic, Mary had been placed in the Southside Senior Center by her younger sister. It was 2009, and at the tender age of 66, Mary had been diagnosed with a surprisingly advanced case of Alzheimer's. She was the third generation with the disease, though the first to be correctly diagnosed. It was her family curse – that and miscarriages.

At the center, she was everyone's favorite. She was good-natured, gentle, accommodating, and usually had no idea who you were. But that didn't matter; Mary would love you regardless of who you were anyway. The orderlies' favorite part of the day was to meet Mary again for the very first time. No matter her mood, she never developed a fear of strangers.

When she met Joe, it was instant friendship. Joe was a big old bear of a man, with a gruff outside (and, to be honest, an inside to match), but he had a tender spot for the small woman with the big smile. He would always include Mary in anything his group did. She seemed to enjoy being included despite not knowing what was going on. And Joe, she never forgot.

They would play bridge, and deal Mary cards. She would be playing Blackjack. They would laugh, and declare her the winner. Mary liked that. And so, life would go on at the center — until the darkness came. It came in the form of dreams and false hope. Mary had forgotten that darkness is quite adept at disguising itself as light. The dreams had offered Mary the life she almost had, the one that got away. It had been her drug, and would have been the death of her, save the courage of her lovely Sir Black Knight.

And there he lay, his lady fair holding his massive hand, the size of two of hers. She held it through visitation hours. She held it when the nurses came to take her to her room. She held it as she refused to leave his side. She held his hand to her tearful eyes as two orderlies tried to pry her free. And she held it as Singer threatened to cut them with the kitchen knife he had secreted if they didn't "Goddamn leave Mary the Hell alone."

Mary, to that point, had never strung more than two sentences together to the best of anyone's recollection but Joe's. But in the chaos in room 318 of the Southside Senior Center in Poquoson, Virginia, a small miracle happened.

Mary began to sing.

At first, the shouting nurses, the grunting orderlies, and the wildly swinging (from his wheelchair) Singer thought angels had entered the room. Singer's immediate thought was that his friend Joe had died, and the angels were a-calling him home as Joe had always promised Singer they would.

Her singing was perfect pitch, a mezzo-soprano with the just the right vibrato. It was the same voice that had sung the hippies' lives in Haight-Ashbury. It was the magic from the poet whose words would make her students weep, in class, unabashedly. It was the voice of the woman who had been damaged by the callousness of the one man she had allowed herself to love. And it was the song of a patient whose consciousness had been restored by a man who loved her — simply because she was.

Everyone in the room stopped at the same time. The only sound was Mary's sweet voice … and if you listened very closely, you could hear violins in the distance; maybe it truly was the angels a-calling for Joe. When she paused, one could imagine hearing the drumbeat of Mary's tears falling on her Joe's cheek. Other residents, hearing the commotion then the singing, showed up one by one, and formed perfect, concentric rings of wheelchairs outside of Joe's door.

In a quiet rhythm, either to her song or to an inner voice only the faithful could know, they closed their eyes and prayed, heads and torsos moving to and fro. Sweet Mary would sing their prayer, but she would not let her Joe's hand free.

No one ever again tried to make her.

22 – MARY MARGARET'S RENAISSANCE

As the days passed, more of Mary's memories began to return. She could recall details of her life that she thought lost forever. She was not cured, but she was certainly better. No one was more aware of her growing cognizance than Mary herself.

The turning point, as far as she was concerned, was simple. It was when her friend Joe had entered the nightmare world in which she was trapped and freed her. Of course, she had been interviewed by the doctors, the staff, and even a counselor hired by the drug company running the research project. To all, she gave the same story, relating how in recent years she had begun to have increasingly vivid dreams that had begun taking over her life. In the dreams, she was no longer alone. She had not been hurt and abandoned by her cheating husband. She was a wife, a mother, and happy.

In her fantasy world, she had not dedicated her life to teaching ungrateful students. Instead, she was a poet, an artist, and a fairly successful singer-songwriter. In the real world, her weakness had always been her sensitive, nurturing personality. Throughout her life, many had taken advantage of it, and her. The price she had paid for her sensitivity was a lifetime spent alone, doomed to die by herself without even her memories as comfort.

But her strength had, in her opinion, always been her strong mind, and her imagination. She had reveled in her world of books, finding comfort and escape in their words. So, when the dreams began to become mixed with real memories, she found herself slipping willingly into their whispers of oblivion. The times her mind left her frail body, and transported her to a world with her two sons had been a drug she could not and did not want to resist.

But then she met Joe, and Joe was real. He was here, and a friend. More importantly, he was a reason to live in the now, instead of the land of what-ifs. Joe used to tell her on many a night that her imagination is what had caused her pain.

"Those damn books let you sit in your big house alone and hide. Your husband hurt you, and instead of grievin' and movin' on, you just ran away inside your little library and hid," Joe had told her one night.

"You don't understand," she had argued, crying, "my library, my journals, my poetry, they were my children. Those were the only things that kept me sane."

"Livin' alone for thirty years ain't sane, Mary. You were made to love people. Maybe God didn't give you children of your own, but he gave you the heart to love other kids. You could have adopted. You could have let yourself love again."

Mary had rejected Joe's arguments as insensitivity and retreated even further into her private world. Now, sitting at his bed, Mary regretted that the very few times she had been coherent had been spent arguing with him. Now, it was clear her dreams were indeed her prison.

She had been trapped in a nightmare world. True, the brain scans taken by the drug company had seen no such world. In fact, all they found were the clusters of amyloid plaques that signaled memory loss, But to Mary, dreams had been her reality — she, with her boys in the French countryside. She had forgotten her entire life, and in its place was a false dream world on which she had become emotionally dependent. Like real-life drugs, it took more to achieve the same result. For a time, brief visits to her other self had been enough. She dreamed, the times would be satisfying, even exhilarating. But lately, days on end had been spent dreaming. Increasingly, she felt darkness: a sorrow and emptiness that wasn't there before. Mary needed longer and longer visits just to find the peace that had drawn her into the world in the first place. She had allowed herself to drift into her world of dreams in order to find love and connection. And, ironically, as her disease made the journeys easier to take, she had become separated from the people who really loved her.

But Joe was a stubborn old man, and he refused to lose. Somehow, and she still didn't understand how, he managed to find his way to her in her dream. The spiders, the snakes, all her fears had come to life at once, as if her own mind was being used against her. It would have trapped her there or killed her, or worse. Joe, impossibly, saved her.

Mary sensed a presence … not so much a person as a … force. Something was feeding off her fears, her dreams. And, as she allowed herself to become a part of that world, it had grown stronger. Now Joe was in that dark place. In his dreams, he was still young and needed. He was Mary's knight in shining armor. Mary was terrified. Joe had freed her, but at what cost? Whatever she'd sensed there did not want him to free her, and it absolutely did not plan to allow him to free himself.

Mary sat by his side in the day and lay next to him at night — it was all she could do. It was the least she could do. She was still all imagination and no strength. She had never been able to fight back, only to love. Her entire life, she had allowed herself to be a victim, and a victim is not what Joe needed now.

So, she would sit, and wait for him to free himself. And no force on earth could make her stop waiting. She had waited her entire life. If the staff would not help her, and no one chose to believe her then she would wait for her Joe.

And she would not go through her dream doors. Never again.

23 – CHARLIE GETS A PHONE CALL

"Charlie! Telephone!" Charlie's sister, whom he affectionately called Troll, was yelling. The two kids had a profound, mutual, love-hate relationship. They loved how deeply they hated each other. Unconditional hate is a rare and beautiful thing. It wasn't so much that Charlie and Layla were night and day. Having someone as your opposite at least gives you a frame of reference to work with. They were more like night, and, say, cheese. Understanding one would provide no insight at all into knowing the other.

The two kids' concepts of humanity were wholly unrelated. For example, Charlie spent a great deal of time in his head. He liked people, but didn't understand them, and had a lot of trouble figuring out how to interact with others. Still, he tried to treat everyone with dignity.

Layla, on the other hand, was very outgoing. She received most of her energy from her interactions with people, and defined herself as a people person. Despite the vast number of people she knew, Layla treated almost everyone the same — like they were pond scum. And, over the years, there were few people she treated with more contempt than anyone who seemed to like Charlie. So it wasn't surprising that Layla was shocked that someone called her house asking for her baby brother.

"Who in the world is so desperate they're calling you?" Layla asked, prompting Charlie to snatch the phone. Layla was still holding the phone to her ear when she asked the question.

"Look, why don't you go pollute the river by drowning yourself?" Charlie snapped. He didn't want to admit he had no clue who would call him. He didn't know anyone in his school who had ever asked him for his number. "He-hello?" he said, frowning at how tentative his voice sounded.

"Hi Charlie. It's Robin." Charlie had another stroke.

Shoot.

He knew he should say something, but his heart was pounding, and he couldn't hear himself think. "Say something, idiot," Charlie thought in his head.

"I said 'hi.' And you are being really rude!"

Shoot! Shoot!

Not in his head.

"N-no, no. Not you. I-I'm sorry," Charlie was backpedaling quickly. "I'm ... I was talking to myself."

"Oh. You do that a lot don't you?" she asked, her voice instantly light. Robin had the singular talent of forgiveness. She was rather like a puppy in her ability to be kicked one second, and wag her tail at you — metaphorically speaking — the next.

Charlie nodded, more relieved at the softening of her tone than embarrassed. He then realized she could not see him nodding, and said, "Yeah, I guess so."

"Well, you should probably try to do that quieter."

Despite himself, Charlie laughed. "I'll try to remember that," he said afterward. "Not that I mind at all, but how did you get my number?"

Robin was quiet for a long moment. Finally, she said, "Okay, I can't think of a good lie where this seems like an accident, so I'll tell you the truth. The school gave my mom a directory, and there were only two guys named Charles in the sixth grade. I figured you were probably not the one named Hsu."

"Oh, no. He's Asian," Charlie answered

"*Brilliant Charlie, you're doing swell.*" Chuck could be very sarcastic.

"Yeah, I figured. Anyway, I can't talk long. I'm not supposed to be on the phone after eight-thirty. I just wanted to talk about the dream stuff. It's really been bugging me. Can I text you?" Robin didn't strike Charlie as the bold type, so he reasoned this must be important.

"You can, but my mom checks my cell to make sure I don't use it after eight o'clock during the week. I can use it on the weekends all I want though."

"Oh, okay."

Robin grew quiet. Charlie was harder to reach than the Dalai Lama, as she was now beginning to discover. Charlie thought for a few

136

seconds then offered, "I do have a laptop though. I can use that whenever I want."

"I don't have a computer in my room," Robin sighed, "and I don't want my mom seeing me talk about dreams and stuff. She'll think I'm cracking up again or something." Charlie caught Robin's use of the word "again," filed the information away, but said nothing.

"Well, if you give me your cellphone number, I can send messages to it, and we can talk that way." Charlie hated geeks, but that didn't stop him from acting like one.

"Okay, cool! Look, I have to go take a bath. You guys have caller ID right?"

"Uh huh." Charlie replied.

"Send me an SMS at, say, ten o'clock. My mom will be asleep — I have an idea about the dream stuff." Robin's voice had become animated.

Hearing the excitement in her voice got Charlie's adrenaline pumping again. "Okay," he said, "I'll text you 'hi' at ten. If I don't hear back, I'll assume you couldn't do it. All you have to do is reply, and it'll come to me." Charlie loved being in tech support mode.

"Won't your mom get mad if you're on the computer? I mean, you're kind of in lockdown mode, right?"

Charlie laughed. "Yeah, my sister calls my mom 'The Warden.'"

"That's what I used to call my dad," Robin said, with none of the humor in her voice that accompanied Charlie's use of the nickname.

"My laptop's a notebook, and fits under my covers. No one comes in my room anyway once I close the door. I think they hate my orange and green walls."

"Um, okay, you definitely don't get to choose colors in the house."

"Yeah, that's what my mom says," Charlie laughed. "It keeps my sister out, that's what's important. She says it 'clashes with her sensibilities.' She clashes with my nerves."

"Okay, but I meant you don't get to paint the kids' room. Anyway, I gotta run. TTYL."

Charlie looked at the phone as if Robin could read his confused look. He didn't know what kids she was talking about. It also took him awhile to figure out "TTYL," since she actually pronounced the letters "tittle."

"You speak in text, Mercedes," Charlie said.

"You remembered my middle name?"

"Yeah ... why, was I supposed to forget it?"

"No, silly. I love my middle name. Mom's yelling. Gone. Bye."

The next sound Charlie heard was an almost painful click, followed by silence. He looked at the clock, which read "8:51." Forty-one hundred and forty seconds to wait. He suddenly had the urge to take a shower instead of hopping in the bed dirty like most nights. In fact, he realized, it had been too long since he changed his sheets.

"It's not a date, doofus," Charlie said out loud, followed almost immediately by, "I have really got to stop doing that."

***

Charlotte was very impressed that Charlie voluntarily put his "stinky sheets" in the hamper and got clean ones. She was even more impressed when she heard him take a shower at night, and not just in the morning, as was his habit. She and her husband, Alan, were in a particularly good mood. Alan had arrived home late, having picked Charlie up from school an hour and a half after being called, due to a flat tire and a run to the grocery store. Charlie had stormed inside in a foul mood. Surprisingly, Charlotte had taken Alan's side. That bit of support and connection had lasted them through dinner. She stood watching her husband, with his curly, sandy blond hair just beginning to show signs of graying at the temples. Her two children looked exactly like their father, she thought, having gotten little more than melanin and musculature from her. It was enough that their marriage had become strained from too much career and not enough relationship work. Now, her youngest was adding to her turmoil by trying to grow up on her.

She pouted at her husband. "See, now he's on his best behavior hoping I'll take him to visit Pops."

"I don't know," Alan replied with a smile, his eyes on Monday Night Football. "Layla said a girl called him."

"Wha-a-t? Some little heifer is after my baby? I'm too young for my baby to like girls!" Charlotte said, with only slightly feigned horror.

"Well, she called him, doesn't mean he's interested yet," he said.

"Oh, he's interested — that explains the shower."

Alan continued to stoke the growing fire. "I don't know, maybe he is getting a girlfriend. I say we ask him about it, maybe invite her over this weekend. Could take his mind off Joe a bit," he said, a distinct twinkle in his eye.

"Oh no. I am not setting up a dating service for my eleven-year-old son." Charlotte said, her arms folded, and her neck beginning to roll.

Alan grinned, his deep dimples showing. "Twelve. He'll be twelve in like, three weeks."

Charlotte began to realize that her husband had been egging her on, and smiled back. "Twelve sounds too grown. My baby is still eleven for now, and eleven is too young for girls to be chasing him. As his father, I think you should go talk to him and make him have girls stop liking him right now."

"He can't help it," Alan laughed. "He looks like his dad."

"I know, but girls are calling him anyway!"

"Hey!" he said, throwing a pillow at her. "These dimples worked on you." Alan grabbed his wife and pulled her into his lap.

"You and your dimples need to let me go," she said, making no attempt to move. "You are supposed to be on my side, by the way."

"The boy has no friends, hardly ever speaks at home. Hell, he talks to himself more than us. Let the heifers call the boy," he said. "Whatever a heifer is."

"You're not concerned that some girl is calling him at night?" she asked.

"Shoot, I'm glad he has a friend. Makes me less concerned about his turning out to be a sniper or something."

Charlotte pushed herself off her husband's lap abruptly. "That's not funny. He's just shy. I used to be shy too you know. You could be a little more sensitive towards him."

"Hey, I was just playing. And I am sensitive towards him, but I think he needs to spend more time with kids his age, and less with old people."

"Alan, Grandpa Joe is his family."

"I get that Charlotte … " he started.

She was growing tenser, and cut him off in mid-sentence. "Those trips to the home are sometimes the only chance I get to spend time with him. We only get a few more years with Charlie being a kid. I would like to not have all those pass by while he's gallivanting out with some badass kids. "

Alan turned away from Charlotte; he was now sour-faced. "Whose fault is it that you don't spend more time with him?"

"Thanks, Alan. I don't have the advantage of working from home. Thanks for the support."

"Starting your business was your dream," he said. "Working from home wasn't mine. I gave my dream up for the damn family."

"You gave your dream up because you didn't have the guts to go for it. Now you're mad at me because I did. Well, I'm sorry, but your issues are not my fault."

Charlotte left her husband and went up to their bedroom. Alan sat for all of five minutes trying to enjoy the game then turned it off, and went to talk to his wife.

Just a normal Monday night.

24 – LET'S DO IT AGAIN

At precisely 10:00 pm and fifteen seconds, Charlie sent a single text message: "Hi." He waited the fifteen seconds so that it didn't seem as if he had been watching the clock for the last ten minutes — which of course he had. He wasn't sure that fifteen extra seconds was nearly enough time to appear casual, but he didn't want to risk Robin's thinking he had forgotten and turning off her phone.

Robin: "Hey Mr. Patterson :)," his computer read.

Charlie: "Are you in bed?" he texted back. Asking a girl if she was in bed made Charlie blush, and he was very glad he wasn't on webcam where she could see it.

Robin: "yeah u?"

Charlie: "Yes, I am."

Robin: "lol"

Charlie: "What's so funny?" Charlie asked, not getting the joke at all.

Robin: "u use proper grammar and punct — its cute :)"

Charlie could close his eyes and see her smile.

Charlie: "oh, sorry," Charlie answered, making sure not to capitalize the first word. He could be cool if he wanted to.

Robin: "it's ok — I like it — did u get home ok?"

Charlie: "yeah finally. my dad picked me up after it was dark"

Robin: "wow that sucks"

Charlie: "yeah, I was real mad, and he got into an argument"

Robin: "u and him?"

Charlie: "no, just him. I wasn't listening."

Robin: "lol!!

Robin: "so ur prolly wondering y I called huh?"

Actually, Charlie was mostly grateful and hadn't taken the time to wonder yet. However, now that Robin mentioned it, he was curious. Nonetheless, he offered a guess so that it didn't seem like he was desperate for company.

Charlie: "i was guessing the dreams, huh?" It was a facile guess, as she had already told him as much.

Robin: "it was just 2 dreams though right?"

Charlie hesitated then opted for the truth.

Charlie: "not exactly."

He practically chewed off his fingernails in between his text and her response.

Robin: "what does that mean?"

Charlie: "well, in one, we were in school."

Embarrassing.

Charlie: "I was a mouse."

Robin: "that was you??? lol!!!"

Charlie: ":(“

Robin: "oh i'm sorry. it's cool, u were a cute mouse :)"

Charlie: "thanks, i think"

Robin: "yw. but there were 3 then. I also dreamed u on the bus. remember? it was the 1st time we spoke? “

Charlie: "yeah!"

Charlie hesitated for only a moment. Then he closed his eyes, and went for it. She had called them best friends, and best friends don't laugh at you. It was a law, or something.

Charlie: "don't think I'm weird, but I've been dreaming u all summer."

No response.

Charlie began to panic. Finally, Robin answered.

Robin: "me too. almost every night. I was never going to tell u though. :)"

Charlie: "This makes no sense! How can we be in each other's dreams???? i never even used to remember dreams."

Robin: "I wish I didn't remember mine. I have the same one all the time."

Charlie: "what is it?"

Robin was silent for a long time.

Charlie: "you still there?"

Robin: "I'm here. I dream about my sister. She died in a car accident."

Charlie: "wow, that's harsh! you don't see her die, do you?"

Robin: "no, I couldn't handle that. I think I'd go crazy."

Charlie: "I'm really sorry. how old was she?"

Robin: "16. I miss her so much."

Charlie: "I can imagine."

In truth, Charlie could imagine it. He couldn't relate to having a sister that he liked, must less longing for her after she was gone. But he could imagine what it is like to love someone who left you — like his Grandma Kate had.

Charlie: "when my grandma died, I stayed mad a long time"

Robin: "yeah it's mostly like that"

Robin: "Can I tell you a secret? I mean really trust you? Tell the truth."

Charlie did not hesitate a second.

Charlie: "Until I die."

Robin: "stop making me like you"

Charlie had his third serious stroke of his very young life.

Charlie: ":) That's usually not too hard a thing for me to do."

Robin: ":(Don't talk like that. Anyway, my secret...."

Robin: "Sometimes I think she did it on purpose"

Charlie was stunned. He hoped she did not mean what she thought she meant.

Charlie: "did what? u mean like suicide??"

Robin: "yes"

Charlie: "with your dad in the car? she wouldn't do that then, right?"

Robin: "I'm not sure, but yeah. that's what the dreams keep saying"

Charlie: "Wow. why? was she sad?"

Charlie: "Stupid question — I'm sorry"

Robin: "No, it's ok. She was acting weird before she died.

Robin: "She & dad fought a lot then."

Robin: "I think something bad happened."

Robin: "Why would she just do that instead of telling me? I could have helped"

Charlie: "When did this happen?"

Robin: "6 months ago — think it's why mom wanted to move — fresh start & all"

Charlie: "Is there something I can do?"

Robin: "ur doing it now"

Charlie: "Maybe u should talk to someone — school counselor or something"

Robin: "not ready for that — ur the 1st person I've told"

Charlie: "wow"

Robin: "enuff of that — tell me 1 of ur dark secrets"

Charlie thought for a long time then decided (as usual) on honesty.

Charlie: "Most people think I'm weird, and I'm not"

Charlie: "School is so easy I can't pay attention so I veg out"

Charlie: "I hate being at home and I hate being in school"

Robin: "what about ur family?"

Charlie: "I'm close to G'pa Joe, but nobody else — I'm just not like them"

Robin: "me and my mom fight a lot. I love her though"

Charlie: "At least u have friends"

Robin: "I guess — I think I have a boyfriend too"

Charlie's heart sank. For a few seconds he considered just turning off the laptop, which by now was making his covers hot anyway. Instead, he decided to just wait.

Robin: "r u asleep?"

Charlie: "No, I'm here"

Robin: "ur not happy for me?"

Charlie: "sure. yay."

Robin: ":)"

Charlie was annoyed that his sarcasm did not translate well via text message.

Charlie: "Who is ur boyfriend? Bryan?"

Robin: "Who is Bryan?"

Charlie: "The twin."

Robin: "Ew! No!"

Charlie was glad that the Cheshire Cat Twins weren't involved, but still, he felt the masochistic need to twist the knife deeper into his heart.

Charlie: "Well, who is it?" He had actually typed "the lucky guy" but deleted it and typed "it" before hitting send.

Robin: "u can never tell anyone"

Charlie: "ok"

Robin: "I mean it — I'll kill you — I know how"

Charlie: "Shaking in my slippers"

Robin: "not jammies with feet? anyway its DeShaun Yancy"

Charlie: "Thugsalot???? r u serious??"

Robin: "lol! he would like that name"

Charlie: ":(“

Robin: "Yes"

Charlie: "Why would u like him?"

Robin: "Well, he was kind of being a bully at first"

Robin: "but I could tell he likes me"

Robin: "he called me railroad tracks — said I was all straight lines and braces"

Charlie: "I can see why you'd like him"

Robin: "lol! brothers are so protective"

Charlie's mood darkened even further. While he had heard that some men had occasionally, through cunning and wile, managed to escape from the Friend Zone, no man had ever successfully broken free of Play Brother Island. That desolate place was where wannabe suitors were so uninteresting the female of the species declared them to be siblings. Charlie was doomed ... it was fourth down and thirty, and he was out of pass plays.

Charlie: "Brother huh?"

Robin: "Yeah, I know it's fast, but I have a gd feeling about u."

Pause.

Charlie: ":) me too"

Charlie's reply was sincere. Guys like him weren't actually supposed to get their dream girls, at least not on the first try. And, the prettiest girl in school had just had a good feeling about him. He had accepted the first of many valuable lessons he would learn about women over the years: when they throw you a gift, catch it, and hold onto it like it's a treasure. That would be a lesson Charles Robert Spencer Patterson never got wrong.

Charlie: "DeShaun wears braces himself."

Robin: "I know, that's why I think he likes me"

Robin: " the 1st 2 weeks I was being bullied by boys, esp. DeShaun"

Robin: " I'm such a nerd. I figured maybe he was doing it because he secretly liked me"

Robin: "I used to always wonder if my dad really loved me too

Robin: "you can never tell with guys"

Charlie: "God, you text as fast as you talk."

Robin: "Keep up, Dimple Boy"

Robin: "DeShaun still acts like he doesn't like me, but he does"

Charlie: "Did it ever occur to you that he acts like he doesn't like you because he doesn't like you?"

Robin: "Of course it did. But then I decided I'm cute."

Charlie actually leaned forward and stared at his laptop, hoping that somehow she could see him looking at her like she's crazy. It didn't work. Texting was a poor substitute for videoconferencing.

Charlie: "That makes no sense."

Robin: "Why, don't you think I'm cute?"

Now Charlie was not stupid. His Guy Alarm went off, and he instantly knew this was a Trick Question. He could answer "no," and she would be hurt and offended, and he would probably be sent from Play Brother Island to ex-friend land, which is reputed to be a prison island far off the coast. Or, he could say "yes," and admit to his feelings. Now, if she thought those feelings were innocent, he was safe. But if she sensed he meant he *liked her* liked her then he was equally doomed, and would be banished to a life of being pointed at and whispered about by every female on the mid-Atlantic coast for having a pathetic, hopeless crush.

Not that he was subject to exaggeration or drama.

The real trouble with Charlie's current situation was that although he knew this was a Trick Question, he had no idea how to avoid the trick. So, he did the only thing a self-respecting male of the species could do. He decided to play dead.

If he just didn't move, she might figure that he was having some brilliant thought, or a brain hemorrhage or something. That had to be better than typing "Not Fair!! I saw you first!!" which is what he was deathly afraid he'd do if he allowed any of his fingers to move. After exactly two minutes and thirty-seven seconds, Robin took a photo of herself pouting, green eyes and all, and sent it to him with the text, ":(is that a no?" She looked adorable in the photo.

Shoot!

Checkmate! In the chess game of "How do I look?" a perfectly executed stonewall move by the male could be overtaken by an equally shrewd "ask the question again, with a vulnerable face" move by the female. In short, Charlie was dead meat. There was no recourse but the truth.

Charlie: "Of course ur cute. ur the prettiest girl in school. u can do better than him."

Pause (for stroke).

Second pause.

Robin: "thank you. u didn't have to say that."

Charlie, of course, knew that he absolutely did have to say that. It was clearly written in the rulebook. Rather, it would have been written in the rulebook if every man who tried to write the rulebook had not gone completely insane first.

Charlie: "He's a jerk, u aren't. Do better."

Robin: "I just figured I wld try with him. What if he loved me and was just afraid?"

Robin: "I need to see past his flaws"

Charlie: "Ur seeing past reality. He's a jerk, and ur only 12."

Robin: "closer to 13"

Robin: "Do you think he likes me?"

Charlie: "Do spiders like flies?"

Robin: "LMBO!! Stop it I'm serious!"

Charlie: "Okay. Does he make you feel good?"

Robin: "Not when I'm talking to him"

Charlie: "Then it doesn't matter how he feels abt u. Do better."

Robin: "ur a good brother"

Shoot.

Charlie: "thx"

Robin: "So, about my dream experiment"

Charlie: "What is it?"

Robin: "We agree on a dream, and see if we can have the same one."

Charlie: "Wow. Ok."

Charlie: "What's the dream?"

Robin: "You think of one"

Charlie: "It's ur idea. I don't have a gd imagination."

Robin: "Everyone does"

Robin: "Ok, let me think"

While Robin thought about a good dream to have, Charlie found himself starting to yawn. He was beginning to fear he might drift off before they had agreed on a test dream.

Robin: "Ok, I got it. The first test will be simple. We just get one word. Ok?"

Charlie: "Sounds cool"

Robin: "ready?"

Charlie: "Yep. What's the word?"

Robin: "As soon as I send it, we log off and go to sleep"

Charlie: "Ok, sleepy anyway."

Robin: "Ok."

Charlie's heart was beating with anticipation. He privately wondered if he'd be able to fall asleep after getting himself so worked up. That thought was immediately followed by the horrifying thought she would text the word "boyfriend" and he would be subject to a night of dreaming about Robin and Sir Thugsalot in a tree "k-i-s-s-i-n-g." To his relief and amusement, she sent the last text of the night:

Robin: "Dragons :)"

25 – DRAGON QUEST

Charlie awoke to a damp, cool morning. He was lying on the frosted grass of a plateau, overlooking a series of rambling hills that curved into the distance. A deep pass, once a river, carved its way through the base of the mountains. Over untold millennia, the river had deepened the valley and abraded the mountains into a series of steep hills. A dense forest of ancient pines hugged the hillside, all but blanketing the valley. From his vantage, the dried riverbed looked like a jagged scar cut through a field of green.

Despite almost constant moisture in the valley, the hills shed their vegetation as their altitudes increased. Near the summits, they were little more than dark rock and low scrub brush. A dense fog obscured all but the very peaks of the furthest hill. The skies were cold and gray, with only muted sunlight filtering through the high clouds. The entire setting was laid out as if it were a painting rendered in shades of gray. Charlie inhaled, taking in the thick, clean air, and exhaled, his face ringed by the visible water vapor heated by his lungs. "We're not in Kansas anymore, Toto," he said to no one.

Even though he had spoken in hushed tones, he could hear a faint echo reverberating from the distant hills. Not knowing what lay in the valley before him, he resisted the urge to shout his name and claim the valley for his. His training had taught him to be wary. He was a hunter, but could just as easily be prey. Charlie touched the ground next to his makeshift bed of soft pine needles and picked up his heavy oak staff. A large arrowhead made of heavy iron formed the business end of the weapon.

149

Charlie wore brown cloth breeches and a cloak made of deerskin, collared with white ermine. "Shoot, I look good," he said, admiring his handiwork and stroking the fur of his collar. "And this collar is really soft against my face."

He strained his memory, trying to recall on which adventure he had trapped the weasels and stripped the fur that now caressed his cheek. It was late autumn now, and the fur was white, so surely it had been the prior winter. Charlie stamped out the remainder of his campfire with his heavy boots, and began the descent towards the valley and the mountain pass where the Great Beast was said to winter. It would be a good hunt — for either the dragon, or himself.

"This is so cool," he giggled.

He took long strides down the hill and approached the evergreen forest. He would need to cut through the thick brush to find the entrance to the path he could see easily from his prior vantage point. As he walked, Charlie felt something hard and round poking him in the back of his neck. Reaching around gingerly with his right hand, he pulled out a long sword the likes of which he had never seen.

"Oh my God, " he gasped. The sword glimmered even in the subdued morning light. The blade itself was nearly two feet long, just the right length for a boy his size. It was made of what appeared to be a solid piece of ruby, except that it was cold and hard to the touch like steel. The ruby blade itself was translucent, and the sky appeared to glow the color of a lava flow when Charlie looked through it. As he held it up to the muted sunlight, the sun's dim rays pierced the blade and intensified, setting a small fire in the grass around Charlie's feet.

The blade was curved like a scimitar, widening to six inches before tapering to a fine, perfect point. The longest side of the blade had been honed to a razor's edge, with the short beveled edge cut into deadly serrations. The net effect of the dual cutting edge was a weapon that could easily slice deeply into flesh, and rip tissue apart on its way out.

Charlie opened his hand and examined the hilt of the sword. The sword's grip was tapered to the exact size of his hand, and made from a dark wood he had never seen. From the feel, it had obviously been hand-made for him. The pommel of the sword's hilt was made of solid gold in the shape of an eagle, a single small ruby for an eye on either side. He dropped his wooden staff, and took the sword in both hands, wielding it with the expertise born of hundreds of hours with video game consoles. The sword was perfectly balanced to his developing frame, which made it feel deceptively light.

"Wow, Robin must have thought this thing up," Charlie gushed, breathlessly. Seeing the dense brush in front of him, Charlie took the sword again in his right hand, the staff in his left, and sliced at a small tree no more than eight feet tall that was directly in front of him. At first, he assumed he had missed, as he felt no resistance at all from the small tree. "Crap," was his single word reaction. He had to do better if he was to become a Slayer. At once, the top half of the tree slid to the ground with a rustle of leaves, leaving only a stem four feet high, sliced at a smooth forty-five degree angle. Charlie broke out in a broad grin.

He began marching through the brush, his blade whirling, slicing, tearing through shrubs and brush with the practiced ease of a hot knife through a jungle made of butter. After some ten minutes, Charlie, now drenched in sweat, mercifully reached the damp coolness of the pine forest. He holstered his sword, trotting among the trees with ease and using his staff to probe the ground. As the hill bottomed out into the valley, he found the ground under his feet suddenly hard. He stopped, kicking away a covering of pine needles, and found the start of an asphalt road.

"Whoa. Okay, I didn't see that coming," he said.

Charlie began walking, and after a few hundred yards, the road curved past the foot of the nearest hill, and quickly broadened into an abandoned highway. The roadway was still dark and misty here in the lower elevations, and Charlie could see no more than a few hundred feet ahead at a time. To Charlie, it looked as if he were now walking along an ordinary country road. Nonetheless, the heavy silence made him feel ill at ease, and he kept his sword close at hand. After another thirty minutes' hike, the forest began to thin, with the rich loamy soil of the hills turning to blackened rock. Unsure how he knew, Charlie understood this was the start of the land they called the Dragon's Lair. He must move with caution from this point on.

He found a small clearing on the side of the road. It was one of few flat spaces in the narrow valley. Here he stopped to rest and eat, removing his provisions from a sling he held beneath his cloak.

"Peanut butter sandwich, Oreos, and an apple? Really mom?" he asked, his hands raised, palm up. "I'm here slaying dragons and I get peanut butter?" Even in a dream world of his own creation, Charlie got no respect. Still, the journey had been long, and the pace quick, so Charlie sat on the precious patch of soft ground to eat. After wolfing down his food, Charlie washed down his meal with water he kept in a leather cask strapped to his back, opposite his sword's sheath. He lay on the ground, resting, looking up at the sky. The sun had fully burned off the fog and mist here, and Charlie could see the sky for the first time. Rather than the familiar blue, it glimmered in green and yellow hues, and the air appeared thick, as if made of clear white smoke.

As he watched, a small translucent cloud passed overhead, moving rapidly. It was thin enough that he could barely make out its movement against the sky. "There must be a storm coming for that cloud to be blowing like that," he said, hoping he could find shelter in the barren terrain ahead. As he watched, the cloud suddenly reversed course then began a dizzying descent toward the hillside.

"What the?" Charlie murmured, sitting upright as he watched. "What kind of cloud does a nosedive?"

Some two hundred feet above the ground, a deafening screech sounded, as if a hundred eagles had all screamed at once. Charlie could see long limbs and taloned feet emerge from a huge body that was just now becoming visible as it neared the ground. At once, the air was filled with a chemical smell, a biting ammoniac odor that was mixed with the cloying perfume of rotting flowers.

Charlie gagged, and held his sleeve to his mouth, instinctively crouching on hands and knees. Whatever was diving from the sky, it was no cloud. "Ohmigod, ohmigod, ohmigod," he found himself muttering, at first wondering who was stupid enough to be talking with that thing out there. Once he realized it was himself, he clamped his sleeved arm tighter to his mouth, as protection against both the smell and his habitual muttering.

The air brightened in a brilliant horizontal flash, as if lightning had emerged from fifty feet above him and decided to travel in a line parallel to the ground. Charlie jumped at the light, falling backward and dropping his sword into the soft ground. From the sky came a broad, white stream of supercooled air from just below a huge pair of crystalline eyes that varied in the reflected light from pale yellow to a pinkish brown. It was a dragon, and it was on a hunt.

Charlie lay flat against the earth, happy that his clothing provided adequate camouflage. His eyes followed the stream of air to the top of a ridge half a mile away, where a small family of goats had scampered up the side of a nearby mountain. He could hear their panicked bleating, mixed with the sound of rushing air and the dragon's screeches, now echoing from both sides of the valley. The supercooled air hit the animals in a blast. All of the goats stopped, frozen rigid where they stood. The dragon swooped in, now in full display, grabbed two goats in each of its forelimbs, and swooped back up toward the sky, barely slowing. Within fifteen seconds, it was gone, and the world had returned to silence.

Charlie exhaled, panting, only now realizing that he had forgotten to breathe during the attack. He looked at his sword, which was sticking hilt first into the muddy soil. Charlie grabbed the handle and pulled the sword out with a loud slurp.

"I'm going to need a bigger sword," Charlie said, frowning at his now far-less-impressive sword.

The dragon had been hunting its prey, camouflaged from the ground by blending into the sky above it. It had smartly waited until the sun had burned off the gray clouds in order that its color not stand out against the cloud cover. It had been moving fast, in a power dive - like an osprey in a full dive into the sea. The sound was mere cover, the shock waves of its bellow bouncing around the canyons and masking its approach vector from its prey. It was a perfect killing machine.

"And it was cold, the air was cold, not fire." Charlie said, panting excitedly. "I hate the cold. With my luck, it'll breathe snow, and I'll end up a Popsicle. A freaking goat-eating snowmaking machine. Great."

The gray morning had turned to midday, and the sun was high in the green and yellow sky. Amidst the towering hills that surrounded him, Charlie no longer felt like a mighty warrior, but rather, small and insignificant. As he had for the greater part of his young life, he was feeling very much alone, and in over his head.

26 – NOT THE SAME DREAM AT ALL

"Wow! What was that thing? That was so cool!" came a voice some fifteen feet above him and to his left.

Charlie screamed. It was not a manly scream, nor a mighty roar of anger. He simply closed his eyes, jumped halfway out of his skin, and screamed like a little girl.

"Sheesh Charlie, scream much?" Robin asked, her face revealing not even a hint of humor. She was coming down the hill, and was being followed by what appeared to be a large pink dog. Robin was wearing a flowing gown that looked to be woven from fine strands of opaque beige glass. As she neared, Charlie could see it was actually made of some type of cloth, but it sparkled in the sun as she moved. The right side of her gown was slit, and underneath Charlie could see she was wearing trousers of fine, soft leather. Her hair was no longer dark brown, but deep red, framed by a headband made from the same material as the gown.

She wore a huge oval shield on her back that was decorated with letters that Charlie could not make out. The shield was wider than she was, and seemed to be perfectly balanced as she walked, as if it had no weight at all. It showed the markings of aged wood, but shone with reflected sunlight like brass. Charlie looked expectantly at her feet for a pair of golden slippers or leather sandals. Instead, she wore a pair of her very own black combat boots. Although he had been vaguely aware of looking for Robin, until she showed up, he had forgotten about their experiment. Indeed, he wasn't completely aware he was dreaming. Seeing her brought him back.

"So, you like gowns huh?" Robin asked with a wry smile.

Charlie felt a surge of embarrassment. He resisted the urge to blurt an affirmative that would reveal he had been staring again. There was, after all, a chance she was guessing, and hoping he would show his hand. He could play poker if she could. It was one of his favorite video games.

"Yeah, it's okay," he said, with feigned nonchalance. "You look nice ... although I don't think it's much good for climbing down hills."

Robin rolled her eyes in mock annoyance. "Whatever," she said. "I was wearing jeans. I didn't look like this till you showed up," she said, squinting accusingly at him. "You better not be having weird dreams about me, buster. I'm your sister now."

"Me? I didn't even know you were there. I was looking at the dragon, and had forgotten all about ... "

"Yeah, I saw that," she interrupted. But I don't think that big huge thing was a dragon. He seemed awfully ... mean." She pointed to the animal behind her. "That is a dragon. Her name is Hannah."

"Hannah Leigh, actually," clarified the small dragon, peering around Robin. "I'm very pleased to meet you." She extended a small pink arm as if to shake.

Charlie, who, fortunately, had put his sword in his sheath, slapped both sides of his face at once, shaking his head. "That's not a real dragon," he said, annoyed that Robin had completely gotten the concept wrong.

"Charlie Patterson! You are being very rude," Robin scolded.

"Um, sorry. It's nice to meet you too," he said grudgingly, leaning around Robin to address Hannah. Then he added, "Could you excuse us for just a second?" pulling Robin aside brusquely by the arm.

"Isn't she adorable?" Robin asked, smiling at the dragon, which waved back in response.

"Uh, yeah," he answered unconvincingly. Charlie looked at Hannah closely. She was no more than five feet tall, and was standing upright on her hind legs. Her skin was reptilian leather, soft and pebbly, and covered with pink suede. Her saucer-like eyes stamped a permanent lost puppy expression on her cartoon-dinosaur face. She had a small tail, the shape of a lion's, and it was only around two feet long. On her head, she wore a rose-colored round helmet embellished with the letter "H." A small tunic of the same rose color as the helmet covered her white chest. She was, in a word, adorable.

"She's pink!" Charlie said, arms extended, exasperated.

"Actually, she calls herself light rose," Robin corrected.

"But look, this is silly. You said 'dragons' and I found a real dragon. We aren't having the same dream at all!

"Of course we are, silly," she said sweetly. "I'm right here. The experiment worked." Robin thought for a few seconds then frowned. "Are you wishing I hadn't shown up? I can leave if I'm not wanted."

"No, I'm sorry … it's … this is so girly. It's embarrassing"

"Not as girly as that scream you let out when I showed up," Robin giggled.

Charlie chose to ignore her insult, though he did place his hand on his sword's hilt in an attempt to appear somewhat more menacing. Robin snatched the staff from Charlie's left hand and walked off to rejoin Hannah calling over her shoulder, "You don't scare me, Dimple Boy. You would never hurt me." Charlie smiled, since she was completely correct.

"Come on Hannah, we need to help the hero here find some ugly dragons."

Hannah looked confused and slightly afraid. "Why would you want to do that? You already have me." She exhaled a small puff of fire as if to prove she was an actual dragon.

Charlie just responded with a shrug and started up the road he had been traveling before. Before he got far, however, Robin and Hannah called him in unison. "Hey, let's go this way," they said, pointing up the hill in the direction whence they came.

"I'm afraid to ask why," Charlie said, not moving.

Hannah answered first. "It's just … a little gloomy this way. Trust me, you don't want to go where that road leads."

She looked in the direction of the hill where the goats were, now with only half of one goat remaining, the frozen top half having been shattered into pieces by the dragon's tail when it flew off. Charlie didn't actually want to test himself if the dragon came back for seconds, so he followed the girls up the hill.

At the crest of the hill, Charlie stopped, dumfounded, while Robin beamed. As far as he could see, the land was rolling hills of rainbow-colored grass and flowers, all swaying in the breeze. The flowers were, in fact, miniature fireworks, all sparkling and popping in the sun. Robin plucked one and handed it to Charlie. The sparkles danced and crackled, but only tickled his hand when they touched him. Charlie sniffed, and the flower, and the very air around him, smelled exactly like warm chocolate chip cookies. He was glad he had lunch.

Splitting the hills were six streams comprising multi-hued water that changed colors as Charlie watched. The streams converged into a mighty river, and where the different colored waters met, they formed what looked like an enormous kaleidoscope. The surrounding landscape was dotted with waterfalls, although it wasn't clear where the water was coming from, or, in fact, where it went once it cleared the falls.

"Shhh, listen," Robin smiled, her finger to her lips.

As Charlie listened, he could hear the waterfalls, not the normal sound of running water, but screams and giggles of delight, as if each droplet were a kid on a rollercoaster. Charlie began to grin, and looked at Robin with awe. Robin caught his gaze and grinned back then pointed to the sky. The sky was no longer the green and yellow of Charlie's sky, but a midnight blue, and the air was filled with smiles. Big smiles, little smiles, smiley faces, and huge grins filled the sky from horizon to horizon.

"The smiles are kind of like stars in our world, except you can see them in the daytime," Robin explained.

"See, I told you I didn't have a good imagination," Charlie said. "This is amazing."

"Really? Robin asked, genuinely flattered. "Do you think I did this? I thought it was just kind of here."

"This part is your dream. In my dream I was a dragon slayer."

Hannah whimpered at Charlie's response, and hid behind Robin's gown, frowning at him.

"No, no! Only the large, cold-breathing kind," Charlie hurriedly explained.

"Oh, well. I don't like that kind. They aren't very cute at all," Hannah agreed.

"I think I'm supposed to find a castle or something. All I'm sure of is that I have a quest, and I have to fight a dark lord in a castle." Charlie continued.

Robin looked skeptical. "Are you making this all up?"

"No, but I don't know how I know either," he said. "It's like there's a voice in my head. I kind of … woke up here, and I had memories, like I actually lived here. It's weird, now that I think of it."

"That happened to me too. Apparently, I'm some kind of animal trainer, or psychic or something-or-other." Robin seemed unperturbed by the fact. "Well, this is the way. It's the same direction as your road. Just not as creepy."

Hannah asked, "Are you sure it's a dark lord in a castle, and not a black knight in a house?"

"What's the difference?" Charlie asked.

"Well, there is the Black Knight, of course, but he lives in a white house. Then there is an Overlord in Castle Black. The big dragons protect him."

"Let me guess — the black knight is evil, right? They always make the evil knights black," he said, annoyed.

"Dude, you're being silly," Robin chimed in.

"Oh, no, the Black Knight is actually pretty nice. We had tea last week. You might be thinking of the Overlord in Castle Black." Hannah answered, unruffled.

"Well who is the Overlord? Is he black too?" Charlie asked, getting confused.

"I don't know what color he is," Hannah replied, coyly holding the ends of her tunic, "but I imagine he's not a lovely rose color like a certain dragon we know and love."

"Besides," added Robin, "this is your dream, not hers. Why would you assume the evil knight is black?"

"I wasn't assuming," he said. "I just misunderstood."

"Why does your dream need a stupid evil knight anyway?" Robin asked.

"Oh good grief," Charlie groaned. He frowned and began walking ahead. After twenty yards, he stopped and turned to face the girls who were both standing with their arms folded, unmoving.

"It's not my dream, Robin, it's our dream," he called out. "We're supposed to be a team, remember? Now would you please come on?"

Robin grabbed the staff that had been sticking in the ground. "I'm coming, but not so you won't be mad. And not if you're going to be all yelly at me." Her lip was poked out, but her eyes were smiling at him.

Charlie took a deep breath and said, "Sorry."

Yelly?

"Good. Don't make my eyes green. You wouldn't like me when my eyes are green."

"You're so scary," Charlie said sarcastically.

"I could be, you know," Robin said. "I'd be famous, like the She Hulk. I just don't want to as I look too nice today to rip through clothes."

Charlie and Robin walked for what seemed like hours; time was a difficult thing to judge in the dream world. The blue of the sky had begun to fade into mottled green and yellow hues. Even the smiles began to fade a bit, looking less like happy faces and more like ordinary stars, as the features of each face blurred in the twilight sky. Behind them, darting in much the same way as a bumblebee does, flew Hannah, who had been chattering happily for most of the trip, but now was silent, except for the occasional smoky huff of exertion.

"Hannah, you're awfully quiet sweetie," Robin said after a while, turning to her friend.

"I (huff) am (huff) a little (huff) winded," Hannah answered, the flapping of her small wings sounding like a giant mosquito.

"Let's stop and rest then," Charlie said. We're almost at the top of this last hill. Maybe we can get our bearings. Besides, all that huffing is starting to singe the hair on the back of my neck."

"Sorry," Hannah said, plopping on the soft grass all at once.

"It's okay, not your fault you have dragon breath," Charlie offered by way comfort.

Robin poked Charlie repeatedly on the arm, smiling. "Stop being such a bully."

"I'm not," he insisted. "I like her. Besides, calling someone dragon breath isn't an insult if they're an actual dragon."

Robin rolled her eyes, but began to giggle, when they were interrupted by a muffled cry from Hannah. Both kids turned to see what was wrong. They saw Hannah sitting on her haunches, both hands in front of her mouth.

Robin silently mouthed, "What is it?"

In answer, Hannah pointed a rose colored hand (with brightly painted pink nails) at the valley that separated the hill they were on from the jagged mountains beyond. There, resting among the trees and brush that dotted the otherwise rocky valley was the dragon they had seen before. It was lying next to an enormous bonfire. Visible in the fire's light were the charred bones of several animals among a pile of sharpened sticks.

Charlie pointed to the bones and whispered, "Those must be the goats. Looks like it likes to heat up its frozen dinners."

"Yuck. Goat kabobs," Robin said, sticking out her tongue.

"Looks yummy," said Hannah, licking her lips.

The dragon yawned and stretched, twisting its neck like a prize fighter before a match, and rose to its full height. In the fire's glow, they could see it was a magnificent beast, towering over the small trees under which it had been resting. It stood thirty feet high, and measured a full fifty feet in length, including its thirty feet of tail.

With its head erect, the kids could see its chest and neck were covered in iridescent plates of overlapping armor. They were light green and yellow in color and covered the dragon's entire underside. This gave it the dual advantage of protecting it from weapons launched from below, and helped it blend into the sky's matching colors when viewed from underneath.

The protective armor that guarded the beast's underside gradually changed to a thick pebbly leather skin, much like the texture of their friend Hannah's skin. However, instead of suede, a soft, downy fur covered the behemoth's skin. Viewed from above, the dragon's body was a thick coat of tan and green, with patterns that resembled that of a jaguar's. It had the advantage of being camouflaged both while in the air, and when on ground amongst the trees and brush.

The dragon's head was reptilian, though with a lion's broad nose. The mouth was filled with rows of shark-like teeth, and a forked tongue that constantly tasted the air around it. Its head was crowned with a mane of long, thick golden fur that draped almost to the ground. It was broadly muscled, with a thick cluster of rippling sinews at its shoulders, to which were attached its wings.

It spread its wings, warming their sixty-foot span near the fire. Its wings resembled those of a bat. Attached to the powerful shoulders, they were what once must have been — an evolutionary eon ago — a third set of limbs. Now they were mostly thin bone and tendons that allowed the dragon to flap its wings in a rotational pattern similar to a hummingbird's. At the tip of each wing were five clearly visible, but non-functional fingers.

The beast walked on four thick legs, the front two ending in taloned feet with large opposable claws. Balancing the huge beast was its thirty-foot tail that ended in spikes.

"That thing is made to kill," Charlie gasped, clearly awestruck. In his excitement, he had forgotten to be afraid. "Look at the spikes on its tail, I bet that could kill anything he hit with it."

"Oh, his tail would kill you without the spikes," Hannah corrected. She looked a trifle embarrassed. "The spikes are just for ... well, getting a girlfriend."

"Oh, a mating thing," Charlie parroted.

Hannah giggled, and held her hand to her mouth. Apparently, as dragons go, Charlie's beast was fairly attractive.

"So, slayer boy, what is this quest we're on? Are we supposed to fight that thing?"

Charlie blanched for a second, and then regained his composure. "I'm not sure, I think we're supposed to get to the castle on the top of the mountain. I get the feeling we have to get by that thing to get there though."

As if on cue, the dragon raised its head, gave a deep bellow that rippled the muscles of its chest, and exhaled a white-hot burst of flames that arced a hundred yards to the mid-point of the dark mountain ahead of it. When the flames ended, the dragon lowered its head, its crystalline eyes glistening. For a split second, as the night closed in on the mountain, all was dark. Then, as the dragon's fire ignited the molten rock that pooled in hidden chasms in the mountain, the mountain itself seemed to erupt in flames. The flames crackled and danced, lapping against the already blackened mountain.

The trio's eyes followed the flames up the side of the black rock and there they could see at the top, a huge structure, hewn directly out of the rock of the mountain itself. Hannah seemed to shrink as the dark castle came into view. She was clearly frightened. "That's Castle Black," she said quietly. "If you're looking for the old man, that's where you'll find him." Her voice had seemed to change abruptly.

"What old man?" Robin asked, looking at her friend with a confused expression.

Hannah pointed at Charlie. "He knows who the old man is. But I must warn you, the Overlord knows about you now, and he will not surrender the old man or the others willingly. Good luck on your quest, you're going to need it."

"What do you mean good luck?" Robin asked, turning toward Hannah.

"I'm really sorry, love. I can't do this," Hannah answered. Her eyes were wide with panic. She mouthed, "I'm sorry," once more, and took off, disappearing into the darkening sky.

After she was gone, Charlie added, "You really need to do a better job of picking friends."

"Oh, you mean like yours, Captain Obvious?" Robin said, testily pointing to the large dragon. It was pacing back and forth with the easy languor of a hyperactive toddler on crack. The iridescent scales on its chest and neck, and its eyes, reflected the fire dripping from the mountain. Dancing with the dragon's frenetic movement, the reflected fire gave the dragon the appearance of being made of flames. The illusion made the two kids shudder. They suddenly felt very alone.

Robin placed her hands on her hips, and looked angry, her eyes green even in the dim light. Charlie, remembering the slaps in the last dream, took a step backwards.

"So, what are you not telling me? Who is the old man, and who's the Overlord?" Robin asked. "And quit jumping around like that. It's making me nervous."

"I don't know what she was talking about," he answered. "She was yours, not mine. And I'm ducking because you have a longer reach than me, and you get violent."

"No, you only dream I get violent. I never hurt anybody. That's my problem."

The dragon chose that moment to interrupt their debate. It turned its head toward them and roared, louder than before, head tilted to the sky. Remembering the flames that previously followed the dragon's bellows, Charlie and Robin dove to the ground. Robin's gown immediately turned into blue sweat pants and a black t-shirt. Her hair was in a single ponytail, in its natural dark brown hue.

"What the heck is that?" Charlie asked, pointing to her new outfit.

"It's what I wore to bed. I'm trying to wake up," Robin answered, her eyes clamped shut.

The dragon sounded once more, but no flames followed. Instead, in a rich baritone that echoed from the mountain, it said in clear tones, "If you want your old man, you'd better come get him boy. He won't last much longer." The dragon followed this with a deep laughter, loud enough to cause a few small rocks to become dislodged on the mountain. "You'll have to come though me though," it taunted. The dragon crouched for a brief moment then launched itself in the air with a great gush of air from its wings. It flew quickly, directly at the two.

"He means my G'pa Joe!" Charlie yelled over the noise.

"He means to kill us! Run!" Robin answered, pulling Charlie by the collar.

"What's your favorite fast animal?" Charlie suddenly asked, running at full speed with the dragon in close pursuit.

"What? You're doing surveys *now*?"

"Trust me! Name one, I can't think!"

"I don't know, Game Show Boy! Survey says, 'Run!'"

Robin seemed to shift into a higher gear than Charlie's shorter legs were equipped to travel, as the dragon's abundant teeth snapped closely behind them. A gust of air rushed past Charlie's face as it filled its lungs for another blast. Charlie was two full steps behind Robin, muttering animal names, most heavy, slow, and powerless. "Um, yak!" he called, as the air grew hot, a line of flame sailing barely an arm's length over their heads.

"Yak?" Robin, stopped, and stared at her friend. "How about a unicorn?" She was looking at him as if he were an idiot.

Charlie caught up to her and closed his eyes. The dragon stopped, and exhaled a thin stream of frigid air in their direction. The two turned, and gasped, as their frozen death approached. Robin screamed, and Charlie clenched his eyes shut once more. Charlie felt the temperature plummet. Something hard and muscular slammed into him and sent him and Robin airborne. The kids, expecting death by dragon, screamed in tandem, as they bounced down a short hill. The top of the hill was now covered in ice.

They could hear the dragon's angry screeches, and bursts of white light and cold air raked the sky as it searched its lair for the two. When that did not work, it flew higher in the night, pulled back its head, and bellowed, a long stream of fire lighting the night sky. The hot air from the flames mixed with the cooler air from its previous icy belches, and the superheated, rapidly expanding air hitting the supercooled air began to cause bellows of thunder. From below, the dragon began to look like an angry thunderstorm in search of victims.

As the night was lit with orange flames, Charlie and Robin looked at the ground near them, wanting a place to hide. There, three feet away, they saw what had knocked them down the hill and saved their lives. It was a golden mare that stood eight feet high at the shoulders. It had wings the color of spun honey, and a gold and white flowing mane that grew from the crown of its head to its shoulders. On its muzzle was not one, but three horns. One was long and gold, the other two, shorter and made of ivory. It was a gorgeous unicorn with soft, pebbled skin.

"It has three horns," Robin said, her mouth agape. Her eyes were an incredible blue.

"Uh, I was thinking triceratops before you said unicorn," Charlie said sheepishly.

"Triceratops?"

"Yeah, well you said yak was stupid."

"I did not."

"You said it with your eyes. Anyway, I couldn't think of anything that was fast. I told you, I don't have a good imagination — I'm too logical, Dad says." He paused for a second then added, "Maybe our imagination got merged."

The tricorn bent low, head bowed to Robin. She grabbed its mane, and swung her leg over the large back. Robin then leaned over toward Charlie, hand extended.

"Climb aboard Dimple Boy; let's go kick some dragon butt … and get your G'pa Joe."

Charlie grinned, and grabbed Robin's hand. She was back to wearing the gown and leather pants. She was holding the long staff in her left hand, and the shield was strapped to her back. As Charlie pulled himself up, she turned to face him with a puzzled look on her face.

"Do you hear that buzzing sound?" she asked.

Charlie looked to the sky to see if it was the dragon coming back. "No," he said.

Robin looked around, and then said, "Oh crap. That's my alarm clock." Then poof, she was gone, and so was the tricorn, spilling Charlie to the ground with a thud. Some five seconds later, the ground began to shake, and the mountain in front of Charlie began to crumble.

27 – THE FRIEND ZONE

"Get up, Turd!" It was Charlie's hated alarm clock, also known as his sister, Layla. "Time for school, fool. I'm sick of waking your butt up every day." Layla stormed out, purposely leaving his door open. "I hope you're naked so Mom can see what a turdy little creep you are."

Charlie blinked, disoriented. His heart was racing, and he felt more alive than he ever had before. He threw off his covers, pushed his door closed, and turned on his laptop, drumming on his desk impatiently while it booted up.

After thirty seconds, he ran to the bathroom to relieve himself. He figured that would show his mom he was awake so she didn't send his nosy sister back into his room. When he came back into his room, the computer was on, and he had a video message. It was Robin. He clicked it, almost afraid to see if Robin had the same dream he did. Know-it-all Chuck inside his head was busy informing him that the entire dream, including Robin, could have been his sole imagination. He opened the message window, and grinned.

Robin's face was in close-up, her braces gleaming, and she was yelling into the computer. "Yay! That was awesome!! I never dreamt like that before!" She frowned. "What happened with your great-grandpa?" Another frown. "Where are you? Wake up already!" She turned, and yelled something, presumably to her mother, then turned back to the computer. "Save me a seat on the bus or I'll beat you! Bye! Hugs."

Charlie was breathless. It had happened to her just as it happened to him. Their experiment was an absolute success. But Robin asked a great question. What exactly was going on with G'pa Joe, and how did the dragon know about it? For that matter, how in the world could he be having the same dreams as Robin? For the first time in his life, Charlie could not wait to get to school.

Especially if there might be hugs.

***

The school day was a blur of monotonous reality for Charlie and Robin. They were both excited from their unfinished adventure the night before, and emotionally drained. Although physically rested, both felt as if they had not been asleep at all. The memory of the dream was as clear as the morning's breakfast. After tangling with dragons, reading, 'riting, and 'rithmatic were mundane beyond reason. Charlie thought he might actually, finally, die of boredom.

Even Jannet's almost constant eye rolling failed to get Charlie's attention today. It took all his concentration just to avoid falling asleep in class. He did not mind sleeping in school, but he was afraid the dream would continue, and he didn't want to go on without his partner. Although he was nervous about the prospect of facing the huge dragon alone, he was more afraid of Robin's reaction if she found out he had not waited for her.

By the time the seventh period bell rang to end the day, Charlie was dragging. It was only the prospect of talking to Robin again that gave him any energy at all. In the morning, they had just enough time to compare notes on their dream and confirm that they had indeed shared the adventure. Robin had told about "waking up" in a world of sky-filled smiles, fireworks flowers, and brightly colored water, with a cute pink dragon standing over her.

"Are you dead?" had been Hannah's first words when Robin opened her eyes. That surprised Robin, as the little dragon had waited politely until Robin awoke to ask her the question. It made Robin think that Hannah had completely missed the concept of death. Charlie and Robin had gotten a good laugh out of that.

Twenty-four thousand, nine hundred and thirty seconds after school started, Charlie was standing outside, panting, and waiting for bus number six, and Robin, who forbade his getting on the bus without her. He was trying his best not to pace back and forth. As he attempted his most casual look – which was being undermined by his constant, impatient frown – he became aware of Bryan and Brandon, both of whom were staring at him. Now on a normal day, Charlie would have just looked down, irritated, and pretended not to notice. This was no ordinary day. After all, he was now a dragon slayer (*almost*) and slayers do not allow themselves to be stared at.

"Do you guys need something?" Charlie surprised himself by asking.

Twins Flynn visibly flinched, neither being prepared for a vocal Charlie. After a beat, they both recovered. Brandon spoke first. "We was just wondering."

"What's up with you and Robin?" finished Bryan.

Charlie sighed and shook his head. His logical left brain decided the question was stupid, and Charlie only answered stupid questions when asked by teachers.

"Well?" asked Brandon.

"We're friends."

"We figured that," Bryan said. "Are you trying to score?"

"Score what?" Charlie asked, feigning ignorance. He wanted to make them say it out loud.

Twin Flynn obliged, speaking in their normal seesaw pattern.

"Dude."

"You know."

"Score."

"Get with."

Charlie shrugged, and opened his hands in the universal "no comprendo" gesture. "No comprendo," Charlie said, being literal, as he often was when annoyed.

"Let. me. talk. slow. genius. Does DeShaun know you're hitting on his girlfriend?" Bryan grinned.

"*Aw heck naw! Let's mess him up!*" Charlie's right brain offered up, proving, finally, that Charlene liked girls — well Robin, anyway.

Fortunately, Chuck was still firmly in control. Charlie replied, as calmly as he could with his heart pounding through his chest, "DeShaun is not her boyfriend, Bryan."

By way of answer, Bryan and Brandon merely gestured in unison by lifting their chins, motioning for Charlie to look behind him. Charlie turned in the direction they were looking. Through the main doors came Robin, looking as cute as usual, her eyes pointed to the ground, and a demure smile on her face. She was wearing a lovely green sweater, and DeShaun Yancy's left arm draped around her neck. Charlie's heart would have sunk, but he was determined not to let the twins, DeShaun, or Robin, for that matter, see him react. DeShaun walked Robin ceremonially to the bus stop, looking around like a hawk that had just stolen an egg.

"What up DeShaun?" Brandon said, grinning in Charlie's face the entire time.

Robin followed Brandon's eyes to Charlie's face, and her smile quickly evaporated into a disappointed frown. Her reaction made Brandon giggle into his shirt.

Charlie was irritated that he was not being as inscrutable as he hoped, and took out his cell phone. As his parents argued the previous night, the subject of Charlie's being at school after dark with no cell phone had come up. The only bright spot in Charlie's now-ruined life was the fact that he was allowed to play games on his phone after school, which he began to do now. He and Robin had been so excited on the morning bus ride he had neglected to tell her.

"I thought you couldn't have your phone at school," Robin said, frowning harder.

Charlie just glanced at her and returned to his game. He was aware of her expression dropping, and secretly wondered if her eyes had begun to turn green. He chose not to look. Bryan, being a tad more serious than his brother, picked up on the energy, and walked away, pulling his brother with him. The next few minutes before Mrs. Thornwood drove up with the creaky old bus were spent with Robin pretending not to notice Charlie existed, Charlie returning the favor, and DeShaun nodding at everyone like some pimped-out bobblehead, so they would notice he was now with the prettiest girl in the seventh grade. As the bus pulled up, and Mrs. Thornwood gave her usual "hurry up" greeting, Robin glanced at Charlie to ensure he was looking. He was. Robin, full of drama, kissed DeShaun on the cheek. Charlie threw up a little in his mouth. It soured his expression even more.

Charlie waited until all the other kids were on the bus, hoping one of them sat by Robin. He was too hurt and angry to face her, but didn't want to insult her by walking by either. To his dismay, as he climbed on the bus, he could see her sitting alone, staring out the window in DeShaun's direction. Charlie had no choice. He sat down in the first seat, by Mrs. Thornwood. The driver looked at him with a surprised sneer then in her rearview mirror at Robin.

"Aw, the puppy love is over already? What a shame," she grinned then pulled the door shut and hit the gas.

"Bite me," Charlie said under his breath.

Thornwood hit the brakes, lurching all the kids forward, and glared at Charlie.

"What did you say?" she asked, her brown teeth almost gnashing at him. She had the expression of a walking corpse whose lips had rotted off.

Charlie looked up from his video game, and said in Chuck's perfectly calm, left-brained voice, "I'm not playing this game with you today, lady. " He then looked at her with the same practiced blank stare he had used to back off Ray Romatowski.

"We'll see about that Charlie Pee Pants," Thornwood snarled.

"Whatever, psycho," Charlie said, imitating her snarling expression. He got up and walked a few rows down the aisle. Every head on the bus was watching him, in something akin to either horror or admiration. Charlie reached Robin's seat, and sat down next to her without a word. Thornwood looked as if she was considering whether she could get away with busting a cap in Charlie's disrespectful little butt, but apparently decided it wasn't worth it.

"This ain't over, kid. Not by a long shot," she muttered, driving off the school lot.

Charlie was certain she was smiling. If it was a game, he did not want to play it.

Robin looked up at Charlie, her eyes a dim, misty gray. "You are being a jerk, you know," she said.

"Yeah, I know," he said. "I'm sick of people messing with me."

"I wasn't messing with you," Robin said defensively.

"And I didn't say anything to you," Charlie countered.

"Fine. I don't want to argue."

"Good."

The two sat silently after that, neither looking at the other. As the bus finished the ten-minute ride to Robin's, she simply excused herself politely, and walked wordlessly off the bus. Charlie watched her leave then leaned back into his seat. He was still mad, but now at himself. After all, Robin had done nothing worse than walking out of school with someone she had confessed to having a crush on.

To her best friend. Me.

He pounded his fist on his forehead, pulled out his cell phone, pulled up Robin's number, and sent a single text message. "I'm sorry," was all it said.

After some thirty seconds, his phone buzzed with the reply, "It's ok, ur very protective."

"Yeah," he texted back. He thought it better to let her believe his anger was protection.

"Are we going to try dreaming again?" Robin asked.

Charlie thought about that until the next stop then answered. "If you think we can."

"What does that mean?" Robin asked.

"We can try. Have a good night," Charlie responded, letting her know the discussion was over.

He turned off his phone, rationalizing in his head his mother's warning against too many text messages on the next bill. He felt as if he had just been dumped, without even getting the chance to tell Robin he liked her. He was sure he would have worked up to that — eventually. A ballplayer should not strike out while still on the bench. Charlie's mood continued to darken, so much so that he didn't even notice when Mrs. Thornwood half-whispered a threat as he left the bus.

"I'll let you have that one, Charlie. But don't push it," she said through clenched teeth.

As the evening wore on, Charlie made the decision that he would approach the dreaming scenario differently. The previous night had been fun, mostly, but too unpredictable for his liking. Before these vivid dreams began taking place, Charlie remembered almost nothing of dreams. The prior night's dream, however, had stayed with him through the waking hours. He could recall it in more detail than his school day, but he was not sure how long the memory would remain. After dinner, Charlie retired to his room, and began a dream log on his laptop.

"You never know when you might need to recall some crucial information," Chuck had decided. Charlene was too busy sulking to help.

As Charlie sat typing, he brainstormed about the previous and current night's adventure, thinking aloud as he typed. "Hannah talked about 'being in the stream,'" Charlie mused, "We have to find out what the stream is. Also, find out more about the Overlord. Whoever that is, he might have something to do with why we're having these dreams. And, if we're supposed to fight his dragons to get to the castle, we better know what we're up against."

Charlie stopped typing for a moment, fingers poised over the keyboard. He was forgetting the most important point of the conversation last night: G'pa Joe. "G'pa! Thought: does this dream world have something to do with G'pa's being … sick? He tried to rescue those kids on the river," Charlie wrote. "What if he got trapped? We need to find him if he's stuck in the dream world."

Charlie stopped typing and shook his head as he read what he had just written.

Trapped in a dream world. That's nuts.

Somehow, however, it felt like the right answer. There was no logical explanation for what was going on. Therefore, the answer must be something illogical. But to solve the riddle, he needed to remember more about the other dreams he had with Robin. His dreams became more vivid when Robin first came on the scene. What if she had something to do with this?

"Question:" Charlie typed, "what if Robin is a dream wizard or something?"

Charlie stopped typing, and shook his head. He considered deleting what he just wrote, but instead, hit save again, and continued talking it through.

"Okay, now I'm being silly. Wizards are for books, not real life. Besides, what if it's me? I need to see if I am pulling in people in the dreams, or if it's her."

Charlie cocked his head, stuck out his tongue, and tapped his temple.

"What am I forgetting?" he muttered, still tapping. "Doors! The dream with the rabbit guy there was a door I went through. What if there are other doors? Not like a cartoon, but something real, like a portal? Can I make other doors if I concentrate?"

Charlie wasn't sure he was making sense. All he knew is he needed answers. A talking dragon implied G'pa Joe was trapped in the dream world. G'pa Joe himself had told him little kids minds might be trapped there, and it was making them seem … senile. What if that is what happened to him? Could he connect with G'pa Joe's dreams somehow?

Charlie almost sent a text message to Robin to discuss it, but then thought of their conflict earlier. He had a better idea, one that she might not like, but which could prove to be very interesting. It would likely be hurtful for one of them, but sometimes one has to take risks. Charlie was almost twelve, and had never taken any. As a result, his life never felt like it was his to control. Tonight would be his first step toward changing that. His plan was risky, but he was going to take a chance — for himself, and to help Robin … even if she did not know she needed help.

At around eight o'clock, Charlie told his parents that he was tired and was going to bed early. Of course, his mom was worried he was coming down with a fever, but he assured her he just had trouble falling asleep the night before, which was common for him. Charlie got ready for bed, and sent a text message to Robin.

"Hey, I'm going to bed. Working on the dragon dream."

After a few minutes, Robin texted him back, "Don't you want to try a new one?"

"Can't. Need to see if G'pa Joe is there," Charlie answered.

"You think that was real?"

"Don't know. Could have just been me worrying. Need to find out."

Chuck had been constantly telling him his seeing G'pa Joe in his dreams was understandable, considering how worried Charlie was about him. After all, he used to dream about Grandma Kate when she was sick too. One dream even came after she passed away. Charlie sensed this was different, however. What with dragons and skies full of smiles and waterfalls to nowhere, his great-grandfather had been the last thing on Charlie's mind. But still, G'pa Joe had been mentioned in another dream.

Charlie found it surprisingly easy to fall asleep. He was counting sheep, but in his dream state, the bleating they made kept waking him up. So instead, he started counting kittens. One minute he was lying in bed, and the next minute, his room was filled with a dozen softly mewing kittens. Kitten number thirteen, a red tabby, jumped right on Charlie's face scaring him into sitting bolt upright.

"Where'd you come from boy?" Charlie said, lifting it up in one hand.

He wasn't sure if he was awake or asleep, but he could feel the soft fur and it certainly felt real. To check, he lifted the tabby to his face. He immediately sneezed — hard. Allergic. Yep, he was awake all right. The tabby squirmed, twisted out of Charlie's hand, and ran out his open bedroom door.

Shoot!

"I left the door open. Mom will kill me if she sees I somehow dreamed up a bunch of cats." Charlie hopped out of the bed and after the wayward kitten. As he reached the hallway outside of the door, he immediately knew something was wrong with the house.

Isn't mom's room on the right?

"*Left, right, it's next door, what's the diff?*" Charlene chimed in, not seeing the problem.

Charlie walked to the right, where his parent's room should be, and found himself at school. He was dressed in the same outfit he wore to school. It was 3:54 pm, just before the final bell was to ring. Charlie was standing outside of wood shop. He looked around, got his bearings, and smiled. He knew exactly where he was, and why he was here. As real as it felt, allergic reaction or no, he was sound asleep. His plan was starting!

At that moment, the bell sounded and the classroom door flew open, slamming into the wall next to Charlie, almost knocking him into the green stone. The students, none in any of Charlie's classes, piled out quickly, one by one. There, strutting as proud as a peacock was DeShaun "Fancy" Yancy.

28 – SIR FANCY YANCY

DeShaun Yancy was not the sort of kid to be dreaming about school, but Charlie was influencing his dream. "Hey Fancy. It's me, Charlie Patterson. Uh, you don't really know me probably." Charlie took the liberty of calling DeShaun by his nickname.

"Yo, yeah, I know who you are. What's dealing, son?" DeShaun replied.

DeShaun was always recognizable by the large diamond earring he wore in his left ear. Charlie had always felt earrings were for pirates and girls, so he wasn't jealous of DeShaun's bit of finery, but he couldn't help but feel envious of the personal freedom it expressed.

"Uh, nice earring. My mom would kill me if I got my ear pierced."

"Yeah, thanks," DeShaun said, looking around, likely for Robin. "Is that what you stopped me to say?" DeShaun was clearly ready to move on.

Charlie bristled at being treated like part of the fan club, but he stayed focused. DeShaun looked at Charlie with upraised eyebrows, his large brown eyes looking simultaneously bored and alert. DeShaun was dressed as he had been in school, in a red hoodie, baggy gray carpenter jeans, and a gray baseball cap with a red lightning bolt on the front. Hats were expressly forbidden in school, but rules never seemed to apply to DeShaun.

"No, no," Charlie said, painting a nervous smile on his face. "Uh, Robin asked me to come get you. She's not taking the bus, and wanted me to bring you to the grove for some reason."

"Okay, okay, baby girl is fast! That's blazin', that's blazin',"

DeShaun said, excitedly. "Well, take me to your girl." DeShaun cocked his hat at a forty-five degree angle and adjusted his clothes and jewelry.

DeShaun was the typical player type, Charlie surmised. He was a year ahead of Charlie, but had come from the same elementary school, having once lived on Charlie's street. His father was an attorney and his mother was chief engineer for a local government contractor. DeShaun carried the demeanor, speech, and dress of a kid who had grown up in "da hood," but in fact had grown up in a million-dollar house in one of the newer developments in the area. DeShaun was about as "hood" as Charlie was, with the primary difference being Charlie still played with radio-controlled cars, and DeShaun played with girls' affections.

Fools like DeShaun are the reason hip-hop is dead.

Charlie led DeShaun out the back doors that bordered the shop classes, to where a small grove of pine trees stood near the school. The grove was part faculty smoking area and part make-out territory during those times there was no faculty around. As soon as the duo hit the line of trees, they ran into a dark, wooden fence, standing seven feet high.

"Yo, when they put this up?" DeShaun asked. "That's whack, they trying to keep kids out the grove?"

"It's okay," Charlie said, holding up a small key he had just thought up, "I have the key." For fun, he made the key look like his sword.

Charlie stuck the key in a door in the fence, and turned till it clicked. Next to him, he could see DeShaun rubbing his hands together, excited at the prospect of privacy with the pretty girl. Charlie pushed the door open with a satisfied smile.

"She's all yours," Charlie said, gesturing for DeShaun to enter with a sweeping hand.

DeShaun rubbed his hands together one last time then took a hop-step and virtually danced through the open door. As soon as he stepped through, he was no longer in his own dream, but had entered Charlie's. Charlie had correctly surmised the best way to reach DeShaun was to concentrate on the last place he was when he had strong emotions. That would have been the time when Robin had decided to be his girlfriend, at school. From there, it was a small thing for Charlie to start remembering his own dream, and bring that dream world back from his memory. Charlie, as has been noted before, was a very smart kid.

DeShaun's red hoodie had become gleaming, silver-colored armor that was covered by a red silk cloak with the emblem of a lightning bolt on it. The gray jeans were likewise the bottom half of an official suit of armor. He wore no jewelry, but was carrying a beautifully jeweled sword.

Shoot.

Even in Charlie's dream, DeShaun was fancier than he was. And he was a freaking knight for crying out loud. So far, this wasn't going exactly as Charlie had hoped. Nonetheless, Charlie figured he would have to go through with the plan. Either he would be happy, or Robin would. If it were she, well then that would have to be good enough. Charlie was dressed as he had been in the dream the night before, and was holding the same ruby sword. DeShaun, now completely immersed in Charlie's dream, looked admiringly at the ruby, and nodded.

"That's sweet, lieutenant. You think you can get me one of them in diamonds?" he asked.

Charlie just shrugged. He wasn't about to suggest that all DeShaun had to do was think one up for himself.

"Dimple Boy! I was looking for you!" It was Robin, waving from a patch of trees at the base of the mountain they had reached the night before.

Robin squinted at Charlie and the mystery knight as they approached. DeShaun had his visor on, and all Robin could see was DeShaun's dome-shaped helmet with the small horizontal slit for his eyes.

"Hey baby!" DeShaun called out, lifting his visor. "Your boy told me you was waiting for me. Damn girl, you look hot."

Robin looked shocked, followed by angry, and then she grinned, all in the course of about five seconds. Charlie was counting on her believing this was his way of apologizing for being a jerk earlier. She was wearing the same outfit she wore the night before, but this time in silk the color of her hazel eyes. Her hair was back to its normal dark color, and it was wrapped in a transparent red scarf that perfectly matched DeShaun's outfit. Charlie sighed audibly. DeShaun, meanwhile, tried to hug Robin, which proved to be impossible while wearing a suit of armor.

Let's see you get your arm around her neck in that, dummy.

DeShaun leaned over and gave Robin a quick kiss, which made her eyes close and Charlie nauseous. For a second, Charlie was afraid their braces might lock and he would suddenly be in a nightmare, but Robin looked uneasily in Charlie's direction, and pulled back, smiling demurely.

"Can I speak to you a second, Charles?" Robin asked, motioning to

Charlie with her finger. "We'll be right back, Boo," she added to DeShaun.

Charlie threw up a little in his mouth again at the word "Boo" and being literal, held his hand to his mouth while puffing out his cheeks. Robin continued talking to DeShaun, pretending not to notice Charlie's dramatics.

"Go feed my three-horned unicorn, Boo. Her name is Aegis, and she can fly." DeShaun began walking toward the now-visible mare the mention of "unicorn." She had been standing quietly by, but was almost impossible to see against the darkness of the advancing night. Aegis' brilliant golden hue darkened as twilight approached until, as night fell, she appeared to be all black.

"Oh, and be careful, it turns out she's part dragon," Robin added in afterthought.

Hearing the word "dragon," DeShaun stopped dead in his tracks. "Pardon me?" he said, forgetting for a second that he was "hood."

Robin laughed, "Oh, it's cool. She's on our side."

She pulled Charlie aside as DeShaun tentatively approached the tricorn. Charlie watched with some amusement as the tricorn lowered her horned head and pawed the ground every time DeShaun approached. Clearly, it was not enamored with Robin's new boyfriend. Eventually, DeShaun gave up, and went to look for his own horse, which, he announced, as a knight, he surely had.

"So what's going on, Charlie?" Robin asked, pulling her friend by his ermine collar.

"Nothing's going on. What do you mean?" he said in feigned innocence.

"Don't give me that. After all the 'do better' stuff, and your tantrum earlier, suddenly you invite my boyfriend to your dream."

Charlie bristled at both "tantrum" and "boyfriend," and answered, frowning, "Okay, let's be real. You think he's great. I think he's not."

"I knew it!" she said, crossing her arms.

Charlie continued, undaunted. "Which means one of us is wrong. If I'm wrong, I'll apologize and be happy for both of you. Either way, I don't want him to mess up our friendship."

"Okay, I'm not sure I like this, but I'll try," she said after a long pause. "I don't see why I can't be friends with both of you."

Charlie grinned. "I'm sure DeShaun will be your knight in shining armor, and you will have bolth of us," he said, mocking her New Mexico accent.

Robin grinned and stuck her tongue out. Before Charlie could respond, she turned and ran over to where DeShaun was, hiking up her ankle length gown, and tying it in a knot on her right hip, just below the waist of her leather pants. Charlie had to admit, he liked her style.

Just as the last bit of sunshine danced below the horizon, Charlie, Robin, DeShaun, and the tricorn were poised at the foot of the mountain upon which Castle Black sat. They had managed to slip unseen through the territory in which they had encountered last night's dragon. The face of the mountain consisted of sheer vertical rock some three hundred feet high. Surrounding the rock on all sides was a dense thicket of barbed vines on which grew black flowers with noxious fumes. Only two people could fit on the back of the tricorn, so they were faced with the choice of leaving one behind, or finding an alternative way up the cliff.

To this point, Robin and DeShaun had been treating the excursion as if it were a walk through the park. They flirted, held hands, and walked Robin's pet tricorn, mostly acting as if Charlie were not there. Charlie walked ten feet behind them, ignoring the pair and looking for signs the dragon might be returning, or a path that would lead them to the higher elevations. They could make out the dark silhouette of the castle against the dimming sky, and could occasionally make out activity — small dots circling at its perimeter, but could find no way up the mountain. Charlie wondered aloud how the castle dwellers got supplies up the mountain.

His reply was giggles from the lovebirds, and a "Chill out, dude" from DeShaun. Charlie gave DeShaun a look that would have melted his armor had the older boy had the courtesy of looking at him.

"Chiggity check yourself before you wreck yourself, fool," Charlene surprised Charlie by responding in his head. Charlie, impressed, thought he might need to find a new name for his emotional side.

Charlie felt the rock face, searching for small cracks that would make handholds. It was cool and smooth against his palm. He had never tried rock climbing, but had read up on it on the internet earlier in the evening, and was willing to give it a try. Just as he felt a thin crevice around four feet up, they heard what sounded like a flock of eagles all screaming at once.

Charlie and Robin immediately went on alert, with Robin's bright eyes searching the night sky, and Charlie retrieving their weapons. He handed Robin her shield and long spear as she scoured the now dark, moonless sky. Robin grabbed both articles without as much as a glance at Charlie, who proceeded to check the harness on Aegis, the tricorn.

"There!" Robin whispered, pointing just above the horizon, due west.

"What? What y'all looking for?" DeShaun asked. His voice quivered and he followed his companions' eyes as they scanned the dark sky. Just visible was a long silhouette framed against dim purple clouds. It was the dragon, and he was home.

"Dragon," was Charlie's single word reply.

DeShaun lifted both eyebrows and looked from Robin to Charlie and back.

"You mean that real? I thought you two was just doing some Dungeons and Dragons kinda shit. What we supposed to do with a damn dragon?"

"Kill it," Charlie said. He barely looked at DeShaun, and instead started hacking away at the barbed vines behind him. If there were to be a battle, they would need a lot more legroom than they had currently.

Robin had turned and faced her boyfriend at his outburst, her mouth forming an "O." A large black bird fluttered overhead, catching Robin's attention. *"You know what Mommy always says about trouble,"* the raven said to her, speaking in clear tones. *"You don't know what a man is worth until he faces down fear."*

Robin pulled Charlie aside. "Did you make it say that?" she asked.

"Huh? No," he answered.

She left him, her eyes still on the bird, and approached DeShaun, placing her hand on his chest, "We have to fight the dragon to get to the castle and help Charlie's great grandpa."

"Hold up. We supposed to slay dragons and shit to rescue some old dude from a castle?" DeShaun said. "You two are tripping."

"Why are you talking like that DeShaun?" Robin asked, using her most soothing tones.

DeShaun, seeing her smile fading, smiled broadly and said, "Sorry, baby, I just get all worked up before a fight. We'll do what we gotta do."

Robin beamed then looked over at Charlie with a "See, I told you so," expression on her face. It was not gloating, Charlie noted; it looked more like relief than anything else.

Robin kissed DeShaun on the cheek. "So you'll help us?" she asked.

"Sure," DeShaun replied. Charlie did not think he looked particularly sure.

Before Robin could kiss DeShaun again and make Charlie finally vomit up his dinner, there was another ear-piercing screech, followed by a horizontal flash of white, ice-crystallized air. The dragon was moving fast, and flying in an erratic pattern. They could make out its aerial maneuvers by the trail of cold air that burst from its lungs. A thunderous roar followed, along with crimson flames that started in an organ fed by flammable secretions from its digestive system.

The dragon climbed, did a 180-degree turn, exhaled cold air then dove at a steep angle and discharged flames. The pattern would repeat — climb, twist, fire, climb, dive, cold — for a solid five minutes. It was in pursuit of something like a brand new F-35 after an enemy fighter. Whatever it was after was fast and small. None of the three kids, all peering in the sky with hands above their eyes, could make out the target of the dragon.

Finally, the dragon seemed to slow, and let out a screech and a burst of flames that arced at least a hundred feet in the air, illuminating the night sky like a flare. There, flying at them at breakneck speed was a very small pink dragon dressed in black from head to toe.

Hannah had returned, and she was moving as fast as her little bumblebee torso could go. At first glance, the kids thought she might be attacking them, and Charlie instinctively jumped on Aegis' back, stood upright, and pulled out his ruby sword. If the little dragon meant them harm, Charlie meant to separate her rose-colored head from her shoulders.

29 – CROUCHING CHARLIE, ANGRY DRAGON

"Wait Charlie! Give her a chance!" Robin called out.

Charlie lowered his sword, but did not climb down. Hannah's panicked expression was visible now. She wasn't attacking; she was flying for her life.

Charlie, seeing her wide-eyed terror, laughed, and sat down, hugging Aegis before sliding off. The tricorn had responded to Charlie's every movement, adjusting her body position to keep Charlie steady. It was as if the tricorn and Charlie had become one being.

When Hannah approached to within ten yards, she began windmilling her wings backward. The effect was much the same as one would get by raising a car's convertible top at fifty miles per hour. The wings became vertical in the onrushing air, and sent Hannah tumbling in mid-air, tail over fire breath, careening towards the group of kids below. All three kids dove for the ground, while Aegis deftly lifted herself aloft at the last second, allowing Hannah to bumblebee herself underneath. Hannah bounced off the hard rock face of the mountain with a high-pitched "Oof!" and landed in the single patch of briars that Charlie had not yet cleared.

Robin and DeShaun rushed over to see if the little dragon was all right. Charlie stayed back, still unconvinced of Hannah's intentions. He eyed the group, his hand on his sword.

"Pooh balls," puffed Hannah, standing and brushing barbs from her black turtleneck sweater, "that didn't go at all like I had hoped." She was panting, and as she did, the air around her glowed red with her exhalations. "Did (puff) you see (puff) me get in (puff) a few licks there? (Puff, bend to the knees.) (Puff.) I think I got him once."

DeShaun and Robin just glanced at each other. No one had seen anything but the big dragon.

"Uh, yeah," Robin said cheerily, "Yay! You rocked!"

Charlie just shook his head. "Not that we aren't glad to see you Hannah, but what are you doing here? You kind of abandoned us last time, you know?"

Hannah lowered her head. "I'm sorry about that. I got scared. It's been a long time since I faced ..." Her voice trailed off. She looked up at Robin with misty eyes. "But then I was at school, and, uh, I felt bad for just leaving you like that. So that's why I'm here, and why I have on my tough clothes."

She pulled at the hem of her sweater and twisted her mouth as if to fight off dragon tears. "My daddy gave me these clothes. They make me feel brave, like him."

Robin walked up and hugged Hannah then introduced her to DeShaun as her "Boo." Charlie finally actually threw up in his mouth and made a sour face for the second time today.

Aegis made a sound that was suspiciously akin to laughter.

"Are you okay, Charlie?" Hannah said, a mischievous grin on her face.

"I'll live," he said, looking at Robin. "Just been feeling a little nauseous all evening."

Robin rolled her eyes. She walked over to Charlie and poked him several times in the arm. "You are such a pain," she said.

"Yeah, I love you too," Charlie answered. It did not sound nearly as sarcastic as he had meant it to sound. Audible sarcasm, as opposed to the in-your-head kind, took a lot of practice.

Robin's eyes got huge with Charlie's declaration, but she remained silent.

"Look," Hannah stated, looking at each of the three kids, "you guys still sure you want to get inside Siri's castle?"

"Whose castle?" Charlie asked.

Hannah met Charlie's stare. Her voice sounded deeper and more confident. "Siri. That's the Overlord's name."

"You've met him?" Robin asked.

"Yes," Hannah said. "A long time ago. But that's a long story." She brightened, adding, "Maybe instead of fighting big dragons, we can have a picnic, and I'll tell you all about it." When Charlie and Robin only stared, their arms folded, Hannah's posture sagged. "We're going in the castle, aren't we?" she asked.

Charlie and Robin nodded. DeShaun looked at Robin, and sighed at her response.

Hannah continued. "I can lead you there."

"Thank you," Robin said.

"There are dragon guards outside the castle walls that protect it from anyone who makes it up the mountain, or tries to get there with a flyer," Hannah said, indicating the tricorn.

"What happens if we get inside?" DeShaun asked.

"Inside there are all kinds of terrible things that guard the castle, Hannah said. "The old man will be in the tower. Our only chance will be to try and sneak in without being seen." She frowned at DeShaun. "Not sure shiny clothes were the best choice."

DeShaun blanched. He opened his mouth to speak, but caught the determined look in Robin's eye, and sighed once again. Charlie wanted to giggle.

"My daddy led a group in once, but we were caught. Only two dragons made it out." Hannah stopped, and wiped away tears, which hit the earth, and quickly boiled away..

"I'm so sorry," Robin said, putting her arm around Hannah. She quickly jerked it away. "Holy crap you're hot!"

"Sorry," Hannah said. "We dragons run hot when we get emotional."

Robin was blowing on her beet-red arm, and was not listening.

The dragon continued. "I remember the passage my daddy told showed me. I can get you in, but if we get caught, we're dead. We won't be a match for the castle's terrors."

DeShaun looked like he might faint, but stood fast.

"Can we trust you to stay this time? I mean, why would you risk yourself for us?" Charlie interjected.

Before Hannah could respond, the group heard a thundering cry, and a heated blast of fire-fueled air roiled in their direction. Instinctively, Robin spun the shield she carried on her back, holding it in front of her. DeShaun and Charlie, who had been standing close by her, managed by sheerest luck, to be protected by Robin and her shield. Fire followed the hot air and hit the shield, spreading around the group like an aurora during an eclipse. The force of the blast pushed the slender girl back two feet, but DeShaun grabbed her by the shoulders and held her in place.

Hannah, who had been behind the group, launched herself, and flew away from the large dragon. Charlie watched, assuming she was about to bolt once again. Instead, the little dragon circled around the larger one, and began blasting it with her own bursts of fire from behind. Although the dragons could exhale fiery cannonades from their own fire-producing glands, the delicate fur and skin made them sensitive to external heat. Another dragon could burn them — even a small one. During their long march the night before, chatterbox Hannah had disclosed that fire-breathing was originally only used for mating displays, before a sudden reduction of their natural habitat caused their behavior to include to territorial battles to the death. The dragons' skin had not yet evolved a strong defense against their own fire.

The attack on the large dragon was enough to make it bellow in rage and pain. It whipped around in midair towards Hannah. The little dragon did a surprisingly deft barrel roll, avoiding the blast of supercooled air the dragon blew in her direction. She then stalled, as the big brute's inertia carried it past. This took her under the large dragon's underside, and she blew a white-hot stream of fire along its entire belly. Although small in stature, Hannah's fire was hotter than the larger dragon's; her flames extruded in a small laser-like stream that could easily cut the toughest flesh.

As Hannah's flames tore through the large dragon's armored plating, the group on the ground could see that her foe was green, and smaller than the goat-hunting dragon from the previous night. Its features were identical, except the fur on its coat was a solid green, the result of generations living in the evergreen forest from which it came. In addition, on its head were two very sharp horns, identical to the ones that Aegis had over her traditional golden unicorn horn. Aegis, as Robin had guessed, was part evergreen forest dragon (on her mother's side).

"That's a different dragon," Charlie shouted, pointing. "That means there's more than one, could be many. We need to get going."

"Already on it," Robin yelled back, grinning. Aegis had responded to her non-verbal signals, and was bent over at her side. Robin grabbed the mane with one hand, and pulled herself on the tricorn. "Come on!" she shouted, reaching for DeShaun.

Charlie allowed himself to feel anger for the briefest of seconds. Robin had chosen, not wisely, but too well, he told himself.

"*Stupid Shakespeare class*," Chuck complained.

Charlene, to the contrary, loved Shakespeare.

As DeShaun and Robin launched in the air, Charlie paced back and forth on the ground.

I've got an idea.

On the ground, he was useless, but if Hannah could now fly like a jet fighter then Charlie needed to be a fighter pilot. He whistled, waving his ruby sword to attract Hannah's attention.

The flash of red from the sword caught Hannah's eye, as she was flying away from the green monster. Seeing Charlie, she veered right, heading in his direction. Aegis and her two passengers were charging from behind the green dragon's left side as it closed in on Hannah. Sitting astride Aegis, Robin had the long spear in her left hand, and was holding the shield to Aegis's side with her right. DeShaun was sitting behind Robin holding tightly onto her waist with his eyes clenched.

Although Hannah was flying as fast as she could, the large dragon, fueled by anger and pain from its torn underbelly, began to close on her. She began a series of zigzag maneuvers, narrowly avoiding the green dragon's alternating fire and ice bursts. Each blast was closer to Hannah. If one hit her directly, the force would almost certainly have knocked her out of the sky. Aegis remained in hot pursuit, but was slowed by the added weight of her two passengers. Just as it looked as if Hannah was about to become a very small dragon kebob, Aegis, now within thirty feet of the dragon, gave out a low bellow, reared back her head, and let loose a burst of flames a foot wide and forty feet long.

The force of the exhalation caused Aegis to rear up in mid-air, knocking the shocked Robin into DeShaun, and DeShaun was sent tumbling over Aegis' back. At the last second, he grabbed the tricorn's beautiful tail, and there he stayed, hanging on for dear life. Robin meanwhile, was laying flat on her back across Aegis' broad torso.

The blast from the tricorn hit the green dragon in its tail area. Part of the flame, in a twist of unfortunate luck for the dragon, entered its … nether regions, and burned through part of the dragon's colon. The great beast let out a mighty roar of pain, and went tumbling into a cluster of nearby trees. There it lay, blowing cold air up its butt as hard as it could.

Hannah, in between bursts of terribly insensitive giggles, used the opportunity to land and pick up the clapping Charlie, who was jumping up and down like a lunatic. As Charlie calmed himself long enough to climb on Hannah's back, he hugged her tightly, and leaning in, kissed her on the cheek.

"I have to ask," Charlie said, as the pair took off, "no offense, but yesterday you flew like a bumblebee. How come you can fly so well now?"

Hannah giggled, "Thank you, I think. The truth is, I don't fly very well unless I'm excited. You should feel my heart pumping."

"I bet your dad would have been very proud you," Charlie said softly.

Hannah's big puppy dog eyes were wide with excitement. "Thank you," she smiled in her dragon smile way.

Charlie held her tightly and the two soared higher, trying to catch up to Aegis. The tricorn was headed toward the mountain with Robin now sitting upright and shouting encouragements to DeShaun who was still hanging onto Aegis' tail.

"How's the view?" Charlie asked as they pulled along DeShaun. After looking at DeShaun for a few seconds, Charlie asked, reflexively, "Dude, are you crying?"

"No," DeShaun lied. He gave Charlie a nasty look, and asked if he could get a little help. Egged on by Robin's giggles, Charlie and Hannah flew behind and under DeShaun. As they reached him, Charlie pushed DeShaun up by the feet, and he landed on Aegis' back, this time facing the rear of the tricorn.

"Poor baby," Robin said, reaching behind herself to pat DeShaun on the back.

"We need to head there," Hannah said, pointing to an area very near where Charlie had cleared the brush earlier. "That's the entrance to the tunnels that lead up to the castle."

The group began flying to the spot, but slammed into a malodorous wall of ice-cold air. The air was filled with the now familiar rotten flowers and ammonia smell from the dragon's breath. The blast hit Robin on her left side, away from the shield, and she spilled over the side of the tricorn, falling the fifteen feet to the hard ground below. She landed on her shield, which absorbed most of the impact from the fall; still, landing on her stomach winded her. Robin lay still and silent below.

"Robin!" Charlie shouted, fearing the worst. He didn't know what happened if you died during a dream, but he didn't want to find out. The stench of the dragon's breath had been so strong that Charlie's eyes were watering and the tears were crystallizing in the frigid air. It looked as if he were crying pearls of ice for his fallen friend.

"Hot air!" Hannah shouted in a warning. By now, they had figured out the large dragons always alternated hot and cold air as the two different organs fully recharged themselves between blasts. This had the secondary effect of creating currents of superheated and rapidly cooling air that created the thunder that often accompanied a dragon attack. The combination of sound and the fury of fire and ice created a mindless, chaotic panic that had been known to stampede entire populations of otherwise intelligent beings into running blindly off cliffs.

A huge blast of orange flames erupted from a green dragon with a mane of light brown hair that was flying above the small group of warriors. It had no horns, and was at least seventy feet from head to tail. It was a male of the species Charlie had first spotted upon entry into this world the night before. Without the protection of Robin's shield, the group was hit by the full fury of the great beast's flames. Charlie and Hannah went down first, badly singed from head to tail, but otherwise intact. Hannah was scorched the worst, and appeared to be in shock. Rather than attempt to re-board the shaken little dragon, Charlie ran to where Robin lay, his clothes smoldering in the night air.

In the sky above, DeShaun had managed to turn himself the right way on Aegis' back, and was attempting to rein in the angry tricorn.

"Down! Down, you stupid damn horse!" DeShaun was yelling, pulling at the tricorn's reins, and trying to force a landing.

Instead, Aegis, despite burns to her head and chest, flew forward, heading for the large dragon from behind. She was taking care not to get in the beast's line of fire. The dragon was heading for Robin. Charlie was holding Robin's shield with one arm, and the slender girl with the other. Robin was longer than Charlie, so it was all he could do to keep her protected behind the shield.

The dragon blew an icy blast at the duo, attempting to freeze and shatter their weapons. As it bellowed another blast of its private inferno, Aegis hit it from behind with her own salvo. The attack hurt the large dragon just enough to send its cannonade of fire sailing over crouching Charlie's head. The dragon bellowed, enraged, whipping its tail with the force of a howitzer, and cracked several of the tricorn's ribs. Aegis and Shaun went tumbling ten feet to the ground.

The monster dragon rose high in the sky, let forth a tremendous high-pitched screech, and entered a dive, heading for the group. DeShaun, who had limped up behind Charlie and the now-awake Robin, was holding his sword nervously in front of him. The dragon bellowed fire, with Charlie holding it off with their shield. The dragon hovered in front of the kids, raising a cloud of dust and ashes with its fanning wings. It was belching fire, and trying to smash the shield with its tail.

"DeShaun, kill it with your sword!" Robin yelled.

Before he could move, the dragon blew an incredible blast of cold, making the shield brittle. It then belched fire, knocking them down.

"One more like that and we're dead!" Robin said, standing back up, the shield in front of them.

As the dragon sucked in a huge gasp of air, preparing for the kill, DeShaun turned, and began to run in the general direction of anyplace else.

"Wake up! Wake up! Wake up!" he yelled, disappearing into the forest.

Charlie had an idea. "Let the dragon freeze the shield then drop it," he said to Robin. "When I say 'now' raise it."

As expected, the dragon blew a torrent of supercooled air, turning the shield into a smooth, round sheet of ice. As directed, Robin dropped the icy shield. Immediately, with a triumphant roar, the dragon inhaled, and blasted a focused stream of fire directly at the pair of warriors.

"Now!" Charlie said, rushing forward. He lifted his ruby sword, and focused the thin blast of the flames, which penetrated the sword like sunlight through a magnifying glass. The heat energy formed what looked like a laser light of concentrated fire. Robin lifted the frozen shield, reflecting the energy off the mirror-like shield. The heat energy bounced back at the dragon, piercing its armored underbelly. It fell to the ground in a thundering heap.

Charlie snatched Robin's staff, and charged the dragon. As he approached the dazed beast, he planted the staff firmly in the hard earth, launching himself on the great dragon's chest. He drew his ruby sword, poised to slash its throat. His face was contorted with rage and determination. Boiling pale yellow blood oozed from the beast's chest. It was hurt, and helpless. One thrust from Charlie's ruby sword would end its life.

"Mercy," the beast rumbled in a deep baritone voice.

"You showed us none, why should we?" Charlie said, the sword still in both hands, raised above his head. Charlie had never killed anything, not even in a dream, but he didn't think his doing so now would be a problem.

"Well, for one thing, I know something you need to know," the green dragon replied, its voice quavering.

Robin walked up to the dragon, having retrieved her long staff and pointed it at the dragon's heart.

"What do you know that we care about?" she asked. She was still looking at the forest into which DeShaun disappeared.

"That you're headed for a trap," the dragon replied.

30 – THE NATURE OF THINGS

Robin and Charlie looked at each other. Charlie lowered his sword, but still held it firmly in both hands. "Go on," he said.

The great dragon, its confidence growing, spoke in deep, hushed tones. "Your little dragon friend works for Siri. You are being led to your death."

"That's not true!" Hannah yelled from behind them.

Robin frowned at the large dragon, and shook her head. She drew back her spear, preparing to shove it into the dragon's throat, and kill him.

The green dragon's gray eyes grew wide, and he spoke rapidly, his voice sounding like an adolescent boy's, "Dude, wait! Seriously! Why do you think I'm here?"

"He's lying," Hannah said to Robin, her small hands extended. "He's working for Siri, not me. We need to go, now!"

"What's your hurry, little dragon?" The large green dragon sneered. "Afraid you've been exposed as a traitor?"

Hannah blew a short burst of flames in the larger dragon's face, causing it to wince. She looked at Robin then Charlie. "He knows we're here. We have to go now!"

Robin turned back to the large dragon. "I'm not buying this," she said. "Hannah is my friend, I can tell."

"You mean like he was?" the large dragon said, pointing to the trees into which DeShaun had fled.

A pained look crossed Robin's face. She glanced again at the forest, and lowered her spear. She turned to Hannah, then back to the large dragon. "I don't know what to believe," she said.

Hannah stared at Robin, and her eyes narrowed into slits. "You two are just as stubborn now as you were the other night with the old man. I am tired of this game, and I am especially tired of children," she said.

Robin's expression grew taut. "What other night? We just met you last night."

Hannah launched herself in the air. "Idiots!" she said bitterly. "Siri is going to kill you both." Hannah launched herself in the air. "When he does, don't call me. I might even help him."

"Wait!" Robin called out.

"If you're too stupid to see I'm trying to help you, you're a waste of my time," Hannah snarled in answer. She turned, and flew off toward the forests whence she'd come.

"I don't believe it," Charlie said. "She freaking flew off again!"

The large dragon spoke. "Beware those who offer themselves as guides. They will promise dreams, and dreams will be your prison."

Charlie raised his sword again and held it to the dragon's throat. "Not now, dude," he said. "I'm not in the mood. She may be a coward, but I really liked her."

"She's not who you think her to be. She is not a dragon," the large dragon said. It smiled, and added, "And she is not a rabbit."

The dragon looked Charlie steadily in the eye. Charlie lowered his weapon, and Robin, following his lead, did so as well. "She's Abner?" Charlie asked.

"One of her many names," it said, nodding. "She has traveled the Stream for a great while, and know its ways well."

"Exactly who is she?" Robin asked.

The large dragon did not answer, but looked away. Charlie raised his sword, sticking the tip in the dragon's neck just far enough to draw a trickle of blood. The dragon sighed, emitting a noxious cloud of hot gas. "A nobody — one of Siri's minions," it said, frowning.

Charlie jumped off the dragon, and onto the ground. "How is my G'pa Joe involved in this?" he asked.

"He's bait, but it is you Siri wants. You are the One, and he will do anything to keep you here. You must leave the Stream, and never return."

"I am The One?" Charlie asked, incredulous.

"Dude, please. You ain't Neo," the dragon said, once again sounding like an adolescent boy.

"Auntie Em, I don't think we're in the Matrix anymore," Robin said absently.

"What stream are you talking about anyway?" Charlie asked.

"This dream, all dreams, and beyond, all are known as the Stream."

"That's a dumb name," Robin said, and threw a rock into a nearby river. She sat in the dirt on the riverbank, and stared at the multi-colored water.

"Hey, I didn't name it," claimed the dragon. "I guess they call it that because there's a ... thing ... that flows among all the dreams."

"Consciousness," Robin said, not looking up. "The 'thing' is called a consciousness."

The dragon looked up at the high peaks, and then spoke in soft tones. "Siri would kill me if he knew I was talking to you."

Robin looked at Charlie, but said nothing.

According to legend, told the dragon, there would be "One who would find the path." The Stream was said, from its distant inception, to be an "in between" place. In between what, no one exactly knew. The Overlord, and Stream travelers like him, had come to believe it to be the place between dreams and reality. The Overlord intended to control the Stream, and thereby come closer to control the world beyond.

"Control the dream, influence the mind, enslave the spirit," was the dragon's explanation.

As one would expect, there were few who could travel across dreams. Of those who could, most were merely observers, or, at best, could interact with, but not influence others in the dream world. A rare few could travel within the Stream and manipulate the dreams of others. As far as anyone knew, only Siri, the Overlord himself, could make even minor changes to the Stream.

That is, until a boy not yet twelve caused worlds to collide with one anguished cry. Like Robin, the Overlord had felt the death of that young world. It was one he had designed. The pair had his drawn his attention. The power to make worlds collide, or change stars into smiles tends to get noticed, in even a dream world.

"So what is this 'One' I'm supposed to be?" Charlie asked, between skipping stones across the rainbow river.

"Not you, both of you. At least that's what Siri thinks." The dragon had eased its body in the river, allowing the water to soothe its wounds. "The legend is there would be One, who was as two halves of a whole."

"Yin and Yang," Robin offered. She was listening, but appeared bored.

"Yeah, whatever," agreed the dragon. "Anyway, this One is supposed to be the key to the path between worlds. Siri wants that power."

Charlie fixed his gaze firmly on the dragon. "Wait, you're telling me he thinks me and Robin can somehow control the dream world and the real world?"

The dragon shrugged. "Something like that." Robin tilted her head in response to the seemingly insignificant gesture.

"That's nuts," replied Charlie.

"Whether you are really the key or not doesn't matter. What matters is he thinks you are."

"Which means? Robin questioned.

"Which means he wants to either catch us, or kill us," Charlie finished.

"Either one, pretty much," the dragon said. There was little emotion in its voice.

"To be honest, this all seems silly to me," said Charlie. The situation they found themselves in was devoid of logic — at least the kind of logic in which he found comfort. So, by very definition, he found it to be a world of foolishness. "Why would anyone care about being king of the dream world? Just go tell this Overlord guy we're not interested. He can be the One, or the king of the dream fairies, or whatever the heck he wants."

The dragon shook his head. "Not that easy. See, this place is like a drug. It gives you whatever you think you want. A lot of people have tried to leave, almost none do — at least not alive." Its demeanor had changed noticeably, and it no longer seemed very dragon-like at all. "He would never believe you'd leave and not come back."

"Dream crack." Robin was speaking in-between gnawing at her cuticles. "By the time folks in here realize they've been dreaming, they can't get out. Or, you get powerful in here, and then you take the power with you when you wake up." She stopped talking to focus on picking loose polish from her fingernails.

The dragon looked at Robin with its mouth sagging open. "How did she know that?" he asked Charlie, his neck straining downward as he half-whispered in Charlie's ear.

"She doesn't really know how she knows. She just seems to know how this place works." Charlie yelled in Robin's direction. "Not in advance though, that would be too helpful! Just *after* bad things happen."

"Deal with it, Dimple Boy. I'm a dream genius, not a fortune teller."

"Dragon, if we can change dreams, we can undo whatever it is this Siri guy is doing, right?" asked Charlie.

"Right," the dragon replied, nodding. "If you two are the One, that means you can not only get in people's dreams, you can get to Siri."

"I still don't get why you think we're the One," Robin said to the dragon.

"Not me, Siri," it replied. "You keep merging your dreams like they're one thing. When you enter each other's dream, it changes."

Charlie thought of how fluid his dreams with Robin were, even from the start. He had even wondered who had been dreaming whom. "I get that," he said. "Like the tricorn."

"You share dreams, and the history in this place changes, yo," the dragon said, no longer even trying to sound like a dragon. "Before you, there was no such thing as a tricorn. Now there's a whole race of them, and they are part dragon. Somehow, I'm even related to them now." The dragon stood up in the river, and walked to the riverbank. It began shaking itself like a wet dog, and drenched Robin and Charlie. The dragon, now standing at its full height, was oblivious. "People wake up, but the dream remains. Instant history," it said.

Robin, who was wringing river water from her hair after being soaked by the dragon's impromptu shower, stopped and stared into the distance, a smile growing on her face. "So when I decided it would be cool if tricorns were part dragon ... "

" ... Suddenly I'm a three-horned flying horse's uncle," finished the dragon.

Robin grinned excitedly.

Charlie's reaction, however, was quite a bit more subdued. He began pacing. "Who is Siri?" he asked.

"Nobody has a clue," the green dragon answered. "All we know is he's real, not just here in the Stream."

Robin thought a bit, and then interrupted, "So if Hannah/Abner works for him then you think she was trying to take us to him?"

"I'd bet my life on it," the dragon said. "Whoever this Hannah is, they're a traveler like you, and they're somebody close to you."

"How do you know that?" Charlie asked.

"The closer you are, the easier it is to walk in your dreams," was its reply. "That's why Siri hasn't found you yet. He can't really ... feel you, except here."

"What about my G'pa … Joe Tettleton? What about him?"

The dragon's voice softened, and it looked down. "If he's here, he's lost. Be sad, say a prayer if you do sort of thing, and then leave, and don't come back."

"Like all those little kids," Charlie said, his voice trailing off.

"I don't know nothing about little kids," answered the dragon.

Robin looked directly at the dragon for first time since he began speaking. "Let me know when you decide to get to the truth." She yawned, and turned her attention to the multi-colored river before her.

Charlie scowled. If Robin thought the dragon was being untruthful then he did too. "If this is true, why would you tell us all this now after trying to kill us?" he asked.

The dragon tilted its head to the sky, and emitted an ear-shattering bellow, followed by a bright stream of fire that wilted the surrounding brush. Charlie instantly drew his sword, but sheathed it when he noticed that Robin had not reacted to the dragon's exhibition. The dragon turned its head to Charlie, and spoke. "When I found the Stream, I felt powerful — a terrible fire-breathing dragon." The dragon sniffed, exhaling a warm puff of smoke. "What a joke."

Charlie looked from the dragon to Robin, as if she were a lie detector. She normally seemed attuned to anyone near her, but he now found her to be unreadable. Frustrated, he looked again at the green beast, coming as close to eye-to-eye as one can get to something so enormous. "Who exactly are you?" He asked, squinting.

"He's just some kid dreaming all of this — like us." It was Robin's voice, and a statement, rather than a question. Charlie turned to face Robin again. She was throwing hunks of meat to a school of two-headed fish that watched her from the river. She caught Charlie's eye, and smiled. "Piranha with a head at each end. I'm calling them Feedme Biteyous."

"Did you do that?" the dragon asked Robin, fascinated. "Cool!" There was no trace of ferocity in its voice.

To Charlie, the voice sounded familiar. "You're really just some kid?" he fumed, as realization set in. "Then why the heck did you attack us?" It was one thing to fight dragons. It was a different thing entirely to be dragged into a pointless fight with another kid. He disliked fighting — but he hated having his time wasted.

"Out there, I'm nobody — a thirteen-year-old 420 geek with bad teeth. I figured I could maybe take out three loser rich kids, and make myself feel like a winner for once. I should have known better." The dragon slumped to the ground, its expression troubled.

"Figures a stoner would be a dragon," Robin mused. "Must be something about all the smoke."

"We aren't rich kids, dude. Neither one of us," Charlie corrected, scowling.

Robin began looking at the dragon in earnest. As she studied the creature's sad eyes and its bowed body language, her demeanor shifted from apathy to interest and finally to her usual empathy in the course of only a few moments. She nudged Charlie, gently urging him to silence. Seeing pain, her habitual nurturing had begun to reemerge. Her eyes shifted from a dull gray to a warm hazel. Charlie, seeing this, found his tension easing.

The dragon continued to talk, as much to itself as to the kids. "He promised me I'd be powerful, but now I'm just a loser in a dragon suit."

Robin walked over to the dragon, and placed one hand on its leg, which was as thick as a tree trunk. "Who promised you?" she asked, stroking its soft green fur.

"Siri, but he's like a pusher. It's all a lie. When I saw the little dragon, I guessed what she was up to, and decided to stop her."

"You could have killed us," Robin said gently.

"Trust me, you'd like that better than being caught by Mr. Personality up there," the fire breather said, indicating the castle on the mountaintop. It stood, shook its immense body, and threw back its head, eyes to the now-rising sun. "My name is Willie — Willie Green, dragon breath extraordinaire, and I'm tired of never being one of the good guys." With no more than a thought, Willie transformed into a normal, pimply-faced teenage boy.

Charlie stood, mouth agape, while Robin studied Willie's face. "I don't think we've met," she said.

"Uh, he's Willie — class bully for life who goes to our school — Green," Charlie said, wisely leaving off the green teeth part. He turned to Willie and added, "No offense."

"None taken. I kind of like the title actually," Willie said. "Now wake the hell up. This has started to get boring."

Charlie opened his eyes, and he was standing on his bed, holding the lamp from his nightstand in both hands.

"Toto, I think Kansas is about to get very weird," he said, lying back down. "God, I hope I don't dream about Oz next," he said, quickly wishing he could take the thought back.

31 – THE SHAPE OF THINGS TO COME

"Gawd Reyna, do you think you two can stop flirting long enough for me to finish the stupid painting?" Robin sighed, while Reyna continued blowing flutters of air against the nape of Charlie's neck.

"We aren't flirting, Mercedes." Charlie defended, his voice a booming baritone.

The tall, buxom Robin eyed him narrowly. "That was a pretty quick answer, buddy boy." That he was scratching his neck did not help his defense.

Reyna lay back against her seat and laughed. She turned to Charlie, tousling his curly hair affectionately. "We are totally flirting, sweetie," she said. Charlie's only response was a deep blush that bloomed crimson through his caramel skin. His obvious discomfort only made Reyna laugh harder. Reyna turned to her sister. "I love that he calls you Mercedes when you've gotten on his nerves. Just like Mommy."

Robin gave her sister a puzzled look, and was met with a smile.

Charlie watched her, and recognized the look. Something felt wrong to Robin, and she couldn't figure out exactly what. It felt wrong to him to, for that matter. He tried to remember how long Reyna had been visiting, when Robin had begun this latest portrait. He had memories, but it was full of holes and unanswered questions. He knew he had been with Robin for a number of years, but couldn't seem to remember any of them.

"Reyna," Robin asked as if reading Charlie's mind, "remind me exactly how long you're staying with us, and why you're here? That is, if you can stop teasing my husband long enough to answer."

She called me husband. That can't be right.

Reyna smiled and blew her sister a kiss, which Robin instantly returned. "Well, I just thought maybe you two needed a reminder about the meaning of family," Reyna said.

"What do you mean?" Robin asked, wiping paint on her tunic. "I adore my family. I adore my husband." Reyna leaned over and kissed Charlie on the back of the neck, making him squirm. Robin responded by throwing an unused brush at her. "Not as much as you love him, apparently." Reyna burst into another round of raucous laughter.

"Do you know why we're here again, hermana?" Reyna asked.

Again. Charlie was more confused than ever.

"Yeah, I'm trying to paint a stupid family portrait."

"Right. And how is it going so far?"

"Terribly!" Robin complained, smiling.

Reyna continued. "So, we're family, right? And you adore us?"

"Reyna, I swear to God if you don't shut up I'm going to paint a mustache on you." Reyna responded with a third burst of laughter. "Sit up Reyna!" Robin bellowed. "Now you've ruined the wrinkles in the backdrop, plus you've got the two monsters going again." Robin threw up her hands, set the brush on her easel, and rushed over to fix her scene for the fifth time in about an hour.

Reyna only laughed harder. And, to Robin's dismay, whenever Auntie Reyna laughed, so did the two kids, who were now rolling on the carpet and ruining their once-perfect hairstyles.

"You are such a pain," Robin said. She then kissed Reyna on the cheek.

"I love you too," Reyna replied.

Reyna blew kisses at her niece and nephew, who were alternating between giggling and bobbing and weaving, trying to read their mother's eye color. Green eyes meant they were in big trouble. "No se preocupen, mi hijos," Reyna soothed. "Her eyes are hazel. We're safe. She loves this."

"I do not. My eyes are totally liars," Robin said, adjusting her backdrop. Charlie, also noticing her eyes, tried to kiss her on the cheek, but she shrugged him off. "Go away, traitor. I have one green eye for you, buddy," she said, feigning annoyance. When he attacked her cheek for a second kiss, she did not object. "You're still about 56 million demerits in the hole, buddy boy."

Charlie shook his head. "No matter what I do, I fall deeper in demerit debt. I'm like a love sharecropper."

"That's right. That's why you're stuck with me for life. You owe me, Dimple Boy." She poked him repeatedly in the side until he sat up straight. "Now please stop wrinkling the backdrop, honey," she said, kissing him on his forehead.

"Mommy," called three-year-old Chance's small voice, "I thought I was Dimple Boy." His arms were folded, and he did not look happy.

Robin looked at him, her face wrinkled with confusion. Then, as if a light switch had been turned on, she brightened, and kissed the boy's dimpled cheek. "You are baby. Your daddy wishes he was as cute as you." Chance beamed, and Robin resumed fixing her backdrop.

The "backdrop" was in actuality a hand-sewn gold lamé bedspread that lay over the antique sofa that served as the centerpiece of Robin's makeshift studio. As she fussed over details, Charlie's eyes took in the room. It featured a two-story cathedral ceiling that provided a sense of immense space in what was actually a small room. One wall was covered with a floor-to-ceiling brick fireplace, from which roared a fire that constantly threatened to lull the entire gathering to sleep. Robin's easel was flooded with indirect light from an enormous window overlooking the Chesapeake Bay.

Above them, the high ceiling was dotted with skylights from which were draped translucent cloths of muted burgundy and olive that complemented the hand-sewn drapery on the windows below. The detail of the tapestry was exquisite, each decorated with yellow thread which, from the floor, appeared to be abstract patterns, but which were actually the names of deceased family members that would "always smile down on the family." The burgundy ceiling tapestry cast the entire room with a faint red tint from the sunlight. The room was littered with lamps, some on furniture, most on the floor. The lamps cast the entire room with a pale yellow fluorescence. With the daylight easing into twilight, the studio itself seemed afire, with flames that burned bright red in the day, now dulling to a muted yellow.

"Some room, huh?" Reyna asked Charlie.

"Yeah, it's … nice." He met Reyna's hazel-eyed gaze, and added, "Where exactly are we?"

"Well, this used to be your family room, but you gave it to Robin as her studio for her last birthday. You only use this place on weekends."

"Uh, oh, okay." Charlie was whispering. "Um, I don't seem to remember that — or anything else, to be honest. Y-you're Reyna?"

Reyna grinned, and gave Charlie a peck on the lips. From behind, Robin plucked Charlie on the ear. "No lips, you two," she said, though her words sounded more like laughter than scolding. "You guys are so in love, it's ridiculous."

"That's right," Reyna answered, not taking her eyes off Charlie. "We're both in love with you."

As Robin returned to her easel, Reyna filled Charlie in on more details. She told him though he had given the family room to Robin as her space, she soon decided she could not work without her "people" surrounding her. Most of her work was painted in the "red room," which gave it a distinctive feel that outsiders could not mimic. It had made the two of them quite wealthy, Reyna disclosed.

"I'm rich? Cool!"

"Well, not just from the painting," Reyna said. "You two have another little venture going that brings in the big bucks."

Charlie cocked his head, trying to remember any of this. He drew a blank.

"Would you stop with the stupid 'I'm solving a puzzle' look, Mr. Patterson?" Robin managed to yell, despite having a paintbrush between her teeth.

"Sorry," Charlie answered. The room smelled peppery, and sweet, mixed with cinnamon or cloves. "What smells so good?" he asked.

"Some homemade scented oil that your wife mixed up. She won't tell her *only sister* what's in it," Reyna added, raising her voice at the appropriate time.

"Deal with it. We artists are secretive," Robin replied.

In response, Reyna stuck out her tongue. She then amused herself by kissing Charlie on his neck again. Charlie felt himself blushing, trying desperately to ignore Reyna's huge eyes, and the shoulder-length curly hair that was tickling his cheek. He had kids, two, apparently, but couldn't remember having been kissed by a pretty girl before.

Heck, I don't even remember being kissed by an ugly girl. When did I get married? It was all too confusing.

Robin rushed over to the two, frowning. She quickly extended her hand toward the pair on the sofa, and Charlie shut his eyes and winced, preparing for the inevitable slap. Instead, Robin re-wrinkled the bedspread that Reyna had once again disturbed.

"You can stop flirting at any time, you know," she said, looking sideways at him.

"I-I'm sorry. I-I don't know what to do," he stammered.

Robin frowned at him, and continued working on the bedspread. "Oh, I don't care, silly. It's just Reyna. I'm just pulling your chain." She looked at him with a somber expression. "Can't you read me yet?" She moved to reposition the two kids, whom had begun a shoving match. "There," she said proudly, after fully two minutes. "Do not move again for the next fifteen minutes, or I will hurt you both," she said, pointing a sharp finger at her sister and husband.

"Your threats would be more believable if you didn't smile when you made them, little bird," Reyna said, sticking out her tongue.

"Oh that's mature," Robin countered. "Since when do angels flirt and poke out tongues?"

"I never claimed to be an angel, little bird," Reyna laughed. "I'm more the oracle type."

Angel? Wait, yeah. Her sister died. What's going on?

Charlie was more confused than before, but found himself asking a question that even he thought was stupid. "Oracle? You mean like, a database?" Charlie asked.

"No goofball," Robin said, frowning in concentration. "She's the Ghost of Christmas Yet to Come."

Charlie shook his head, and turned to Reyna, a pained expression painted on his face. "God help me, Reyna, I completely understood that."

Reyna gave him a look of mock consolation. "Poor Charlie," she said soothingly, stroking his cheek with the back of her hand. She turned to Robin and wagged a long finger. Her dark curls bounced in harmony with her movements. "You broke my sweet Charlie. He used to be so wonderfully logical, and now look at him. He's, he's all ... Robinated," she said, gesturing with her hands.

"He is," Robin beamed. "It took me fifteen years, but I fixed him. He would've been, like, a scientist if I hadn't rescued him. Now would you please stay still? You know Charlie gets all ... emotional ... when you jiggle around like that."

"I'll have you know, I never jiggle. Not since I died anyway. Besides, it's not my fault your husband loves me."

"Everybody loves you," Robin said, once again setting down her brush. "That's it. I've lost the mood ... " Robin stopped in mid-sentence, a look of surprise coming over her face. She placed both hands on her forehead, began to sway awkwardly, looked at Reyna, their eyes locking in a brilliant blue embrace, and fell to the hardwood floor with a thud.

Charlie was certain Robin had been smiling when she fell.

"Mommy!" her daughter called, worried. "Are you okay?"

Reyna smiled reassuringly, and stroked her niece's long brown hair. "She's fine Reggie, it's just time to wake up. Today's a school day, and she has a bus to catch."

"She's okay, Rocky," Reggie parroted to her brother. "Can she come back to visit me in another dream?" Reggie asked Reyna.

"Sure, baby," Reyna said, hugging her, "but you have to wake up for school soon too."

Reyna turned to Charlie, whose face was a twisted marriage of worry and bewilderment. He willed himself to stand, but remained motionless on the sofa, helplessly looking from Robin to her sister and back. Reyna smiled at him, and stroked his cheek once more. "Sweetie, do you know why I've been flirting with you?" she asked.

"Uh, not really, no," Charlie responded, his eyes still on Robin.

"Because you're letting me. Love, you have to stop being so passive. You are the alpha, the lion. I need you to never forget that — too much is depending on it."

Charlie stopped looking at Robin and turned to her beautiful sister. "I understand," he said. It was not an intellectual, but an emotional understanding. He felt the truth of Reyna's words, and intended to take them to heart. Since hearing Reggie's mention of dreaming, Charlie began to realize that this was, in fact a dream. It was a strange, realistic, beautifully confusing dream, but chimera nonetheless.

"Don't be afraid to love her, little brother," Reyna said, smiling mischievously.

Reyna stood, radiant, beautiful. As she rose, she took the bedspread with her, draped over her shoulders like a shawl. She walked, barefoot, across the carpeted floor with a grace that belied footsteps; she seemed, rather, to float. Her delicate footfalls were precise, and though with each step she stomped towards the floor energetically, her feet barely touched the carpet before rising again. Reyna stepped rhythmically, turning first east then west with each step. As she spun, Robin's son and daughter began grinning and clapping with Auntie's steps, until eventually they could hold back no longer and joined in the silent dance.

Reyna wore only a simple blouse, blue peasant skirt, and the old bedspread, but she was the embodiment of grace and beauty. She was Reyna, but she was more than that — some wordless other that dare not be named, lest it be damaged by such banal things as labels. Her skin began to bleed a brilliant azure light that made Charlie and the children shield their eyes. Reyna had become a lovely blue bird, masquerading as a woman.

"Wh-why are you dancing?" Charlie asked. His face had twisted into a frown.

"We are celebrating."

"Celebrating what?"

"That, I can't tell you, not yet. Besides, it's time to wake up."

"Wa-wake up?" Charlie asked, his confusion and fear growing.

"It's okay, love," Reyna soothed. "You won't even remember we were here. But your heart will remember."

"I don't really understand," Charlie replied. He was frowning.

"I know, sweetie. You are both still so young for this." Reyna paused, and for a brief moment, allowed herself to look troubled. Then with a deep inhalation she declared, "But you and Robin are now the One. That is all you need to know." Reyna turned, looked at her still immobile sister, and blew a solitary kiss. It left her mouth as light, shaped like full lips, glowing a dazzling blue, and nestled lovingly against Robin's cheek. Robin smiled in her sleep ...

***

... and awoke with a start. It was eight in the morning, and she had only a half hour to get dressed and ready for school. Reyna had shown her the dreams again, the wonderful, confusing dreams.

"Possibilities, little bird," was all Reyna ever said about them.

Robin did not really believe them to be true. She had learned long ago not to believe in fairy tales. Still, one thing was certain; she had some boyfriend issues she needed to deal with.

32 – AFTER MATH

Charlie's excitement from the night's adventures lasted exactly fifteen minutes. That was how long it took him to shower, brush his teeth, and hear his parents in a raging argument. He could not tell what they were arguing about, but he didn't have to. By the time he had come downstairs to breakfast, his father had left the house, the door slamming behind him. That troubled Charlie the most, as his dad worked from home. Layla sat expressionless, which Charlie knew was a cue not to ask his mother what had happened. If his insensitive sister was being wary, he knew to consider the morning's events to be an emotional minefield.

"I need you come with me this morning," Charlotte blurted.

Charlie's question caught in his throat, and he nodded head without saying a word.

"We're going to stop by the Senior Center," she added. "Pops is okay, but he's not responding, and I promised to take you by there for a few minutes to see if that gets him going."

Charlie reminded his mother that he had a math test later that day (without disclosing that he had failed to study.) She assured him they would be back by then. They arrived at school at 11:45, having spent almost two hours at the Center. G'pa Joe had been quiet and sullen, and he did not seem to know who either of them was. By the time Charlie reached school, his mood was a perfect match for G'pa Joe's.

This was aided, in no small part, by his mom's revelation that his dad would be moving out "for a while." She did not call it a separation, although Charlie was bright enough to understand that was precisely what it was.

That they were in time for his math test did nothing to brighten Charlie's day. By the time his test ended at 2:05 p.m., he still had not seen Robin, or Willie for that matter. He had seen Jannet, and was even somewhat happy that she was in all but one of his classes. Her voice grated his nerves like nails on a chalkboard, but at least they were familiar nails. He desperately needed something to feel normal.

While Charlie stood at his locker, he was startled by someone poking him in his side — his secret ticklish spot. Charlie, startled, jumped backwards, hitting his head on his locker, causing it to rattle back and forth..

"Ow! Crap!" Charlie said, grabbing the back of his head with both hands.

He was greeted by the sound of laughter, from, of all people, Willie Green. At five foot seven, Willie was six inches taller than Charlie, and two inches taller than Robin, who was standing behind him, giggling through her hand. He was a good-looking, if slightly goofy, acne-faced kid, his flaxen hair cut short with just a shock of longer hair sticking almost straight up in the front. Willie had crooked teeth that had obviously not been taken care of, and he tended to avoid smiling because of it. That, combined with his linebacker physique had created the reputation he had nurtured for years.

Willie stared at Charlie, his long blond eyebrows arched questioningly. "Dude, you really need to watch out. You might hurt yourself," he deadpanned.

Charlie ignored Willie's bad breath and responded. "How did you know that was my weak spot?"

Before Willie could say a word, Jannet peered around his right side, and grinned. "I know all your secrets … Dimple Boy."

Charlie gave Robin an angry stare. This was really not the day for folks to be making fun of him. Annoyed, he pushed his locker shut and started toward his Spanish class. He noticed Robin's hurt expression, and Willie's look, which was something between amusement and annoyance.

"Chill, Dude," Willie said, grabbing Charlie by the arm. Willie's one-handed grab completely stopped Charlie in his tracks. "Jan's just teasing, man. What's wrong with having a nickname? Hell, how'd you like to be called Greenteeth?"

Charlie tried as best he could to look blank. He had a horrible feeling his entire face would be smashed in if Willie sensed amusement.

"Yeah, I know kids call me that," Willie sighed. "I always thought it was cool that you never did."

Charlie felt as small as the mouse he had once dreamed himself to be. It seemed whenever he felt especially trivial, it was always in front of Robin.

"In case you didn't know it, Einstein, girls happen to think dimples are cute. For a brainiac, you can really be thick sometimes." Jannet spoke in her customary tactless way. Pausing, her arms folded across her chest, she added, "You can thank me for the compliment now."

"Whatever," Charlie grumbled. He had no idea which part of Jannet's speech had been "the compliment."

Robin gave Charlie a look with her huge eyes that made him forget he was angry. "I always call you Dimple Boy," she said. "How come you never told me you don't like it?"

"You never make it sound like an insult," Charlie responded, looking at Jannet.

"Nice try Patterson. I gave you your compliment for the year. I won't repeat it."

"I'm sorry, I must have been daydreaming when you were complimenting me. I only noticed you were making fun of my friendship with Robin."

Jannet walked up to Charlie, the tip of her nose brushing his. She was not frowning, Charlie noticed. Her expression was neutral, in fact. Still, she conveyed her displeasure well enough that Charlie had a déjà vu moment wherein he thought he was about to be slapped — twice. When Jannet abruptly raised her hands to her hips, Charlie winced, which made Robin giggle through her hand again.

"Okay, listen up Patterson," Jannet said. "Willie was telling me about this really weird dream he had. He described it to me in detail, even though he never remembered a dream before in his life. Then your friend Robin came up, and she knew his dream — even parts he didn't remember."

Charlie, taking a page from Jannet's book, simply rolled his eyes, turned away, and resumed walking to class. Jannet looked astonished. She ran in front of him, her hands still on her hips.

"I have known you since you were four years old, and at no point have you been even marginally interesting," she said. "Now I hear you're traveling in dreams and flying on unicorns. If you think for a second that you get to do this without me, you are sorely mistaken." She paused and scrunched up her freckled face. "Even if that means I have to be your friend." She frowned, as if thinking of what to say next. Her eyes brightened, as did her expression … then she smiled at him.

She was being friendly, which Charlie found to be annoying. "They're tricorns, not unicorns, and you can spare me the friendship."

"That was uncalled for," Jannet said, her face turning scarlet.

"Sheesh, you two act like brother and sister," Robin said, shaking her head.

"Yeah, I'm thinking they love each other," Willie laughed, and began making kissing sounds. He was interrupted by the sixth-period bell, and made a pained face. "Look, I got to head to my tech class. Jan, you tell him our plan." Willie then turned, and ran down the hall to the industrial arts wing.

"Wait up!" Robin said, running behind him, equally late to her Algebra class.

Jannet and Charlie went into the classroom, and were greeted by a substitute teacher. Señora Hawkins apparently had the flu, and the 24-year-old substitute spoke no Spanish, which made her Charlie's favorite Spanish teacher ever. Class became a free period, the sole bright spot in Charlie's day.

"For the record Patterson, I wasn't trying to make fun of you."

Charlie was stunned that Jannet was still talking to him. They had had an unspoken agreement since the third grade that although they always competed with each other, they never, ever acted like friends. This was as if Iran was suddenly calling Israel and inviting it over to tea. It was just … weird.

"I actually think it's sweet you have a friend who's close enough to give you a nickname. You never let anyone get close to you."

"Yeah, I guess," Charlie agreed. "I got tired of being made to feel weird. It was just easier to feel alone."

"That, I understand. People think because you're good at school that means you're like, a robot, or something. I refuse to act stupid merely to fit in." Know-it-all Jannet was starting to seem like just another vulnerable kid.

Charlie decided maybe now was the time to stop fighting. To change the subject, he started with the obvious. "No offense, but I somehow never pictured you with Willie."

"No, it doesn't jump out at you, does it? Well, he's not my boyfriend. I mean, he's cute and all, but he's kind of a "here and now" type of boy. I think about the future a lot."

Charlie was taken aback that Jannet had even thought of a boyfriend.

"I'm into ideas, and he's into things he can touch. I like him a lot, but we don't really like the same things." She leaned over and whispered. "I'm helping him with his classes. He came to me a few weeks ago and said he wants to do better in school."

"Willie? Wow." Charlie asked. "I thought he just made people do his homework when he needed a better grade."

"He really isn't a bully, Patterson," she said. "If he wants to do better, it's my Christian duty to help."

Charlie knew Jannet was very religious. Once she had invoked the "Christian duty" clause, she was committed. By age six, she had talked openly about having been drafted into God's army. Charlie figured helping Willie Green was the equivalent of being shipped overseas into battle.

"God is very funny, you know?" she continued. "Who knew? Willie is really, really funny. I love hanging out with the big goof."

"Big, bad Willie Green is funny?" Charlie asked, incredulous.

Jannet nodded excitedly. "He's a practical joker. Do you know that rumor he failed, like, three grades?"

"Yeah," Charlie said, not admitting he always assumed it was a fact.

"Willie started that himself. He never failed. It turns out his dad is six foot eight."

"Why would he want people to think he's dumb?"

"Because, people would be afraid of him, or feel sorry for him, and help him with homework. Willie could convince a cat to take a bath. I tell him he needs to do well in school so he can get a job as a salesman and get rich."

"Wow, I had him totally wrong. I kind of had him pegged to be a repeat offender."

"Ha! Just you watch. He'll be class president one day." Jannet's normally somber expression exploded into a broad grin.

Charlie tried to remember seeing Jannet grin before today, and couldn't. The very fact that she did made him start grinning back. Then he started giggling until tears threatened to attack his cheeks.

Jannet frowned. "Are you okay?" she asked. "What's so funny?"

"Just this day. Everything is all mixed up," he said.

"Oh, irony," she said. Jannet was eleven, with the vocabulary and speech pattern of a college freshman.

"Willie is funny, not a bully," he continued. "You are talkative and acting like the cheerleader type. I'm almost scared to know what comes next." He considered mentioning his parents seemed on the verge of a break up, but decided against it. Jannet's parents adored each other, and he did not want her sympathy.

"Look Patterson, I'm not good at touchy-feely stuff, so I'll make this easy, okay? I do not dislike you. If I did, I wouldn't sit next to you every class."

"I thought you did that just to bug me."

Jannet rolled her eyes. "For seven years, Patterson? Really? I'm not insane. Look, never mind. What's important is that I know you guys have this little dream club going."

Charlie looked around and made a shushing noise. He leaned in closer to Jannet. "It's not a club. We didn't even know Willie was there. Robin and I were just experimenting."

"I know. Willie said you guys showed up in his dream. He doesn't know how you do it, but he thinks it's … bad somehow. But he can't remember why when he's awake."

"I remember what he said. The dreams are like we were there for real. I remember every bit."

"That's why you need it to be a club. You can help each other. And I can help too."

"You? How, are you dreaming like that too?" Charlie asked warily. He was on the lookout for whoever might be the Abner character.

"Me? No, I don't think so. I never remember my dreams," she said.

"You're lucky. I'm starting to wish I didn't either," he said.

"I have a great imagination, Patterson, and I love the idea of dreams and walking through a world that links people's imaginations. In fact, I intend to get a Ph.D. in psychology one day, so this will come in handy."

Charlie looked at Jannet's clothes which looked like they had come from an nineteenth century Sears & Roebuck catalog and had trouble believing she was imaginative. He obviously looked more than a little skeptical, because Jannet followed his gaze to her dress and tugged at the sleeves, disdainfully.

"This is not me, okay? My mom is a very conservative Seventh Day Adventist, and she makes me dress like this," Jannet said, almost apologetically.

"My Aunt is Adventist, and she doesn't dress like that. You sure your mom isn't Amish?"

Jannet frowned, and Charlie could just imagine the icicles reforming. But after a few seconds, she stuck out her tongue gleefully. "Watch it brown boy. Remember, I know all your secrets. Do we need to discuss the third-grade sobbing incident with Miss Robin?"

Charlie put both hands together and pleaded, "Oh please, no! I'll never insult your lovely dress again. In fact, I don't know why the Amish don't get the fashion props they deserve."

"That's more like it," Jannet said. Despite a smile, she began chewing on her lower lip, which Charlie knew meant she was nervous. Not many things made Jannet nervous, but she clearly was, her eyes averted. She was quiet for a long time, her silence punctuated with her stealing glances at him. Finally, when Charlie began to wonder if her lip would bleed, she blurted, "I really want in your group, Charlie."

Charlie thought about all the years he and Jannet had spent disliking each other. To him, the idea of their spending time together on purpose seemed like a bad idea.

Jannet, used to observing her silent rival, quickly added, "I know what you're thinking, and you're wrong. I've always liked you — a lot." Then, a deep exhalation later, "I'm really sick of not being your friend, Charlie. It isn't fair."

Charlie was stunned, felt guilty, and then was stunned once more. "I'm sick of it, too." He was surprised to realize he meant it.

Jannet smiled, but otherwise did not pause a beat. "We have a plan. I've spoken to the principal, and he's agreed to let me form a Future Psychologists of America club. You're the newest member. The first meeting is tomorrow after school then we meet every Thursday after that."

"Me? I can't be in a club. I don't have any way to get home."

"*My dad moved out, and he can't pick me up,*" his left brain added.

Aloud, he only said, "Besides, I don't want to be a psychologist."

"You don't have to, dummy. The club is you, Willie, Robin, and me. We meet after school once a week to work out the dreaming ... plan it, you know."

"Oh. Oh!" Charlie was becoming enthusiastic. "But I still don't have a way home."

"You have your cell phone now, right? Instead of playing games, maybe you can use it to tell your mom you joined a club. We can all take the late bus that's for the cool kids who are in activities. It'll take us wherever we need to go."

Charlie knew for a fact that neither he nor Jannet had ever been in an afterschool activity in their lives. It was likely both their moms would see this as positive. Jannet's cleverly picking a future-oriented group title would certainly gain his mom's approval. Besides, this could not have come at a better time. Anything that would keep him away from home for an extra hour would bring welcome relief.

"I'll call my mom between classes. One last thing — how come you get to call me brown boy, but I don't get to call you white girl?"

"Because that would be racist."

"What? That makes no sense."

"It completely does. You are in fact, brown. I am not white. I'm pink with beige spots."

"What difference does that make?"

"'Brown boy' is simply descriptive. You don't want me to call you Dimple Boy do you?"

Charlie narrowed his eyes in response. "How 'bout you stick to Patterson?"

"Yeah, I thought so. That name is property of little Charlie's girlfriend."

"She's *not* my *girlfriend!*" Charlie said, exasperated. He had never had such a long conversation with Jannet, and she could frustrate him even during a short one.

"No, but you like her." She closed her eyes and held up her hand as Charlie started to protest. "It's okay, stop being childish. Look, the prettiest girl in school considers you to be her best friend."

Charlie stopped frowning abruptly. "How do you know?" he asked.

"I just met her today, and she's already called you that twice. If Dimple Boy's her special name for you, be happy. I don't even have a nickname."

Yes you do, Plannet.

He didn't verbalize his thoughts. Instead, he said, "Jan is kind of a nickname." Jannet grinned in response. Charlie did not grin back, as he was now embarrassed. "Is it that obvious?" he asked. "I mean, that I like her?"

"Uh huh. Except to her, apparently."

"Good, she doesn't need to know. Anyway, she loves DeShaun." Charlie spat out the boy's name as if it were a disease.

"Oh, I don't think so, I saw him trying to talk to her after lunch, and she totally ignored him. So then, he got mad and grabbed her shoulder …" Jannet started giggling.

"What? What happened?" Charlie asked. His heart was pounding.

"Mistake. Girlfriend popped him dead in the mouth. Boy ended up in the nurse's station getting iced up. I don't know what he did, but he must have screwed up big time. His lip looks like a flat tire."

"I know what he did," Charlie said, a smug smile creasing his lips.

He got played.

"So your only problem is you're too short for her. Ha!"

Being friends with Jannet the Plannet was going to take some getting used to.

33 – LIAR, LIAR, DREAMS ON FIRE

The remainder of Charlie's day and evening had been a jumble of emotion and activity. His mother was shocked but delighted that Charlie had responded to her news of the separation by finding comfort in a group of kids his age, and gladly gave him permission to join the group. The first official meeting of the Future Psychologists of America group convened on Thursday, and Jannet immediately decided that Robert's Rules of Order should be followed. However, since none of them knew what the rules were, they decided instead, "members should raise their hands like a civilized group."

They then agreed they should have a leader, just in case they needed to make decisions. Charlie had pointed out there were four people in the group, and if they agreed to vote democratically, they could end up tied on everything. Willie pointed out his family had always voted Republican, but they assured him that's not what they meant. No one but Jannet seemed to know he was joking. Jannet quickly picked up on a boys-versus-girls threat, but Charlie really meant Robin and himself versus the intruders, and he considered saying so, but he still wasn't entirely convinced of Willie Green's not being a bully.

To Charlie's surprise, the group voted him the president of the club by a three-to-one margin. Charlie was the dissenting vote. He didn't want the job, but Jannet had pointed out that he was the only one organized enough to take notes. Part of the reason Charlie had maintained good grades in school, she noted, was the fact he would read and take notes on subjects in advance. He didn't study, but that was because he had mostly memorized the material while writing his notes in class.

"How long exactly have you been spying on me, Jannet?" Charlie asked.

Jannet answered quickly. "Since you were four. You're weird, but you're pretty predictable too. Leaders should be predictable I think. But they need us free-spirited types to balance them out."

Willie began snickering, while Robin and Charlie laughed openly. She frowned, and tugged at the sleeve of her dress again. "It's the clothes!" she protested. "These are totally my mother. My style is very artsy — neo hippy in fact."

"You know, a lot of hippy clothes were really very conservative," Robin enthused. "Maybe you can convince your mom you can have your own style and still dress like …"

"My grandma!" Willie laughed.

Jannet and Robin began fussing at Willie, and the room soon turned into a cacophony of insults and giggles.

"Guys," Charlie said, holding his hands up, "um, we only have thirty minutes left, and we still haven't talked about the dreams at all."

"See, that's why we made you the leader," Robin said, her hazelly-grayish-blue eyes shining.

Charlie smiled, and blushed under his light brown skin. He silently thanked his mom for the melanin so no one could tell.

Willie began by telling the group of what he knew of the dreams, most of which he had told them when he was the dragon. Before the three met in the Stream, he had remembered nothing. But now, it was as if some invisible barrier had been breached, and all the dream memories were flooding out. Charlie and Robin had been surprised to find that Willie had been having dragon dreams almost nightly. He was one of many dragon guards of Siri's castle. Willie had rarely seen him, but he was supposedly something of a wizard — a maker of dreams and stealer of minds.

Siri drew in unsuspecting people by preying on their loneliness. Willie compared it to being in the best amusement park or video game you could imagine. The only problem was you were never in control of the dream; you just had to ride it out.

Willie said, "For instance, kids have always been afraid of me. So, I learned to like that. In the dreams, I got to be a big, bad dragon. "

"It gave you what you wanted," Charlie said.

"Yeah, plus somewhere to be. My home life kind of sucks." Willie got quiet, and looked at each kid as if deciding how much he could trust them.

Robin placed one hand on his arm and said, softly, "Go on, we're listening."

"My mom drinks — a lot. My dad left a couple of years ago because he couldn't deal with it. Now she just drinks more than ever."

Charlie looked at Willie, and was beginning to feel less sorry for himself.

"Some days I don't even get dinner unless I go to the store myself," Willie continued. "I even drove her car there once, and no one cared."

"I'm so sorry, Willie" Robin said.

"It's okay, I'm used to it now. It's just that ... most days I feel like any place would be better than home. The dreams gave me somewhere to be."

"Couldn't your dad help?" Robin asked.

"Naw, I think he just stopped caring," he answered. Willie was doing a good job of being stoned-faced, as long as you looked past the deep pain in his eyes. "I got an Uncle Willie, he was always cool ..." Willie stopped, and his eyes glistened for a moment. He inhaled sharply, and continued, all the while looking at the ceiling. "He's got problems, though. We're not sure where he's at."

"Willie, I think you're wrong," Jannet said. "You think you aren't good with people, but you've been getting kids to do your homework for years."

"That's 'cause they are afraid I'll kick their butts," Willie pointed out.

"Willie Green, I haven't seen you fight anybody since the third grade," Jannet said, her hands on her hips for effect.

"Now that you mention it, I haven't either," Charlie said.

"See?" Willie said, pointing to Charlie. "But he still thinks I'm a bully. That's why kids help me."

"It's not why I help," Jannet said. "I help because you're nice, and you make me laugh. Most of the kids just want to belong to your gang."

"I don't have a gang," Willie said, frowning.

"I know that, but your friends think they are your gang." Jannet was relentless. "See, that's the point. You think you aren't good with people, but they follow you around just so they can sit in the back of the class with you and feel cool. I bet in your dreams you're like leader of the dragons or something, right?" Willie smiled a surprisingly sweet, almost shy smile, and nodded. "I knew it!" Jannet exclaimed.

Charlie thought about what both Willie and Jannet were saying. Something was clicking in place, but he still wasn't quite sure what it was.

"Let me think out loud," Charlie said, surprising himself. He generally only did that by accident. "You got trapped in the Stream because you thought you were bad with people. But Jannet thinks you could talk a cat into taking a bath." Willie looked at Jannet and grinned. She looked horrified, and threw an eraser at Charlie, who had not realized it had been a private comment. "Sorry, Jannet," Charlie said, noticing that she had rolled her eyes at him.

Robin added, "So let's say this Overlord guy is evil. Maybe evil works by telling you whatever you want to hear."

Charlie nodded. "My grandma used to always say evil lies," he said.

"The devil is a liar and the father of lies," Jannet offered. "That's from John, 8." The group of kids looked at her in unison. "Hey, it's what we do," Jannet shrugged.

"Cool," said Robin. "If we are dealing with evil, we need somebody from the home team."

"Home team," Willie repeated, laughing.

Charlie could not quite put his finger on it, but he was certain there was more. He remembered the numerous times that G'pa had joked about how old and useless he's become. The faraway look in his eyes had told Charlie that he was not really joking. He was old, but not happily so. He was not well educated, but he was wise, and worldly, and had experienced heartache first hand, and largely defeated it. The sad irony was that G'pa Joe was important to Charlie precisely because he was old. But if G'pa Joe was trapped in the Stream, Charlie reasoned, it was probably because he no longer had to be old — he could be the young lumberjack Charlie and Robin had seen, or the Huck Finn wannabe Charlie had met on the blue river.

Robin interrupted Charlie's musings just as the bell rang, signaling an end to after-school groups. "There's more," she said. "Remember that dream on the bus, when all the little kids went by?"

"Yeah," Charlie said then turned to explain to Willie and Jannet. "We had this dream with a bunch of kids that sounded like sheep."

"They were being herded by these creepy guys in hoods," Robin said.

"G'pa Joe and I saw a bunch more later, in a different dream," Charlie said.

"Are you thinking this Siri person is behind this?" Jannet asked.

"I don't know," Robin said. "But if her is, we need to be much stronger."

"God gives you weaknesses because that's what He wants you to work on," Jannet declared, exiting the classroom.

"Maybe we don't really know what makes us strong," Charlie said, standing to leave.

"Judging by the dreams so far," added Robin, "I'm guessing we're gonna get a chance to learn."

The thought stopped Charlie in his tracks, as his friends' footsteps echoed in the empty corridor. "That's what I'm afraid of," he mumbled, turning the lights off behind him.

34 – THE LONG, DARK ROAD

Joe Tettleton hadn't seen everything in his 85 years, but, as he often said, he had seen most of it. Born in the Jim Crow South of Lee County, Alabama, he had risen from the abject poverty of a third-generation sharecropper to what passed for prosperity in the great cities of the north. At fourteen, young Joe had quit the fields, grabbed his daddy's old suitcase, and headed off to see the world. His trip north had been an adventure in itself, and it couldn't have been more difficult if he'd been a runaway slave. At least then he might have had Harriett Tubman on his side. An ill-schooled, idealistic teenage boy had no business on the road by himself.

There he'd met a young man who called himself Tennessee Toot. It was originally a shortened form of his given name, Toussaint Hebert, but later referred to the tarnished horn with the slightly bent bell from which he managed to coax "heaven's sweet song" for enough coins to eat. Fortunately, Toot liked Joe enough to let him tag along up north. It was a give-and-take relationship, though. Joe would give Toot everything he had, and Toot would take it. But Toot's worldview and dry sense of humor made Joe laugh, and he didn't mind trading half of what little he had for Toot's tips on how to find food and keep from getting killed. Toot was just shy of twenty, old and experienced as far as Joe was concerned, and he could use a big brother about now.

Joe was big, and strong for a kid, but he had learned on his first day out that big and strong is just strong enough to get you in trouble if you didn't know where not to be, or who not to mess with. Joe's daddy had always taught him never to call another man "sir" unless he had earned it. Toot taught him to call everyone sir unless he happened to be holding a gun at the time.

Joe loved his papa, but he had never risen much above the level of indentured servant, so Joe took his advice with a grain of salt. At least Toot had a gold tooth that shone when he smiled like a million bucks. That bit of gold was probably worth as much as anything his daddy owned, Joe figured. Toot's light skin also shone like gold in the Alabama sun, and that had to be worth a bit of something up north as well.

Short, slightly bent, with a walk that looked half strut and half limp, Toot managed to look stooped and humble when those in power gave him their "You best not look me in the eye, boy" stare, while strutting like a prized rooster among his own people. Toot wore his hair slick and conked. He would have been horrified to be seen with his hair any other way. See, he was no longer a country boy. He was citified, and that meant hair that was black, slick, and very good. Well, in point of fact, Toot's hair was red, but one gets the meaning.

"See," Toot would say, "as black folk, it often comes down to hair. We Negroes know our hair is bad, but we keep it in its place, and it don't cause no trouble." Joe thought Toot's hair was just about the finest thing he'd ever seen. Toot was still dressed the part of the city slickster he had been before trouble with another man's wife had chased him temporarily back south. Once in Detroit, he would trade up from his current wardrobe to a genuine Zoot suit with the reet pleat.

But this was not Detroit. This was some other place, one created by fears, hopes, memories. It was a place of dreams as well as ill will. It was precisely as real as one believed it to be. Here, in the Stream, belief was everything.

To G'pa Joe Tettleton it was one hundred fifty miles northeast of Birmingham, Alabama in the summer of 1942. He stood in his oversized coveralls, next to Toot, on the intersection of two unmarked, dusty roads. Toot and Joe had just left one of many two-bit towns, hustling the poor folk for a bit of change. To them, Toot was a city boy, whose clothes were the height of fashion — if a bit dusty and ragged at the hems. If you stood too close, you would notice both he and Joe smelled like two-day old socks from head to toe, and their breath could make a baby cry. But from across the street, if you squinted just right, Toot looked real fine — like a fine, yellow cockroach in a pork pie hat, being trailed by a big brown-skinned hick wearing suspenders and a stupid grin.

They had a plan, these two. With a few bits of labor here and there, and the coins Toot earned with his trumpet, the duo had earned enough for the train to Detroit. The problem was, here they stood, with nightfall rapidly approaching, and there was no train station to be found.

"Now, I knows it was here, big Joe," Toot said. "I swear I took the train right from this spot no more'n three years ago, when I hit Detroit for the first time."

Joe was more amused than concerned. Even as naïve as he was, he had come to realize that not everything that Toot swore to be true could be taken as gospel. "Don't worry none, we'll find it," Joe said. Joe's surety was rattled by Toot's unexpected response.

"Naw, Joe. You don't understand. See that low plain, yonder?" Toot pointed to a stretch of farmland that slid downhill as the eye traveled. "Y'all go round about twenty miles there, and that's where I come from. I know this part of Tennessee like I knows my name. Ain't no way those tracks ain't here. No way at all."

Joe picked up on Toot's nervousness, which gave him pause. Still, this far from his Alabama home, everything was new to him, so he saw no particular reason to fear something as minor as someone tearing up some train tracks. He was no longer a clodhopper in ancient brown shoes handed down from God-knows-who. He had left a nervous country boy, but now he was an adventurer, a young man on his way.

"Maybe white folks tore up them tracks to keep us Negroes from going up north," Joe joked.

"Well, if that's what it is, it was most likely the folks up in Detroit what tore up the tracks. Not all the colored folk who head up there mean to do good."

The sun was rapidly setting in the western sky, painting it with rich purple hues. Toot insisted this was not a place to be caught after dark, so the duo decided to retrace their steps to town, and seek other transport. They followed the same road from which they had come, this time heading due east, away from the setting sun. After some twenty minutes, Toot pulled to a stop.

"Joe, this here's the road we took right? I mean, I ain't drunk or nothin', right?"

Joe looked around, trying to get his bearing. The road looked familiar, but instead of farmlands that bordered a town, there were desolate fields behind them, all tatters, abandoned crops, and ruin. Before them stood rows of abnormally tall wheat, eight feet high, fully twice what it should have been. Joe and Toot turned in all directions, but nothing seemed familiar.

"Toot, I ain't even sure this is the same road we was on when you asked me that question." Joe tried on a laugh, but it didn't fit, so he quickly discarded it.

Toot spun left and right, looking here and there. "Ain't nothin' like it s'posed to be," Toot said. "Since when do folks round these parts grow wheat?"

Joe was taller than the older Toot by quite a bit, but still he sidled a bit closer for reassurance. "What the heck is going on, Toot?" he asked. His voice did not sound fearful, but wary. Even at fourteen, fear was not a familiar companion of Joe's.

"Don't know, Joe, but I knows we best keep walking."

The two continued heading in the direction that should have taken them to town. Although the landscape had changed, they decided that heading in one direction beat traveling in circles. They had barely crossed the Tennessee border, and east would eventually take them to Chattanooga, as long as their legs and shoes held out. The two marched on, past sunset, through the rising of the moon, deep into the Tennessee night. Still, the landscape was disconcertingly unchanged. It was high wheat field, empty pasture ... wheat, pasture, wheat. The trees, though present, were sparse, as if it were perennially a warm winter night in this part of the world.

After traveling for hours, Toot's ungainly walk had begun to take its toll, his slight limp becoming more noticeable with each passing yard. Eventually, he had begun to lag behind Joe — first a step or two, then a yard or five, and finally more than was comfortable for a small man in the dark. "Big Joe," Toot called out. He was whispering, though they had yet to pass a farmhouse, and nary a bird had been seen. Toot was bent at the waist, his right arm extended, waving Joe back. "You is still a young cat, Joe. I can't keep up. I'm gonna' to have to rest."

Joe walked back to his companion without a word of complaint. "Well," Joe said when he had re-joined Toot, "it don't make much sense to keep walkin'. I can't even tell if we're gettin' anyplace." He looked up one end of the long road, and down the other. The dark landscape was overbearingly constant.

"It do all look alike," Toot agreed. "Maybe we should just sleep out here under the stars, and get our bearings in the morning."

"I'm for that. My blisters don't much want to go on anyway."

They made camp, which consisted of improvised beds of broken wheat, and the small bundles of their meager belongings as pillows. It was not their first night with only the moon's pale light for shelter. Within the span of a few mosquito bites Joe was too tired to scratch, Toot was sound asleep, and snoring softly. Now walking for miles on a lonely road would normally have been enough to lure Joe to sleep, but something ... was off.

Joe closed his eyes for one more fruitless attempt at sleep, the sound of late summer crickets buzzing under Toot's snores. From the dying brush that bordered the tall wheat field, he heard a sharp snap. It was not loud, not something that on an ordinary night would have caused anyone alarm.

This had not been an ordinary night, and Toot awoke with a start. He was fully alert, his eyes peering into the dark. For the first time in his young life, Joe Tettleton became afraid. It was not the sound, per se, or the emptiness of the dark night. It wasn't even the strange yellowish tint of the full moon. It had been something in Toot's eyes — a remembering, a fear that had awakened him. There was a — something — out there, and Joe didn't think he wanted to know what it was.

"Is ... is that you out there?" Toot asked. His voice was dry, ancient, broken. It lacked the strong resonance of a man not yet twenty, yielding only the rasping of a lifetime's despair. Toot sounded as if fear had aged him decades.

The stillness of the night was broken by a second sharp snap. Joe recognized it as the same sound the dry wheat stalks made as they broke them for their beds. Someone, something was coming through the field. The happy sound of crickets calling for end-of-season mates stopped at once. A rumbling approached, slowly at first then quickening. Joe was standing, wondering when he had stood up, his fists balled into taut knots. Toot was holding his knife, extracted from its hiding place with the swift skill of a deep-country ninja.

"There!" Toot whispered, pointing to the edge of the nearby wheat field with the gleaming point of his knife. Joe squinted, peering into the moonlit night. "See them eyes?" Toot asked. He moved closer to Joe, or Joe to him ... neither was quite certain which.

In the Tennessee night, through an eight-foot wheat field that should not have been, came the low murmur of machinery, though there had been no sign of man for miles. Peering from where Joe searched for the source of the sound, were eyes, gleaming yellow in the night.

They were not alone.

"Come out of there now, you hear me?" The ever-so-slight quiver in his voice betrayed Toot's brave words. "I ain't playing, boy, y'all come out where I can see you. I will cut you a new one, I damn mean it." Toot's fear was cranking up the adrenaline in his brain, and adrenaline was turning fear to anger. Anger, Joe had learned, made Toot dangerous.

The rumbling sound grew louder, and a brilliant light burst through the murky darkness. The shaft of light blinded Joe, and caused both he and Toot to turn away, as if in pain.

Then there was silence.

35 – UNTIL COMES THE MORN

Charlie peered through the eight-foot-tall grass he found himself in. He had awakened in the Stream, lost in a field with no transportation. After walking for less than a mile, he had come to the conclusion he would spend an entire night's dreaming walking through dark fields. On a whim, he had decided what he really needed was an off-road vehicle that was positively brimming with awesomeness. What he had ended up with was a 1940 's Quad. That in itself was surprising, as he had never heard of such a vehicle. It was the color of dingy sand and resembled a World War Two army jeep with a sloping canvas roof. Charlie was too excited to discover he could drive in his dream world to be disappointed. With lucid dreaming, he was learning, almost anything was possible.

After plowing recklessly through dry brush, he had spotted an opening, and sat idling. While not afraid, some unspoken voice urged caution. Charlie turned off the Willys and waited.

"I ain't gonna say it again there now boy," came a timeworn voice from the darkness. Charlie had spent sufficient time at the Senior Center to recognize the elderly.

Resultantly, as he emerged from the field, he was taken aback to see a short teenager and a huge monster of a boy near his age. The older one was brandishing a knife, while his companion stood in the shadows.

"Oh … oh, I'm sorry," Charlie offered. He surmised they had been asleep, and were startled by his intrusion.

Toot laughed nervously, but did not lower his knife. "What's your name, boy? What the hell you doing out here this time of night?"

"My name's Charlie. I don't really know what I'm doing here." The situation called for honesty in Charlie's estimation. "I was lost and trying to find my way out."

Joe approached Charlie without hesitation, despite Toot's admonitions to the contrary. Joe offered a smile, and a hand already big enough to envelop Charlie's. There was no glimmer of familiarity, still Charlie did not hesitate to return Joe's handshake, offering a dimpled smile of his own. There was something about the big boy's demeanor that appealed to him.

"My name's Joe. This here's Toussaint Hebert, but folks just call him Toot. He's harmless, unless of course, you ain't."

Joe looked at Toot, who lowered his knife just a bit, but made a point to look as menacing as possible. "You still too damn friendly for your own good, Tettleton," Toot frowned. Toot seemed to mistake Charlie's look of utter shock for fear, which, fortunately for Charlie, finally convinced Toot he was harmless. Toot slid the knife back into the sheath he kept tucked inside his waistband, and extended his hand. "Boy, you don't know how glad I am to see you ain't nobody else. They's still Klan 'round these parts."

Joe hushed Toot, and invited Charlie to sit, which he gladly did. Charlie was watching the fourteen-year-old version of his great-grandfather with great interest. He had never seen him so young and powerful. He had seen him at nineteen, and as a man in his twenties. Neither was as impressive as the high-school-freshman-aged Joe, already built like a pro linebacker. If he so desired, Joe could snap Charlie like a twig. Still, there was the same gentleness, the quiet power he had always observed in G'pa Joe.

Toot asked how he had come to be in field, and what was making all the noise as he had approached. Charlie tried to explain, but to little avail, as he did not know how he had come to be there himself. It didn't much matter, as it turned out. Toot heard the word "car" and in a blink, the three of them were driving break-neck down a dark country road with Toot at the wheel.

"Where exactly are we going?" Charlie finally asked.

Toot answered without turning his head. "Chattanooga."

"Like the Choo-choo?"

Charlie meant that to sound like a joke. Instead, Joe 's laughter was a shade mocking. "Charlie boy, you ain't more'n a few minutes off the farm, are you?"

Toot started laughing as well, and Charlie briefly considered being offended, until a hearty slap on his back from Joe convinced him it was all good fun. It was ironic, he decided, being considered to be a hick, given the fact that Joe's southern accent was worlds thicker than he'd ever heard it. Besides, the fact that Joe still called him "Charlie boy" made him grin. They drove on for an hour, following the moon-cast shadows east. For a time, it was jovial, with Joe and Charlie hitting it off like two old friends. Of course, Charlie knew that they in fact were. Joe, as he would in the Center, regaled him with tales from back on the farm — new ones that G'pa Joe's conscious mind had long-since forgotten. Charlie would remember them, and this night forever. Not all for joyous reasons.

As the moon took refuge behind thick clouds, the paved road ended, changing to road. In the distance, barely visible at the horizon, was the low form of familiar dark mountains. The hair on Charlie's neck stood on end. He tried convincing Joe and Toot they should turn back, but Toot would have none of it. Joe watched his new friend's growing ill ease, and gently urged Toot to listen. Toot, happily barreling down the dirt road, did not. Finally, Joe, from the back seat, placed one hand on Toot's right shoulder firmly enough to make him wince.

"Damn, Joe," Toot complained, standing on the brake. "You liked to broke my shoulder."

"Sorry Toot, but sometimes you don't hear so good," Joe replied. Charlie stifled a giggle with his hand. This was the same G'pa Joe he knew all right. Once Joe decided a thing, there was little room for argument.

Toot turned to Charlie, smoothing wild, red hair from his eyes. "So what's so damn important back there you need to see, boy?"

"It's not what's back there, it's what's ahead," Charlie answered.

Joe and Toot sat in expectant silence. "We listening," Joe finally said, since Charlie offered nothing further.

Charlie inhaled. "That's where the Overlord lives." He pointed in the direction of the mountains at the horizon.

Joe followed Charlie's gaze down the road then back. "Overlord? What, you some kind of runaway slave?" Joe threw back his head and laughed, but Toot quickly quieted him.

"Shush now, Joe. What you mean about this Overlord, boy?"

Charlie spoke in soft tones, trying to sound as calm as possible. It was clear neither of his companions knew they were dreaming, and Charlie's truth would resonate of insanity. If he were to save Joe, he would need to be believed.

Joe was in the Stream, and his mind was being drawn to the dark lord. Charlie had fallen asleep, and entered the Stream almost immediately. Without plan or purpose, he found his G'pa Joe. Something was guiding him, bringing them together. At first, he assumed his great-grandfather's mind drew him into his dream. But time had passed, and Joe had no inkling who Charlie was. The looming mountains had re-awakened the quickening fear in Charlie. He had been so engaged in enjoying meeting his great-grandfather as a boy, that he had neglected to get him out of the Stream.

Now he was being pulled deeper in its midst, but not by Joe. The Overlord was luring them all.

Charlie had no way of knowing Toot's real truth. At first, his adventure with Joe was purely a figment of Joe's mind — some misremembered episode attached to a dream. It was Charlie himself that had drawn Toot's mind to Joe's. He had been the bridge to a sleeping, elderly Toot, somewhere on a city street. His old friend Joe Tettleton and their adventures as "Tettaton and Toot" had been merely a passing thought. But Joe's strong memories, aided by the power Charlie had in the Stream, had joined the two old friends' minds for real. Toot could feel Siri, had begun to remember as soon as Charlie arrived. Even the sorry state of his existence had not dulled his ability to see.

There was something in Charlie's eyes, in his voice that rang true to Toot. "Tettleton, I think we need to get the hell outta here. This here boy done give me the jitters."

"Now you both gone crazy," Joe said. "Fine, if you want to go back the way you know is nowhere, that's alright by me. As long as we keep moving, I don't much care."

"G'pa ..." Charlie started then caught himself. "Joe, we really aren't safe. I'm not making this up." Charlie tried his best to explain to Joe that they were in danger, that something had created this place for them. Joe was having none of it. "Look at this place," Charlie said desperately. There's one road, nothing anywhere else, just empty space. And that one road leads someplace you don't want to be."

"What you know boy?" asked Toot. There was fear and darkness in his voice. "You know about ... him ... don't you?"

Charlie looked Toot in the eyes. They were old and tired, even in their present nineteen-year-old form. Charlie did not need to ask to whom Toot was referring. It was in his eyes. He simply nodded.

"I knew I wasn't crazy," Toot half-whispered. He stamped on the gas, but the old Willys didn't move. There was no sound, the engine simply stopped.

"What's wrong?" Charlie asked.

"Guess I drove her too hard. Looks like we walking again."

Joe sighed, and jumped out the back of the Willys. He prostrated himself on the dry grass, yielding, finally to the night. He intended to sleep. From a distance, Charlie began to hear the murmur of distance voices. He looked to Toot, whose wild-eyed look of fear spoke volumes. Something was coming. Something bad.

The two smaller travelers begged Joe to get up. When he refused, they tried to drag Joe down the road. Joe responded with stubbornness, much the way he would respond to most things that tried to force his hand during his life. Charlie, pleading, was tugging on Joe's left arm, with Toot straining, both hands on Joe's right wrist, and his feet practically spinning in place like a tire in deep mud. If the voices weren't coming closer, it would have been comical.

Charlie began calling Joe by his "real" name, G'pa Joe, in hopes that it would awaken him to his dream state. By now, fear and adrenaline had awakened Toot's octogenarian mind, although he could no more wake up than he could make himself actually nineteen again. If they could not convince Joe — G'pa Joe — that he needed to fear, to run, there was no hope.

"G'pa," Charlie pleaded, "you gotta believe me. This is a dream, and you have to wake up!"

Joe, by now, was tired of the game, and easily pulled his hands from each of the pair's arms, rolling over to sleep. "Y'all better leave me alone, now boy," was Joe's intended last words on the subject.

"Toot, what do we do?" Charlie asked.

Toot smoothed out his hair, and took a deep breath. The distant sounds were a gathering rabble now, loud enough for individual voices to be distinguished. Joe was still deaf to them, but Toot ... Toot knew their song, and it was the song of gathering death. Wiping his brow, he smoothed his hair once more. Toot always said he thought best when he looked his sharpest. "Charlie, you need to do something to convince this big lunkhead this ain't 1942. Something big."

Thinking on his feet was never something Charlie had done well. He banged his temples, as a damnable, high-pitched giggle lilted over the high wheat fields, filling the previously empty night with sonorous, gleeful despair.

"Betty Lou!" Charlie shouted suddenly.

"Boy, we don't need no damn woman," Toot said. We need a way the hell outta here."

"Betty Lou isn't a who," Charlie answered, running to the dead Willys. "It's G'pa's one true love." Charlie was at the jeep now, and placed his hands on it, his eyes closed. He called out to Toot, "I don't care how you do it, but get his attention."

Toot thought for about five seconds, pulled Joe's arm, once more, and discovered he was sound asleep. His eyes widened, as through the night, five hundred feet away, eyes appeared, moving in their direction. Toot unzipped his fly, and …

… woke Joe up. It is quite likely that Joe would have killed Toot in his dream state, if the latter had not wisely run toward Charlie, who was standing, grinning next to Betty Lou. She was young, beautiful, and blue. Betty Lou was G'pa Joe's 1957 Cadillac Eldorado convertible with the 365 V-8, and the cherry red interior. G'pa Joe kept a photo of her in his room at the center, in a place even more cherished than that of his late wife.

"Oh. My. God. Betty Lou, baby, where you been girl?" G'pa Joe, speaking in a high-pitched scream, was positively in tears. He was once again lucid.

Before they had the chance to celebrate, a shaft of moonlight crept from behind low clouds, illuminating the road. There, clear as day was a procession of what appeared to be a gathering of the Ku Klux Klan, most dressed in the most garish pink Klan robes hell ever saw. They were in no hurry, with the procession looking like a nightmarish parade.

"What's with the pointy pink hats?" Charlie asked, looking at Joe. He was not overly concerned.

"Them ain't pink hats, son, that's the damn Klan." It was Toot's voice, and he was already moving.

The trio, stuck in a hellish version of the 1940s south, jumped in Betty Lou, and tore out of there in the general direction of the hell out of dodge.

"Betty Lou does purr, don't she?" Joe said, as Charlie and Toot eased into soft laughter. Their levity was short-lived, however. Behind them came the wail of sirens, closing fast. Charlie turned and saw an array of 1940s era police cars and pickup trucks. A coven of pink-garbed Klansmen, some with police badges, filled the vehicles as if they were clown cars. They were hooting, hollering, and shooting wildly at

Joe's car. For a time, the old Caddy held her own, until the road suddenly narrowed. Joe pushed Charlie's head down on the floor, as he weaved to and fro, dodging bullets and curses alike.

An old black and white pulled along Joe's left side, the driver laughing demonically. "Now y'all best be pullin' over, y'heah?" he called, cackling. The driver spoke in the same accent as did Joe, but to Charlie, it seemed to hold none of the same easy charm. This man meant harm. He pulled the steering wheel hard to the right, sending the Cadillac barrel rolling into a clutch of trees. The sound of crunching steel and splintering wood tore the night air, the Caddy's engine choking from a low purr to a pitched whine. Joe and Toot lay limp in the car, which had miraculously come to rest right side up. Betty Lou was little more than twisted metal, the grill of the Caddy smashed toothless into the trunk of a huge oak. Charlie lay twenty feet from the car, having been ejected as the car spiraled off the road. He was conscious, but barely.

As Charlie blinked from the glare of the dozen sets of headlights, he was greeted by the sight of two women pulling Joe out of the wreckage. They were both dressed in nuns' habits. One wore a pink coif, the headpiece normally seen in white under a black veil. Her veil was an iridescent pink, which was offset not by a crucifix and rosary, but by large round rose-colored glasses. The other nun was similarly garbed, with a more-traditional white coif and cap, under a lovely black and gold lace veil. The remainder of the klavern wore traditional Klan robes, except being in varying shades of pink.

The klavern was pulling an old wooden trailer that resembled an antique circus wagon. It was little more than a flatbed, upon which stood a barred cage. In it, however, were not lions or tigers. There was no animal trainer. Instead, the cage was filled with small children, some seated, some standing, all dirty. Their faces were dark with despair.

One by one, the Klansmen removed their hoods, and advanced toward the three boys. The nuns, and all the other's whose faces could be seen, wore white makeup reminiscent of clowns. The Klan, Charlie had no emotional ties to, and did not fear. But Ku Klux Klowns?

Charlie. Hated. Klowns.

The entire group was dressed similarly: all bizarre, all clowns, all oddly beautiful. One, clearly the leader, as evidenced by the words "The Leadur" embroidered in white lace on the back of his magenta robe, stood forth. He began to preach, as the Klowns swayed and called out to the rhythm of his words. He did not preach of God or

Satan, of Good or Evil. He preached merely of nothing, of hopelessness, of dying alone and living to die. Charlie could not stop listening, though he could not make out the words. It was a sermon of the mind, and not the tongue. Charlie tried to speak, to move, but could not. The Klowns placed a pink noose around Joe's neck, and looped the other end over a branch. This was not to be a capture, but an old-fashioned lynching.

As if on cue, when the Leadur, or Siri as he was otherwise known, was finished, the two Klowns pulled the rope and hoisted Joe toward the treetops. Joe's eyes opened from the shock and pain, and there he danced, ten feet up, grasping at the rope in desperation. His fingers bled, but still he danced.

The Overlord removed his hood, and looked at Joe, smiling. In an effete, cloying voice he said, "You really should have just come on your own, and helped me lure the boy. Now I have the boy, and don't need you." Charlie could not make out his features, as Siri, covered in the same white clown makeup as the others, still managed to be in shadows, even in the bright moonlight. Charlie could only make out deep pink lipstick with matching eye shadow, and a clownish pink flower on his forehead, nearly as wide as his head. Evil had a sick sense of humor.

Charlie's anger grew at Siri's mocking, singsong tone. He closed his eyes, and fought against the power holding him immobile. The power was Siri's mind and no one had ever overcome it. Charlie concentrated; sweat dared to run down his cheek, or perhaps, a traitorous tear. His eyes moved to his G'pa Joe, now eighty-five, with bulging eyes. Charlie moved, ever so slightly.

Before Charlie could lift himself from the ground, however, he heard a shrill, off-key cry from the dark night above. It sounded almost like singing.

What now?

Charlie hesitated, but only long enough to notice that the Klowns and Siri had stopped, and were staring into the darkness. Whatever was coming was not of their doing. The knowledge that there might be something more horrific than them took Charlie's breath away.

"Woot! Woot! Woot!" The cry was loud, fearsome, ... and familiar. A second later, several of the Klowns' vehicles erupted in flames. Charlie heard Toot's voice cry out. Again the Klowns turned, their own painted faces now mirroring fear. From above, a thin line of flames lit the night, burning through the rope that held G'pa Joe. He fell to the ground in a heap.

Charlie followed the line of flames to the source, and there he saw Robin, standing atop an enormous brown dragon. She was pumping her fists, and singing, badly. The shrill cry, it turned out, had been her rendition of the theme from "Rocky."

"Woot! Woot!" she screamed again, her fist pumping. She made eye contact with Charlie as her dragon swooped, grabbing three Klowns at once. Charlie shuddered to think of their fate.

In a flash, Charlie was up, and in a dead run. Without any conscious thought, his ruby sword appeared in his right hand, and without slowing, he sliced two Klowns fully in half at the waist. Charlie was a fury of beautiful violence. He was his pack's alpha now, with the heart of a lion and the mercy of a praying mantis — which was none. He sliced and tore, severed and shredded. Those he missed became dragon fodder. Many of the Klowns evaporated into dust as they met their fate. Like the wolves before, most were figments of Siri's mind — most, but not all. Those sorry few who were real would never visit the dream world again.

Charlie turned, and Robin was on the ground now. She was not alone. Charging through the oversized wheat field came — a herd of cows. They had long red hair, wide, sharp horns, and puppy dog faces covered by shaggy hair. They looked like a cross between a bull and an English sheepdog. They would have been adorable, except they were ten feet high, and stampeding toward the remaining Klowns.

"Miss me?" Robin asked, grinning.

"Um, what in the heck were those?" Charlie asked, indicating the cows, which had disappeared in the distance, chasing a large group of Klowns.

"Scotch Highland Cattle. I made them bigger," she said, grinning.

"No duh."

Charlie saw Siri, who was watching, but not reacting in any discernable way. Charlie lifted his sword, and charged toward where Siri was standing, but was met with only empty space. Moving with the speed and grace of a cat, Siri had maneuvered behind Charlie. With one deft motion, Siri disarmed Charlie and caught him around the throat with his strong, bony hands. Charlie smelled sickly sweet perfume, as he stood motionless, Siri's six-inch nails just drawing blood from Charlie's neck.

Robin was busy wielding her long staff against a pair of Siri's bodyguards. Toot was nowhere to be seen. Charlie struggled vainly against Siri's thin armed, vice-like grip. He was coughing, Siri's grip tightening with each exhalation. Siri turned to face Charlie without releasing him. His head turned from side-to-side as if he were deciding whether to purchase an overripe watermelon. Charlie could not speak, but the anger that flashed in his eyes spoke volumes. It was rage, but not fear. He was, finally, G'pa Joe's progeny, and fear would never again be a close companion.

Siri raised his free hand, the long, dagger-like fingernails poised to end Charlie's life. Charlie met his gaze, but did not blink. It was fear he wanted, and Charlie would not give him the satisfaction. Nightmares, however, do not like to be faced. Siri struck, his blow certain to end the boy's impudent life once and for all. Siri looked at Robin, whose dragon had turned her attackers to powder. She was too far away to reach Charlie.

"Come, little girl," Siri called in his creaky voice. "Maybe you can get here just in time to watch the boy die."

In his arrogance, however, Siri had forgotten one old, run-down Toot Hebert, who had lived most his life without having done anything of significance. As Siri moved to plunge his fingers in Charlie's heart, killing him in his sleep, Toot slid his own knife deep into Siri's back. Siri howled, clutching at his wound in agony, as Toot leaned on the knife with all his might. Dropping Charlie to the earth, Siri disappeared with little more than a soft popping sound.

Once again, it was night, and silent, save the sound of late summer crickets. Gone was Siri, gone were the Klowns, and gone was the cage full of children. Also gone was G'pa Joe.

Charlie spoke, his voice a thin rasp. "They've got him. He's my great-grandfather, Toot. I have to find him." Charlie moved to follow the klavern that had dragged off G'pa Joe, but Toot grabbed him by the shoulders.

"You can't help him now, son. All you'll do is get yourself killed." Charlie gave a weak protest, but he knew Toot was right. He was no match for Siri, not yet. "Don't worry none, I'll keep an eye out on old Joe. I owe him that much."

Robin joined them, and placed a tentative hand on Charlie's shoulder. "He's right, Charlie. We'll have to find him another time."

Charlie began to cry, wiping angry tears with the back of his hand. "I failed him again, Toot. I can't let you get hurt too trying to fix my mistakes."

"Look Charlie, I ain't never seen no fighting like you done, except for Joe, that is. You is definitely his seed. I aim to make sure you get the chance to grow up."

Charlie shook his head no. "You hurt Siri, and he's not going to let you get away with that."

Toot looked at Charlie, his own time-hardened eyes filling with tears. "That's okay. I wasn't about nothing before, so it don't much matter what happens to me. You just live your life, and grow up to be the kind of man Joe expects. That's how you can thank me."

With that, Toot hugged first Charlie then Robin, and took off running behind the klavern. Charlie stood for a time, telling himself to follow Toot, to ignore the warning. He did not have the heart, and sat in the dry grass, and wept. Robin sat beside him. She did not speak, and did not touch him.

She simply remained by his side, until dawn woke them both.

36 – INSIDE OUT

Robin awoke on Friday, October 12 with a migraine that made her want to pull her head off. Around 8:00 a.m., when she realized it wouldn't come off, she began to cry. Around 8:15 a.m., she began to feel nauseous. Her mother, having seen this frequently, and having experienced it countless times herself, quickly gave Robin meds, and put her back to bed. Robin had been having migraines on and off since she was six years old, but now that she was in the throes of puberty, they had become both more frequent and more intense.

She spent the morning in bed, and the early afternoon dozing on the couch in front of the television. Her headache medicine made her sleep, and as usual, she had been having disturbing dreams. At 3:00 pm, she was sitting in a warm tub, surrounded by Bratz dolls she had since she was four. At 4:00 pm, she was drinking hot chocolate in hopes that the caffeine would stave off the migraine before the drink made her nauseous again. By 5:00 pm, she was feeling better — well enough to eat — and had switched to diet colas.

Robin's mom warned her against drinking too much caffeine lest she not be able to sleep that night. In fact, not being able to sleep was precisely Robin's plan. She was sick of the dreams — sick enough of them to risk a caffeine-charged rebound headache. She was tired of seeing her sister's accident, despairing of hearing the sounds of Reyna's late night tears, sick from knowing why, but convincing herself that she didn't. Her one blessing was that many times she would remember only the emotion, but none of the details of the dream. On many nights her mind would begin to dream the moment she fell asleep — long before the REM sleep that induces dreams were even possible. In point of fact, many of her dreams were simply memories that her conscious mind had suppressed.

"*You can't stay awake forever,*" her inside voice reminded her.

Robin knew it was true. Moreover, she had already started the cycle of thinking about Reyna, and trying not to. The more she tried to stanch the flood of thoughts, the faster they broke through the dam her mind attempted to build. Since the death of her beloved sister, Robin's inside voice had been increasingly vocal. She'd had negative thoughts as long as she could remember. And, as long as she'd had them, she felt somehow apart from the feelings they conveyed. She referred to those other thoughts as her inside voice, because it was to her as if there was another — someone — inside of Robin — someone who was bitter, easily frightened, distrustful. More recently, since the dreams had started, Robin had begun to feel like her inside voice was no longer content to remain inside. Frequently, the struggle to suppress the voice resulted in a migraine.

The adventures with Charlie had been a godsend. They could explore worlds of their imagination, and there were no horrors to waken her in the middle of the night, making her afraid to go back to sleep.

"*That's how the other kids get hooked in the Stream, you know.*" her inside voice said. "*The big kid said so.*"

"The big kid has a name — it's Willie. Why don't you ever try to think of people by their names?" Robin countered. Unlike Charlie, whose inner debate was a silent, sometimes subconscious battle, Robin often spoke to her inner voice aloud, as though it were another person.

"*Boys aren't people. Boys become men, and you know about men.*"

"Actually, I don't know what you mean, and I don't want to know," Robin said. She put on her headphones, the noise-dampening ones, as if they could somehow reduce the static inside her head.

"*It's time you knew. I hate that you pretend not to know.*"

Robin began to sing, and managed to still the argument with herself. It would not last, she knew that, but for now, she could pretend herself a little peace of mind. For long-lasting peace of mind, she knew she needed help. Back in Albuquerque, she could always count on her friend Becky to be there. She and Becky Davis had known each other since daycare and had sworn to be best friends forever. However, Robin had been calling and emailing Becky regularly, but had gotten no response for over a week. She needed someone who would be there when she needed them, not eventually.

She briefly considered contacting Jannet, who seemed really smart and nice. But Robin had picked up on the fact that deep, emotional conversations were really not Jannet's strong suit.

Back home in Albuquerque, Robin had been immensely popular, with a clique of pretty girls surrounding her, keeping her mind occupied. She was sure, if she tried, she could connect with girls in her school here in Virginia, but she no longer found that to be satisfying. She missed having a sister and confidant. A circle of giggly acquaintances was no substitute.

"*Why don't you call that big-head boy with the dimples — Charlie Brown? You can play Lucy,*" her inside voice chimed in. "*All we need is a football.*"

Robin was surprised because she thought she had turned that part of her psyche off. It was becoming increasingly difficult to silence the nagging voice. Trying would only worsen her headache. "Don't call him that; he's my friend, and his name is Patterson, not Brown," she said. "And I thought you said all boys were bad."

"*Well I was right about DeShaun, wasn't I? You know what boys want, and it ain't friendship.*"

"Then why would I call Charlie, if he doesn't want to be my friend?" Robin asked aloud.

"*You need someone to talk to besides yourself, dummy. Plus, we can both laugh when you pull away the football.*"

"Just go away," Robin said bitterly. She was starting to cry in frustration now.

Robin realized perhaps her other — she could not bring herself to use the word "self" — was trying to tell her something. Since Charlie had first shown up in her dreams, she had a good feeling about him. It was trust, and she could not remember ever having trusted a male before. Maybe even the bitter part of her who nagged her from within even trusted him a little. She decided she did need to talk to him, and hoped he was allowed to talk to girls on a Friday night. Charlie had been distant for almost a week, sullen even.

Robin went to the family room, and sat next to her mom who was attacking a bag of microwave popcorn as if it were made of the most decadent chocolate. Her mother, Gloria, was the spitting image of her daughter, save for shorter hair and fifteen surplus pounds. The sound of her mom's lips smacking in concert with the glisten of spittle on her licked fingers churned Robin's stomach again. She had spent half the day alternating between riding her sheets in a horror storm, and hugging the only available port — the white ceramic one that had demanded the contents of her stomach as tax. Robin forced herself to look away from her mother's vomitorious snacking, and focus on the task ahead.

Gloria was watching what her father used to refer to as "The Weepy Women's Network." He had perfected the art of barbed cynicism. It was an art form in her dad's hands, and one to which Robin's inside voice had apparently decided to take an apprenticeship. Experience had taught Robin to wait until a commercial break if she had any hope of getting a positive response from her mom. Cable television had become her closest companion. On this cold autumn night, she wrapped herself in a velvety blanket, a bowl of comfort food at hand, and prepared for an intimate evening with Mr. Sony, her one true love.

Robin must stalk her mother's attention if she was to be successful. She would sit in the big recliner, just out of her prey's line of sight, in her mommy blind, and await her opportunity. At some point, the mommy would wander close enough to Robin to be engaged. There would be an instant when Mr. Sony ceased his wooing, and the mommy's attention would be exposed to Robin for the pounce. At the appropriate time, in between adverts for tampons and Midol, Robin saw her chance.

"Mommy, why is it your station seems to think that the only thing women do is have periods?" Robin asked, hoping to get her mom's attention through charm.

"That isn't true baby. They also think we clean, get headaches, eat chocolate, and go through menopause."

"Still, shouldn't there be more commercials about investing or stuff like that?

"No, those women are watching the news. Apparently women who emote don't think about their future," Gloria replied, smiling. She patted the burgundy sofa cushion, inviting Robin to join her. "So, what do you want, mi hija? I know you well enough to know if you try to make me laugh, you probably want something."

"Um. I don't know, Mommy. Okay, I lied. I do know."

"Uh huh," Gloria said, smiling.

"Anyway, there's a boy in my school, we're just friends, you know. It's not like a boyfriend thing, he's like a brother."

"He's like, 'a brother,' or he's like your brother?" Gloria teased.

"Well, both as a matter of fact," Robin giggled.

"Good, brothers rock. Mine always watched out for me."

"Yeah I know, especially Tio Rueben. He acts like the sister police."

"Well, honey, he is a cop."

"Oh yeah. I didn't think about that." Robin cuddled up to her mom, sliding under the blanket she habitually used when watching TV. "So, my thing is, I want to talk to Charlie — my friend — but I don't know if it's okay to call him at night. I did once before, but I don't want to get him in trouble."

"Well, why are you calling?" Gloria asked, her eyebrows rising.

"Uh, I just wanted to talk about the, um, psychology club. Plus it's his birthday this weekend, and I want to make sure he's not going to spend it alone. His mom and dad have been having problems."

"Oh, that's a shame. It must be hard."

"Yeah, I think it is," Robin said, "even though he won't really talk about it. So, I just wanted to see how he was."

"Is he having a party? Everyone should have a birthday party."

"No, I don't think so." Robin worried about him, and wanted, *needed* to help. "Not everyone likes birthday parties."

"Why would anyone not like a birthday party? I just don't understand that at all. Well, maybe you can take him to the movies or something for his birthday."

Robin considered reminding her mom of the horrible last birthday Reyna had, but decided that would just lead to another argument. Her mom seemed to be dealing with Reyna's death by keeping all the feelings locked inside like a dormant volcano. Robin didn't want to be there when the eruption finally happened. Mount Gloria was likely to erupt all over anyone nearby, and Robin did not want to end up a scorched shell like those poor people in Pompeii. Besides, she liked the movie idea. Spending a day with her bud could be exactly what both of them needed, and agreeing with her mom was imminently safer.

"I would love to do that!" Robin enthused. "But do you think his mom would let me? Charlie says she's pretty protective."

"Tell you what, baby." The next commercial, I will call his mom and see what we can arrange."

True to her word, the very next commercial, which given the state of cable television, turned out to be exactly ten minutes later, Gloria called Charlotte Patterson for the first time. The two mothers, much to Robin's relief, seemed to hit it off right away. They were both hard-driving career types, and both recently single moms, for very different reasons. Charlie, it turned out, had neglected to mention his dad had moved out "temporarily," though Robin had deduced as much.

Both women also had beautiful, brilliant kids who seemed very lonely and in need of a good friend (from a good family, of course.) After a forty-minute conversation, during which both Charlie and Robin paced back and forth in their bedrooms and sent each other "Is your mom smiling?" and "I think they like each other," text messages, Gloria knocked on Robin's door.

"Okay mi hija, your mama has worked her magic," Gloria announced, beaming.

"What? What? Tell me," Robin really needed some good news.

"First of all, I really like his mom. Her name is Charlotte. She's part-owner of a small engineering company in Hampton." Robin gave her mother the blankest expression she could muster up. "My company has done business with them. They are a good outfit," Gloria added, unfazed by the zero-emotion stare.

"O-o-okay," Robin said, trying to stay patient. "And this means what?"

"This means that he comes from good people, so I'm not so worried about my little girl being around him alone."

"Oh. Oh! That's good then." Robin was grinning now, her bluish-gray eyes beaming.

"Those eyes. Your daddy gave you the most beautiful eyes."

"Mo-om-my! Please, I'm going nuts! All Mexindirishfrenchican girls have eyes like this. What did she say?"

"You and your sister with that stuff," Gloria said, shaking her head and smiling. She was torturing her daughter on purpose of course, because, well, that is one of the most fun parts of being a parent. Nine months of pregnancy's discomforts followed by twelve laborious hours of agony needed to be repaid slowly. Seeing Robin literally bouncing on her mattress, however, apparently made Gloria feel sympathetic and nostalgic. "You used to bounce in your little jumper like that when you were six weeks old," she said.

Robin fell over backward on her bed and groaned. "I'm adopted. That's it. You found me while on vacation in Mexico, and took me home with you."

Gloria picked up a pillow and smacked Robin in the head with it. "Smarty. She said she thought it would be a great idea if you took Charlie to a movie."

"Yay!" Robin yelled, energized. Her phone buzzed a simultaneous, equally enthusiastic response from Charlie.

They were to go to the mall, and have lunch first. Layla would be hanging out at the mall with friends, and would look out for the two younger kids.

"I'll drive you to the mall tomorrow at 11:30," Gloria said. "Charlotte said, and I agree, that her teenage daughter didn't need to be driving you guys."

"Mommy, you rock!" Robin exclaimed, giving her mom a big hug.

"Claro que sí. But I'm not finished." Gloria smiled and lay down on Robin's bed. She was back in torture mode.

"What? Mommy, come on, you're making me crazy," Robin said, frowning anxiously and bouncing up and down once more.

"*No, you were crazy before she came in,*" her inside voice sneered in her head.

"You and Charlie are really close, huh," Gloria said, her light brown eyes shining.

"Yeah we are, Mommy. He and I became friends really fast. It's funny, 'cause we're really different."

"Different is good. Sometimes we need someone who is strong where we're weak. Your father and I couldn't have been more different."

"*That's for fricking sure!*" Robin's inside harpy shrieked.

"So Charlotte and I have decided that we should all be closer. You need family here, baby."

Robin hugged her mom tightly, and squeezed the parasitic voice right out of her head for the rest of the night.

37 – IT'S ONLY A DATE IF SHE SAYS SO

Robin showed up at the Mall looking gorgeous. From her demeanor, it appeared she didn't have a clue she looked gorgeous, or at the very least, she was good at hiding the fact, if she did. She was dressed in black and white, her favorite, with a simple black button-down top, open at the neck. She wore a short, mid-thigh skirt, off-white, and overlaid with black lace. She also had on a black leather jacket that stopped at her hips; the sleeves were slightly rolled up, coming to her mid-forearm. She tied it together with black stockings and her oft-present calf-high black combat boots. The only deviation from her aesthetic was an oversized black purse she carried on one shoulder. She wore her hair simple and straight, hanging down her back except for long bangs that covered one eye, and a rebellious lock of hair that hugged her chest.

For jewelry, she wore a plain choker made of a thin strip of black leather, and matching bracelets — three of them — on her right wrist. On her left wrist, she wore the turquoise bracelet her sister Reyna had given her. Robin's small hands were covered with what looked like weight-lifting gloves with the fingers missing, except they were made of a soft black lace. Her fingernails were a brightly painted turquoise, the color of her bracelet — the shock of color standing out like neon against the black. And, if Charlie could have seen them, he would have found the nails of her cute bubbly toes were painted alternately the same turquoise and black. She had told her mother that it mattered what color they were, even if only she knew. She would feel mismatched, and somehow, people would know from her expression.

She didn't consider herself to be Goth at all; rather, she was "cute, with an attitude."

Gloria responded by saying she looked more like, "Cute, on a date." Robin vehemently disagreed.

As usual, she was walking with her head down and her eyes averted, meeting no one's gaze. She recognized Charlie only by his red high-top sneakers. These, however, were leather, and new. She looked up when she saw them, grinning at him with one eye and a dazzling smile full of braces. Charlie, to her surprise, was dressed in black jeans, offset by a gray button-down shirt that he wore loosely over a white wife beater. He had on no jacket, but wore a black leather vest and sunglasses on the top of his curly head.

Robin pretended not to notice how adorable he looked. She hoped.

Charlie showed little reaction when he saw her, but he did cast his eyes toward his sister. That was code for, "You look great, but I'm not going to let Layla know how glad I am to see you." One of Robin's very favorite things about Charlie was how easily she could read him. His mouth was silent, but his eyes were being all flirty again.

He very politely shook hands with her mom, and followed the appropriate protocols for ensuring she did not leave believing him to be a deviant of some sort. Robin was delighted that her mother left thinking Charlie a "polite young man" and Layla, "quite mature for her age."

Robin's grin widened when she noticed how Charlie was looking at her. Although she didn't want the attention of many boys, she didn't want not to be noticed either. Being a girl was a complicated, delicate balance. She reached in the large bag and pulled out a tightly folded package. She handed it to Charlie, with a simple, "Happy birthday," and a shy one-eyed smile.

"Thanks," Charlie said, adding, "you didn't have to get me anything. Besides, my birthday isn't until tomorrow, officially."

"I know, but I wanted to. It isn't much — I kind of got it secondhand. I wanted to give it to you in private, without a bunch of people watching."

"And that's why you chose the mall."

"Shut up!" she said, laughing.

Charlie opened the bundle, and held it open in both hands. It was a jeans jacket, a lovely find from her favorite secondhand store, in a size slightly larger than he wore. On impulse, she had dyed it black. The jacket's front pockets were stressed, and there were small worn areas in discrete places on the jacket itself. On the jacket's back, which was delicately hand stressed, but not torn, there was a beautiful hand-painted rendition of the green dragon that Charlie had defeated, Willie Green's alter ego. Its head was thrown back and mouth open defiantly. Below, as a sort of coat of armor, was a ruby-red sword that was crossed with a shield that looked remarkably like the one Robin had carried in the dream. On the shield were the words "Dream. Believe. Do."

Charlie was awe-struck. "Where did you find this? It's awesome. Thank you!"

"The jacket I got from "Found Treasures," which is my favorite store. I kind of made it my own. I don't like giving people stuff that I buy — I'd rather make something myself."

"Did you paint this dragon and stuff?" Charlie asked, gently caressing the dragon.

Robin swept the hair from in front of her eyes, and met his gaze with a growing confidence. "Yeah, and I stressed it myself too. I love doing stuff like this."

"Wow, you should sell this stuff," Charlie said. He gave her an awkward hug, made even more awkward by her height advantage over him. "Thank you so much."

Robin smiled, and said a painfully soft, "You're welcome."

"You should make one of these for yourself." Charlie said.

Robin shrugged noncommittally. "I dunno. That's yours; I wanted you to have something unique."

Charlie grinned and put on the jacket. "It matches my clothes."

"Yeah, I don't know why I made it black." Charlie was staring at Robin's feet. "You like my boots?" she asked, to change the subject. Too many compliments about her art made her feel weird.

"Yeah I've got to get me some boots like that. Well, a guy version, I mean."

Robin laughed. "I only wear guy's boots. I have these in two colors. My mom got all mad at first, 'cause I dyed a pair blue without asking her. They were tan. I hate tan. She should know me by now — why even be surprised?"

Charlie took two steps then stopped. "Hey, *I'm* tan."

"No, you're more a dark ecru, or maybe a light russet," Robin said, squinting with one eye through her hands shaped into a square.

"Are those even colors? Only a girl would know a million names for brown."

To their delight, rather than some stuffy restaurant, Charlie's sister agreed to let them eat in the food court — alone — while she and her friends sat nearby and ignored them. Layla surprised him by giving him thirty dollars for the food and movie.

"Here twerp," she said, handing him the money.

"What is this for?" he asked, eyeing her suspiciously.

"Happy birthday. Don't say I didn't give you anything."

Charlie was surprised enough that he hugged her, but then must have realized what he was doing and they both jumped back as if they were two magnets with the same polarity. Robin just stood by, shaking her head at them. Ten minutes later, they sat eating at the food court.

"The dragon is really cool," Charlie said to Robin in between bites of bourbon chicken with rice. "How did you do it?"

Robin smiled shyly, and wiped tomato sauce from her mouth with the back of her hand. "Oh, I painted it with some old fabric paint I had left over. Do you really like it?"

"I like it a lot. I didn't even know you were an artist."

"Well, I'm not really. I used to want to be a fashion designer — or a writer — but I don't know anymore. I don't think I'm good enough."

"You look good enough to me. Besides, you're only in the seventh grade. Picasso probably wasn't great in the seventh grade either." Charlie picked up the jacket from the back of his chair. "Bet he never painted dragons," he mused.

"Thanks. I thought you should have a trophy for defeating your very first dragon. I find a lot of stuff at thrift stores and change them. I promised Jannet I would take her to one."

"You definitely need to get that girl off the prairie."

"That's so mean," Robin said, giggling.

"You know, in the fourth grade, she dressed up like a mummy for Halloween. Nobody noticed."

"Ohmigod! Is that why Carlton calls her Mummy?" she asked. Charlie nodded his head in the affirmative.

Robin began to laugh harder, and started flapping her hands as if they were two hummingbird wings. She and Charlie spent the next ten minutes laughing about the kids and teachers in the school, with Charlie making her laugh, and Robin flapping like a little bird. At one point, her laughter became loud — a deep, raucous laughter, accompanied by her head thrown back, her eyes wide, irises rolled up in her head, and her hands flapping at her face.

Charlie grinned at her. "You're going to take off one day, flapping," he said.

"If I could, I'd be famous," Robin answered, calming down enough to eat a French-fry.

"You know what I like about the way you laugh?" he asked. "The way that you look like you might be going insane, and just when I'm about to go for help, you stop."

"I'm crazier than you think, Dimple Boy," she answered drily.

Charlie frowned, and tilted his head at her, but said nothing. They continued to eat, Robin occasionally looking at him with her one visible eye. Finally, Charlie spoke. "I saw DeShaun on Friday — he was asking me about you."

Robin looked at him blankly. "Was he?"

"He looked pretty bad." Charlie's expression was unsympathetic.

"Good. Nobody grabs me like that."

Charlie looked at her, and one dimple began brazenly flirting with her.

"Quit it, Dimple flirt." Charlie could not have looked more confused. This satisfied Robin, and she continued. "It started with the dream, see? It bugged me the way he just ran off when things got rough. I knew it was only a dream, but I wondered if he was like that in real life."

"I did too," Charlie confessed. He seemed to be having a hard time not grinning.

"Then the next day, I just — casually — mentioned I had a dream about him and we were fighting dragons but he left, and he got all defensive and angry. He even called me a name, so I just walked away. Then he follows me, and when I wouldn't turn around, he grabs me by the shoulder. I guess I lost it. Afterward, I guess he felt all bad because he kept calling me and texting me how sorry he was. Big huge jerk."

"Typical."

"Do you know ... do you know that fool had the nerve to tell me he loves me? I said ... listen," Robin said, touching Charlie's arm, "this is great ... I said, 'Okay, if you love me so much, what's my middle name?' He just stood there looking stupid."

"How can he not know your middle name?"

"Yeah, right? That's what I said! So I told him I didn't need him around to tell me how great I am one minute and then act mean to me the next. I said, 'In fact, I don't need you around to tell me how great I am even if you're never mean. That's Charlie's job. Go bully someone else.' You know, I've never been tough with anyone before. It was kind of weird, really."

Charlie sat staring for quite some time. Robin had said her little speech all in one breath, while chewing. "Wh-what did you mean it's my job?" he asked.

"You know what I meant," she said, smiling, "you just want compliments." She obliged. "You're my best friend, okay? It's your job to pick me up when I'm down."

"Best friend huh?" Charlie responded, again, one dimple showing as he tried not to smile.

"That one-dimple thing is going to get you in trouble with girls one day."

"Why?" Charlie said, looking confused. "I thought I had two."

"Not always. And when you have one it's … distracting."

"Oh."

"Hey!" she said, leaning in closer, "I didn't know black guys could blush."

"I'm only half black. So I blush half the time."

"Is that true? That's sounds like it would be true."

"No, it's not true, goofy girl. I just made that up. Sheesh."

"Stop making fun of me. And, by the way, you said 'sheesh.' You're totally starting to talk like me now."

Charlie feigned a look of horror. "Oh. God. No."

"Soon people will think you really are my little brother," she said, sticking out her tongue. "We may even consider you for citizenship as an Mexindirishfrenchican American — immigrant status only, of course."

Charlie's expression sagged.

"So do your job, and cheer me up. I've been really sad. If I wanted to be miserable, I would have come here DeShaun."

"First, why are you so sad? Second, why were you girlfriends with a guy you don't even seem to like? Girls are so weird."

"Second question first," Robin offered, after a deep breath and a long pause. She leaned closer to Charlie so no one around could hear her. I guess I liked DeShaun because he was kind of mean, but nice sometimes."

"Say what?" he said.

"My daddy used to act like that and I would wonder if he really loved me. I guess I figured that if DeShaun acted like that, maybe he really loved me too. But then I just decided it doesn't matter if he does — he's stupid."

She looked into his eyes, searching for an understanding and a connection that he was too young to completely get. Still, she tried. She told him it was hard to explain to him, to anyone, that it was as if there were two halves of her, and one was okay with her being treated poorly, because she was used to it. It was all she knew, and sometimes comfortable is the enemy of logical. She was nearly thirteen, and not ready to trust a boyfriend yet. In a way, it was a disposable relationship. Charlie was different. He was her best friend because she already trusted him.

"I feel honored," Charlie said, grinning.

Robin looked down at the table. She didn't want to be looking in his eyes when she spoke. " I know you like me, Charlie," Robin said softly, "but I really just need a friend."

After a long silence, he answered. "It's okay. Jannet says I'm too short for you anyway."

Robin shook her head. "You're too nice for me. I wouldn't be able to handle that."

"Too nice? I didn't know nice was a bad thing."

Robin started to answer but sighed instead. "I guess I don't really know how to be liked," she said.

"Yeah, I know what you mean," Charlie said. He was looking past her, and she followed his gaze to Layla, sitting with her friends. "I guess if someone liked me a lot it would feel strange," he said.

Robin felt pained by his words, though she knew he meant no harm. "I do like you a lot, silly. But you need to make more friends than just me. You can't put all your balloons in one basket."

Charlie shook his head, and laughed. "Eggs — it's all your eggs in one basket."

Robin blinked at him. He was being all logical again.

"You know, a basket of eggs? A basket of balloons would float away."

"Oh. Well I'm from Albuquerque. Our baskets are big, and have balloons attached."

"Your logic makes my head hurt," he said.

"Why?" she asked. "We don't get eggs in a basket. We get them from the grocery store in the little box thingies."

Charlie began to giggle, which annoyed her.

"You're serious, aren't you?"

"Of course I'm serious. 'Eggs in a basket' makes no sense at all. Who does that?"

"Please stop," he said, holding his head, all the while laughing. "You might be causing permanent damage."

"The point is, I'm not used to nice. There's nothing wrong with you, but I don't need a boyfriend, I need someone I can count on. Besides, all that marriage stuff is later."

Charlie cocked his head and looked at her like she was crazy. "What marriage stuff? I didn't ask you to marry me. I was just wondering why girls are 'friends' with guys they like, and date guys they don't like."

"If you can figure that out, you'll be rich. You are way too logical. And your kids are just like you."

Charlie leaned over the table, staring at her. "I'm like, twelve. What kids? You are so weird."

"And yet, you love me," she said, wiping her mouth with her napkin.

"Huh?"

"You really need better dreams, Charlie." Robin said, standing up. Layla was calling them to leave, as the movie was starting soon. Robin walked close to him and said, "I need to talk to you later, okay? I — I've been having these dreams, and they are driving me nuts. You are the only one who would understand."

Charlie nodded. "Maybe we can talk after the movie. Layla said mom won't pick us up until 3 o'clock," he said.

Robin grinned, and wrapped her arm around Charlie's, almost making him drop the tray full of trash. They walked to his birthday movie arm-in-arm, with Charlie walking slowly, looking around, as if they were on the red carpet. Every few steps Robin would accidentally hit him with her oversized purse.

"You keep hitting me with that," Charlie said, not really complaining. "What in the world do you still have in that thing?"

"Lots of stuff, secret girl things. Like, I have three different kinds of lotion." She pulled out two to demonstrate.

"Okay, I give up. Why?"

"Because, I buy it, but then after awhile I get sick of it. But I don't throw it away, because I might secretly like it. So it stays in my purse."

"How do you 'secretly like' something?"

"It's easy. Plus, I usually have my emergency flip flops," Robin said, looking in her bag to check.

"What? What in the world are emergency flip flops? I wasn't even going to ask you why you wear those things when it's cold outside."

"Because my toes don't like shoes — unless they're boots. They get claustoephobic," she said.

"Of course," he said, his eyes rolling.

"And I carry emergency flip flops 'cause you never know when the pair you're wearing is gonna break. So you have to be prepared. I keep mine in here." She pulled out a pair of plain black flip flops then put them back in the bag.

"Every time I try to follow your logic, I get a headache," Charlie said, laughing.

38 – BEST. MOVIE. EVER.

This was turning out to be the best movie ever. Just as they got in line to buy tickets, Charlie saw Bryan and Brandon with their father standing in line to see the latest comic book adaptation. To Charlie's surprise and delight, Robin immediately asked if they could see that one.

"You're a boy, so you're supposed to like this stuff. But, if you want to see, like, a romantic comedy, I will 'cause it's your birthday. However, I'm not responsible if word happens to get around school on Monday that you're secretly a girl."

"I can't believe you're blackmailing me on my birthday. I'll agree, but just so you can see how dumb a superhero name Dimple Boy is," Charlie said.

Robin laughed and poked Charlie in the arm, which she was still holding onto. Charlie laughed too and looked up, just in time to see Twin Flynn in a dual-open-mouthed stare. Their dad bought tickets for himself and the twins, followed in line by Robin, Charlie, Layla, and her two friends. Despite having just eaten, they all loaded up on the expensive junk food that was requisite for movies. First Brandon then Bryan then Brandon again then both turned to stare at Charlie and Robin at approximately fifteen second intervals. They never said a word; instead, it was as if they hoped that at some point, they would look, and Charlie would have magically disappeared. The more they looked, the more Robin would frown, and hold Charlie closer. This, of course, caused them to stare even more frequently.

Robin held onto Charlie near the theater door to see where Brandon and Bryan sat before she chose a seat. Twin Flynn and dad went down front. Robin sat in the first row of the second seating area, safely separated from the twins by four rows and a wide aisle.

"Those boys are like, double creepy. They follow me around sometimes, but they never say anything. Not even, 'Hi.' I once dreamt they kept chasing me through some cornfields."

"Stephen King would be proud of you."

"What's their deal?" Robin asked, her feet on the rail in front of her.

"I dunno. Serial killers, maybe. Plus, you make guys nervous."

"Me? Why would I make guys nervous? I don't do anything."

At first, Charlie thought she was fishing for a compliment, but something in her eyes told him she was sincere. "You really don't see how guys look at you?" he asked.

"I don't really pay boys any attention. Why?"

"You need a better mirror."

"I don't get it," Robin said.

"Okay. Guys are always supposed to be cool, right?"

"Uh, no."

"Look, if you go to try to talk to a girl, and she blows you off then all the guys you know will laugh at you for, like, the rest of your life. And, if she happens to be really cute then pretty much all of the girls you know will rag on you too."

"Oh. I didn't know there were so many rules," she said, munching on popcorn.

"Yeah. So, if you're a dude, you have two choices. One, you walk up, act all confident like you own the world."

"DeShaun," she said.

"If the girl blows you off, you act like you were doing her a favor anyway. I call that the Pimp."

"I call it being an idiot," she said.

"Same thing. Or, two, you just kind of hang around, and hope she says something. I've never seen that work, but guys still try it. That's called the Sad Sack. The twins are Sad Sacks."

"Interesting, especially that you took the time to give them names. So which one do you do?" Robin asked, raising one eyebrow with her finger.

Charlie recognized her attempt at mocking the look he often gave her when she was being weird, which was usually. "Me? Neither one," he said. "I don't really like girls yet."

"Uh, I'm a girl. You might have noticed my long hair."

"That's different. Besides, I figure if a girl really likes me, she'd let me know."

"Girls don't let guys know that, silly. Maybe we'd flirt with you, or act like we don't like you, but girls hardly ever just come out and say they like you."

"Why not?" Charlie's left brain was still in control. His right brain would have rolled its eyes — if it had eyes.

"That would be the girl version of the Sad Sack," she said. "You should try walking up, being confident — but normal, not a jerk — and just say, 'Hi.'"

"Does that really work?"

"Not usually, no. But the other stuff never works."

Charlie munched on a handful of popcorn. "See? That's why I'm not into girls — too complicated."

"Nuh uh, girls are simple. Boys just don't pay attention to the rules." She grinned, and grabbed a handful of Charlie's popcorn.

"Hey! I thought you can't have popcorn with your braces."

"I don't have popcorn. This is your popcorn, so it doesn't count." She was throwing one up at a time, and catching them in her mouth.

"You have the strangest logic in the world."

"Logic is for people with no imagination." She shook her head. "My Dimple Boy is so clueless."

"Well, that explains why I'm in the movies with you, and not a cute girlfriend."

Robin punched him in the shoulder. Hard. "I'm very cute."

"Ow!" Charlie said, and was promptly shushed by someone behind him that could only be his adorable sister. "Why are you always hitting and poking me?"

"Because, you're a pain."

"I'm a pain? You're the one who hits."

Robin smiled just as the lights dimmed. She leaned over to Charlie and whispered. "How come you know so much about what people do when you never say anything to anybody?"

Charlie answered without hesitation. "I have to be around people, so I watch them. Besides, I do talk to people. I talk to you. I'd say I talk to Jannet, but she's not a people."

Robin hit Charlie in the shoulder again. Charlie mouthed the word "ow" and rubbed it discretely.

"Don't be mean. She is too a people. I like her. And of course you talk to me, I'm very special."

"Yes you are," Charlie replied, and when Robin gave him a big smile, he added, "in the little school bus kind of way."

Robin punched him hard, in the exact spot as before. This time when he yelled at least five different people told him to hush.

"Would you stop doing that?" Charlie whispered. "They're going to throw me out."

"Then put some bass in it, dude," she answered, her braces gleaming in the dim light. From the front, they could just make out Brandon's head giving the pair one last gaze by the light of the previews. "I swear, if those weird boys look back here one more time, I'm gonna throw your popcorn at them." She was talking, not whispering.

"They're probably just looking to see if we're making out," Charlie whispered, "but you're not my type."

"I am so your type. You adore me," Robin whispered back, leaning in, but not looking at him at all.

"In your dreams, Mercedes," he said.

"In yours too," she replied, smiling.

***

After the movie, Robin, Charlie, Layla and her two friends, were hanging in the seating area in the middle of the mall, doing what normal kids do at a mall, namely, nothing. Layla would smile at boys who walked by, and then frown at or ignore them when they approached her. Her friends occupied themselves by laughing at the ordinary-looking guys who got dismissed, or asking Layla what her problem was when she humiliated cute boys.

"You know," Robin said to Charlie, "your sister is really, really pretty. But she's a little mean."

"She's a psycho," Charlie said flatly. "I once saw her speed up in her car because there was a squirrel in the road. She's just nuts."

Robin looked at the pretty, lean-muscled teenager with the curly brown hair, caramel skin, and deep dimples. Then she looked at Charlie then back at Layla then Charlie. "You know," Robin said, staring at Layla once again, "you and your sister look exactly alike. Except she's all cute," she added, giggling.

"What? We look *nothing* alike! That psycho and I are barely related."

"That's mean, Charlie. She is your sister. You have to love her, it's the law."

254

"What? That's not a law. You're making that up."

"Well it should be a law. It's in the Mexindirishfrenchican constitution. She's a big sister and she has the right to your love." Robin looked at Layla, who was now happily dancing to music that existed only in her warped, but lovely head, after publicly humiliating another would-be suitor. "Even if she is really scary," Robin continued.

"Yeah, right? Can you imagine her dreams?" Charlie said. "Even the dragons would be afraid of her."

"Maybe she's just hurting, and needs help." Robin said, her smile wilting like a rose. "I couldn't help Reyna, and look what happened." She wiped away a sudden tear.

"Hey, that wasn't your fault," Charlie said. He paused then went on. "Is that what your bad dreams are about? You said you've been sad, but we spent this whole time acting silly."

Robin looked at Charlie, and blinked back more tears. "Yeah, I needed silly — even our popcorn fight." Robin painted on a weak smile, and turned back toward Layla. "You're my bestie, that makes Layla my sister, and I want to like her. But she has to like herself first."

"You always change the subject to other people," he said, "My mom will be here soon to get us, and you still haven't told me why you're sad, or about the nightmares."

Robin took a deep breath and slumped back into her seat. "I don't remember everything about the dreams. I don't want to remember them, really. The only part I remember is the accident — Reyna's accident."

"You were there?" Charlie asked, horrified.

"No, I was in school when it happened. Reyna's school got out before mine, and Dad went to pick her up so she could practice driving. In the dream though, I'm in the back of the car."

"That sucks," he said.

"It's like I can see them, but they don't know I'm there."

By this point, Robin's eyes were misty. From the corner of Charlie's eyes, he could see Layla looking at them with some interest, and an expression he hadn't seen on her before ... it looked almost like concern.

"Charlie, in my dream, my dad is screaming and grabbing the wheel, and yelling at Reyna to slow down. She's crying and yelling something back at him, but I can never make out what she's saying. She just keeps speeding up, faster and faster." Robin paused, and slumped deeper in her seat.

"Go on," he said, putting his hand on her shoulder.

"Next, he's climbing into her seat, and right when he's just about to take the wheel from her, she turns it really hard. I hit my head on the window, right before the car hits a tree." Her voice softened to almost a whisper. "Then I wake up."

Charlie was quiet, unsure of what to say or do. "I'm really sorry. You shouldn't have to see that."

"Yeah, it bites. I dream that all the time," she said. Robin turned her back to leaned over towards Charlie then put her head on his shoulder, her back to him. "I keep remembering things too; bad things. My father wasn't a very nice man. He used to yell at my mom all the time. I remember hiding under the bed once and he didn't know I was there. It was this big huge bed, and I could get my whole body under it. I think I was around four."

"Wow, you remember stuff that far back?" he asked.

"Yeah," she sighed. "My mom had been late getting dinner; she was in school trying to get her degree, and my dad said he was sick of always having to wait for her. Then, Charlie, he punched her — right in the face. She hadn't even said anything, and he just hit her."

Charlie just closed his eyes — his own parents' issues suddenly felt far less dramatic.

Robin kept talking, her back to him. "He said it was a warning, and he wasn't blankety-blank waiting for dinner again. My mom couldn't go to her school for days 'cause her face was so messed up. But dinner was never late again."

"Did he hit her a lot?" Charlie asked. He couldn't imagine his dad hitting his mom. Not and living to tell about it anyway.

"Yeah. She tried to hide it, but we could tell. Then when Reyna was thirteen, three years before she died, he started in on her."

"On your sister?" Charlie asked, incredulous.

"He would yell at her in front of all of us. She would come into my room at night sometimes, crying, and just get in the bed with me. I would wake up and hold her, and then she'd go to sleep. That would happen a lot too — right up until a little while before she died."

"Didn't your mom try to do anything?" he asked.

"No, she was terrified of my dad. We all were."

"Did he ever hit you?" Charlie asked, struggling to get the words out.

"No," she said. "My dad would come in to check on me while I slept sometimes. I would pretend to be asleep, and he would just stand there. Then he'd leave."

Robin grew quiet, and Charlie took that at his cue to say something, though he didn't know what. "Do you … do you think your sister got in an accident on purpose?" Charlie asked after what seemed an eternity. Then he quickly added, "If it's too hard to answer, you don't have to say anything."

"No, I have to tell somebody. They sent me to counselors and stuff, but I didn't want to talk about it. My mom won't ever talk about the accident. It's almost like she thinks Reyna went away to college or something."

Charlie remembered how he acted when his grandmother died. "Sometimes it's just too hard to admit they're really gone," he said. "Pretending is easier."

There was another long, silent pause. Finally, Robin said, "Yes, I think she did it on purpose. I don't know why. I don't know why I have the dreams either."

"Maybe she wants you to know the answer," Charlie said softly. "My Grandma Kate used to say that sometimes angels try to reach you through dreams, like in the Bible. Maybe Reyna is trying to reach you."

"I believe Reyna's my guardian angel. I had some really nice dreams with her in them this summer. But this sucks. If I have that dream much longer, I'm going to go nuts. I'm afraid one night I won't wake up, and I'll actually have to watch her … die." The tears were coming now, and she kept her arm on her face so that no one would be able to tell.

"We won't let that happen," he said. "Maybe we should have it together."

"I'm not ready for that yet. Let's think of something easier first."

"Okay," Charlie promised.

"Charlie?" she asked, "You'll be there when I'm ready, right?"

"Of course," he said. "You saved my butt from Siri, remember? We're a team."

Robin sat up straight, and looked at Charlie, her eyes scanning his face. "Some team, she said. We can walk in people's dreams, and we're both afraid to go to sleep."

"Yeah," Charlie agreed, "but it could be worse."

"How?"

He pointed to a tall, skinny girl with blonde hair walking through the mall. She was being trailed, by some fifteen feet, by Twin Flynn. Their dad was nowhere to be seen. "You could be that girl," he said.

Robin shuddered, and crouched down behind Charlie. "Sheesh. Is it three o'clock yet?" she asked, as Charlie laughed.

39 – FULL OF HOT AIR

On the night prior to Charlie's birthday, G'pa Joe's mind was still imprisoned in the Stream. The walls of his cell were stone, hewed from the mountain in which it stood. There was a single glassless window carved into the ceiling some fifteen feet above. Moonlight shone through the bars that secured the window, leaving shadows like an elongated game of tic-tac-toe on the rock wall. The floor was red clay, or blood-soaked dirt. In the dim light, his eyes could not tell which.

He looked to the far end of the barren cell, which was an opening secured by intersecting steel bars. Beyond was only darkness. He was not certain for how long he had been a prisoner, but, chained as he was, with his long arms extended to the ceiling, he no longer cared. He was death, who had once dreamed he was a man. His "body," which in fact was a metaphysical representation of his mind, was bruised, battered. He had been beaten, hard, and often. But he had a strong mind, and had suffered much worse during war at the hands of those far more frightening. It was the solitude that tormented him now. They had tired of trying to force his family's secrets — Charlie's and Charlotte's — and had abandoned him to die, alone.

He would welcome the relief, but it was not forthcoming. Siri had him beaten, burned, shocked, and cut. He had movies played in his mind of the deaths of those he loved. He suffered sights no man should see, but he had not bent, had not broken. Finally enraged, Siri told him of an "emissary" who would bring "the damned children" to him. Siri could not find them, but in the Stream, they were strong. Siri could feel their strength, and he was scared. G'pa Joe could feel both his fear and hatred.

Robin routinely changed worlds to her liking with no more than a thought. Charlie had twice found Siri's domain without looking. It was as if the Overlord were a magnet, drawing Charlie to himself. The legends had foretold there would be One such as the boy, and Siri meant to discover the truth. Siri had raged about not believing "the foolish myths," yet still G'pa Joe could tell he feared them. G'pa Joe was old, and of no use, except as bait. Siri did not know why the boy wanted to save the old man, but, as he had hissed in his deep, effete voice, "Every fish needs a worm." G'pa Joe was his.

As G'pa Joe sat considering his fate, begging God for death, a large white bird squeezed through the narrow bars in the cell's ceiling. It was glorious, its feathers radiant with light. They streamed behind the bird as if it were a luminescent bird of paradise.

"Hi G'pa Joe," said the bird, standing on the dirty floor between G'pa Joe's dangling legs.

"G'pa? You a friend of Charlie's?" he rasped.

"Yes, and I'm here to bring you a message of hope." Its wings fluttered, filling the cell with light. "I cannot stay long, for the dark one returns and he will take you to a place even more desolate. But don't fear or despair, all is as it should be."

"I understand," G'pa Joe said. He had long known the legend of the One. "Are you sure it's my boy Charlie? You sure he's ready?"

The bird looked at Joe, and his chains broke, freeing his hands. The old man fell to the cell's floor in a heap. He lay there, looking up at the bird. "Not yet, and not alone," it said. " But he will be. And you know what must be done."

Joe sighed, and nodded. "But how do I know he'll be okay? I mean, the wrath of God ain't exactly been beating down evil's door up in here. I don't want my boy killed."

"Nor do I. Remember, the One is two. They must both be ready."

"So, who's this other one?" G'pa Joe asked, squinting at the bird's light.

The bird did not answer at first, but leapt to the window, preparing to take flight. "My sister, and we have a date," she answered, and squeezed once more through the bars, departing into the night.

"Well, I guess that tells me what I need to know," he said, smiling for the first time in a great while. He stood, walked to the door, and sat, anxiously awaiting his captors' approach.

***

Sometime around midnight that same night, Robin lapsed into a deep, but troubled sleep. She had spoken about her dream to Charlie, and went to bed trying very hard to focus on the fun they had at the mall, and the not the memories of her recurrent dream. Unfortunately, trying not to think of her fears almost always guaranteed that she would be able to think of little else.

Earlier, she had tried texting Charlie, hoping to engage him in a silly conversation that would mask her fears. One of Robin's primary coping strategies was keeping her feelings bottled up inside and acting as if everything were great. By so doing, she hoped that people around would adore her and give her loving energy that would in turn offset her own internal struggle. Tonight, however, Charlie was nowhere to be found. So instead, she had read her favorite of L. Frank Baum's Oz books, or more specifically, about the bunnies of Bunnybury. She had thought there could be little that was further from real life's pains than the Land of Oz — perhaps Wonderland, but she had not been able to locate her copy of *Through the Looking-Glass*.

So, to bed she had gone, with hopes of dreaming of Bunnybury, and, perhaps, to finally meet Dorothy Gale in person. Instead, she found herself on a familiar street, Indian School Road, in northeast Albuquerque, New Mexico. It was a cool February afternoon, with traces of snow still lingering on the winter desert landscape. The cloudless sky was turquoise, the Sandia mountains lit by the afternoon sun. In around ninety minutes they would appear to glow with a distinct pink color that some thought to resemble watermelon pink, rumored to be the origin of their name. In truth, the name had likely come from the squash that grew nearby that the Spanish thought were watermelons. Still, Robin had preferred the first explanation, and felt a familiar longing at the sight of her "watermelon mountains."

She wore only her blue silk pajamas, yet felt none of the cold. She knew by virtue of the now-familiar bicyclist in the orange jumpsuit who would pass by and wave — now — that her sister would be driving by in exactly six minutes and thirty seconds. Once, she had gone to sleep wearing her watch, and had thought to time the interval in her dream. Six minutes and thirty seconds until the dream once again turned into a nightmare.

Her brain told her to run, to return whence she came, but to no avail. It was, as it always was, as if she were rooted to the spot. She would not leave, and when Reyna drove by in the battered Ford Taurus, Robin would find herself swept inside, as if the car were a vacuum and she were little more than a dust bunny.

Five minutes, six seconds to go, and a roadrunner scampered across the street in search for a winter meal. The sky would now be clear except a Southwest Airlines jet on approach from Denver … and … and a balloon, low to the ground, flying erratically, parallel to the eastern mountains.

"What the heck?" Robin asked, staring at the balloon. "That's new," she muttered, mildly annoyed at the change in protocol.

As she watched, the balloon began to drop from the sky. It was tan in color, connected to a basket that was decorated in bright red and blue. The balloon approached the open field across the street, and was now no more than twenty feet off the ground. Thirty seconds earlier it had appeared to be miles away, and now could be no more than fifty yards from where she stood.

"That guy is moving way too fast, he must be out of control," she said aloud. "And who in the world decorates the basket instead of the balloon? How odd."

It was indeed odd, as she could feel no breeze; the air was cold, though calm, and quiet. As the balloon descended to a height of ten feet, it leveled off, and, to her surprise, instead of landing in the field, made a sharp right turn across the street, directly at her. Part of her mind told her to run, but a hot air balloon does not bring to mind imminent danger, so she decided to see exactly who was there. Maybe Reyna had decided to take a balloon home today instead of practicing driving. Robin stood on tiptoe in an attempt to see if her sister was in the balloon's basket, but she could not see her. In fact, she could make out no one in the balloon at all. It looked as if she had discovered nothing more foreboding than a runaway hot air balloon.

The balloon slowed, and moved to within five horizontal and ten vertical feet of Robin. As she tiptoed, shielding her eyes from the afternoon sun, the balloon slowly rotated 180 degrees, revealing a particularly cute decoration that looked like a face, with two remarkably lifelike dimples.

"Oh, there you are!" came a voice from the balloon. "Hi Robin. I hope you're not angry I came."

"Is, is that you Reyna … or Dad?" The voice did sound more masculine than her sister, but not exactly like her father either.

"No, it's me, Charlie," said the voice.

"Charlie?" Robin laughed out loud. "Ha! Where are you? I can't see you at all from down here." Robin stifled a laugh, thinking it funny that he was so short he couldn't be seen above the basket. "Can you stand on tiptoe so I can see you?"

"Huh?" Charlie said. His confusion turned to amusement as he realized her mistake. "Oh, I'm not in the basket, I'm above it." Charlie grinned, and a huge set of teeth appeared on the side of the hovering balloon. His speech sounded like the hissing of escaping air. With each sentence, he dropped another inch or two.

"Whoa! How did you make it do that?" she said. "That's kind of creepy."

"Robin, I am the balloon, goof. You should try it. Flying is amazing. I was just floating over the mountains. Did you know there are a bunch of trees on the other side?"

"Uh, yeah, I was born here. Why are you … *how* are you a balloon? How on earth did you find me?"

"Could you jump up in the basket first?" he asked. "It's a little hard to talk to you from this far away. If I land, I might not get back off the ground. Takeoffs are a little trickier than they look."

"I can't get up there, you're like a zillion feet up."

Charlie answered, "More like ten, and sure you can. Look, I was on the internet reading about this stuff before. It's called 'lucid dreaming.' All you have to do is to remember this isn't real life."

"You are very confusing, Balloon Boy," she said with a frown.

"This is your dream, and it's all happening in your head. That means you can make it do anything you want."

Robin was not convinced. "I don't know how to do that," she said in an uncharacteristically whiny voice.

"You are the boss in here. Just imagine you can jump as high as you want," he said.

"I don't know Charlie, I'm a little scared. What if I miss?"

"You won't miss, and even if you do, you can't get hurt. It's just a dream. Besides, you're the girl who showed up in my dream, riding a dragon."

He had a point. "Okay, but you better catch me, buddy. If I die in here, I'm not going to speak to you again."

"Uh, okay," he said.

Robin closed her eyes, and jumped. She imagined her legs were springs, and sure enough, they coiled up, and sprang her fifty feet into the air. Robin opened her eyes, saw that her head was above the top of the Charlie balloon, and began screaming. She stopped in mid-air, cartoon style, for two full seconds. Then she began to fall — fast.

"Help!" she screamed.

"Just slow down. Use your imagination!"

Robin thought of the old cartoons, and yelled, "Air brake!" at which point a lever appeared. She pulled it, and screeched to a stop, eleven feet from the ground. "Bugs Bunny rocks," she said, wiping nervous sweat from her brow despite the cold.

"Oh brother," Charlie balloon said.

Robin took a cautious step, and to her surprise, she didn't fall. In fact, she walked straight ahead, in mid-air, and stepped down into the balloon's basket.

"Welcome aboard Patterson Airlines," Charlie balloon grinned.

"Charlie Patterson, that almost killed me. But it was exciting, I must admit." She peered over the side of the basket. "So, why are you a balloon, and what are you doing here?"

"Okay, I was on the internet like I said," he replied, his balloon face looking very much like a movie projection. "First I was looking up how to control dreams, but then, I thought you might have the dream again since we were talking about it."

Robin frowned. "I don't think I'm having the dream at all. I'm just waiting for my sister to pick me up."

Charlie's voice was calm and reassuring. "Oh, well, she will probably be by soon. But she's not going to pick you up, today."

"No?" Robin asked.

"No. Today we're going to pick her up."

"Yay! She'll love that! Reyna loves balloon rides."

"That makes it easier," he said. "I was worried she might be afraid of heights."

"No, Reyna rode at the Balloon Fiesta last year with her boyfriend. My dad was *so* angry at her afterwards." Robin, programmed by her subconscious to repeat the dream, still did not understand she was asleep. She began to worry that her dad would never let Reyna ride in a balloon with a boy's face talking to her.

"Well, we should probably start moving, or when she comes by, we'll be going too slow to catch her," he said.

"Oh, okay. Fly on, Dimple Balloon!" she gushed. "Charlie, you didn't tell me how you found me."

"I don't know, exactly. I was looking at Google Earth, and trying to remember as much as I could of the city map, trying to make it real, you know?"

Robin nodded in agreement then said "Yes," when she realized Charlie was looking at the road below him, and not her.

"So, I was reading about Albuquerque, and they kept talking about balloons. First I thought it would be cool to ride one then I thought, shoot, why can't I just be one?"

"Good for you!" she said grinning.

As they drifted, waiting for Reyna to drive by, Charlie related that he had imagined himself made of fabric then inhaled deeply. As he did so, he said, his head began to inflate with hot air. After a number of attempts, he finally got aloft, and floated off. From there, it was a simple matter of following his phone's GPS to Albuquerque. Charlie's imagination was rooted in reality, it turns out.

"Once I got close to New Mexico, I think I entered your dream," he said. "Then, boom. I was here. It is so cool to fly. I have to dream this again."

"This is pretty fun, I must admit. You were so clever figuring out how to get here. I'm proud of you," Robin smiled.

"Thanks," he said. He blushed, which made flames ignite, and raised the balloon slightly. "The hard part was finding you in this big city. But I just seemed to fly here all by myself, like you were pulling me to you. I was even looking in the wrong direction."

"When we fought the Klowns, it was like that for me," she said. "I just flew right to where you were, even though I didn't know you were in the dream."

Charlie smiled. Robin's awareness was returning. "Do you remember the dream stuff, Mercedes?" he asked tentatively.

His use of Robin's favorite name momentarily focused her attention. "I do now. But I should be all mad at you. You agreed we wouldn't do this yet."

"I know," Charlie answered, shouting over the wind. They were now floating at some twenty knots. "But I also promised you I'd be there when you did. I didn't know another way."

"Well, thanks," she said, adding, "You're very sweet."

Charlie balloon let out a gush of wind that dipped them lower to the ground. "Sorry, he said. I did that by accident."

Robin, who fell over in the basket when they dropped, smiled and said, "Gas much?"

As if on cue, cars began to appear, and the heretofore-empty road became busy with traffic. Robin's look glazed over once again, as her subconscious restarted the sequence of her recurring dream. Charlie saw the change in her demeanor, and shouted to get her attention.

"Okay, Mercedes, which one is your sister's car?"

"What?" she asked dreamily.

"Your sister's car, which one is it? Focus, okay?"

Robin nodded, and said, "It's a piece of crap blue Taurus. My dad doesn't give a hoot about her having a nice car."

"I see it!" Charlie said. "It's the one with the white smoke. Hang on! We're going in."

"Why are you calling me Mercedes?" She sounded more asleep than awake.

"Because it always gets your attention."

Charlie balloon accelerated to an incredible thirty knots, matching the speed of the Taurus below. Robin could see Reyna through the windshield. She was almost an exact double of her sister, the only differences being age, a more adult figure, and light brown hair. She appeared to be crying and yelling, though Robin could not make out the man next to her. The sight of her sister shocked Robin into alertness.

"Okay, now when I say go, I want you to imagine yourself picking her up," Charlie shouted.

"Picking her up? How?" She was more than a little frantic.

"I don't know. You're the creative one. Create something!"

Robin felt as if she would collapse. "I'm not so good under pressure."

"Robin, that overpass is coming up. We have to do this now. Listen, this entire world is only happening in your mind. You made it." Charlie was talking and watching the upcoming overpass closely.

"I made it?" she asked.

"You. And you can make your dream into anything you want it to be! In this place, you are the leader — so lead!"

Robin bit her lip then closed her eyes. "Lower!" she yelled to Charlie.

Charlie dropped to within two feet of the speeding car, matching its speed perfectly. When Robin opened her eyes, a key appeared on the top of the car that looked exactly like one from a sardine can. Robin grabbed the key and turned it, unpeeling the top of the Taurus, exposing its occupants like two little fish. Reyna and her faceless father both looked up. Robin reached down, her arms having grown at least five feet longer, and grabbed Reyna under each armpit.

"Up, now!" she yelled.

Charlie exhaled, and the Charlie balloon shot skyward, ascending sixty feet in a matter of seconds. From that height, they could just make out the small figure of a man attempting to climb over the seat and grab the steering wheel. Reyna looked scared at first, then stunned, and finally her expression eased to amusement. She began grinning, and looked up at Robin, her legs dangling freely in the air — now one hundred feet above ground.

"Hey, little bird," Reyna said. "You finally learned how to fly."

Robin began to cry — a trickle at first, followed by earth-wrenching, ground-soaking, desert-flooding sobs. As she cried, her teardrops caused a mighty rain in the winter desert, and confused cactus plants began to blossom below. As the afternoon sun pierced the desert shower, a lovely rainbow, all in shades of purple appeared below the Charlie balloon.

"Wow, I've never seen a rainbow like that one," Charlie said.

"Yeah, it's my favorite color," Reyna said, smiling at Robin. "You remembered, huh little bird?"

"I would never forget anything about you," Robin said.

"But you have baby," Reyna replied. "Pull me in."

Robin pulled her older sister into the balloon, and they held each other, sobbing and laughing, as Charlie floated over the Sandia mountains, headed east.

After a time, Reyna pulled herself away, and kissed Robin on the forehead. "You forgot that I was happy sometimes, baby girl," Reyna said, wiping Robin's tear-soaked cheeks. "It wasn't always bad."

"No it wasn't," Robin agreed. "I just miss you so much."

"Then how come every time you come to visit me, you only show up here? Why can't we, like, go on a picnic or something? Sheesh, I could even take you to the Frontier for some green chili."

"Oh man, I miss green chili so much. I ask for it in Mexican restaurants in Virginia, and they have no clue what I'm talking about," Robin lamented.

"See? We need to have some next time you come. I'm glad you miss me, and I wish I could be there for you. I mean for real."

That brought more desert rain from Robin's eyes. "I hate that you're gone, hermana," Robin said.

"But I'm still in here," Reyna said, tapping Robin on the head, "so find the good places, and dream about those. Stop dreaming about losing me. Besides, you have it wrong anyway."

"I do?" Robin asked.

"Yes. I didn't wreck the car on purpose. Don't you remember I promised you I'd never leave you?"

Robin shed new tears and nodded yes.

"Well, I wasn't lying, little bird. I didn't kill myself, I promise." Reyna was holding Robin's face in her soft hands. "You need to let it go, not try to understand it."

"I just can't stop thinking about it. There's something more, something I can't remember."

"I know, sweetie, there is a lot more. You'll remember it when you need to — when you can handle it. For now, déjalo ir." She kissed Robin on the forehead.

"Okay," Robin said, smiling. She was reliving the comfort of being a little sister.

"If you want to remember me then remember when I was happy, okay?" Reyna looked up at Charlie, and cupped her hands to her mouth. "Hey, hermanito!"

"Huh? Oh, hi," Charlie said. He seemed uncomfortable talking to Robin's dead sister.

"Thanks for bringing her by little brother," Reyna smiled.

"Shh, stop calling him that," Robin said, shaking her head vigorously.

"What? You didn't tell him?" Reyna asked, speaking under her breath to Robin.

Robin answered, "No," using only her eyes.

Reyna looked up at Charlie and grinned, "Never mind, my bad … primo."

Robin frowned and folded her arms.

"You two look alike and act alike. It's really weird," Charlie said as he started to descend onto the top of the nearest mountain peak.

"That means he adores you," Robin explained. "I just knew he would."

40 – IT ISN'T ALWAYS A PICNIC

When the Charlie balloon touched down, it had become a lovely summer day. Gone was the cold, snow, or any trace of rain. Robin and Reyna climbed out of the basket and sat down on a blanket that had conveniently appeared nearby and filled itself with food. Charlie exhaled, and he deflated, eventually laying sprawled out flat on the ground. Then, as Reyna and Robin applauded, he shrank to his normal shape. He was wearing bright blue and red pajamas. Charlie looked down at his PJs, blushed, and immediately changed into jeans and a t-shirt. Robin had likewise changed to jeans.

"You are something else, Dimple Boy," Robin said.

"That means she adores you too," Reyna said.

"Shut-*up*, Reyna!" Robin said. "No I don't."

Charlie smiled, deciding that both versions of the story were probably in fact Robin's, coming from her mind. He didn't mind the conflicting reviews at all. "See? When we are in dreams we don't like, we can just change them," Charlie said. He hesitated, pain flashing across his face. "I wish I had learned that a week ago."

"You did fine last week," Robin said.

Charlie shrugged. "Not really, but I'll do better next time. We just have to learn to take control of the dream. We have to learn to laugh at the scary parts."

"Or, you just pull yourself away from the scary thing like you did with me," Reyna added.

"Right," Charlie said. "The internet said to think about something that makes you happy."

"Like picnics with my big sister," Robin said, beaming at Reyna.

"We can do anything we want because it's our dream," he replied. "We can have anything in it we want." Charlie reached into his pocket and pulled out a pair of black flip flops. "See, I brought you these. Emergency flip flops."

Robin laughed and put them on her pedicured (with turquoise and black nail polish) feet.

"This is our world, and there is nothing to be afraid of," Charlie said.

Reyna stood and smiled. "I knew we picked the right guy for the job. Thanks for looking out for my little bird," she said to Charlie. "You know, she always used to think she was so funny looking. You make her see herself for who she is, and that's great."

"I never realized how much I look like you," Robin said, smiling at Reyna.

"I always did, hermana," Reyna smiled back. She looked at Charlie and said, "I'm glad she has you."

Charlie listened, wondering if Robin even knew she was talking for her sister.

"Just one warning though, okay?" Reyna continued. "Yes, this is your world, all that's true. But someone else has made it his world too. Be careful."

"You mean Siri?" Charlie asked. "Yeah, we've met." His eyes flashed momentary hatred.

Reyna nodded, her expression somber. "If you go walking around in folks' dreams, teaching them how to fight back — well, he's not going to be happy," she said. Reyna turned to Charlie. "Do you know why you're here?" she asked.

"I get the feeling you're not gonna say it's for a picnic," he answered.

"No," she said, smiling. "I mean, why you're in the Stream. Why you are here in Albuquerque."

"Uh, I was just trying to help Robin."

"And you have, and I'm grateful. But see, that's the point. That's why you're in the Stream, both of you."

"I don't get it, Reyna," Robin said.

"Charlie, do you remember what you told Robin your Grandma Kate said about angels?"

Charlie looked at Robin, with some sadness. He was concerned that she still had not figured out she was making Reyna come to life. "Yeah, of course I do. She said angels visit in dreams sometimes."

"She also quoted you scripture," Reyna said. "Remember Job?"

Charlie looked at Robin with surprise. "How'd you know that?" he asked, directing his question to the younger girl. "I didn't tell you that."

Robin looked back at him, confused. "Why are you asking me?"

Reyna smiled, and shook her head. "Sweetie, I'm not just part of her imagination, any more than I'm part of yours. You have to stop thinking like a scientist if you're going to survive in here." Reyna leaned over and gave Charlie a peck on the lips. This time, Charlie actually had a stroke. At least he thought it was a stroke, as he saw a flash of white light, and fell to the ground in a heap. After a few moments, he awoke with a start, to see Robin leaning over him with a broad smile.

"My Reyna's an angel!" she yelled the second his eyes were open, which scared the bejeezus out of him, and almost caused a heart attack.

"Hush, goofball," Reyna said with a laugh, and pushed Robin over on her side. Reyna was dressed in all white. "Do you believe me now when I say I'm really here?" Reyna asked.

Charlie sat up, and nodded. "Robin would never have kissed me on the lips," he said. Robin nodded in agreement.

"You can't handle my kisses," Robin said grinning.

"Merced, if you don't hush, I swear," Reyna said.

"You sound just like Mommy," Robin said, her arms folded glumly.

Reyna shook her head, and continued. "Charlie, what was it that your Grandma Kate would say?"

Charlie had to think hard to recall. He had long-since filed away most of his Grandma Kate memories to rarely used sectors of his brain. They had become too painful to access frequently. After a time, he remembered, and recited the words she used to tell him whenever he had a nightmare. "In a dream, a vision of the night, when sound sleep falls on men, while they slumber in their beds, then He opens the ears of men, and seals their instruction."

"Exactly," Reyna said, nodding and smiling beatifically. "And some versions say 'terrifies them with warnings.' But here in the Stream, you need to pay attention to both the instruction and the warnings."

For the first time, Charlie knew Reyna was not just some imagined rendezvous with a lost sister. Perhaps she had started out that way, but now it was much more. This was important, a message of some sort. "I get it, I think," Charlie said. "Reyna, which one are you?"

"I'm both, little brother, and I'm not just speaking for myself," Reyna said, with sadness in her voice. "There is much expected of you here. You must both remember to stay on the right path, and to fear nothing but straying from it. Your fear is his strength." Reyna bent over and kissed Robin once again on the forehead. She kissed Charlie on the cheek, making him blush clean through his brown skin. "Bye little one, see you again soon okay?" Reyna said to Robin.

"Don't go yet," Robin whined. "I'm not ready."

"It's time, little bird. I have to go, and you and Charlie have work to do."

Reyna gave a small wave, and turned to walk down the mountain. Robin jumped to her feet, intent on retrieving her sister. She began to run after Reyna, calling and waving for her to come back.

Charlie, having a bad feeling, began to follow the girls. He reached the downward slope just in time to see a dirty blue Taurus with trailing white smoke driving along the side of the mountain. It was holding onto the rocky surface despite being at an impossible angle with respect to the ground. Robin yelled for Reyna to "Watch out!" but instead of turning, Reyna gave Robin a last little wave. The Taurus slammed into Reyna, sending her flying fifteen feet in the air, her legs and arms dangling like a child's rag doll.

"Reyna!" Robin screamed, and began running towards her sister, now sprawled on the ground, limbs bent akimbo. She dissolved into the ground like the Wicked Witch from the Wizard of Oz. From the window of the car, Robin saw a large white rabbit with amber eyes and two rows of sharp teeth grinning at her. Robin screamed and stopped in her tracks.

The shark-toothed rabbit turned the wheel, and the car began chasing Robin up the side of the hill. Robin turned and ran, stumbling over the low shrubs that dotted the landscape. Simultaneously, Charlie began bolting down the hill toward Robin, just as she fell sprawling in the brown dirt. The car, spewing smoke, gunned its engine and began bearing down on the girl. Robin, seeing the vehicle driven by the maniacal rabbit, rolled out of the way just as the vehicle zoomed by, missing her by inches.

The car now veered left, and began to circle for another run. Charlie, seeing Robin's peril, began racing headlong toward the vehicle. The rabbit's gleaming, drooling grin was visible as it leaned forward into the steering wheel. The engine roared to life as it bore down on the boy. Robin, seeing her best friend no more than ten feet from his death, leapt to her feet and sprinted behind the car.

The Taurus, still racing impossibly up the steep hillside, hit a dirt mound and became airborne, its dented grill arching towards Charlie. In horrible, beautiful, slow motion, the car, tires spinning, and engine revving in a deafening roar, crashed headlong into the boy. Behind the car, Robin screamed in angry despair as the car crumbled into the dirt, grinding Charlie under its weight.

The world became shatteringly silent, with only the sound of pebbles falling to the ground, amid a thick cloud of dust.

"Someone's crying," Robin said aloud. A tear dripped onto her bare foot, and she touched her damp cheek. It was she who was crying. After interminable moments, the dust cloud settled again to earth, revealing the mangled remains of the Taurus. The car had smashed headlong into the ground, and rolled over onto the passenger side. There was no movement from the vehicle, and only a bloody, hairy paw sticking out of the shattered driver's window was visible. The rabbit, expecting Charlie to run, had not counted on smashing into the mountain.

Robin walked slowly to the car, fearful of finding her friend in the same state that she had imagined her sister on many a night.

"I'm here," came a voice, followed by a thick, dusty cough. It was Charlie, sitting on the ground, the Taurus' fiber bumper wrapped around him.

"Ohmigod!" Robin shouted, and ran to embrace her friend. She was crying, and laughing. "Why aren't you dead?" she asked then clapped her hand over her mouth.

Charlie pulled himself from his friend's embrace, and lay back on the ground with a loud moan. "This isn't my dream, and I decided not to believe this stupid rabbit could hurt me with a car that no longer exists. Besides, I've had just about as much of rabbits as I can stand."

"Wait," Robin said, her face flushed. "You risked your life on a hunch that this wouldn't be real if you didn't believe it? Are you nuts?" She was either angry or overjoyed, but it was not clear which – likely to either of them.

"It wasn't a hunch," he said sheepishly, "it was ... deductive reasoning. Besides, I couldn't just let it run over you."

"Okay, Sherlock Homeboy," she said, shaking her head. "You are either a genius, or an idiot."

"Both, actually," he said. "That hurt a lot."

Robin's face distorted in anger, and Charlie instinctively raised his hands to protect himself. However, he was not her target. Instead, she stomped over to the car, jerked the still stunned rabbit out through the broken window, and screamed, "You are not a rabbit, and you are not real! But you tried to kill my best friend, and now, I am pissed."

The rabbit opened its eyes wide, which were now a glaring red. "You are going to die, you little bitch," it snarled.

"Definitely, you lop-eared, buck-toothed rat. But not today." She grabbed the rabbit's long ears, snatched them to her face with all the strength she could muster, and whispered the single word, "Hamster."

The scene immediately changed. No longer was she on a mountain in New Mexico. Instead, she was in a ten-by-ten foot white room with a single door. Below her, on the floor, was a small, brown hamster. Robin picked it up, and looked at it carefully. It wiggled its nose cutely, but otherwise did not move. As she lifted it closer to her nose, it suddenly began barking and snarling — sounding exactly like a large, angry Rottweiler.

"Jesus!" she said, almost dropping it. "I want you out of my dreams!" she yelled.

"Not until you are mine, or as dead as your sister," it snarled. It began laughing at her, the sound rising to a deafening crescendo.

Robin, in a fit of rage, took the hamster, and flung it across the room, slamming it against the far wall. It hit hard, but made only a muffled thump, leaving a bloody, brown mess.

She turned, her lips still twisted angrily, and walked out the door. Outside, waiting for her, was Charlie.

"Well, I guess you handled that," he said looking at the smear on the far wall. "Are you okay?"

"Yes," Robin said, wiping away an angry tear. "I don't like hurting things, but that felt good. Besides it wasn't real, I could tell."

"Um, why a hamster?" Charlie asked, still staring at the furry smear.

"I'm not afraid of hamsters."

"Oh."

"Reyna said some nightmares are warnings," Robin said. "So we're warned. The Overjerk wants a war."

"You want a war, I'll bring you a war!" Charlie yelled into the empty hallway.

Robin giggled. "You totally stole that line from the movie tonight."

"Hey, I already told you I don't have a good imagination. Jeez-o-flip."

"You are such a dork," she said, still laughing. "Plus you really need a better expression than 'Jeez-o-flip. It's embarrassing, frankly."

"I love you too," Charlie muttered, sarcastically.

"I know you do," she said, teasing him. "Who doesn't?" she added, grinning.

"At the moment? Hamsters," he replied, shuddering.

41 – THE LONG AND WINDING HALL

Robin looked down, focusing her attention on the ugly yellow carpet. They were standing in a long hallway, having left the room where Robin killed the demonic hamster. "Were you just thinking about The Wizard of Oz?" she asked, frowning.

"No, why?"

"It's just that the carpet looks kind of like the yellow brick road. I was wondering if you did that."

"It wasn't me," Charlie said, shaking his head. "Never mind that, I have a theory. We showed up in each other's dreams by accident, right?" he asked.

Robin shrugged. "Who knows? We still don't understand how it works."

"However it works, we seem to be connected to each other here. It seems like every time I have an intense dream, you show up."

Robin nodded. "Lately, so do you." She smiled at him. "Like tonight, for instance."

"Willie seemed to think there's a connection to this … Stream," Charlie said.

"So what does that have to do with your Yellow Brick Rug?" she asked, pointing down the corridor ahead.

"Huh? Nothing! And it's not my rug!" he said, more amused than frustrated. "I haven't seen that movie since I was a kid."

"You're still a kid, and it was a book before it was a movie."

"Oh, I didn't know." He shook his head again, as if shaking out Robin's stream-of-consciousness thought flow. "I was thinking the

276

Stream's like the internet. Like, at home we have a wireless network right?"

"Yeah, we do too."

"And you and I text or videoconference in kind of the same way."

"Right," she said then paused, and smiled. "I get it. You think this Stream is like dream Wi-Fi."

"Exactly. I remember before the Abner dream, there was a hallway the not-a-rabbit took me through. I don't think it's a real place, though."

Robin grinned. "Well, I like it better than the idea of becoming an airhead like you did before."

"Gimme a break. You made me fall asleep thinking about balloons. Anyway, I was thinking that maybe I connect to others' dreams like a network. For the internet, all you need is the IP address."

"Why didn't you just use a dream IP directory?" she asked with a straight face. Charlie frowned in response. "It was a joke, dude," she said. "Relax."

"Oh," he said, sighing in relief. "Since there is no directory, I wondered if I could connect by concentrating on the person. I made this hallway as a way to help me focus."

"Ha! It is your yellow brick rug! I knew it."

Charlie clamped the heels of his hands over his eyes, and shook his head.

Robin chose, at that point, to stop tormenting him, lest he really think her dumb. "Maybe at first we can just connect to other people who are kind of gifted somehow," she said. "That would explain how we came across each other."

"That makes sense."

"So maybe it just takes more work to connect to everyone else. These doors might lead to other people's dreams."

"It's worth a try," Charlie said. The hallway was narrow, barely wide enough for the two kids to stand side-by-side. The old wood floor was covered by a strip of beige carpet, imprinted with a pattern of golden bricks. The walls on either side were plain, with poorly painted molding near the floor and cracked crown molding near the ten-foot high ceiling. "Doesn't look like anyone's been here for a while," Charlie said.

Robin followed Charlie's gaze down the hall, and squinted, frowning. The dim corridor was replete with doors. Each door was different: in style, color, and size, even in shape.

"Why'd you make it so big?" she asked.

"I didn't. I only made a small hallway that looks like the one in my house."

"Well it's too dark in here," she said. "Isn't there a light switch anywhere?" She turned to the wall behind her, and began caressing the cool, gently pebbled surface with her hand. After some time, she felt a plastic switch. "Ah, here," she said, flipping on the lights.

The hallway immediately became illuminated with the warm glow of incandescent lights, shining from evenly spaced brass wall sconces. Despite the even spacing of the identical light fixtures, the hallway was inconsistently lit, the result of random burned-out bulbs. There were dark spots, some brightly lit ones, and others that cast the hall in a dim, yellowed glow. The shape of the wall sconces produced shadows that looked eerily like four-armed spiders along the entirety of the hallway.

The hallway itself curved in each direction, extending hundreds of yards before the walls bent out of their line-of-sight. In some of the more well-lit spots, they could see other hallways that intersected at varying angles.

"This place is a maze," Robin whispered.

"Yeah. I'm wondering if it was a good idea turning these lights on. I mean, we don't know who's inside this place," Charlie paused then added, "Or lives here."

Robin shivered. "Well, maybe you're right, but I'm not walking down these creepy halls with no lights on. We can go green when we wake up."

"Yeah, I agree. Just let's be careful, okay?" he said, looking at the spider-like shadows on the wall. "Even the shadows give me the creeps."

Charlie stood beside a wooden door. It was plain and brown, the only décor being carved rosettes in the corners of the frame. Most of the other nearby doors were more ornate. Charlie touched the plain, brown door. It was warm to the touch.

"Let's try this one," he suggested.

She frowned, and regarded the plain door. "Yuck. That one is boring."

"I like it."

"Why do you want to go through there? The others are much more interesting."

"I dunno. It just feels … right. C'mon, let's try it," he enthused. "You get to pick next."

Robin sighed and shrugged. She walked over to where Charlie was standing. She had changed into black jeans, a tapered cowl neck blouse that was ribbed at the neckline and stopped at her hips, a pair of large gold hoop earrings, and the black flip flops her gave her.

"Um, why did you change clothes?"

"Because, it's a new dream, silly."

Charlie sighed and shook his head. "Why does that make sense?"

"Because I'm cute."

Charlie began banging his head on the wall.

"Never mind, Dimple Boy. Let me show you something." Robin put her finger to her lips then giggled. "Got it," she said. "Wait, watch this."

Robin dramatically grabbed her upper right arm with her left hand then folded her right arm over to grab the left arm. She looked at Charlie, gave a devilish grin, and then blinked, while nodding her head. Charlie was immediately dressed in cream-colored leather boots, baggy black carpenter jeans, and a long sleeve powder blue shirt with ribbed collar that zipped all the way up the front. Underneath, he wore a sky-blue t-shirt. On his right wrist, he had a simple gold chain-linked bracelet.

Charlie looked at the outfit, fingering the soft weave of the shirt. The jeans had a leather tag on the back pocket with the logo "Merced" on it.

"Well, do you like it?" she asked excitedly.

"Yeah, these are spice," he said.

"They are what?" she asked. "Spliced?"

"Spice. It's what I say. I don't like other people's slang, so I make up my own."

"Spice?" she asked, grinning.

"Yeah, spice," he said defensively. "You know, hot, with a nyceness. That's spelled n-y-c-e." His voice trailed off at the end, as he met her gaze.

Robin repeated his spelling aloud, her grin broadening.

"You know, like New York City nice," he explained. He was all but pouting now.

Robin laughed. "That's hysterical. Who makes up their own slang? Whom do you even use it with?"

"I just use it. Sometimes morons like DeShaun will think it's popular, and they start using it too. When it spreads, I stop using it, and make up more."

Robin was guffawing, her eyes threatening to roll up in her head again.

"Well, he was using 'that's blazing' the other day. That one was mine too," he said, defensively.

"Nyce, huh? You are so funny," she said, gently poking him.

Charlie's face lightened when he realized she wasn't really making fun of him. "You always laugh at me when I'm being serious," he said.

"Well, you do the same thing to me," she said, still grinning at him. "Okay, so you like them," she continued. "Well you better, 'cause I designed them myself. Except the shoes; I hate shoes."

"You did this? Wow! See, I told you that you could be a designer."

"Check the socks."

He pulled up one pant leg to reveal calf-high gym socks the color of his shirt. "See, details matter, even if folks don't see them," she announced.

Charlie was both impressed and pleased, and told her so. He grabbed the doorknob then stopped short, looking suddenly uncomfortable. "Um, did you do my underwear too?" he asked.

"Ew! No! I'm not covering your junk! Ew!"

"Okay, okay, I was just checking — man!" he exclaimed. Charlie grabbed the doorknob once more then turned toward Robin again. "How come when it's a guy's ... stuff ... they call it junk? They never call a girl's stuff junk."

"That's 'cause ours can make babies. Yours can only make trouble. That's the definition of junk."

"You have an answer for entirely everything."

Robin just poked her tongue out at him. "Would you open the door already please, dimple perv?" she asked with a smile.

Charlie grabbed the doorknob. "I'm not a perv, I'm a scientist," he said.

"Same difference."

Charlie twisted the doorknob, and pushed the door open. On the other side, they saw a strangely lit hallway glowing with a yellowish tint. Directly across from them, they saw Charlie, his back turned, standing next to Robin, with both looking into a door.

"Okay, that's a little weird," both Charlies said flatly.

"Wow. I look pretty cute," the Robins said.

Charlie turned to look at her, and the doppelganger Charlie in the room ahead simultaneously turned to look at the second Robin. In stereo, the two Charlies said, "Would you please focus?"

Both Robins placed their hands on their hips and said, "I am focused. Stop being all bossy, please?"

Charlie and Charlie Prime both apologized, to which the dual Robin's responded by suggesting he close the door, as the scene was starting to give her a headache. Charlie did so, and it immediately locked with a noisy click.

"Very weird. I'm guessing that was your dream," Robin said, whispering.

"Why mine? It could be yours too. He paused then added, "Unless someone else is dreaming about us."

"Please, this place is creepy enough without you making me all paranoid. Can we just move on?" Robin asked, moving away from the door to walk down the corridor.

"Sure," Charlie said following her. As he caught up to her, he stopped then held up one finger. "Wait, I'll be right back."

Charlie reached in his pants pocket, and pulled out a black felt tip marker. He went to the door they'd just opened and wrote "CHARLIE PATTERSON" on it in large block letters. He had to tell her what it said, as she saw only gibberish.

"I figure that of the two of us, I'm more likely to be thinking of puzzles and paradoxes and stuff," he said.

"Parawhatsis?" Robin asked.

Charlie smiled and rejoined her. "Give it up, Robin. I've figured out you've been playing dumb."

"Yeah, that's a hobby of mine." Placing a finger to her lips, she said, "Do me a favor. Write 'G'pa Joe' on the door too." He gave her a questioning look, and she replied. "Just a feeling."

He ran back and wrote G'pa Joe's name on the door also. They began walking slowly down the hallway, looking at each door they passed. One was small and round, another a set of double doors made entirely of polished brass, with a sign on the door. Again, Robin couldn't read it.

"Are you just pretending not to be able to read it?" Charlie asked.

"Nobody can read in their dreams," Robin said. "I read that somewhere."

"Yeah, Jannet told me the same thing last week. She was talking about the left brain and stuff. I didn't get all of it, but she said they say because part of your brain is turned off, you can't read in dreams."

"Then how come you can?"

"Practice. I created a dream where I was standing, looking at a stop sign." He shrugged. "I just kept staring at it until I could read the word.

Now, I can read whenever I want."

My Dimple Boy is so smart.

"Anyway, the sign says 'No Soliciting.'"

"Humph, must be some rich kid," Robin sniffed, walking by.

"So, what's your method of choosing what door we go in?" Charlie asked.

"Oh, I'm just vibing on it."

"You're doing what?"

"I'm just checking them out to see which one has a vibe that feels interesting," she said, still eyeing the doors. "These all feel like kids' dreams. I don't want to deal with fairies and unicorns and nightmares just now … oh! That one."

42 – CRAZY OLD TOOT, WHO DON'T GIVE A DAMN HOOT

Charlie turned to where Robin pointed. Here the doors were quite different. On a corner, their very first intersection of the bisecting hallways was an old, metal-framed glass storefront door. There was writing on the door that was written to be read from the other side of the glass. Charlie and Robin peeked in and could just make out a metallic mesh grate and a concrete stoop on the other side of the door.

"That one? Why there?" Charlie asked, trying to see in the darkness.

"I don't know. It's just different. And look, it's like we're on the inside of the place, named ... whatever those jumbles mean, and that's the street. I wanna go exploring."

"It says 'Booker's Barber Shop,' the letters are just backwards."

"Not to me, those don't even look like letters," Robin said, cocking her head. "I think that one is a picture of a pig."

She turned the knob, and stepped through without a moment's hesitation. Charlie sighed, shrugged, and followed her through. On the other side, it was snowing briskly, light flakes of dry snow swirling in the breeze. It was cold, but not wet, as if some Hollywood director had insisted on realism in his special effects, but couldn't quite work out how to make the flakes melt. Despite the billowing powder, there was a clear blue cloudless sky — summer's clarity in clear defiance to the conditions on the ground below. In the still silence of a winter's snow, Charlie could hear the raucous cries of unseen seagulls. He looked left, down the sidewalk covered in dingy snow, barely making out the figure of a small, stooped man in a dark coat. The coat was a shambles, a remnant of what it used to be. Once woolen, and handmade by some designer's apprentice, it was now a hollow shell, its lining long ago shed by the ravages of time, heat, and well-soaked, wallowed-in filth. It partly covered the man, the shredded back of it exposing his dirty white shirt. It couldn't have offered any protection against the elements.

Robin followed Charlie's gaze, and seeing the man, immediately trotted over to where he was. Though cautious, even frightened in the hallway minutes before, she now had a mission, a fellow traveler in need, and she was on alert.

The man's name was Toussaint Hebert, once Tennessee Toot, now just "Crazy Ol' Toot, who don't give a damn hoot." He had been living on the streets since the early part of the 1980s, and, despite all odds, had survived into his late eighties. He would tell himself, out loud, and often, that he was only alive because, "God don't want me, and the devil don't want me in Hell." True or not, he had survived on a diet of thrown-out restaurant food, leftover tourist fare, cigarettes, and fifths of the cheapest rotgut gin man could produce.

Toot had stopped feeling the cold hours earlier, as he slipped into what was meant to be a final winter's nap. It was three a.m. in northwest Washington D.C. — Fourteenth Street, Northwest, to be exact — and Toot had found a spot on his favorite heat vent near Jimmy Booker's old barber shop. The shop had closed down long ago but Toot didn't mind. He had tried for some time to force his way inside, hoping to dull the chill in his bones and escape the growing blizzard — to no avail, however. The city knew well how to protect its precious abandoned buildings from squatters. Toot's body could not escape the cold, and as his teeth chattered and his body slowly began to shut itself down, his mind found an escape. In his fantasy, he was no longer in the nation's capitol, and it was not winter, not at all.

Toot had moved from Detroit during the Second World War, a few years after his friend Joe "up and joined the army." He had pimped, and hustled, and hoed around a bit, until a short stint in jail set his life even more adrift. After committing a pointless little burglary, he had entered the State Prison of Southern Michigan full of bluster, his gold tooth checked in with his other valuables. But Toot was a small man in a big prison. Without the protection of his brawny protégé, Joe, Toot had been easy prey for the long-term, hard-core residents. He had left prison less than three years later, a changed man.

Toot left the Jackson, Michigan prison, and left the state almost as quickly. He knew the state of Michigan had better things to do than chase down a small-time burglar who skipped parole. Toot was New York State's problem now. For a time, living in the Bedford Stuyvesant section of Brooklyn, Toot had done okay. He had even gotten a job sweeping up at a local barbershop, which had become his haven. He would listen to the gossip, sometimes share his stories of life on the road or in the southern juke joints. Toot worked for the smallest wage imaginable, but he had a place, finally a home, and life had been good. He worked hard to keep "his" floors swept spotless, and would reward himself with weekend trips to Coney Island, or even to the Jersey Shore.

It was as good a time as Toot's life had ever been. However, by the mid-1950s, Toot had started to drink on those weekends when he didn't have the money for the beach. Then he would drink his way through those cold winter nights, and eventually, through the pain of spring's colors with no one to love, or autumn's glory with nothing worthwhile to show. The barbershop kept "Old Toot" as long as it could, until they finally had to let him go. At the end, he had worked there two decades longer than the current owners had.

Toot had been a citizen of the streets ever since, eventually finding his way to Washington, D.C. to live on the streets amid a renewed urban landscape. As Toot's mind slipped into its final unconsciousness, it created images of the time his life had meaning. As it had done a week earlier with Joe, his mind had taken him to his past. In Toot's mind, he wasn't sitting in the snow; he was on the Jersey Shore, and life was good.

It was all swing and sway, and time to jive, and life was still worth having. His footprints were in the sand, the wet sand, cool, and soothing against the arthritic heat. His final trip was a far walk from caring how he looked, whether vagabond or wayward grandfather escaping the howls of beloved progeny. Simply, he knew relief, and, for a brief instance, he was flourishing. Memories forced themselves into his mind like an unwelcome guest, and he was all Zoot suit with the reet pleat, all conk and circumstance, and So. Damn. Ready. He was Toot, Toot the Red, Little Detroit Red, and he was at the top of his game.

And, at the Jersey Shore of his mind, he was young, with hair of red, and he was fine, in his mind, and bright yellow, back when it meant something. His ladies would beckon with eyes afire or dance a hip sway his keen hands could read in the midst of a purple jitterbug jump, hot in the smoky darkness. Allreet! He would jive and sway and the ladies they would swoon. Their faces revealed little of the sweat on their backs or twixt their flabby folds. But Red he was, blood red he was, and there would be no blacklisting for the Red on a jitterbug night. In his beleaguered mind, he was cool, real cool, like black ice on the winter pavement. He was fine, so fine, it was almost real — fine.

Yet, even in his snow-clouded mind, a still voice, soft and silent like the mounting snow, knew these were not those days. His body had grown numb against the cold, and so he let himself believe it to be summer. In his imagined summer's heat, with punctured youth and humbled gait, he had slid his jittery toes deep in the sand (snow), and remembered the heat. Toot was hot, and cool, and, far away in the purple darkness …

… he was no more than fifteen minutes from death.

"Charlie, something's not right here," Robin said, feeling Toot's brow.

"What do you mean, not right?" he asked. All Charlie could see was an old bum playing in the snow.

"I don't know, it's just something I feel — a vibe I guess you could call it." She squatted down and lifted a handful of the cold, dry powder. "This is snow, but it feels like sand when I hold it. See how he's playing in it? He's actually digging his toes in the snow."

Charlie leaned over, and waved his hand in front of Toot's face. "It's like he doesn't even know we're here." Charlie looked at Toot closely. "Something is … it's like I know him."

"We've been brought here to help him," Robin said.

Charlie's left brain was about to argue with her. He had always relied on logic in conflicts to get him through. Although his emotions were as strong as anyone's, he had never found them reliable in a crisis. His strength, he had always believed, was that he became calm when everyone else was becoming agitated. That was what happened with Jay Romatowski; Charlie was calm, and that calm rattled the bully's confidence.

This, however, was different. This was Robin, and everything he knew told him to trust her. They were different, these two — but perhaps the differences were what made them the right team.

"Look Charlie, remember when you said what we think is our strength is what we are supposed to overcome? In our last meeting, you were saying it's like a crutch. And both you and Jannet started saying how what we think are weaknesses are just hidden strengths we're afraid to use."

"Yeah, I remember. My grandma Kate used taught me that."

"Well this time I need you to not try to guess the answer, or think about all the facts you learned on the internet. I need you to not be a scientist. I need you to just look at him and feel what he's going through." Robin was tearful at this point. "I need you to trust me."

Charlie knelt down in the snow, and closed his eyes for a second. He took in a deep breath, and exhaled deeply. At that moment, Toot closed his eyes, and began a soft moaning sound, slumped over in a heap in the middle of the silent sidewalk on 14th Street. Charlie looked at him, and began to think aloud. He reasoned that he needed to talk, rather than be in his head. "I keep hearing seagulls, but I haven't seen one. It's snowing, but the sky is clear. The snow is cold, but it doesn't melt, and you say it feels like sand."

"Uh-huh, and I hear the birds too, but I didn't know what they are," she said.

Charlie opened his eyes. "He looks lost — lost and sad, like he's somewhere else … somewhere … oh my God! He's at the beach."

"The beach!" Robin exclaimed. "That's why the snow feels like sand."

"Yes, that's why things seem mixed up in here!" he blurted. "It's cold, but he thinks it's the beach. But I don't get why we see it so mixed up."

"Maybe we're not all the way in his dream, Charlie. Remember G'pa Joe? He was seeing stuff we didn't see — fighting against ghosts or something, like we only saw part of the dream."

"Okay then," he said, "you're the expert in here. What do we do?"

"Me? No way, you're the leader. I don't know what to do." Robin stood and took a step backward.

"We don't have time to argue. If he's in the snow playing like it's the beach, he's going to freeze to death. Look Mercedes, out there you guys made me the group leader."

"I don't know what to do," she whimpered.

"I'm good at puzzles, and pretty good at planning stuff out. But in here, it's all about imagination and emotion, and you're made for that. You need to lead now. So lead!"

It was Robin's turn to close her eyes and inhale. Toot groaned audibly, and slumped into Charlie's arms.

"Hurry up Mercedes! You can do it, I promise."

Robin nodded, and squatted down in front of Toot. "We have to make him feel us, Charlie. Hold onto him, I'm gonna try something."

Charlie wrapped his arms around Toot's torso, and Robin placed her hands on Toot's head, and spoke directly to him. "I need you to hear me. This is not the beach."

Toot groaned in response, but did not open his eyes.

Robin continued talking. "You can't sit here or you're going to die. I need you to feel us, and talk to us." All the while, she was focusing her thoughts on the street scene, noticing the details in the street. She began to describe the street, the closed stores, the swirling snow, and the parked cars.

Charlie looked up, and the sky was now black and cloudless. The air had become visibly colder, their breath lighting up in the now visible sulfur streetlights. "Keep it up, I think it's working," he said.

Toot moaned again, and Robin began to describe his filthy clothes, and the brick barber shop behind them. She looked at the front of the abandoned building where the bricks had long ago faded by the sun and pollution. Clearly visible were the stenciled words "Booker's Barber Shop" imprinted on the bricks. Robin expressed surprise she could read it, but as she concentrated, other details came into focus — the street sign, the no parking sign at the corner, even the DC Lottery sign in the store window across the street. She was lucid dreaming.

"Wake up!" Robin shouted at Toot.

Toot immediately opened his eyes and said, "Hey pretty girl. Goddamn it's cold out here." He looked down, and said, "I can't feel my feet."

"Come on, we have to get you out of here," Charlie said.

Toot looked at Charlie in response to the sound of his voice. "Hey Charlie boy. I didn't expect to see you two again." Robin gave Charlie a questioning look, but Charlie merely shrugged in response. "It's me, Toot … from Tennessee."

"Ohmigod," Charlie exhaled, breathlessly. "C'mon, we gotta help him."

The two slipped on Toot's beat up shoes, and stood him up. They began to walk, slowly, Robin holding his right elbow, and Charlie his left. They walked up 14th Street and then turned onto U street, where a small group of people was visible. They began to walk faster, with Toot stooped over, mostly stumbling through the snow. As they approached the crowd, Robin let out a large gasp.

"Charlie! Those people don't have faces."

"Jeez-o-flip!" he yelled, but continued walking. "Okay, I guess that means he's still asleep. Let's keep going. I don't know what else to do."

Robin thought for a second.

"I do! Hold on!" she said, suddenly running to the street.

She reached in the gutter and pulled out a large, empty drinking cup. Running back to Toot, she bent over and scooped up snow, filling the cup.

"Sorry, old dude," she said, and threw the 32 ounces of new snow in Toot's face.

Toot gasped, and his eyes shot open. "Holy hell little girl! The hell'd you that for?" Toot looked in Charlie's direction. His eyes appeared unfocused. "Joe?" he slurred. He looked around, blinking, and saw the cold, snowy scene unfolding around him. "Oh shit, I need to wake up."

And just like that, he was gone.

43 – "A PERSON STARTS TO LIVE WHEN HE CAN LIVE OUTSIDE HIMSELF" – ALBERT EINSTEIN

Robin and Charlie stood quietly for a second, not knowing what to do next. The faceless crowd in front of them began to melt as if they were wax figures standing too near the sun. Past the crowd was the clear form of Siri and his minions, still dressed like Klowns, all laughing.

"That is one big huge freak," Robin said.

A split second later, the buildings, street, and everything around them began to melt. Charlie and Robin began a frantic search for safety. Robin shouted, pointing behind Charlie.

"There! A doorway! Let's go!"

The pair ran as fast as they could to the open door. Inside, dim lights cast a yellowish haze cast onto the melting snow on the kids' side of the door. The ground beneath them began to dissolve and the door itself began to distort. They had no more than a few seconds left before it would become too twisted to get through.

"Jump!" Charlie yelled.

He and Robin sprinted, and leapt, tumbling through the doorway just as the last bit of ground behind them fell away into a seemingly interminable darkness. They landed in the hallway, in virtually the same spot from which they had entered, falling over each other. Charlie sat up, breathing hard. Robin was bent over, panting and coughing.

"You okay?" he asked. He hesitantly patted her on the back.

The door, no longer made of glass, but now the painted double doors of an ambulance, slammed shut behind them. As they watched, the doors became translucent ... transparent ... gone. Where they stood was only bare wall.

Somewhere on U Street in Washington, D.C. on a freakishly cold autumn night — the night of a rare October snowfall — an old man named Toussaint-Michel Hebert, had closed his eyes. He was embraced by the icy glove of a frozen night while in the throes of a massive heart attack. The paramedics speculated that he had fallen asleep after a daylong binge with the bottle by his side, and, as he fell into an alcoholic stupor, it had begun to snow. Something had awakened him from his deep slumber, and he had staggered to his feet, walking the half-block in the snow to where he had a chance of finding people. But years of alcohol abuse, tobacco, and table scraps of the unhealthiest of diets had taken their toll on his heart, and he had died there, on the street.

They could not have reckoned on the Overlord's contribution.

"I can't believe he made it as far as he did," the lead paramedic said.

"Yeah, the people standing by said he was clutching his chest the last thirty feet or so," said the on-duty Metropolitan Police officer. "By the time someone took the time to check on him, he was too far gone. Collapsed right into their arms, poor bastard."

"Yeah, the cold and booze got 'em, prolly," the paramedic said. "At least he didn't have to die alone."

"True. Most of the time, guys like him, we find half-buried in snow the next morning. Must be a horrible thing, to die alone like that."

Somewhere, deep in a strange hallway, one existing not in a place, but in a stream of thought, a handsome twelve-year-old boy held a lovely twelve-year-old girl as she wept. She had felt something — "a tug" she called it — the moment Toot had died. It was as if someone had forcibly ripped a connection out of her brain. She cried until her eyes could make no more tears; she cried until the pain from having her sister torn from her was likewise finally vented. She cried at the injustice of being given a gift with no instructions for its use.

All the while, her silent friend listened, and stroked her hair, and let her cry. And, when she could cry no more, she stood, touched her friend's tear-soaked shirt, and said, simply, "Come on Charlie, you and I have to go home. We're out of our league here."

Charlie nodded, stood next to her, and together they took a down-hearted left-turn passage in search of an exit. However, search as they might, every turn led simply to more doors, or to dead ends that forced them to retrace their steps. They attempted to find the doorway they had marked previously, but it was nowhere to be found. Frustratingly, when they did reverse their course, they found the hallway to have changed completely, as if it were a continuously changing puzzle box.

Finally, exhausted and exasperated, Robin sat down on the floor in a heap, and began to cry again. Charlie considered consoling her, but instead, sat next to her, and concentrated his energy on not allowing himself to cry too. Truly, he was way past feeling embarrassed at the prospect of Robin's seeing him cry, but he knew if he had allowed himself that relief, at that moment, it would have made her inconsolable.

Robin sobbed softly, more in frustration than anything else, until, her tension abated, she blinked back tears, looked at Charlie, and smiled. "Thanks for letting me cry it out," she said, to his amazement. "I always feel better afterwards. Most boys think you're all broken when you cry, and try to fix you."

Charlie managed to force a weak smile, but said nothing.

"Charlie," she asked, wiping her eyes, "do you ever cry?"

He thought about his answer for a long moment then shrugged. " If you cry alone, and no one hears, did you really cry?" he finally asked.

"Yes," she answered without a second's hesitation.

"Then, yeah," he answered, averting his eyes.

She leaned over, and gave him the single warmest hug of his life. "You are such a goofball, philosopher boy," she said smiling. Then, once more serious, she added, "Thanks for loving me the way I am. I love you too, you know."

Charlie had to concentrate very hard on not passing out.

Robin followed her statement by looking about as uncomfortable as one could look. Charlie stood, and reached down to help her up, but was interrupted by a soft tinkling sound. From a hallway around a corner came a "thump" followed by a scraping sound. Then again, "thump, scrape; thump scrape." Robin looked at him, eyes wide, and reached for his hand, pulling herself up. Cautiously, the two tiptoed to the corner, pausing. They looked to one another for reassurance then peeked, Robin's head above Charlie's, around the corner. There, sitting in the middle of a wooden floor, was a little girl, who appeared to be no more than four years old. She was playing jacks, with surprising dexterity.

As they tiptoed closer, the little girl, fair of skin, with blond hair, said, "Hi Robin. Hi Charlie." She did not turn to face them, instead, focused on her last jacks. "I'm up to twosies," she said. "I never get past threesies, though." She laughed, and looked over her shoulder at them. She was small for her age, but was clearly older than the four they took her for. She was a beautiful child, with round cheeks and crimson-painted lips "Come sit," she said.

Robin grinned, and said, "I love jacks. I used to be really good at this game."

"It is my guilty pleasure," the little girl said. "I must confess I'm not very good at it."

Robin looked taken aback at the girl's clear speech, but did nothing to indicate she was alarmed. Charlie, however, immediately went on the alert. "Hi Abner, I mean, Hannah, he said."

The little girl looked up at him, and then handed the jacks and the ball to Robin, who began playing. "Could you please sit?" the small girl asked. "You're making my neck hurt."

Charlie did as asked, but sat with his arms folded. "I'm sorry, I guess I'm a little tired of games," he said.

"Really?" the girl said. "That's unfortunate. You were chosen in part because you love games ... and riddles, so much."

"Don't mind him," Robin said, smiling. "He secretly loves this stuff." She leaned over and whispered, just loud enough for Charlie to overhear. "He's just being protective of me again."

The small girl smiled, and nodded. "That's what I love about you the most," she said to Charlie. "My name is Gabrielle, by the way, but you can call me Gaby."

"That's funny," Robin said with a laugh. "My friends always called me Gabby. But I don't think they meant it in a nice way. Threesies!" she enthused, throwing down the jacks once again. She confessed that she and her sister had played the game almost endlessly when Robin was a little girl. Playing was having an amazingly soothing effect on her, Charlie noted.

"I know what you're thinking," Gaby said to Charlie. "I'm not who you think I am. Do not be afraid, I come only to bring you good news."

Charlie sat with his arms folded, indicating that he was in no way receptive to Gaby's statement. They had been tricked too many times already in the Stream. Before responding, however, he looked at Robin, who was relaxed, and now in the midst of a lovely little dream. It was precisely what she had needed at that moment. They had tried to help save Reyna, and failed. They had found then lost, G'pa Joe. They had tried to rescue Toot, and he had died. Robin deserved a bit of joy.

Gaby placed her small hand on Charlie's, startling him. "You have not failed," she said. "The work is without end. One can only fail by stopping."

"But the old man froze to death," Charlie said. The emotions he had been withholding burst forth in a gush, taking away his breath. For a moment, he feared he may never catch his breath again. A solitary tear danced at the edge of his eyelids, pondering its descent down his dusty cheek. It thought better, and in its hesitation, was wiped away to its doom by the back of Charlie's hand. "It's hopeless," Charlie finally said. He looked at Robin, who was up to foursies, and oblivious.

Gaby nodded to indicate Robin, and said, "She's okay. She understood why I was here right away. She felt it."

"So why am I here?" he asked. "I didn't feel anything, that's my problem."

"You feel everything, that's your problem. You just haven't learned what to do about it." Gaby reached in the pocket of her dress, and handed him a small object. "Here," she said, have a piece of bubble gum."

Charlie almost cursed aloud then looked at Robin with the jacks, and started grinning. He was being handled, he finally understood, and he needed to follow. He took the bubblegum, chewed hard, and immediately blew the largest bubble he could make. Without so much as a glance in his direction, Robin reached over and popped it with a jack. Pink bubblegum covered his face, his neck, and the entire front of his curly brown hair. The three began to laugh, soft giggles at first, and then loud, boisterous guffaws. Charlie made no attempt to clean himself up at all.

"So do you know now why you're here?" Gaby asked once again.

Charlie, misunderstanding, answered, "Because we needed this?"

"Well, yes, but that's not really what I meant. *You* are why *I* am here. Do you know why you are here, in this Stream, at this time?"

"Because there is no one else," Robin said, and put down the jacks.

"There is always someone else," Gaby said. "But for the people you touch, there is no one else. You are here because you are for them."

"What, what about my G'pa Joe?" Charlie asked.

Gaby shook her head. "He is old, and he is not why you are here."

"Th-then why are we here?"

"Do you remember your struggle against the Klowns, young warrior?"

"Humph. Some warrior I am."

"Hush, Charlie," Robin said. "Yes, we remember."

"Did you happen to notice some children?" Gaby asked.

Charlie brightened into alertness. "Yes! They were in some kind of cage. With all the fighting, I forgot about them."

"We've seen kids like that twice," Robin added.

"They are why you are here, Charlie," Gaby said. "The dark one uses them for his purposes, as if they were batteries."

"Is that why they were there?" Robin asked.

Gaby nodded. "Those Klown demons you fought were created by Siri, using the energy from those children's minds. It is corruption of the most distasteful form."

Charlie nodded; Robin, however, was scowling. "So what do we do about it?" she asked.

"At the right time, you will know what to do."

"When is the right time?" Charlie asked, anxiously. "How will we know?"

Gaby leaned over and placed her hand on his chest, her jade green eyes shining. "You will feel it here," she said. She placed her hand on Robin's head. "And you will know the truth of it."

"But Charlie's the smart one," Robin protested.

Gaby stood, and smiled, brushing the floor's dust from her blue dress. "Intelligence is not about being smart, it's about being, smartly," she said, facing Robin. "As for you Charlie, don't worry about your emotions, instead, trust your feelings."

"I totally don't get that," Charlie said.

"The part of you that you call Charlene understood. Listen to it," Gaby answered, and closed her eyes. She began to emit ultraviolet light, which suffused the hallway. From behind her, translucent wings, as delicate as a damselfly's, spread behind her.

"Awesome," Robin said, in hushed tones.

"We don't really wear these things," Gaby said, "but I figured you would understand better." She began to fluoresce, becoming increasingly brighter and more difficult to see. A moment before she disappeared from sight entirely, she said, "Go, stand, and speak in dreams to your people all the words I have given you."

"What words?" Charlie shouted after her.

"I love you," came the reply, as she winked out of sight.

Charlie blinked, his eyes readjusting. "What do you think that was all about?" he asked.

"I think we were just told to 'get over it, and get to work.'"

"Yeah, that's kind of what I thought too."

"Charlene?" Robin asked, her face twisted in a smirk, and arms folded across her chest.

"It's a long story," Charlie sighed.

They looked around, and though they were still in the hallway, there was only a single door left. It was made of dark wood, deep as ebony. On it was written the words, in block letters, "FREE YOUR MIND."

"Well, let's go to work, Dimple Boy. I want to wake up, so I can get some rest."

Charlie smiled a two-dimple smile. "Yeah, I know what you mean."

44 – FREE YOUR MIND AND THE REST WILL FOLLOW

Robin pushed the door, straining at the effort. Charlie joined in, and felt sand beneath his feet. He tensed, believing they had returned to Toot's final dream. However, Robin's breathless, "Wow," put him at ease. He followed her through the doorway, blinking in brilliant sunlight. Ahead, as far as the eyes could see, were hills of brilliantly colored sand.

No, not sand, this is glass.

Charlie bent down, and let the small pebbles of glass run through his fingers. Excitedly, he turned to Robin, who was doing the same thing.

"This is like being back home, only prettier," she said.

True enough, the landscape was remarkably similar to the New Mexico desert he overflew as a balloon — with one major exception: instead of miles of brown earth and rock, at their feet glistened multi-hued glass. They walked gingerly across the desert floor, careful not to shatter the glass beneath them. To their amazement, the glass reacted precisely as sand would, their feet sinking in the soft "soil." After some fifty yards, Robin removed her shoes.

"Are you nuts?" Charlie asked. "You're gonna cut your feet to pieces."

"Oh, hush. It's just a dream, silly," She said, her black-and-turquoise-painted toes wiggling in the brilliant glass sand. After a cautious few steps, she turned back to Charlie, her braces gleaming in the sunlight. "You gotta try this! It feels just like sand."

"Uh, no thanks," Charlie responded.

Robin shrugged, and handed him her flip flops. "Well then you can hold these for me." Charlie tried to object, but by then, she was off, leaving varicolored footprints behind.

This is our work.

He started behind her. He was grinning from ear to ear, for the first time that he could remember in weeks.

I wonder if Gabrielle is still handling us.

Above them, the sky was bluer than any he had seen. Only Robin's eyes competed with its azure brilliance. The ocean of air was dotted with thin, cirrus clouds, which merged into the landscape at the horizon. Charlie stopped, and cupped his hand to his eyes. "Can you tell what that is?" he asked, gesturing to the distant landscape.

Robin squinted, and shook her head. "Not really." She turned, and her grin widened so much he feared her jaw would come unhinged. "I guess we know which way we have to go."

"How do you figure?"

"Gaby told me," she answered. Charlie responded with only a puzzled look. "She said, 'At the right time, you will know what to do.' Well, I know. We need to be where the sky meets the sand."

"I still don't get how you know that," he said. This Oneness felt like a gift Robin possessed, which he did not share.

Reading his expression, Robin stopped, and faced him. "That's because you think too much. Remember what she said. What do you feel?"

Charlie started to answer that what he felt was nothing, but that was not true. He did feel. Instead, he did what he would always do with Robin: he opted for the truth. "What I feel is stupid and frustrated, because I don't know how to do this dream stuff. I feel like I'm just a kid who's being asked to be some kind of dream superhero. And I feel tired, but I'm asleep, and I'm scared, but nightmares are a part of life here. And …" He paused, suddenly realizing that all the tears he had been withholding were about to cause a desert flash flood.

"Go on, Charlie," she said, gently touching his elbow. "You're doing great."

"He smiled at her, with one-half of a pair of dimples, and inhaled. " And, I don't want to be negative, but if we have to be there," he said, indicating the miles-ahead whiteness at the edge of the desert, "we're in big trouble, 'cause we're never gonna be able to walk that far."

Robin was nodding in agreement with everything he said. When he was finished, she asked, "So what do you want to do about it?"

Charlie shrugged, and lowered his head. A split-second later, he raised it, smiling, and said, "If it's too far then don't walk, dummy." Robin frowned at him, her lower lip poked out, and he quickly added, "No, no, that was kind of what I was telling myself in my head." Quieter, he said, "I call that part of me Chuck."

"Oh, well tell 'Chuck' not to be so rude next time."

Charlie laughed, and started to ask Robin what she thought they should do next; however, he was interrupted by the piercing sound of her whistling. She had two fingers in her mouth, as if she were calling for a taxi.

"Jeez-o-flip," he said, sticking his fingers in his ear, "where'd you learn to do that?"

"Yeah, graceful, huh?" she said, and winked at him.

Charlie looked up, and saw a large golden form flying in from points unknown. It was Aegis, Robin's tricorn, and she was flying as fast as her considerable wings could carry her. Aegis swept in low, her head back, and bellowed a line of fire skyward. On her second pass, she flew slower, but did not stop. Robin reached up, grabbed her long mane, and managed to climb onto the tricorn without its stopping.

"Okay, that was pretty cool," Charlie said, aloud.

On the third pass, Charlie tried the same trick, with no success. Two more passes, and three liters of glass pebbles in his shorts later, he managed to climb aboard the tricorn, and they took off due west, to the horizon.

"Aegis doesn't like to land on the sand," Robin explained. "It gets between her hooves and the shoes, and irritates her. Plus, I think she thought making you try our little trick was funny."

"Yeah, hilarious," Charlie said, as he surreptitiously shook glass sand down his pants leg.

They flew swiftly above the remarkable desert, with Aegis needing no direction. The colored glass portion of the sand did not last for long, transforming, within a few miles, to ruddy earth that was dotted with high plateaus of red rock. Some plateaus were flat, some tall, all standing like monoliths against the barren scenery. Charlie thought it the most beautiful place he had ever seen.

Without warning, Aegis began to descend, flying low enough to the ground that they could see the abundant life at the desert's floor. There were multi-legged creatures that looked like a snake-centipede hybrid, six-legged jackrabbits, and a strange bird that Charlie had never seen. It was feeding on what appeared to be a carcass.

"That's a roadrunner," Robin said. "I think, somehow, we're in the Stream and New Mexico."

"That's weird," Charlie replied. He did not get a chance to say anything else, as he was interrupted by the sound of singing. They searched but could find no source.

"Are you doing that?" Charlie asked Robin. He was seated behind her, but had contorted himself, so as to see her face. He was surprised to see she was crying. "What's wrong?" he asked, as the song continued around them.

"That's my Reyna," she said, wiping a tear. "She's still with us."

"How do you know that?"

"'A Horse with No Name.' That was my grandma's favorite song. She would sing that to us whenever we would go riding on her ranch. Only Reyna would have known that."

Charlie leaned back, and smiled. Then, as the reddish desert soil changed to pure, white sand, he began to sing, "You see, I've been through the desert on a horse with huge wings, it felt good to get out of my brain."

Robin laughed, and joined him, and the now-white desert was filled with the sounds of their singing, and laughter, and joy. Above, circling virtually unnoticed, just east of the sea, was a white bird with beautiful plumage. It circled and watched, circled and watched. Every so often, Robin would look up, and smile as she sang. Charlie did not understand why she did, but found the bird's presence reassuring.

***

After an hour's flight, Aegis eased to the ground. She walked now, her two charges still aboard. The desert floor sloped quickly uphill. They had reached a place of dunes — hills of white sand, upon which were scattered spiny yucca plants in full bloom. At the top of the dune, Aegis stopped, and Robin dismounted, followed by Charlie. Ahead was a caravan, riding across the white sand toward them. Behind the caravan was a long trail of tracks through the sand, which twisted their way to the distant horizon.

"I don't know where they're coming from," Robin whispered, "but I know where they're going."

"To where just we came from," Charlie finished.

"And we can't let them get there."

"Nope." Charlie paused then continued. "I sure wish I knew why."

"Oh shoot," Robin said.

Charlie turned in her direction, and saw she was holding her shield, and the long staff. Each tip of the wooden staff was topped with a heavy metal cap. Charlie felt his hip, and found, to no surprise at all, his sword. "Looks like we have some work to do."

They stood there, at the top of the dune, observing the approaching caravan. There were twenty to thirty wheeled carts, each covered with white tarps. The carts cut a single-file curved line through the desert sand, each pulled by enormous beasts with massive chests. Each of the animals' six legs ended in huge, padded feet, ideal for maneuvering through the desert sand. Their broad, shovel-shaped muzzles were bent low, their nostrils flaring as they labored to climb the dune.

Caretakers led the doe-eyed beasts, prodding them on their flanks with long sticks. These were humanoid, though impossible to see, as they wore long, white hooded cloaks that covered everything but their black skin.

"Wow, I thought *I* was black," Charlie remarked,

"No, you're ecru," Robin asserted.

The caretakers were the color of shadowed black panthers at midnight. Their jet-black skin and golden eyes against the white cloaks was breathtaking. For each cart, there was one caretaker, and a pair of soldiers. The soldiers were dressed in simple blue tunics, cinched at the waist with a wide belt. Each carried a broad sword, a knife, and either a wooden shield, bow and arrow, or a long spear. There were fifty soldiers, one Charlie, one Robin, and one Aegis.

As they approached to within fifty feet, the soldiers stopped, and one called up to the pair. "Who are you, and why are you here?"

Charlie answered, as much to his surprise as anyone's. "We were sent here to meet you."

"To what end?" asked the soldier.

"To free the slaves," Charlie replied, pointing to where the caretakers stood by their carts.

The soldier turned, and laughed. "Those are not slaves, boy, he said. They are guardians of the beasts, and they are with us."

Charlie looked at Robin, who was smiling. "He wasn't talking about them." She turned, and with one swift movement, was atop Aegis and in flight, before the first soldier could move.

Charlie noted that the lead soldier had approached to within fifteen feet, though he looked startled … and … it was only then that Charlie realized it was he who was in motion. The soldier was, upon closer inspection, decidedly not human. Though they had muscular, gray human bodies, their faces featured long brows, furrowed into rows of at least twenty parallel wrinkles. Their eyes were black, and deep-set low on their faces, near the bottom of their ears. They had no noses, and wide mouths with jagged teeth. Their ears were long and pointed, flopping as they ran like cocker spaniels.

The first soldier met Charlie sword to sword. The noisy, metallic clang of the first blow sent Charlie reeling backward onto the sand. Charlie was no physical match, but this was no physical battle. He recovered quickly, looking to strike again before the soldier could attack. The soldier however, was now holding his long spear, which was trembling. In the sand, at his feet, was his sword, broken neatly in two from Charlie's blow. The soldier stabbed at Charlie with the long sword, as a second soldier charged, swinging his sword wildly. Charlie spun to his right, and found himself behind the first soldier. He struck him in his back with the crimson sword, felling him.

The second soldier struck Charlie in the shoulder, drawing blood, but causing no real damage. Charlie's reflexes, honed from hours at video games, were sharp, and he swung upward with his sword even as he was struck, killing the second soldier.

Two down, a zillion to go.

Charlie reached the first cart, as two more soldiers charged. Ahead, Aegis erupted in a line of fire that raked through the charging soldiers like a brush fire through a New Mexico bosque. Atop Aegis, Robin was using her long staff to bash soldiers on their helmets as Aegis swept by in her low-level flight.

Half-a-zillion.

Charlie was smiling, as Aegis and Robin had already taken out the first line of soldiers. Charlie was now in tight combat with two soldiers, and though he was wounded for a second time, their weapons were no match for his sword. He had killed four soldiers, Robin and Aegis fifteen, but there appeared to be more soldiers now than when the fight started.

To his right, he heard Robin's scream, and he was running toward her before he knew what had happened. Aegis was on her side, on the sand, wounded, but alive. One soldier had brought her down with an arrow, and Robin had tumbled onto the white sand. She was covered with dark blood, most of it belonging to Aegis.

"Are you alright?" he asked, breathlessly, as he reached her.

"I'm okay, but Aegis is hurt."

Charlie and Robin were crouched behind the tricorn, who had managed to right herself somewhat, and was now lying on her belly. Four-dozen soldiers convened in a semi-circle around her, weapons drawn, and faces venomous with rage and anger. Behind, the cloaked caretakers stood silently next to their beasts.

"Jeez-o-flip, there are as many now as when we started."

"Yeah, every time we kill one, another appears out of nowhere. It's hopeless."

"So what do you want to do?" Charlie asked. "Aegis can't keep them back forever." Aegis was holding them at bay, raking the sand before her with fire whenever they approached.

Robin said, "Well, we can't get out of here with Aegis hurt, so I guess we just keep fighting."

Charlie looked at his friend, who was bravely attempting to cover up a small wound on her side from an arrow. He himself had a wound on his left shoulder, and his right arm was bleeding. His attention was caught once again by the caretakers, who were watching the scene with apparent indifference. "Robin, I have an idea," he said. "Those caretaker guys, the soldier said they were with them, but they aren't helping them."

"Yeah, well they aren't exactly helping us either."

"Maybe we didn't ask nicely enough," he said.

Robin looked at him, her eyes a brilliant blue. "Are you sure?" she asked, though he had mouthed no question. Still, he knew she understood him perfectly.

"I'm pretty sure," he answered.

Robin stood, and called to the caretaker closest them. He was standing silently, behind the semi-circle of soldiers. "We need you to help us," she called to them. "We can't do this without you."

The caretaker's resonant voice thundered in response, though no face could be seen inside the cloak. "Why should we help you, violent child?"

Charlie stood in answer. "That was my fault," he said. "I didn't understand before."

The caretaker replied. "If you fight as the beast fights then you become as the beast." His black hand swept toward the soldiers before him. The soldiers murmured in response, turning angrily toward the caretaker.

The caretakers aren't as with the soldiers as they think.

Charlie pressed on. "We were sent here, and we need your help to do the work."

"Sent here by what, child?" asked the caretaker.

Robin answered without hesitation. "By Gabrielle, and she said to give you a message."

The caretaker approached, walking through the line of soldiers as if they weren't there. None made an attempt to stop the caretaker, whether due to respect, fear, or complicity, Charlie could not tell. Behind, all of the caretakers had left their carts, and were now standing behind the soldiers, listening.

"And what message would that be, child?" the caretaker asked. He was standing directly in front of Charlie and Robin now. Aegis had made no attempt to stop him. The caretaker was ten feet tall, though it had been impossible to tell before.

Robin looked at Charlie, and whispered, "Do you think it's okay?" She did not look nervous, but calm, as if she were asking Charlie for his opinion about a new jacket.

"If Aegis trusts him, that's good enough for me," Charlie said. Aegis brayed happily in response.

"Gabrielle said to tell you, all of the caretakers, that she ..." she paused, correcting herself in mid-sentence. "That *we* love you," she finished.

"We're here doing her work," Charlie added, softly.

The caretaker stood silently for only a moment before turning toward the other caretakers, who murmured and nodded. "We are quite found of Gabriel," the caretaker said. If you have been sent, then it is to you whom we must deliver our charges. Without another word, the caretaker turned, and, in unison, the caretakers opened their cloaks, wrapping them around one then the next soldier. Each of the soldiers disappeared into the cloaks, screaming, fighting, clawing, and, finally, succumbing. In a matter of less than a minute, the desert was quiet, and the soldiers gone.

The caretakers nodded toward Charlie and Robin, and returned to their carts. Each pulled away the white tarp that covered his cart, exposing cages of small children. The carts were identical to the one that Charlie had seen being taken by the Klowns. The caretakers opened the cages, and one by one, groups of small children, none older than seven, began wandering toward Charlie and Robin. They appeared dazed, as if they had been awakened from a long slumber.

"These were being delivered to the one called Siri," a caretaker stated, matter-of-factly. It was as tall as the first, but the voice was female. "The small ones have much energy," she said.

"But Siri would just keep them all prisoners," Robin complained, "like slaves."

"More like batteries," Charlie added.

The female caretaker nodded. "Clearly, that is so," she said.

"But if you know that then why were you helping the soldiers?" Robin asked. Her eyes were green, but her voice was even.

"We were helping no one," the caretaker replied. "We provide only transport, and keep safe whatever cargo we are entrusted with."

Robin's face changed to fury, and for a moment, Charlie feared her head would explode. "It's okay," Charlie said, trying to calm her. "It's like what my mom calls 'works for hire.' They were just doing their job, like we are."

"Well, I don't understand how anyone can help evil people hurt little kids."

"It is not for us to decide who will hurt, and who will save our cargo," a third caretaker said.

"Then I don't get it," Charlie said. "If that's true then why did you help us?"

"It is as I said," came the first caretaker's booming voice. "We are quite fond of Gabriel. If you carry his mark then you are assuredly ones whom will care for our cargo ..." he paused, his voice softening. "Perhaps the words 'our charges' would be more pleasing than cargo," he said, his head dipping slightly.

Charlie understood. The caretakers were neither good, nor bad. They were entrusted with delivering precious cargo, and would, to whomever they believed were the rightful recipients. Charlie and Robin were the recipients of the children, two of whom were now sleeping at Robin's feet.

"You keep saying 'Gabriel,' Robin said. We met a little girl, who said her name was Gabrielle."

The caretakers laughed in unison. "Yes, that can be quite confusing at first, the female caretaker said. Gabriel ... Gabrielle does not seem to like being one form for very long."

"Nor does she choose a permanent gender," said another. "Most, however, call her Gabriel. Perhaps you have read of him."

Robin gasped and crossed herself. Seeing her, Charlie's eyes widened, and he nodded. "Y-yes, my Grandma Kate told me about him."

Without another word, the caretakers walked back to their now-empty carts, and began turning the beasts from whence they came.

"Where are you going?" Charlie asked. They were miles from anywhere, and Aegis was in no condition to fly.

"We are going home, as you must," said a caretaker, pointing them toward the eastern horizon.

"But we have no way to get back," Robin said. She was looking worriedly at the flock of small children who buzzed around her. They were laughing and playing, but none was more than twenty feet from her at any moment.

"Then child, you must click your heels together three times," the caretaker said.

"Wow! Really?" Robin asked, "Like Dorothy in the Wizard of Oz?"

"No, not really," said the Caretaker. "I was just teasing." All the caretakers, and Charlie, began laughing in unison. "You just have to wake up, child," the caretaker said, turning, as the group began their return trip home.

"You are so gullible," Charlie laughed.

"Oh shut up," Robin said, smiling. "You totally believed him too."

"Did not," Charlie said, totally lying, as his alarm clock began buzzing, waking him from the strangest slumber of his life.

He lay there, thinking of the night's adventures, with amusement, and sorrow, for Toot; with horror, for the beasts that the night hid; and in joy, for a job well done. They had not helped G'pa Joe, but had freed the minds of dozens of small children, directed by – it seemed – the angel, Gabriel.

I am totally wrong for this job.

"*That you think so is precisely why you are right,*" replied a voice in his head. This time, it was the voice of neither Chuck nor Charlene.

Charlie lay there, staring at the ceiling.

If that's the case, then nothing on Earth is going to stop me from saving G'pa Joe.

It was a promise he made to himself, one that burned deeper in his psyche as he lay there, quietly, waiting for the house to grow loud with the sounds of morning.

45 – M&M AND THE GEE UNIT

After a night filled with adventures, Charlie and his mom picked up Robin and headed to the Southside Senior Center. Charlie spent the entire thirty-minute trip chuckling, as Charlotte seemed to be ready to adopt Robin at any minute. He wondered aloud if Mrs. LeBeaux would consider a trade for Layla, which earned him a poke in the head from Robin, whom was seated in the back seat.

"Serves him right," was all his mom said.

Charlotte Patterson was impressed that a girl Robin's age would be willing to spend a Sunday hanging out at an old folks' home, even for the sake of a friend. Robin explained that in her mom's family the elderly were revered, and she had grown up loving their company. In fact, Robin told her, she was excited to meet G'pa Joe, since Charlie had been talking about him virtually non-stop since they met. What neither Robin nor Charlie mentioned was that due to the previous night's dreams, they were now determined to help those they could reach. G'pa Joe, Mary, and their friends were all still within reach.

Just after two o'clock, the trio walked into the small room that served as a party room for special occasions. As they entered, Mary, who was bouncing from guest to guest like a barefoot, gray-haired fairy, greeted them. With her was Abe Singer, Sarge Sargent, Jay Patil, a few members of the nursing staff, and of course, G'pa Joe.

"Hey G'pa!" Charlie said brightly, waving as he entered.

"Hey yourself," G'pa Joe muttered. He looked at Charlie only after a few seconds' delay then his eyes lit up with recognition. "Well, it's good to see you!" G'pa said, looking at Charlie first then Charlotte, and smiling. "I haven't seen you in years."

"Very funny, Pops," Charlotte said. "I was just here a couple of weeks ago.

Nora Radcliffe, the head nurse, walked over to Charlotte to brief her on her grandfather's status. Charlie and Robin stood nearby. Nurse Radcliffe's normal protocol would have been to shoo the kids away, but she knew the close bond Charlie had with Joe, and she spoke to him and Charlotte as if they were equals. "He's probably not being funny," Nurse Radcliffe said. "He's having a pretty good day, as they go lately. He seems to know who people are, although he sometimes thinks he's still in Alabama."

"He hasn't lived in Alabama since the 1940s," Charlotte said, a vertical line creasing her brows.

Charlie, on a whim, looked at G'pa Joe and said, "He's been to Tennessee more recently though." G'pa Joe looked startled. He turned to Charlie and Robin and winked. He was not as far gone as he pretended.

They ate lunch, and snuck Singer some KFC chicken as soon as the nurses left. That made Robin giggle, as she thought it was "very cool" to be sneaking food to the "prisoners."

"Now, this is a smart girl," Singer responded, giving Robin a hug. "I try to tell my own granddaughter they have me locked in a prison, and she just tells me to quit exaggerating. I should introduce her to this young lady."

"That young lady is Charlie's girlfriend," Mary Margaret said authoritatively.

"Ain't nobody ask you nothing, Miss Mary Know-it-all," G'pa Joe said, mumbling through bites of potato salad that Charlotte was feeding him.

Charlie sputtered words that were meant to clear up their relationship.

Charlotte came to the rescue by telling the group that Robin was in fact Charlie's best friend, and that her "baby" was still "too young" to be dating girls. She turned to Robin and said, "When he does, I hope it's someone as sweet as you."

Robin hugged her, and gave Charlie a huge "thank you for including me," smile.

"Bah, the boy's twelve today. That's old enough for a sweetheart," G'pa Joe said. He looked at Robin. "Better eat your chicken, little bird, before that greedy-ass Singer gets to it."

Robin's mouth hung open, and she and Charlie exchanged confused stares.

"Pops, don't be rude," Charlotte said.

Robin smiled. "It's okay, my sister used to always call me that. I like it."

G'pa Joe winked again, and said, "I like birds. Make me feel free, them birds."

The group ate lunch, with the kids spending most of the time laughing at the old folks who sat around gently bickering with and poking fun at each other. After they ate, Mary Margaret walked over to G'pa Joe's boom box and put in a CD she had handpicked. The nurses and a couple of orderlies who had come in to mooch pieces of birthday cake immediately began giggling.

Mary walked to the center of the room, and was joined by Singer and Jay Patil, both of whom had put on dark sunglasses. Singer unbuckled his belt, and his pants immediately sagged below his potbelly, with the last three inches of cuff dragging on the floor. Jay assumed his best "gansta" pose, which looked delightfully ridiculous on a devout seventy-three-year-old Hindu man from Delhi.

"Mom, what is going on?" Charlie asked.

"Beats me, kiddo," Charlotte responded.

"Now, ladies and gentlemen — and Joe," Singer said, poking out his tongue at G'pa Joe and holding a pretend microphone made from a TV remote control unit. "I bring you the world famous M&M and the Gee Unit."

The nursing staff and remaining guests broke out in rather raucous applause, as Charlie, Robin and Charlotte just sat looking puzzled. G'pa Joe plugged his ears with his large fingers.

"Gee Unit?" Charlie asked.

Nurse Radcliffe leaned over. "It stands for Geriatric Unit."

Mary pressed play on the boom box, and a hip-hop beat kicked in. She grabbed the pretend microphone, and immediately broke out in a rap she had written to that particular beat. It would never have been mistaken for "gansta" rap, but it was bright and funny, bubbly and energetic. It was the old Mary of Haight-Asbury — the artsy, poetic Mary. She had come back, and she was home, faculties intact, to stay. Charlie, having known her at the depths of her Alzheimer's despair, looked, incredulous, to Nurse Radcliffe, who simply shrugged.

"Well, we have been trying a new drug," said Nurse Radcliffe, "but even the manufacturers can't account for her recovery. It's a bit of a miracle. We don't know how long it will last, but we're all delighted for the time we have now."

Charlotte pressed to have her grandfather given the same meds as Mary, although she knew that was not possible. Robin again made eye contact with Charlie. Neither believed Mary's recovery was due to drugs. This was somehow connected to G'pa Joe, although they didn't know how.

Nurse Radcliffe looked at Mary, who was now trying to coax Sarge to dance in his wheelchair. "See? She is the absolute life of this place," Nurse Radcliffe said, smiling. "It turns out she's a poet, a singer, a painter, and just a wonderful storyteller. Can you imagine all that personality, all those memories trapped inside, not being able to get out?" Nurse Radcliffe gave an uncertain smile, shook her head, and left, ushering the staff back to work.

Charlie looked at G'pa Joe, and said, "Yeah, I can imagine it."

Robin walked up to Mary and asked, "Are you really a poet?"

"I used to be," Mary said. "In fact, I taught poetry for many years. I taught painting too, but only for fun. Poetry I taught for my career."

Charlie, overhearing, came over and showed Mary his birthday jacket that he was all but sleeping in. "Look Mary, Robin painted this herself."

"Wow," Mary said, "you are very talented. Come by again and we can do some painting together." She leaned toward Robin and whispered. "You know how it is when you're surrounded by non-artists. They just don't get it."

Robin smiled and nodded. "Um, I really liked your raps, especially the prison break one. I kind of write poetry myself."

"Robin, would you be willing to share some of your poetry with me sometime?" she asked.

"Um, I'm like … I don't know. I mean thank you, I'd like to, it's just …"

"I promise, I'm not here to judge it. I just want to share with a fellow artist. The person who painted that lovely dragon has vision I want to see."

"Okay," Robin said with a shy smile. "I do have my journal in my purse. I kind of always keep it with me."

"You kind of always keep everything with you," Charlie said.

"Hush, hater." Robin fished in her oversized purse, and pulled out the small book. "I have one I wrote this morning. It was about something that happened in a dream. It really made me cry — the dream, not the poem."

She looked at Charlie, who was now sitting quietly with G'pa Joe as he stared out the window. "Charlie was there with me," Robin said.

Mary's eyes brightened, and she slid forward until she was sitting on the edge of her chair. "What do you mean, he was there?"

"We've been having the same dreams," Robin said. "We started going from dream to dream — it's like having a stream that connects everyone's dreams, and we can somehow travel down the stream."

Mary leaned forward then checked the room. "I know about that Stream. I've been there too — with Joe."

Robin's face bloomed surprise, and Mary relayed the story of her encounter with the wolves, the snakes, the tree, and her subsequent rescue by Joe. Robin called Charlie over, the two kids now enthusiastically conspiring with Mary. They told her how they had seen G'pa Joe in a dream fighting ghosts. Together, they realized that the kids had witnessed Mary's rescue, but only from the outside, not from within Joe or Mary's dream. The kids then shared their most recent adventures, and, in particular, Siri and Gabrielle.

Mary leaned in and began whispering. She told them that G'pa Joe had rescued her; she didn't know how, but he had managed to bring all of her back. Whatever force he beat to do that, must have become enraged, as he had not been the same since. Mary dabbed her eyes, and looked at Joe.

"I feel like this is my fault," Mary said. "He's always so brave, always the hero, and that's what got him in this mess."

"Charlie's just like him," Robin said without hesitating. Charlie averted his eyes and smiled. "My sister was wise like him."

G'pa Joe, sitting quietly nearby, looked at the trio for the first time. "Yes, she is," he said.

Mary's eyes narrowed. "Hush Joe, you never even met her." To Robin she added, softly, "I'm sorry sweetheart."

"That's okay," Robin said. She looked at G'pa Joe, who was looking at her with a clarity that disputed the reports of his advancing senility. She noticed his use of the word "is" but said nothing.

"I want you kids to be very careful with this." Mary warned. "I think you should stop while you're ahead."

"We will be careful," Charlie said. "But we can't stop just yet." He looked at Robin. "We'll know when it's time, but we've kind of been told now isn't that time." Robin nodded in accordance. "I don't know how to help G'pa Joe," he continued, "but I'm working on that. Until then, there are probably a lot of people we can help."

"Well, actually," Robin added, on impulse, "I think there a bunch of little kids that doctors will suddenly be able to reach."

"Are you talking about that 'premature dementia' stuff from TV?" Charlie asked.

"Yes," Robin answered. "I've been thinking about all those little kids we helped. After hearing Mary's story, I just get the feeling it was the same thing."

Charlie's face flashed brief, but intense anger. "If that's what happens when this Siri character traps kids, I guess we don't have any choice. We've gotta stop him."

Mary stroked Charlie's curly hair. "You are just like Joe," she said. "I won't tell you to stop, I have no right. Besides, you'd no more listen to me than Joe would."

"He is pretty stubborn," Robin agreed, looking at Charlie.

"Just promise me you'll be careful," Mary implored.

"We will," Robin said. She leaned into Charlie and said softly, "We have a lot of work to do, Dimple Boy. Superheroes never rest."

"Some superheroes. Dimple Boy and The Hamster Avenger."

"Yuck. I prefer Dream Girl," Robin said, sticking out her tongue and scrunching her face. "Let's pretend you never saw me do that, okay?"

Charlie laughed, as did Robin. G'pa Joe joined in, though it wasn't clear he knew why he was laughing.

Mary gave both kids a hug, and convinced Robin to let her read the last night's poem. They sat together, talking, with Robin occasionally erasing, and re-writing in her journal. After another half hour, Mary stood, announcing, "Ladies and gentlemen, Miss Robin Mercedes LeBeaux would like to read you an original work she wrote today. It is a large work about one small homeless man." She gently touched Robin's back. "Go on, sweetie."

Everyone in the room, except G'pa Joe, turned attentively to Robin, who spoke, her voice almost a whisper, looking at her paper, and not the room.

"It's called 'At Three,'" she announced. "At Three," she repeated, clearing her throat.

"At three, the gentle night breeze kissed with fetid, frosty breath,
an empty life that no one missed, to give the sleep of death.
His arms are drawn up to his chest, his legs are twisted under.

He speaks no more with mind possessed, from lips now drawn asunder.

His warmth a dying coffee cup, now spilt around his feet
his final hope he vomits up, a victim of the street.
At four, they place him in a vault, don't ask a single name.
At five, decide it's no one's fault - another drunken shame."

Robin wiped the few tears that had formed as she read her piece and allowed herself to see it once again in her mind. The room burst into applause, in particular Charlie, who admitted being stunned his gentle friend wrote with such passion.

"Wow, Robin," Charlotte said, hugging the girl. "That's incredible — especially for a twelve-year-old girl."

"Thank you," Robin said, smiling. "Well, Miss Mary helped me with some of the words. I couldn't think of a good word that rhymed with 'under.' I'd never even heard of 'fetid' before."

Charlotte hugged her again. "That's still extraordinary baby."

Robin looked at Charlie, and said, "So now at least you can feel my tears."

"I always feel you," he said, smiling at her. "Even before we met."

Robin placed both index fingers in his dimples and smiled tears at him. "How about you and your dimples take me home," she said, "I need a nap."

"His name was Toot," G'pa Joe interjected from across the room. No one even knew he had been listening.

"Whose name, Pops?" Charlotte asked, but by then, G'pa Joe's attention was elsewhere. He ignored her question entirely.

Robin and Charlie looked at each other, and Charlie broke out into a smile, which was matched by Robin's. He had been there, and he had been watching. That meant there was still hope. G'pa Joe could yet be saved.

46 – MOUNTAIN MAN

Charlie was sitting in the back seat of his mother's car on the ride home from the Senior Center. As the autumn landscape blurred by, the gentle swaying of the car on the road, and the rush of wind against the convertible's soft top soothed him. Robin was seated up front. He smiled, listening to his best bud and his mother chatting away like two old friends.

Robin had come to Virginia despondent, having lost a large part of her joy with the death of her beloved sister. However, in a few short months, she had found more family — Charlie's.

Charlie thought about the recent events — their discovery of the Stream, and each other, their realization that what they did in the dream state could affect people's lives. Indeed, they had both found confidence in the Stream. Charlie was becoming more outgoing, much more alpha male than lone wolf. For her part, Robin, who had come to Virginia shattered into many fragments, was finding the way to peace. She was becoming whole again.

True to Robin's prediction, the car's radio was filled with news stories regarding a number of local children whom had emerged overnight from varying states of seemingly irreversible brain damage. Doctors were stunned. It would be a story repeated many times, worldwide, over the coming days.

As he drifted into a serene sleep, Charlie's thoughts turned to losses as well. His parents' marriage was crumbling. Charlie had to watch helplessly as his one hero, G'pa Joe, slowly lost his grip on himself, and drifted toward senility. G'pa Joe haunted his thoughts.

So, it came as little surprise when he "awoke" from consciousness standing in the familiar hallway with the yellow brick carpet, outside room 318 in the Senior Center. Once Charlie realized where his dream had taken him, he pushed the door open with a grin.

"Hi G'pa ..." he said, the remainder of his sentence caught in his throat. He was not in the Senior Center at all. Instead, he stood on the westward peak of a great mountain range, overlooking a deep canyon lined by rust-colored cliffs. The cliff's edge was no more than thirty feet from the door. Charlie could see the chasm fell away sharply to the canyon floor several miles below. The mountain range extended as far as he could see, fading in the horizon from the warmly lit reddish peaks nearby, to a dark, snow-capped range in the distance. Cutting through the range was an immense expanse, twice the width of the Grand Canyon's widest point. In the center of the vast canyon was a spire of jagged rock. To Charlie, it resembled an enormous totem.

It was split at the bottom into twin outcroppings several hundred feet thick. A single peak of rock that resembled a torso joined them. It was topped by a relatively square rock that teetered precariously on a thin neck of crumbling stone. The entire structure looked like a primitive stone statue of a man, six miles tall. At the very top, stood a small figure of a man, waving vigorously. It was G'pa Joe.

"Charlie boy," he shouted, "come here." He was separated from Charlie by a horizontal space of a half-mile.

"G'pa?" Charlie shouted back. "How'd you get over there?"

"It wasn't my idea," G'pa Joe yelled. "Now get over here and give me a hug. I haven't seen you in ages."

Charlie couldn't help but laugh. It appeared as if the Stream G'pa Joe was as unaware of what happened in the Center, as the waking G'pa Joe was. "I can't get over there," Charlie shouted. "It's too far."

From the rock, he heard his great-grandfather laughing. After some time, he stopped, and called to Charlie. "Boy, this is your dream. Use your imagination. If you ain't got one in here, where do you have one?"

Charlie thought for some time. He cupped his hands to his mouth, and called out towards G'pa Joe. "Walk!" he bellowed.

"Boy, I ain't walking nowhere," G'pa Joe shouted back. "I'm old, and I'm tired."

"I'm not talking to you," Charlie shouted.

With that, the slender butte on which G'pa Joe was standing began to groan and shake. G'pa Joe looked around nervously and steadied himself on the quaking structure. Suddenly, one of the thick spires

Charlie had decided looked like legs tore itself from the canyon floor below, and took one mighty step toward Charlie. It landed back on the canyon floor with a reverberating thump that scattered the canyon's nesting birds.

G'pa Joe starting hooting, his head thrown back, and his arms wrapped around his belly. As the mountain-man walked obediently toward Charlie, taking two-hundred-yard steps, G'pa Joe had the best laugh he had enjoyed in years. Charlie grinned and began laughing as well, upon seeing G'pa Joe's delight. As the mountain-man reached Charlie's cliff, G'pa Joe hopped onto the plateau and gave Charlie an enormous hug.

"Boy, I've been trying to do that for days," G'pa Joe said. "You have the gift, that's for sure."

"G'pa, you have no idea how glad I am to see you," Charlie said, brimming with adrenaline. "I was afraid you were lost."

"Don't worry about me, Charlie boy. I'm just fine."

Charlie turned and pointed to the door he had entered. "Let's get out of here," he said.

"No, not yet," G'pa Joe said. "There's still work to do here. And you're the one to do it."

"But why can't I do it with you back safe where you belong?" Charlie asked, tugging lightly on G'pa Joe's arm.

"Because, I need to watch over you," G'pa Joe said. "I ain't as trapped as he thinks."

"You mean Siri?" Charlie asked.

"Yeah, you could say that I guess." G'pa Joe looked once again at the mountain-man, whom had begun walking along the canyon, looking very much like a small child exploring his world for the first time. "Old Siri's gonna be some kind of pissed when he sees what you did," G'pa Joe said, laughing as the mountain-man scared a pair of nesting eagles into a steep dive from their perch.

Charlie looked at the now-skipping mountain man, and laughed. "Did he put you there?" he asked.

G'pa Joe nodded, "Yep. That was supposed to be my new prison, I guess. Close enough to the door to see my way out, but too far to jump."

"If it was too far for you, why did you tell me to do it?" Charlie asked.

"Because, I've been watching you and Robin. You two got the gift, I told you. Heck, I couldn't even move before you showed up here."

Charlie looked around, and the view of the canyon was changing before his eyes. The valley was filling itself with flowers, and the sky began to dance with colors and light. The birds that had once filled the crevices in the rocks were in mid-flight, and changing form. They became dragons, and flying dinosaurs, and even a two-headed lion with wings that used to be a pair of eagles. Smaller birds blinked with bright light, and became fairies that lit up the twilight sky like a horde of fireflies.

"What's going on G'pa?" Charlie asked, awestruck. The entire scene was being filled with unimaginable beauty as he watched.

"I think your friend is here," G'pa said, and motioned toward the door.

It opened, and in strolled a yawning Robin. "Hey Dimple Boy!" she said. "Wow, look at this place."

"It just changed to this," Charlie said, eyeing her. "Did you do this?"

"Me?" she asked, grinning as a fairy landed on her outstretched hand. "I just fell asleep when your mom stopped at the store."

G'pa Joe extended his large hand and introduced himself. Robin did not mention they had just met earlier in the Senior Center. In any case, this was the real G'pa Joe, and earlier meetings did not really count.

"Robin, how did you find me?" Charlie asked.

She looked at him with confusion then pointed to G'pa Joe. "He called me. You were right next to him, and he said to come in here."

Charlie spun and looked at G'pa Joe, who simply smiled. "I told you, Charlie Boy, there's a lot to learn. You keep following rules too much. Who said you can't be in two places at the same time?"

G'pa Joe told the two that while part of his mind was engaged with Charlie, other parts had reached out and found Robin, who was asleep near Charlie in the car. Prior to Charlie's arrival, and the power his mind added, G'pa Joe could barely think, much less move through the Stream. Strengthened, he invited her to join them, because he wanted to show them both something.

"Well, what is it G'pa Joe?" Robin asked. She was all smiles and braces, her hazel eyes radiant in the warm evening sunlight. No one but Charlie (and the Reyna bird) had ever called G'pa Joe that, not even Layla. Charlie was as protective with the name as a miser was with his first earned dollar. With Robin, however, Charlie had not even blinked.

"You love this girl huh?" G'pa Joe said, nudging Charlie.

"What?" Charlie asked, taken aback by the question. "I guess so. She's like my sister, except I actually like her."

Robin punched Charlie in the arm. "Stop that," she said. "I told you, she's just hurting, and we have to figure out how to help."

G'pa Joe smiled and swept his arm towards the beautiful canyon. Multicolored waterfalls were bursting through the sides of the mountains. "That's the kind of vision that turned this place into what you see," he told Robin.

"Me?" she said. "I did this?"

"Charlie and I saw nothing but an empty valley. It was like a giant Grand Canyon — beautiful, but not exactly full of life. It became what you see now, because of you." G'pa Joe laughed, slapped his knee, and did a little hop step. "Old Siri's gonna be some kind of pissed when he sees what you did to his prison."

"But how, G'pa?" Charlie asked. He was wondering why the Stream seemed to like Robin more than him, but he wasn't about to say so.

"It's the gift — you two are the One," he said, looking at them both. G'pa Joe took them each by the hand and walked to the edge of the cliff. "Okay, jump!" he said.

Charlie looked at him, eyes wide in horror, but said nothing. Robin looked up at G'pa Joe with a huge grin and said, "Really?" G'pa Joe nodded, and Robin immediately yelled "Generalissimo!" and leapt from the cliff, arms wide, and without a moment's hesitation.

Charlie called to Robin, whom he was certain was now quite dead, and turned toward G'pa Joe — who was obviously a murdering, doppelganger, friend killing, false G'pa Joe. "Why did you do that?" he asked angrily.

"It's called a leap of faith, Charlie boy," he soothed. He pointed to the canyon, where Robin could be seen soaring with a large white bird with radiant plumage that extended for ten feet behind her. "That's her sister," G'pa Joe said. "We see a bird, she sees the real girl."

Charlie was even more frustrated now. He had discovered the Stream, but apparently, his lack of imagination kept him from using it to its potential. "How am I going to be able to help people if I can't even imagine how?"

"You're missing the point, Charlie. She sees things the way they should be, and that's a beautiful gift."

"That's why this place changed when she showed up," Charlie reasoned.

"Yep, but you have a gift too."

"Me? What, I can bore the enemy to death, right?" Charlie asked cynically. "Maybe one day I can do their taxes like dad."

G'pa Joe ignored the sarcasm. "You see things the way they are. No lies, no tricks, you just know." He pointed to the mountain-man that was now sitting on the canyon floor, playing as a flock of firebirds encircled him, making lovely patterns of fire and light. "See, you looked at that rock, and immediately saw the man inside, and freed him."

"That was a man?" Charlie said.

"He's been catatonic for years. He lives in a hospital, and stands in place all day, never moving, never responding. He can, but won't." G'pa Joe took Charlie by the hand. "I used to talk to him a lot, even though he never answered."

"I didn't know," Charlie said. "It just reminded me of a totem pole, that's all."

"Don't matter," G'pa Joe said. "What does is that he'll be making great progress now because of you. You didn't know with your brain, you felt in your heart he was a man."

Charlie looked again, and noticed that the mountain-man seemed to be much less rock, and quite a bit more soft earth. His movements were more limber, freer.

"We did this together, didn't we?" Charlie asked.

"You and Robin," G'pa Joe nodded. "You saw the man, she saw the child the man could be, and gave him a reason to want to be more than he was." G'pa Joe placed his hand on Charlie's shoulder. "In order to make a change, you gotta know what something is, and what it can become. That's what you and Robin did."

"But neither one of us did it on purpose," Charlie said. He did not think he should get credit for something he had done almost accidentally.

"That will come in time," G'pa Joe said, facing the setting sun. "You're learning quickly — like you did with Toot."

"But we failed. He died."

"You didn't fail, he was dying anyway," G'pa Joe said, embracing him. "Because of you, he didn't have to die alone — believe me, that matters. I was with him. He knew it, even though you couldn't see me."

"I hope you're right," Charlie said. He remembered Toot calling his old friend's name. "I think Robin felt you were nearby too."

G'pa Joe smiled, and nodded. "It's why you're so scary to Siri. I was his prisoner, and even he didn't know I'd slipped out. Robin knew right away. Imagine what you can do to him when you both really try." G'pa Joe sighed. "Now that I've gotten off his little prison rock, he's gonna have to put me someplace worse."

Charlie was horrified. "That's why we need to get you out of here."

"No, Charlie boy," G'pa Joe answered calmly. "There are people where he'll be taking me, people who need a leader." G'pa Joe shrugged, looking wistfully at the sunset. "It's what I do, what I've always done. Look Charlie, I have to be honest. This time with Siri was pretty peaceful, as these things go."

"That was peaceful." It was meant to be a question, but the thought stuck in Charlie's head, and it came out as a statement.

"Yep," G'pa Joe said. "The next time you meet, things are likely to get quite a bit … well, Toot might not be the only person we end up mourning. You need to prepare yourself for that."

Charlie was about to object, the rational Chuck portion of his brain calling out for a truce, an end to the nightmare madness. However, before he could speak, G'pa Joe took several sudden steps backward, and then ran full bore toward the cliff. Joe plummeted like a stone for a great distance, waving his arms frantically, as Charlie screamed from above. Finally, when G'pa Joe could no longer be seen, Charlie dove off the cliff, changing his form into that of a giant tan falcon as he fell. Within seconds, he had caught up to G'pa Joe, who he found floating in place, arms folded behind his head, hidden below a low-hanging cloud.

"See Charlie boy," G'pa Joe said, grinning, "all you needed was a reason. You'll do fine."

"G'pa, you almost scared me to death," Charlie complained, his voice echoing as an angry screech against the canyon's walls.

"No, boy, I scared you to life. Besides, you needed to understand why I can't leave. There's work to do, and remembering your mom's next birthday, or Mary's last name just don't measure up to that. So, I'll be right here for a spell, thank you very much." He looked at the ground far below. "I told you, I ain't as trapped as he thinks."

"Why can't you be out there too? Why does being here make you … senile?" The word grated Charlie's throat like sandpaper.

"I'm old, Charlie. There just ain't that much mind left to go around."

Before Charlie could complain again, Robin, now riding on the giant white bird her sister had become, sailed by. "Come on guys, we need to go exploring," she said.

G'pa Joe banked steeply, still dressed in bib overalls and a pork pie hat, and still just an old man, said, "You heard the lady, Charlie boy.

Time to go exploring." As he jetted behind Robin, he called back, "Better hurry. Your mom will be waking you up soon, and I have to get back before I'm missed."

By this time, Chuck, doing the mental equivalent of pacing back and forth in Charlie's head, had just about had enough. "*Okay, that's it! It is time for all of this nonsense to end!*" his imperious left brain insisted.

Charlie shook his head, smiled, and spoke. "End? Are you kidding? We're just getting started."

He turned, taking in the breathtaking scenery, flocked by a swarm of buzzing fairies with grizzled beards, and happily flew off to rejoin his group. It was the beginning of another excellent nightmare.

AN EXCERPT FROM THE FORTHCOMING

Awakening

By Bill Jones, Jr.

Book 2 of The Stream

Available from Panthera Press

Spring 2012

1 – DRAGON, SHALL I SLAY THEE WITH MINE PEN?

Charlie Patterson was dreaming with his best friend, Robin. Most teenage boys were limited to dreaming about beautiful girls, but not Charlie. His dreams were vivid, tactile, powerful, and emotional. In a word, they were real. Better than that, when Charlie dreamed of Robin, it was usually because she was right there, with him, in the dream.

They stumbled across the Stream, the limitless world of dreams and fantasy, during the summer prior to his twelfth birthday. In so doing, they had found each other, and created a bond that went beyond friendship. They were the One, a pair of dream travelers who, it was foretold, would restore the balance of good and evil, of light and darkness in the Stream. One day. For now, however, they were just two kids playing around in a world where one's brightest imagination or deepest fears could come to light.

It was twilight in the part of the Stream in which they found themselves. Charlie was seated in a long, narrow boat on a still lagoon. The landscape was serene, comprising forested lands that bordered the wide lake, with mountains that rose behind them. It was spring here too, Charlie noted, as the trees that dotted the mountainsides were populated with new foliage. The air was thick and humid, though not unpleasant. Low clouds hung in the air, close enough that the tops of the mountains were obscured. The sun had descended behind the mountain toward which they drifted, and its light painted the sky a muted pink that was reflected in the mirror-like lake.

Away from the westward sky, the landscape had turned violet, with the thick fog drifting over the treetops. It gave the lagoon an odd duality, with half the landscape bright and cheery, and half dark and ominous.

Charlie sat in the boat facing the dark half. Robin, by contrast, was standing, dancing in a tight circle, as she faced her lovely pink sky.

"You're all gloominating my dream, Dimple Boy," she said, barely pausing to look at him. "Cheer up."

"That's not a word," Charlie said. "You're always making up words."

"That's what we poets do." She punctuated her statement with a pirouette, then sat facing him. "I'm here because you asked me to help you use your imagination. Now you're complaining that I'm using mine."

"I-I wasn't complaining. Just ..."

"Envious?"

Charlie looked up at Robin, and was surprised to see she was smiling at him. He had never known her to make fun of anything that troubled him, which meant either she could not tell how much this bugged him, or ... "You're about to say something you think is brilliant, right?" he asked.

Her grin broadened, and she poked him in the shoulder. "Quit reading my eyes, that's cheating," she said.

"I wasn't. It's too dark out here. They just look gray."

"Well, it wouldn't be dark if you'd cheer up."

Charlie looked around, noticing once again the fog seemed to thicken as his mood darkened. "I can't help it. I hate writing stupid poems."

Robin grinned wide enough that Charlie was tempted to cup his hands, in case all her teeth popped out of her mouth. He hoped her braces would not cut his hands. "That's my idea," she said. "I want you to close your eyes, and just make up a word. Then we'll just let the dream decide what the word means."

"What? What'll that do?"

"De-gloominate the place, hopefully. And it might get you started on this poem you have to write."

Charlie sighed, and face-palmed. The sound of his hands slapping against his forehead echoed over the quiet lake.

"The phrase you're looking for, I think, is 'liven up.'" The voice came from a small canoe about ten feet away from them, in which was seated a thirteen-year-old boy with black-rimmed glasses and slicked-back hair. He looked remarkably like Charlie, except that he was dressed in a white collared shirt and red bowtie. Even sitting in the canoe, he managed to look as if he were preparing to lecture an algebra class. .

"I beg your pardon," Robin said.

"You cannot just go around modifying the English language as it suits you," the boy responded. "It makes no sense to invent a word for a thing that already has one."

Robin cupped her hands to her forehead and squinted. "Do I know you? You look awfully familiar."

The boy barely glanced in her direction, having apparently lost interest in the conversation immediately. He was now maneuvering a pair of oars and was straining toward the darkened end of the lagoon. A vein bulged in the center of his forehead.

"Dude," Robin said. "You're gonna give yourself a stroke."

He did not respond, but continued pulling at the oars with all of his might. Seated opposite him was a girl, who appeared to be around seventeen. She looked very much like Charlie, with long, curly brown hair, caramel skin, and full lips that were drawn into a tense frown. She was rowing just as hard as the boy, but in the opposite direction. They were, not surprisingly, going precisely nowhere.

"Charlie," Robin whispered. "I think that's your sister."

Charlie's eyes shot open, and a look of horror crossed his face.

Oh God, no. This place is nuts enough without Layla invading my dreams.

Charlie and his sister Layla loved each other. Deep down someplace. It was very deep down, however. Her moving out to live with his father had been a joyous occasion for him. He was certain he would eventually miss her. However, it had not happened yet. He looked over to where Robin was pointing, and his expression turned to a scowl.

"That's not Layla," he said. "It looks nothing like her."

Robin looked again and then turned to Charlie, looking at him as if he were insane. "What are you talking about? If she's not Layla, she's got a twin." She again turned her attention to the pair in the boat, who were now in vigorous argument as to the best way to reach the shore. The girl did, in fact, look precisely like Charlie's beloved sister. "Who's the nerd with her?" Robin whispered.

Charlie felt himself blush. He had met them once before, when he was twelve. He had hoped it would be the only time the two halves of his brain manifested themselves I physical form. "Th-that's Chuck," he stammered. "The girl is Charlene."

Robin's head whipped back and forth faster than spectators at a jackrabbits' ping-pong game. She looked first at Charlie, and then at the two teens in the canoe, who, by now, had ceased arguing, and were busily trying to push one another overboard with the oars. "That explains so much," she said. Her voice rose into a titter, and she began to giggle. Within seconds, she threw back her head, her eyes rolled up until only the whites showed, and she began to howl with laughter.

Charlie closed his eyes and waited for the inevitable finger-pointing cackle and snort, which would be followed, finally, by his best friend's regaining her control. Three minutes later, her laughter abated, he reopened his eyes. It was not her silence, but loud splashes that caught his attention. The other canoe was empty, and Chuck, also known as his logical left brain, was swimming to the shore, having given up on trying to convince his emotional half, whom Charlie called Charlene, to row in the same direction he was going.

Rather than paddle the boat alone, Charlene had followed him into the water. She was walking across the still waters with her fingers in her ears. Chuck, between strokes, was insisting that she sink into the lake, as her actions were both illogical and impossible.

"That's you in a nutshell," Robin said. "You could walk on water if you wanted to, but you'll never let yourself believe it."

"Bah. That's not even real. It's just my mind messing with me, as usual."

"See? That's what I mean. Your stupid logical brain won't even let you see your own dream as real."

Charlie considered reminding her that dreams were not real, but thought better of it. He would have had a better chance of convincing Robin she was a potato.

"Did you notice how they never got anywhere in the boat?" she asked. Her voice had become soft. Charlie recognized her caretaker mode. She had made the easy switch back to being his best friend.

"Yeah," he said, sighing. "That's how I feel trying to write this assignment. Every time I think of something, I realize it's stupid, and throw it away."

"You need to just tell Chuck to go to sleep, and let your

4

imagination free." Robin stood once again in the small boat, which by now had drifted to the edge of the lagoon, and was pointed toward the open sea. She closed her eyes, and lifted both slim arms above her.

"What are you doing?" he asked.

"Being free," she said, lifting one leg into what Charlie imagined was a kung fu crane-style position.

Before so much as another heartbeat passed, an enormous shadow swept over the boat, blotting out the remaining sunlight. Charlie opened his mouth to warn his partner, just as two massive claws snatched her out of the boat.

"Robin!" he screamed, leaping to his feet. His movements, along with the sudden departure of the slender girl caused the small boat to rock angrily, threatening to toss him into the lake. Charlie grabbed the sides of the boat, gripping them with white-knuckled vigor lest he be thrown overboard.

I can't swim!

The boat eased from its pitching and rolling, and Charlie looked up in time to see a thirty-foot green dragon with Robin in its forelimbs. The girl dangled there by both arms, and appeared to be struggling fruitlessly against the beast. Already the dragon's iridescent scales had begun to blend in with the sky, making it appear as if Robin were flying, Superman-style, straight up.

"Save me, Dimple Boy!" she called, as the great dragon disappeared into thick cumulus clouds that had taken possession of the sky. The dragon must have fired a line of supercooled air, as the lagoon reverberated with its shrill screech, and the clouds lit up as if by lightning in the upper atmosphere.

"That wasn't Willie," Charlie said, pacing back and forth in the boat. Willie was Willie Green, a mutual friend of theirs, and notorious for dreaming, every night, that he was a green dragon. With Willie, she would have been safe, but this was a strange beast. Charlie was speaking aloud, which he tended to do whenever he was stressed. "I need to do something ... I need to figure out how to go after her."

As was often the case in his Stream adventures, Charlie was having difficulty allowing his imagination to lead. His deep-seated logic had always been his protection against the world's hurts. Here in the Stream, it was his limitation.

"See? This is why I haven't been able to help G'pa Joe. How can I fight Siri and help free my great grandpa if I can't even figure out

5

how to chase a stupid dragon?"

Charlie thought about Robin's earlier suggestion, and sat again in the boat. He was attempting to solve his problem as if it were a puzzle. If his time in the world of dreams had taught him anything, it was that dream puzzles were not solved by logic. The Stream was a world of interlocking dreams – the worlds created in a single dream lived long past the dreamer's waking. As such, any logical framework Charlie could imagine would be of no use, say, in a world that had been originally created by the mind of a three-year-old child. This lagoon had been Robin's creation. If he knew his friend at all, she had planned this entire adventure, and logic would be of almost no help.

So, I'm supposed to make up a word. Okay …

Charlie tilted his head, stuck his tongue in his cheek, and tapped an index finger against his temple. It was his best thinking position, and he was certain it helped, even though all of his friends said it just made him look stupid.

He stood, closed his eyes, and said, "Crowdacious!" The word made him giggle.

The quiet of the lagoon was interrupted by the loudest caw he had ever heard. The sound caused him to clamp his hand over his ears. Even the surface of the lake rippled from the impact of the sound waves. Charlie looked up, and a saw a massive crow circling down to the water's surface. Each wing was easily ten feet from shoulder to tip, and as wide as Charlie was tall. Had it been able to stand vertically, it would have been two-and-a-half times as tall as an adult human male.

Without another sound, the giant crow alighted on the surface of the lake. "Crowdacious," Charlie repeated, and smiled. Without hesitating, he climbed onto the mammoth bird's back, gripping its soft feathers with either hand. "Let's go catch us a dragon," he said.

The crow flapped its wings, causing Charlie's red shirt to lift above his neck, and his curly hair to fall into his eyes. By the time he had repositioned himself enough that he could see, he, and the bird were a hundred feet above the lagoon. He noted for the first time that it was shaped like the letter "C." It was a hint from Robin that he was on the right track.

Charlie smiled. He was proud of himself for the first time since he had entered this dream. He and Robin were as different as two best friends could be, but lately, he had come to believe they were the

One about whom so much had been made. According to legend, there would be two very different dream travelers would who act as though they were one being. When first told of the prophecy, both he and Robin were skeptical. However, after more than a year of friendship and exploration of dreams, after months of finding and freeing the minds of innocents who had become trapped in nightmares of their own making by the dark lord Siri, they had begun to believe. Neither had been able to match Siri's strength, on the rare occasions when they had confronted him. However, the two friends were able to blend their own strengths and dreams as easily as if they shared one mind.

Here, clinging to a giant crow, with the wind whistling past, was one more example of this. Despite the sun's having set behind the mountain below, another red sun sat noon-high in the sky. When Charlie cupped his hands, shielding his eyes from most of the light, he could just make out three dark areas of shadow across the surface of the sun. He looked down, awestruck with the beauty of the layer of billowing clouds below. The sun had painted them pink, save for the odd shadows on the glowing orb's surface.

Charlie burst out in laughter. The shadows, cast on the surface of the cloud cover, formed a perfect smiley face. Robin was having fun with him, all right.

"Yay!" she called from above him, her dragon diving in from where it had been hidden by the brilliant sunlight. "If I had been the enemy, you'd totally be toast by now." She was grinning, her braces shining in the bright light. "I win."

"You win? I didn't even know we were playing the game."

"Duh. The enemy doesn't tell you in advance they're launching an attack, Charlie. Color yourself toast."

Charlie looked down at his lightly suntanned, caramel skin. "I'm already the color of toast," he said. Robin cackled in response, her long, dark hair framing her face.

"Follow me," she said, "if your big huge bird can keep up."

"Crowdacious," he replied, pulling the crow into a steep ascent behind her.

He could hear her laughing and saying, "Good for you," ahead of him.

The pair flew through above the landscape, mixing briefly with a tangle of smaller dragons, most of which flew like bumblebees, which is to say, poorly. One particularly chubby orange beast bounced off

Charlie's head, sending him, arms pinwheeling, and voice screaming, plummeting to Earth. After falling a few hundred feet, he noticed his crow circling below, and he allowed himself to enjoy the free fall. He landed on the downy feathers of the bird's rump, just as Robin came into view.

She was once again dangling from the dragon's foreclaws, and again appeared to be struggling. On closer inspection, however, it was clear that she was dancing, and the dragon was moving in concert with her movements.

Only Robin could teach a dragon how to dance.

The pair continued their flight, soaring over a dark forest rumored to be inhabited by mythical beasts. It was dark below, despite being bright sunlight above. As they descended for a better view, they were buzzed by a swarm of what at first glance appeared to be angry insects. These bugs, however, had grizzled beards, and cursed like sailors. They buzzed Charlie and Robin, who were waving frantically at them, as the swarm thickened. These were not insects, but small, flying humanoids that were stinging the kids with minute bolts from their outstretched fingers. Charlie could not tell if it was electricity or magic, but it hurt.

"Go away, you stupid gnat fairies!" Robin yelled. Her dragon began raking the air with fire in response to her anger. It worked, finally convincing the swarm to depart, but also caught Charlie's enormous crow in the crossfire. The big bird descended in a power dive to the ground, its tail feathers aflame. Charlie had barely enough time to slide off the bird before it rolled itself in the dirt, putting out the fire. The bird missed crushing him by inches. Charlie lay in the grass for a moment, panting, as his heart slowed its jackhammering to near normal. He was in a field of lovely purple flowers, all of which were shaped like six-pointed stars. He leaned over and sniffed one, and immediately erupted in sneezes. It smelled like black pepper and garlic.

"Jeez," Charlie said, as Robin helped him to his feet. "Next time you decide to fry fairies, wait until I'm out of the way first. This forest bites."

"Sorry, dude. I hate bug fairies. One flew up my nose." She looked at him, a sly gleam in her eye. "Snot very cool." Charlie rolled his eyes in response. Robin's eyes darted up to the sky, and she screamed, "Look out!"

She dove out of the way, but Charlie did not react quickly enough.

He had just enough time to look up, as his angry crow discharged its ... feelings about being singed ... all over Charlie. In other words, he was now covered from head to toe in a Crowdacious mound of bird poop.

Robin's eyes were watering, and it looked as if she were biting her lower lip hard enough that it might start bleeding.

"If you laugh, I swear to God, we aren't friends anymore."

"Oh pooh balls," she responded. "You're no fun at all."

Charlie gave her the longest eye roll he could muster, and then, thankfully, woke up.

His hair was still covered in bird poop.

These dreams are becoming too realistic.

He rolled out of bed, pulled off his stained pillowcase, and headed for the shower. He reached the doorknob, and stopped.

"Crap," he said aloud. "I still haven't written the stupid poem."

Robin's experiment had been no help at all, he decided, and headed for the bathroom, glad, for once, his mother left for work before he awoke. Having to come up with a plausible excuse for awaking with a head full of bird poop was one bit of creative writing he did not need.

Just as he stepped into the bathroom, quite nauseous from the smell, he heard his mother's voice.

"Charlie? Are you up? Don't forget we have the dentist this morning."

Oh goody. And I thought this was going to be a bad day.